AF843341

Holly Hepburn

Christmas All The Way

SIMON & SCHUSTER

London · New York · Amsterdam/Antwerp · Sydney/Melbourne · Toronto · New Delhi

First published in Great Britain by Simon & Schuster UK Ltd, 2026

1 3 5 7 9 10 8 6 4 2

Simon & Schuster UK Ltd, 7th Floor,
199 Bishopsgate, London EC2M 3TY

Simon & Schuster Australia, Sydney
Simon & Schuster India, New Delhi

www.simonandschuster.co.uk
www.simonandschuster.com.au
www.simonandschuster.co.in

The authorised representative in the EEA is Simon & Schuster Netherlands BV, Herculesplein 96, 3584 AA Utrecht, Netherlands. info@simonandschuster.nl

A CIP catalogue record for this book
is available from the British Library

Paperback ISBN: 978-1-3985-1210-8
eBook ISBN: 978-1-3985-1211-5
Audio ISBN: 978-1-3985-6894-5

Typeset in Bembo by M Rules
Printed and Bound in the UK using 100% Renewable Electricity
at CPI Group (UK) Ltd

FSC
www.fsc.org
MIX
Paper | Supporting responsible forestry
FSC® C013604

For Jane and Charlotte and Emily and Anne,
whose brilliance never dims.

CHAPTER ONE

'A lady might travel the Seven Wonders of the World and never see a sight so welcome to her as that of her dearest friend.'

The Mistress of Pendennis, ELIZA NORTON

The great British public could be broadly divided into two sorts of people, Grace Murphy thought as she surveyed the freshly stacked shelves of the supermarket with a faint frown: those who were outraged by the appearance of mince pies for sale in the middle of an August heatwave, and those who welcomed them and everything they represented no matter how many months it was until C-Day.

For years, Grace had been in the latter camp. Her Christmas countdown would begin on the first day of the new school year. She got the box of decorations down from the loft as soon as the leaves started to turn, booked her online grocery slot the moment the notification email landed, spent hours planning the merry mischief her son's Elf on the Shelf would get up to, and took pleasure in ticking off the items on his Christmas list, which was, of course, written long before December. But as Jack left childhood behind, the list had grown shorter and more practical, easy to source on the internet. The elf's antics drew smiles rather than delighted giggles, and she found herself putting up the tree with the cast of *Love Actually* for company, while Jack hid in his room, bellowing cheerfully at his games console. If she was totally honest, decorating the tree on her own hadn't been so bad, especially with a large glass of Bailey's at hand, but wild reindeer couldn't have dragged the admission from her. And this year, there would be no need to hang a stuffed stocking over the fireplace at midnight, nor would her festive food shop contain enough snacks to feed a small army, or one ravenous teenager. This year, for the first time in nineteen years, Grace would be waking up on Christmas Day without Jack. He would be thousands of miles away, enjoying a year on the other side of the world with his father, in Sydney. Three days had passed since she'd held back tears to wave him through the departures gate at the airport and the ache in her chest showed no sign of easing. How bad would it be when the festive period arrived in all its sparkly, full-on glory, and every advert declared the importance of gathering loved ones near? She could hardly bear to think of it.

'What you need is a change of scene,' her friend Keeley had prescribed over the phone, when Grace had confessed she was finding it hard to adjust to the Jack-shaped hole. 'Between an empty nest and the redundancy, it's no wonder you're feeling a bit lost. Why don't you come and stay with me for a few days?'

It was a tempting offer. The Chelmsford library where Grace had worked for the past decade had fallen victim to cost-cutting measures in June, and there hadn't been a suitable position in the city's remaining libraries to accommodate her. She'd reluctantly taken the proffered redundancy package, grateful that her long service ensured it was generous enough to give her some breathing space before having to find something new. Quite what that might be, she wasn't sure. Was there much demand in the current economic climate for highly qualified librarians in their early forties? It seemed doubtful.

'But you're busy,' she reminded Keeley. 'The last thing you need is a house guest.'

'I'm never too busy for you,' her friend responded firmly. 'And it will be nice to have some company. I'll even drop my dirty socks in the middle of the floor, if you like. Make you feel more at home.'

Grace had laughed at that. One thing she hadn't missed in the immediate aftermath of Jack's departure had been scooping up his discarded clothes, empty wrappers and used crockery. But perhaps Keeley was right. Perhaps a break would do her good, even if it was only for the weekend. And the village of Freezy Tye, where Keeley lived and worked, was certainly a charming spot for a mini-break. Nestled in the heart of the Essex countryside, it was as though someone had gathered together all the ingredients of the quintessential English village and painstakingly arranged them for maximum quaintness. Pastel-painted cottages with pristine thatched roofs overlooked a lush village green and lily-covered duck pond, a sixteenth-century coaching inn welcomed locals and thirsty travellers alike, and a flint-bedecked Norman church had presided over it all for almost nine hundred years. Freezy Tye had also once been home to a well-respected Victorian author, Eliza Norton. A contemporary of the Brontë sisters, her work had yet to reach the same level of universal adoration but she had produced a number of sharply observed romantic novels that had a dedicated fan base around the world. Her cottage was open to the public, and was curated by Keeley herself, along with a team of enthusiastic volunteers. Yes, Grace thought as she considered her friend's offer, a few days in Freezy Tye might be exactly what she needed.

'Okay,' she said. 'How soon can I come?'

They had agreed on Friday evening, when Keeley would have ushered any remaining members of the public out of Juniper Cottage and locked it up for the night. 'Not that we've been overrun with visitors lately,' she sighed. 'But at least that makes it easier to close on time.'

'I'll pick up something for dinner,' Grace offered. 'And maybe some cake.' Did mince pies count as cake, she wondered now, her hand hovering over the luxurious crimson and gold boxes. Keeley loved Christmas – she had to, living in Freezy Tye, which had been voted Britain's Most Christmassy Village seven years in a row – but Grace wasn't sure how she'd feel about breaking out the festive food before summer was even over.

'Tempting, aren't they?' A wistful voice at her shoulder caused Grace to turn and find a woman standing there, staring at the shelves. 'My husband mutates into Ebenezer Scrooge if I buy them this early. I have to hide them at the back of the cupboard.'

At least that wasn't a problem Grace or Keeley had to contend with; cantankerous husbands were thankfully a distant memory for them both. 'His loss,' Grace said cheerfully. 'I like them warm, with a bit of brandy butter, but it's probably too soon for that to be on sale.'

'Now you're talking,' the woman exclaimed, grinning. 'Although a bit of clotted cream does very nicely too.'

Praise for Holly Hepburn

'Irresistible love stories in gorgeous locations with characters that feel like friends. A Holly Hepburn novel is a heartwarming treat!'
Miranda Dickinson

'Like a ray of sunshine on a cloudy day, this sparkling story will sweep you away and leave your heart full of love'
Cathy Bramley

'Losing yourself in a Holly Hepburn book is one of life's pleasures – they're the perfect escape'
Milly Johnson

'Wholly satisfying reads – a warm glow is guaranteed when you snuggle up with a Holly Hepburn book!'
Heidi Swain

'I devoured this gorgeous book as quickly as a tin of Scottish shortbread. You'll be on the first train to Edinburgh after reading. Cosy, comforting, escapist and romantic, and in the most wonderful setting, this is the perfect way to start the New Year. Delightful!'
Veronica Henry

'A feel-good story that captured me – then held me until the last page'
Sue Moorcroft

'An uplifting, indulgent treat of a romance, perfect to curl up with on sunny days or cold winter nights. I loved everything about it!'
Cressy McLaughlin

'The perfect cosy romance, I loved hanging out with Fraser and Maura in Edinburgh – a gorgeous celebration of love and the magical city that brought them together'
Laura Wood

'A Holly Hepburn novel is guaranteed to fill your heart with joy'
Isabelle Broom

Holly Hepburn is the author of ten novels including *The Little Shop of Hidden Treasures*, *Coming Home to Brightwater Bay*, and *A Year at the Star and Sixpence*. Follow her on Instagram at @HollyH_Author.

Also by Holly Hepburn

A Year at the Star and Sixpence
A Year at Castle Court
Last Orders at the Star and Sixpence
The Picture House by the Sea
Coming Home to Brightwater Bay
The Little Shop of Hidden Treasures
Escape to Darling Cove
Return to Half Moon Farm
Healing Hearts on Thistledown Lane

It certainly did, Grace decided, placing a box of mince pies on top of the other treats she had piled into her basket. Evidently emboldened, her new friend took one too, and they exchanged a conspiratorial smile as they parted company. On a whim, Grace passed down the booze aisle on her way to the checkout. August might be too early for brandy butter but Bailey's was a different matter. Especially in Britain's most Christmassy village.

The gardens of Juniper Cottage were Keeley Cotterill's happy place. Even now, as the exuberance of the summer blooms began to fade, the flowerbeds were still a riot of colour and scent. These bright, blue-skied mornings were her favourites, when she could wander the cool, meandering paths before the heat of the day had set in and the first visitors arrived.

Sometimes she imagined turning a corner to happen upon Eliza Norton herself, a trug tucked into the crook of one arm as she trimmed the roses. From extracts of letters the author had sent to her sisters, Keeley knew she had been a keen horticulturalist, but gardens had featured prominently in her novels too. Her most swoon-worthy hero, the noble and dashing Captain Forsythe, had proposed to Sylvie de Villiers among the gloriously described orchards of Pendennis House, in a scene that Keeley had always felt was deserving of the most sumptuous BBC adaptation. But for reasons she'd never truly been able to fathom, no one had ever approached the trustees of Eliza's estate with a view to adapting any of her work for the screen. Perhaps it was because none of the novels had achieved the kind of enduring success seen by those of Jane Austen, despite sharing a similar talent for writing sparkling dialogue laced with astute social commentary, and creating memorable characters that lived on in the imagination long after the story had concluded. Austen had been published some forty years before Eliza, and by the 1850s literary tastes had taken a turn for the gothic, so perhaps it was simply that she was writing the wrong thing at the wrong time, but it had always puzzled Keeley that her books hadn't found favour with modern readers. They were well regarded by scholars of nineteenth-century fiction, and had a respectable following among dedicated lovers of historical romance novels, but her name was rarely mentioned alongside those of her more illustrious peers. It was why Juniper Cottage enjoyed a considerably lower footfall than Austen's house in Hampshire, or the Brontë Parsonage Museum in Haworth, but, despite the best efforts of Keeley and the board of trustees who managed Eliza's estate, it was proving difficult to attract more visitors, even at the height of the tourist season. At least that meant the gardens were rarely crowded, Keeley thought as she listened to the industrious buzz of bees in the early morning sunshine.

Reluctantly, her thoughts returned to the conversation she'd had with Malcolm Davidson earlier that week. 'The bottom line is we need more punters,' the trustee had told her at their quarterly meeting in London, his faded blue eyes sombre as he regarded her across the mahogany table. 'What with the repairs to the summer house, and the improvements to the toilets, we're looking at a worrying increase in expenditure this year and visitor numbers are down again.'

It wasn't anything Keeley hadn't already known but she'd still felt the need to defend herself and the team of volunteers who kept Juniper Cottage running on a day-to-day basis. 'The talk by Dr Barnard in June was well attended,' she pointed out.

'Almost forty tickets were sold and we shifted quite a few copies of his book, as well as seeing an uptick in gift shop sales. And we've organised a children's treasure hunt over the holidays, to try to encourage more families.'

Malcolm had rubbed his forehead wearily, bushy white eyebrows beetling as he frowned. 'We appreciate all your hard work, Keeley, but you know the problem – reading isn't as popular as it once was and there are so many other, flashier attractions making a grab for people's attention and money. Virtual reality exhibitions and escape rooms and the like.'

Keeley blinked. 'Surely you're not suggesting we turn Juniper Cottage into an escape room?'

'No, of course not. But the fact remains that we need to freshen things up.' He paused and squared his shoulders. 'To that end, the trustees have decided to engage the services of a creative director. Someone who can work with you on a part-time basis to raise the profile of Eliza and the house, and hopefully encourage greater footfall.'

'Okay,' Keeley said warily, because the title of creative director had the ominous knell of seniority when compared with her own position as curator. 'Do you want me to help draw up the job description? I can put some feelers out too, see if there's anyone who might be a good fit.'

Malcolm's features crinkled into a smile, although Keeley thought she detected a hint of anxiety in his eyes. 'No need. We've, uh, already found someone. Offered him the role and he's accepted. Just two days a week, but every little helps, eh?'

'Oh.' Keeley blinked, taken aback both at the speed with which the trustees appeared to have moved and by the fact that they hadn't felt the need to consult her first. 'Who is it?'

'A chap called Xander Jones,' Malcolm said, and hesitated. 'He's not traditionally the kind of candidate we'd choose but he has a very impressive track record. One of those behind-the-scenes social media wizards. I think he'll shake things up quite nicely.'

The words sent a shiver of foreboding through Keeley. 'Shake things up in what way?' she asked slowly, picturing the understated elegance of the cottage, its rooms painstakingly arranged the way Eliza's diaries had described, with simple printed displays that explained her daily routine and gave context to the items on show. The aim of Juniper Cottage had always been to preserve Eliza's life and work for posterity, much the same as other properties belonging to artistic luminaries did. The idea of shaking things up suggested some of that might get broken.

'Bad turn of phrase,' Malcolm said, his weathered pink cheeks turning even more florid. 'What I meant was, he'll be a breath of fresh air. He put together a presentation with some suggestions and we all agreed they sound exciting and innovative.'

Keeley fought a sudden urge to fold her arms. 'Innovative?'

Evidently picking up on the flatness of her tone, he held up a placatory hand. 'Look, I'm not explaining it very well. The best thing would be for you to meet him, so he can lay out his ideas and you can see for yourself how good they are. He suggested Friday, if that suits you?'

She wanted to reply that it did not suit her; her most dependable volunteer, Hilda, had a funeral to go to, which meant Keeley was short-handed, but she suspected she would only appear churlish if she refused. 'Fine,' she said, swallowing a sigh.

'Wonderful,' Malcolm said, beaming at her. 'Here's his card. I'll leave you to hammer out the details, shall I?'

His bluffness suggested he was trying to head off any more awkward questions but Keeley was determined not to let him off that easily. 'I suppose that makes sense. But I'm still not clear how all of this is going to work. How much authority will Xander have? Who will he be reporting to?'

His brows shot up. 'To the trustees, naturally. Our intention is most certainly not to give you more work, my dear. Quite the opposite.' He threw her an encouraging look. 'We see you as equals, working in tandem towards the same goal, which is to introduce more people to Eliza's work.'

'But what if we don't work in tandem?' she persisted. 'What if there's a difference of opinion – who has the final say?'

'I'm sure it won't come to that,' Malcolm soothed. 'But I want to reassure you again that Xander joining the team is in no way a reflection upon you – we simply thought a fresh perspective might help. Why don't you meet him and hear what he has to say? You might find you're pleasantly surprised.'

There wasn't much Keeley could say to that – not without sounding peevish. She had spent most of the train journey back to Essex scouring the internet for more information about Xander Jones and although she couldn't find a website, she did come across a social media account bearing his name that was full of appealing, artfully composed pictures of stately homes and museums. As far as she could tell, it was a personal account – there was nothing to suggest he was working with any of them. The profile picture was a stylised arrangement of the letters X and J, which she guessed might be a business logo, but there were no images of anyone she might reasonably assume to be Xander himself. When she'd grudgingly sent a brief email introducing herself, he had replied within an hour to suggest they met at Juniper Cottage around twelve-thirty on Friday, and signed off with a smiley face emoji. She'd looked at the cheery yellow face for several seconds, wondering about the kind of person who added emojis to professional correspondence with a new colleague, then berated herself for being the kind of snob who judged others for their emoji choices. But she awoke on Friday morning weighed down by a leaden reluctance, and not even the thought of her best friend's arrival that evening could lift her spirits. She'd applied her make-up with more care than usual, treating it as a layer of armour to defend against whatever Xander Jones might throw at her, and smoothed her long blonde bob into glossy perfection. She had dressed up a little too, choosing a crisp white blouse and navy palazzo pants that made her feel a little like Anna Wintour, and completed the look with a splash of red lipstick.

Perhaps she was wrong to view the upcoming meeting as a battle, she considered now, pausing to breathe in the fragrance of the pink and yellow honeysuckle blooms that hung from the frame of the pergola over the path to the gardens. Perhaps Malcolm and the other trustees were right, and the newly appointed creative director would be exactly what Juniper Cottage needed. But at least she was prepared, even if no battle materialised.

The unexpected arrival of a coach full of overseas tourists was a welcome distraction and kept Keeley busy for most of the morning. Her small but dedicated team of volunteers were distributed between the lower and upper floors of the house and the gift shop, ready to handle ticket sales, answer questions and ensure enthusiastic visitors did not attempt to sit at the desk Eliza Norton herself had used when writing her novels. Another volunteer had stepped in to fill the gap left by Hilda's absence but she was not as knowledgeable about Eliza's life and work, meaning Keeley had decided to put her in the gift shop, while she took up position in the library.

She didn't pay much attention to the man with the blond hair at first. Long experience had taught her there was no such thing as a typical visitor to Juniper Cottage, but on weekdays the demographic skewed towards the older generations. They came in couples or small groups, or in larger numbers as part of a coach party, trooping through the house with varying degrees of interest. Very occasionally, there were school trips, when the rooms were filled with chattering children and the peace of the cottage was vanquished. The volunteers were instructed never to shush them; Eliza had no children of her own but she'd been aunt to a legion of nieces and nephews and her correspondence showed she had adored their visits to the cottage, delighting in their exuberance and noise. But the type of visitor Keeley saw less often were square-jawed, floppy-fringed men in their late twenties, wearing rock band T-shirts and looking like they might be more at home on the beach than exploring the home of an underappreciated literary treasure. Narrowing her eyes, she watched him drift towards the floor-to-ceiling bookshelves, his gaze intent on the leather-bound spines Eliza had lovingly collected throughout her life. She checked the time – just after eleven o'clock. If this was Xander Jones, he was more than an hour early. She tried not to feel nettled. She had planned to give him a guided tour as part of the visit but it seemed he'd decided to show himself around and now she had a quandary. Should she introduce herself, or pretend she hadn't noticed him when he presented himself formally at the agreed time of their meeting? What if she was wrong, and he wasn't Xander Jones at all?

'Excuse me.' An elderly woman materialised before Keeley, her sharp gaze magnified by the thick glasses she wore. 'Could you settle an argument between me and my husband? Is this where Eliza Norton wrote *Where the Wind Blows*? I'm certain it was here in Freezy Tye but he insists it was Cromer.'

At her shoulder was a tall, grey-haired man peering over a pair of gold wire-framed spectacles. He was shaking his head in what appeared to be wry amusement, as though confident his wife was about to be corrected. At the bookshelves, the blond man moved nearer. Was it Keeley's imagination or had he tilted his head to listen? She pushed the thought away and focused her attention on the couple in front of her. 'The answer is both,' she replied, smiling. 'According to her diaries, Eliza first had the idea for *Where the Wind Blows* while visiting her sister on the Norfolk coast one winter. She was inspired by the wildness of the sea and the spell it cast over those who lived nearby. In fact, Gardner Crookshanks was based on a fisherman she met at the harbour once.'

The bespectacled man looked pleased. 'There. Didn't I tell you?'

'But she only *began* the novel while in Cromer,' Keeley went on. 'Her sister was taken ill and was advised to travel to the Continent for her health, which meant Eliza returned to Juniper Cottage sooner than she planned. She wrote the remainder of the book here, and didn't return to Cromer until after it was published.'

Now it was the woman's turn to look triumphant. 'She

finished it here,' she said, turning to prod her husband in the chest. 'That means I win.'

'Hardly,' he sniffed, before turning a suspicious gaze upon Keeley. 'You're a volunteer, I suppose. An enthusiast rather than an expert.'

Instinctively, Keeley's hand moved to the lanyard that hung around her neck, identifying her as Curator. A quick glance downwards told her it was back to front, presenting only a black and white image of the cottage. 'Actually—'

But the woman cut her off. 'Don't even dignify that with an answer,' she barked, then rounded on her husband again. 'There's no need to be rude to this young lady, just because she's shown you up.'

He glowered at her. 'The only person showing me up is you.'

Keeley decided it was time to nip the brewing disagreement in the bud, despite a certain amount of wry enjoyment in the notion that she might be considered young. 'Why don't we agree that you're both right?'

They stared at her, as though she had suggested they each slice off an arm. 'Utter nonsense,' the woman said briskly. 'I'm right and he's wrong. You'd think he'd be used to it after fifty years of marriage.'

'Fifty-one,' he corrected and gave a hollow laugh. 'Believe me, I've counted them.'

Keeley gave up her efforts at mediation. 'There's an original, handwritten copy of *Where the Wind Blows* on display in the smoking room, along with extracts from Eliza's diary, which you might find interesting.' She waved a hand at the door to their right. 'Just through there.'

Continuing to bicker, the pair left the room, leaving Keeley with the distinct impression she had survived a small and very localised tornado.

'I think you may have just facilitated a divorce,' the blond man said, as their voices faded.

'Possibly,' Keeley agreed, noting a distinct Australian twang behind the words that went hand in hand with his light golden tan. 'Although my parents are exactly the same. If Dad says the sky is blue, my mother will insist it is cerulean and an argument will follow. They've been married for over forty years.'

He tipped his head. 'Love wears many disguises, I suppose.' Stepping nearer, he extended a hand. 'It's good to meet you, Dr Cotterill. I'm Xander Jones.'

So her intuition had been correct. Of course it had. 'Hello,' she said, only moderately gratified that he had addressed her using her professional title. 'It's good to meet you too.'

Something of her thoughts must have coloured her tone, because his mouth quirked. 'I know, I'm disgustingly early. I wanted to get a feel for the house before we spoke. I didn't realise you'd be on sentry duty.'

Was that how she'd looked, Keeley wondered. Stiff and guarded? 'We're a little short-staffed today,' she explained. 'But I enjoy talking to visitors. They're always so enthusiastic about Eliza's writing.'

Xander smiled and a distant part of Keeley's brain observed that it caused dimples to appear in each cheek. 'Apart from when they think they know more than you.'

'Even then,' Keeley said. 'If I was a writer, I'd be in heaven. We see all sorts of characters here.'

He raised his eyebrows. 'Do you have ambitions to write?'

She shook her head. 'No. But Eliza's novels are filled with

big characters. Those two reminded me a little of Mr and Mrs Frogmore, in *Manningtree Lodge*.'

He nodded, but Keeley couldn't tell whether he agreed or even if he knew the novel. Checking her watch, she saw it was just after eleven-fifteen. The flow of visitors from the coach seemed to have dried up; could she ask Jenny to keep an eye on both rooms while she met with Xander? The quicker she heard what he had to say, the sooner she could get on with the rest of her day. She really hoped it wasn't going to involve a PowerPoint.

Once again, he seemed to divine what she was thinking. 'Don't let me disturb you,' he said. 'I'll have a wander round and we can meet at twelve-thirty, as planned.'

'No, that's okay.' She craned her head, trying to catch a glimpse of Jenny in the neighbouring room. 'I'm sure one of the volunteers can take over here and I can give you a quick tour.'

'That's kind of you but I'd rather find my own way. I like to get a feel for a place, form my own impressions of what's working and what could be improved.' He offered her a crooked smile that caused a burst of fine lines to radiate from the corners of his sea-blue eyes. 'Would you hate me if I turned you down?'

Keeley couldn't prevent a flicker of irritation. The cottage was laid out in exactly the way it had been when Eliza lived there – nothing about it needed to be improved. And his choice of phrasing grated too; she'd offered to give him a tour, not buy him a drink. 'Fine,' she replied, determined to appear outwardly unruffled. 'Shall I meet you in the gift shop at twelve-thirty, as previously agreed?'

'See you then,' he said, with a carefree wave that somehow only irritated her more. She watched him go, observing the frayed hem of his too-long faded jeans, dangling over the battered Converse he wore, and she found herself wondering exactly how old he was. Her initial guess had been late twenties but the laughter lines suggested he might be older, in spite of the way he was dressed. Younger than her forty-two years, that much was certain, and perhaps that was another reason for the prickle of annoyance that lingered between Keeley's shoulder blades, for all Malcolm's reassurance that his role was in no way senior to hers. But she'd never been one to judge a book by its cover, no matter how tempting it might be. Xander Jones had convinced the trustees that he could bring more visitors to Juniper Cottage, which meant Keeley was obliged to hear him out, in spite of a suspicion he had never so much as opened one of Eliza's novels.

Her resolve to take refuge in professional courtesy was tested slightly when Jenny appeared in the doorway of the adjoining room to mouth 'WOW!' at Xander's departing back. Thankfully, Keeley was saved from having to respond by the arrival of a fresh wave of tourists from the hallway behind her. When Keeley entered the gift shop shortly before twelve-thirty, it was to find Xander leaning against the ticket desk, nodding at something volunteer Elspeth was saying. Elspeth herself looked every bit as starstruck as Jenny had been; her eyes were wide and one hand fluttered at the string of pearls around her neck as she listened to his reply. Keeley kept her expression neutral as the volunteer let out a peal of girlish laughter that caused several shoppers to glance towards her. Another hour – less, if she kept questions to a minimum – and everything could settle back into normality.

'Hello again,' she said, sending a cool nod Xander's way as she approached. 'How do you like Juniper Cottage?'

'It's wonderful,' he replied, and the warmth of his tone suggested he meant it. 'I got a real sense of Eliza's presence. If I closed my eyes, I could almost hear the scratch of her quill.'

Keeley gave him a sharp look because there had been moments, at the end of a long day when the house was empty and silent, that she'd also imagined she could hear the faint scratch of a quill on paper. Once or twice, upon entering a room to check everything was as it should be before closing up for the night, it had seemed to her that the still air had gently swirled, as though someone had departed a split second before she arrived. These were observations she had always kept to herself, however, mostly because it was difficult enough to find reliable volunteers and the last thing she needed were rumours that the cottage was haunted, but also because she had long suspected those almost otherworldly moments were born of wishful thinking on her part. She had read and reread Eliza's novels and diaries so often that the writer felt like a friend, one she longed to meet in real life. The fact that their lives were separated by more than a century was neither here nor there. But she had no intention of admitting that to Xander, in spite of his unsettling echo of her own experience. 'The rooms are arranged as closely as possible to the way they were in Eliza's day,' she said, determined to head off any thoughts he might have about rearranging the furniture. 'Our visitors enjoy seeing how she lived and worked.'

He nodded. 'Of course. That's why they come. But I think there's potential to offer them more than superficial engagement.'

There was a loaded silence, during which Keeley fought to smother a burst of indignation. From the guileless expression on

Xander's face, he had no idea he'd just insulted both her and her team of dedicated volunteers. 'Well,' she replied, managing to compose herself, 'I look forward to hearing your ideas. Would you like a coffee? I thought we might find a quiet table outside the cafe, since it's a lovely day.' She glanced at the rucksack slung over his shoulder and wondered again if he was going to subject her to a slide show. 'Unless you need power.'

'Outside is great,' he assured her easily. 'And so is coffee.'

It wasn't until they reached the cafe that Keeley began to wonder whether Xander might be expecting something more substantial than coffee. The tables were filled with visitors tucking into sandwiches and snacks they had bought, and the air was rich with the aroma of toasted bread. There was also a lengthy queue snaking along the counter towards the tills, but that was less of a problem since they didn't actually need to join it. She turned to Xander. 'How do you take your coffee? I can recommend the cherry Bakewell slice to go with it, or there are sandwiches and toasties if you'd like something more filling.'

He shook his head. 'Just a flat white, thanks. I've got somewhere else to be at three o'clock and it's a bit of a drive.'

Throwing up a silent prayer of thanks to the patron saint of harassed museum curators, Keeley deposited him at an empty table in the shade of a large oak tree and went to make the drinks. As she stepped outside again, the sun slid from behind a cloud, causing golden light to dapple through the leaves of the oak tree, bathing Xander in a gently rippling amber glow in a scene that might have caused Leonardo da Vinci to reach for his paintbrushes. She slowed, momentarily transfixed, until she saw he was tapping at a laptop, and the beguilement vanished.

It looked as though her worst fears were correct. There was going to be a presentation.

'So,' she said, sliding the tray of drinks onto the table and taking the seat opposite him. 'I hope you won't mind my bluntness but I'm not sure I understand why you're here.' He started to speak but she held up a hand. 'Obviously, the trustees want to increase visitor numbers and raise Eliza's profile as one of our great literary treasures, and I assume you have some expertise in that area, since they appointed you as creative director. But what are you actually going to do? Other than suggest the current Juniper Cottage visitor experience is superficial.'

She hadn't meant her final sentence to sound so snippy but the irritation she'd felt in the gift shop bubbled to the surface and escaped before she could prevent it. A faint blush warmed her cheeks, even as she forced herself to hold his gaze. But he didn't look discomfited by her questions. Instead, he closed the computer and eyed her steadily. 'First things first, I'm not here to step on your toes. You're the foremost expert in the life and work of Eliza Norton – you know more about her than anyone and I'd be a fool not to respect that. I certainly didn't mean to suggest that anything about the brilliant way you've preserved Eliza's legacy isn't up to scratch. But the way people interact with the past is changing, which means the way we engage them has to change too.' He leaned back in the seat, his expression almost apologetic. 'It means we have to offer more than a walk around an old house.'

'We do offer more than that,' Keeley replied, stung all over again. 'We run a programme of events throughout the year, including a wealth of talks from notable speakers, and we encourage families with child-friendly activities.'

'And all those things are great,' he said, nodding. 'The sensory trail in the garden is particularly good – I bet toddlers and younger children really get into it, and the way you've tied it into scenes from Eliza's books is clever. But lectures by dusty academics won't increase your visitor numbers by much. Not because they're not interesting, but because the people who come to hear those speakers already know Eliza's work.'

Keeley took a sip of tea, fighting the urge to glare at him. 'We encourage everyone who visits Juniper Cottage to sign up to our mailing list, to help spread the word.'

Xander smiled. 'Again, that's great. Do you have a regular newsletter? Who monitors the engagement rate? Do you prune subscribers who delete without reading?'

She stared at him. 'They're people, not roses. Why would anyone prune them?'

'To avoid contact fatigue, for a start,' he said, shrugging. 'You want subscribers who are happy to hear from you, not ones who automatically hit the delete button because they're not interested in what you have to say.'

The trouble was, Keeley could see his point but she was damned if she was going to give him the satisfaction of saying so. Nor was she about to admit that she had never thought to check just how many newsletter subscribers read the emails she carefully composed every month. She folded her hands in her lap. 'Of course.'

Apparently picking up on her ruffled feathers, Xander puffed out a long breath. 'Look, I'm not handling this very well.' He tapped thoughtfully on the closed lid of his laptop. 'I prepared a whole presentation on visitor engagement and social media metrics but I've just had a better idea. What are you doing this weekend? Could you manage a trip into London?'

'London?' Keeley threw him a startled look. 'Why?'

He reached for his coffee. 'Have you ever heard of Delores Semple?'

She frowned, wondering if he was being deliberately obtuse in an effort to make her feel even more stupid. 'No.'

'She was a costume historian and visual artist who lived in London in the 1980s,' he said. 'Her family was descended from wealthy Huguenot weavers who had settled in Spitalfields in the 1700s, and Delores eventually inherited the family home on Folgate Street from a distant aunt. When she began to clear the house in preparation to sell it, she discovered much of the furniture dated back to the eighteenth century. In the attic, she found box after box of carefully preserved clothing. It inspired her to restore the house to the way it would have been when her ancestors first arrived and she spent the rest of her life doing exactly that. When she died, she left the house in trust as a museum.'

Keeley thinned her lips. 'And you want me to visit, to see how it should be done.'

'Yes,' Xander said, then paused. 'But that's not the only reason I want you to see it. Apart from anything else, I think you'd love it.'

Keeley could picture it now: a rosy-cheeked young woman at the door, bobbing and curtseying as she played the role of parlour maid to the household. Perhaps the lady of the house in an upstairs room, dressed in silks and powdered to within an inch of her life. Her mood darkened a little more. It wasn't that she had anything against actors bringing history to life in museums and stately homes, more that she didn't feel it was something that would work at Juniper Cottage. If that was what Xander had planned, then he was going to have a fight on his hands. 'Unfortunately, I have a friend coming to stay this weekend so I'm not free.'

If her lack of enthusiasm bothered him, he didn't show it. 'One day next week, then. I can arrange an early visit, before the doors open to the public, so you can have a good look round.'

She was tempted to decline again, but knew it would seem uncooperative. Perhaps it was better to agree and get it out of the way. That way she'd have a better idea of how much of a battle lay ahead. 'I'm free on Tuesday,' she said. 'Where in London do you want to meet?'

He grinned, subjecting her to another flash of dimples. 'Liverpool Street station – the house is only a few minutes' walk from there. Shall we say nine o'clock?'

She nodded before she could change her mind. 'Okay.'

'Amazing,' he said. 'Oh, and one other thing. Would you mind very much not looking up Delores or the house? I want you to come to the experience fresh, without any preconceptions.'

Keeley frowned, because researching Delores Semple was the first thing she'd intended to do once Xander had gone. 'Okay, if that's what you want.' She sat back, wondering what he'd been planning to say before he changed his approach. 'Is there anything you want to share about Juniper Cottage?'

'Not at this stage,' he said, and drained his coffee. 'It wouldn't achieve anything.'

She was tempted to point out that his visit had not achieved much either but held her tongue. The last thing she wanted was to goad him into delivering the threatened presentation. 'Well, I'm glad you enjoyed the gardens, at least.'

Xander raised his eyebrows, and once again, Keeley was left with the impression he knew exactly what she was thinking. 'I'm sure you have a million things to do so I'll let you get back to your day,' he said, rising to his feet and holding out his hand. 'Thanks for your time, Dr Cotterill.'

'You're welcome,' she said, grasping his outstretched fingers with her own. 'See you next week.'

Slotting his laptop into his rucksack once more, he smiled. 'I'm looking forward to it already.'

CHAPTER TWO

'There is nothing at all like Christmas to gladden the heart.'

Broadstairs House, ELIZA NORTON

The journey from Upper Benbridge to Freezy Tye should have taken Grace just under forty minutes but she had reckoned without the Friday evening traffic. An accident on the A12 had caused chaos around Chelmsford and every back road Grace took to avoid the gridlock seemed to be full of other drivers who'd had the same idea. It didn't help that a sudden thunderstorm had broken almost as soon as she'd got free of the jam. The torrential downpour had made the narrow country roads even more tricky to navigate than usual, with the windscreen wipers doing little to clear her view, and she'd encountered a flash flood that had forced her to find a different route. Throughout, the rumbling thunder had been close enough to rattle the windows of the car, making her wince. By the time she eventually eased through the gates leading to Keeley's charmingly tumbledown, peppermint-green-walled cottage, more than three hours after setting off, she felt as though she'd crawled over the finish line of an assault course. She really hoped Keeley had wine.

'Come in,' her friend cried, flinging open the front door to greet Grace as she splashed across the sodden gravel with her overnight bag. 'Has it been a total bugger of a journey?'

'You could say that,' Grace said, shaking her head in disbelief. 'I was meant to be here by six o'clock and now it's almost nine. Sorry I'm so late.'

Keeley took the supermarket carrier bag from her and ushered her across the doorstep. 'It's hardly your fault. And you're here now, that's all that matters. I've got a lasagne in the oven and a decent Chablis on ice.'

'You're a lifesaver,' Grace said gratefully, dropping her overnight bag to the flagstones. With a weary sigh, she reached out to embrace her friend. 'It's so good to see you.'

In seconds, she was wrapped in the warmth of Keeley's arms, closing her eyes to breathe in her familiar perfume even as strands of her blonde bob tickled her nose. The stress of the journey fell away and she felt somewhat restored as they broke apart to smile at one another. 'Tea first?' Keeley asked, raising a quizzical eyebrow. 'Or shall we go straight to the good stuff?'

Grace thought wistfully of the carrier bag she'd lugged in from the car, which Keeley had placed on the floor in the hallway, stuffed full of goodies that ranged from Twiglets and Greek olives to mince pies and Bailey's. But the humidity that the storm had done nothing to dispel meant that her T-shirt was clinging to her back and her fringe was stuck to her forehead; what she craved now was a chilled glass of something crisp and classy. 'Wine, please.'

Keeley nodded. 'I thought you'd say that. Why don't you go upstairs and freshen up, and I'll get pouring?'

The guest bedroom at the top of the crooked wooden staircase was every bit as comforting as Grace remembered. Dark polished floorboards gave way to a thick woven rug just inside the door, and pristine whitewashed walls rose up to meet the uneven oak beamed ceiling. Sage green curtains pooled around the lead-paned window, which had been left open to encourage a whisper of cool air to circulate. A walnut sleigh bed had pride of place, spread with a faded patchwork quilt that she knew had been made by Keeley's grandmother, and was dotted with an assortment of mismatched scatter cushions. An antique tall boy nestled into the alcove beside the chimney breast, its many drawers inviting Grace to deposit her clothes, secrets and dreams within, and the opposite alcove held a bookshelf, lined with cloth-covered hardbacks and dog-eared paperbacks that included a full collection of second-hand Agatha Christie novels as well as the entire, special edition *Bridgerton* series by Julia Quinn, complete with gloriously floral sprayed edges. Grace allowed her fingers to trail along their pristine spines before turning back to the bed. Two fluffy white towels lay folded at its foot; she was half tempted to seize one and head straight to the bathroom at the end of the landing for a much-needed, restorative shower, but she was conscious her late arrival had kept Keeley waiting long enough and her own stomach was grumbling, reminding her it had been a long time since lunch. She would shower before bed, she decided, and slip into the blissfully soft cotton sheets weary but freshly scrubbed.

Leaving her bag at the foot of the bed, Grace settled for a splash of cold water on her overheated cheeks and smoothed her limp brown curls into a scrunchie before making her way back downstairs. She'd learned long ago not to try to compete with Keeley in the chicness stakes; even when tumbling out of bed five minutes before the start of a lecture, she had always been effortlessly cool. Back then, her hair had been platinum blonde and her lips scarlet, and Grace might have remained every bit as much in awe of her as the first time they met, if Keeley hadn't also turned out to be lovely and funny and completely unaware of just how striking she was. They had bonded over a shared love of *Jane Eyre* and *Persuasion,* debating the merits of their preferred book boyfriends long into the night – Keeley had been Team Rochester, defiant in the face of Grace's insistence that Captain Wentworth's earnest dependability was infinitely sexier – and nursed each other's broken hearts when real-life boyfriends spectacularly failed to measure up to their literary counterparts. Now, more than twenty years on, their friendship had outlasted their marriages and was stronger than ever, even if they were often too busy to do more than grab the occasional lunch.

'So,' Keeley said, handing her a brimming glass as she entered the kitchen. 'How's the flown chick? Have you heard from him?'

'He's okay, as far as I can tell,' Grace replied. 'He's not the best at communicating but I did get a text to say he'd landed safely, and Kevin called to reassure me he'd met him at the airport.'

Keeley's grey eyes were steady over the top of her wine glass, and Grace was uncomfortably aware her friend saw everything she was trying to hide. 'Give him time. It's a big adjustment, arriving in a new country. He'll start missing you once the novelty wears off and then you'll hear from him more.'

Grace sighed. 'I know. It's just hard. I don't want him to miss me – I want him to have an amazing time and reconnect with his dad and get to know his new family. But . . .'

'You want to still feel part of his life,' Keeley finished gently, as Grace trailed off and tears prickled her eyelids. 'That's perfectly understandable. I'd be the same, in your shoes.'

Except that Keeley wouldn't be caught dead in the scuffed and battered trainers Grace had worn to drive over, she thought a little wildly, and a small sniff of self-pity escaped her. She took a gulp of wine. 'I need to get a grip. Find a job, something to take my mind off how quiet the house is.'

Turning away, Keeley reached for an oven glove. 'Any idea what you want to do?'

'Not a clue.' Grace sighed again, watching as her friend withdrew a golden bubbling lasagne and lowered it onto a trivet. 'I'm pathetic, aren't I? A living, breathing midlife cliché.'

'You're neither of those things,' Keeley replied sternly. 'You're at a crossroads, that's all. Now, if you can grab the basket of garlic bread, we're ready to eat. Shall we sit down?'

Grace did as she asked and carried it over to the small table in the corner. 'Sorry,' she said, sinking into a wooden chair. 'I know every parent goes through something like this when their kids grow up.'

Immediately, Keeley's hand was on hers. 'Hey, don't apologise. I understand. You've spent years putting Jack first, and pouring everything else into your work. Now both of those responsibilities have gone, it's only natural you're feeling a bit lost.' She dug into the lasagne, releasing a cloud of rich, tomato-scented steam. 'You could always volunteer at Juniper Cottage for a month or two, while you figure out what comes next.'

It wasn't a bad suggestion, Grace thought, picturing the sunflower yellow walls and dark thatched roof of Eliza Norton's home, nestled on one side of Freezy Tye's village green. It wasn't as though she needed to worry about money, not with the cushion of her redundancy payment tucked away in her bank account, and it would be no hardship to spend a few hours each week chatting to fellow book lovers. 'Do you need another volunteer?'

'Always,' Keeley replied, without hesitation. 'Things tend to quieten down in the run-up to Christmas but there's still plenty to do. Although you're ridiculously overqualified and far too level-headed to fit in with the rest of the team. You should have seen the way they reacted to the arrival of our new creative director this afternoon.'

'Oh!' Grace's hand flew to her mouth. 'With all the travel drama, I completely forgot you were meeting him today. How did it go?'

Her friend piled green salad onto her plate. 'The meeting itself wasn't anything to write home about. He came, he saw, he didn't have anything useful to say and then he left. But Elspeth and Jenny pretty much lost their heads, giggling and whispering like they'd met some kind of rock star. You'd think they were teenagers, not fully grown women with partners and families.'

Grace frowned. 'Is he good-looking then?'

'He's an Aussie,' Keeley said, and shrugged. 'All blond hair and twinkling blue eyes, a bit like that actor who was in all those superhero films a few years ago.'

'Oh,' Grace replied, widening her gaze. 'In that case, I'm inclined to cut Elspeth and Jenny some slack.'

Keeley stabbed at a lettuce leaf. 'I don't care what he looks like. What bothers me is how much he's going to interfere. He's making me visit a museum on Tuesday morning, so I can see all the things I'm doing wrong at Juniper Cottage.'

Grace felt her mouth drop open. 'He said that?'

'Not exactly,' Keeley admitted. 'But that was the implication. He dressed it up by suggesting it was something I'd enjoy.'

Grace took a mouthful of lasagne, taking a moment to savour the richness of the béchamel sauce mingling with the bolognaise as she considered her friend's words. It wasn't like Keeley to react so defensively to change, especially when it was designed to help increase public awareness of Eliza's writing. Whatever his intentions, it seemed the newcomer had only succeeded in ruffling feathers. 'What's the museum?'

'Delores Semple's house, in Spitalfields,' Keeley said. 'It's quite a small place, I think. Have you heard of it?'

Grace nodded enthusiastically. 'I have. And I think Mr Rock Star is right – you're going to love it. In fact, I'm surprised you've never been.'

Again, Keeley shrugged. 'He made me promise not to look it up, which made sense at the time but seems ridiculous now.'

'No, I think I understand where he's coming from,' Grace replied, chewing thoughtfully. 'It's the kind of place you need to experience to really appreciate it. Reading up on what to expect might take away from that.' She paused to throw her friend an apologetic look. 'He sounds like he knows his stuff.'

'We'll see,' Keeley answered tersely, then appeared to make a conscious effort to soften her features. 'But enough about Xander Jones, he's a problem for next week. What would you like to do tomorrow? I need to work the till in the gift shop all morning but the afternoon is clear.'

Which allowed Grace a lazy morning of browsing Keeley's impeccably curated bookshelves, she thought with a small flutter of pleasure. 'Perfect,' she said. 'How about afternoon tea at that nice garden centre near Flaxwood?'

'Ruggles?' Keeley pursed her lips. 'That works. I could pick up some autumn bedding plants while we're there and you can help me decide where to put them.'

'Sounds like heaven,' Grace said, and winced. 'Ugh, did I really just say that? I told you I've morphed into a middle-aged cliché.'

Keeley laughed. 'If that's the case then I'm one too, but I don't mind a bit.' She raised her wine glass in salute. 'Here's to our garden centre era.'

The mirth dancing in her eyes made Grace feel a little better. She chinked her own glass against that of her friend. 'You know, it doesn't sound so bad when you put it like that. Cheers!'

While Grace was of the considered opinion that August was most definitely still summer, it seemed Ruggles Garden Centre had leapt headlong into autumn. The grand, domed entrance lobby was awash with russet, gold and brown in the form of artfully arranged floral displays and cascading garlands loaded with glistening berries. Leaf-shaped bunting criss-crossed beneath the glass-panelled ceiling, plush miniature pumpkins in purples, greens and creams were piled high on old-fashioned wooden handcarts, while real pumpkins and their smaller, sister squashes nestled in raffia-packed crates on the floor. An assortment of lanterns hung at different heights; Grace could imagine them filled with fairy lights or flickering faux-flames. She lingered beside a display of scented candles, all bearing names like *Fireside Dreams* and *Toffee Apple Delight*, and was tempted to choose one to brighten up her living room when she returned home. Jack had always complained about the smell when she'd lit them previously, calling them 'mum catnip' so she'd stopped buying them. But there was something soothing about the gentle glow of candlelight, and having a room filled with a mood-enhancing aroma. There would be more inside, she supposed. Perhaps she'd pick one up before they left.

'This is nothing,' Keeley said, when Grace commented on the abundance of autumnal decorations. 'You should see the pumpkin patch they open in September – it's like walking into Stars Hollow. I half expected to find Lorelai running the cinnamon bun stall.'

Grace smiled, because they'd both loved the idyllic small-town setting of the *Gilmore Girls* television series. 'Sounds like I need to come back next month.'

'Definitely,' Keeley nodded. 'We could take a pumpkin-carving class.'

At that, Grace's spirits dipped, because carving a too-big pumpkin for Halloween had been an autumn tradition Jack had loved when he was younger. But it had been years since he'd shown any interest and Grace couldn't remember the last time she'd bought one. These days, she left a bowl of sweets on the doorstep for visiting trick-or-treaters, with a note to help themselves. 'Maybe,' she said.

Her friend eyed her knowingly. 'You're allowed to make new traditions, Grace.' She pointed to a poster advertising an autumn wreath workshop. 'I remember you producing the most glorious wreaths for your front door in Christmases gone by. Fancy seeing if you've still got what it takes?'

What it took was a base, some greenery and an eye-watering amount of floristry wire, Grace thought, but it was true that making her own festive wreath had been one of the Christmas rituals she'd enjoyed the most; she and Keeley had occasionally managed to align their diaries to attend a workshop together. And then one year she'd been poorly, and she'd found an old artificial one in the loft that had done the job almost as well, and somehow she'd never found the time to get back to making her own. Much like mixing her own Christmas cake on Stir-Up Sunday, or baking a gingerbread house to decorate once school had broken up, or filling the house with the scent of homemade mince pies. There didn't seem much point in going the extra mile when Jack was too busy growing up to notice. But dipping her toe back into something creative with Keeley could be fun. Maybe she was right – it was time to make some new traditions, for her own enjoyment rather than to please someone else. 'I'd like that. But only if you have time.'

'I'll make time,' Keeley said. 'Now, do you mind if we head to the cafe first? I didn't have time for lunch and I'm starving.'

By a stroke of luck, they found a table in one corner of the busy courtyard, shaded by a large parasol, and before long they were working their way through a delicious selection of sandwiches, delicate pastries and mouth-watering scones presented on an arched brass stand. Grace felt her enjoyment was only improved by the exquisite rose-painted tea set it was served on. The overall effect was gloriously old-fashioned; she felt as though she'd slipped into a bygone era, where the taking of tea was the lynchpin of good society. 'This is lovely,' she told Keeley, when a lull in conversation allowed her to gaze around in appreciation. 'Thanks for inviting me to stay this weekend.'

'Totally my pleasure,' Keeley said, leaning back in her seat with a contented sigh. 'I've been so caught up with work recently that I've forgotten what it's like to take a bit of time for myself. And I can't remember the last time I ate here – I usually make straight for the plants and get through the tills as quickly as I can. I'd forgotten how decadent an afternoon tea can be.'

Decadent was an excellent description, Grace decided as she sipped her Earl Grey, but calorific was another – her stomach was groaning and there were still several scones and cakes left uneaten. 'We'll get a box to take them home in,' Keeley said, rubbing her own enviably flat stomach. She looked around for a member of staff. 'They can be a teatime treat tomorrow, before you leave.'

Once the leftovers had been packaged up, Keeley led the way through the various rooms of the garden centre towards the outdoor plants. 'They really go all out for Christmas,' she said as they passed a tempting display of velvety red and orange toadstools. 'The rooms are transformed into grottos, arranged by colour and theme, and each one has a fully decorated tree in the middle to make it easier to visualise how the baubles and ribbons on the shelves will look. The arrival of the preview evening invitation in November sets off my "Christmas is Coming" klaxon.'

Even now, three months from the frenzied whirl of the festive period, Grace could picture the scene. 'No wonder Freezy Tye wins the Most Christmassy Village award every year, with this place on the doorstep.'

Keeley shook her head. 'Ruggles is fantastic, but the planning for the village displays starts long before the decorations go up here.' She smiled. 'Let's pick out some plants and I'll introduce you to the secret of our success.'

Mystified, Grace could only follow her friend to the outdoor nursery, where rows of low wooden shelves stretched into the distance, filled with pots of joyful colour. Bees buzzed around clusters of lavender, the scent of roses drifted from a nearby display and a pair of unrepentant blue tits chased each other across the space between shelves, in search of seeds or worms or both. She watched Keeley briskly assess the assortment of autumn bedding plants and select several plugs of cheery pansies and a number of bold pink cyclamen. 'These will brighten things up,' she said, loading them into the pull-along basket. 'We have a professional gardener at Juniper Cottage and I'm always stealing his ideas, although on a much smaller scale.'

Pausing for Grace to collect one of the scented candles she'd noticed earlier, they paid and made their way back to where they had parked. But instead of steering the car towards the exit and the main road, Keeley turned left, to where the smooth tarmac of the garden centre car park gave way to a wide, three-bar gate and a dusty track beyond it.

'We're not going home?' Grace asked, frowning as they bumped along the less well-maintained road. Sturdy hedgerows on either side hid whatever lay ahead from view.

'No, Alice,' Keeley said, with a mysterious smile. 'We're going to wonderland.'

Before Grace could ask what she meant, the car rounded the bend to reveal a tall, oak-beamed barn. A cheery red and white sign above the plain wooden door bore the name 'Santa's Secret' but there were no other obvious clues about the building's purpose. She glanced at Keeley in bafflement. 'What is it?

A getaway for Father Christmas when he wants a break from the North Pole?'

Her friend laughed. 'No, this is Freezy Tye's secret weapon in the battle to remain Britain's most Christmassy village. You'll understand when we go inside.'

None the wiser, Grace followed Keeley to the entrance. 'After you,' Keeley said, holding the door back and sweeping an arm to usher Grace inside.

The room Grace stepped into was disconcertingly not what she was expecting. Instead of the open space suggested by the barn's exterior, she found herself in a square room, enclosed by four white walls and a ceiling. Two closed doors punctuated the wall opposite the entrance, plain and nondescript. A counter ran along one wall, upon which sat a number of old-fashioned electronic tills. Michael Bublé and Shania Twain crooned in unison from an unseen speaker, dreaming of a white Christmas with little regard for the fact that it was August. A young woman stood behind one of the tills, tapping at the keys and chatting to the customer in front of her as she worked her way through the contents of her shopping basket. She glanced up and smiled. 'Welcome to Santa's Secret. Have you visited before?'

Keeley nodded, bending to pick up a shopping basket from a pile near the right-hand door. 'Don't worry, I know my way round.' She gave Grace a mischievous look. 'Ready?'

'I suppose so,' Grace said. 'Lead on.'

Nothing could have prepared her for the assault on her senses as she stepped through the door on the right. The barn had been divided into corridors, using the same white walls as the entrance hall, but that was where the similarity ended. Boxes of tinsel in every conceivable colour stretched along the wooden trestle tables that lined one wall, shimmering strands spilling over the cardboard rims to trail haphazardly onto the table top and merge into rainbow puddles. Bolts of fabric in reds and greens and golds, patterned and plain, peeked from deep shelves on the opposite wall. Strings of sequins cascaded from rolls hung from hooks on the walls, dazzling under the fluorescent strip lights, while loose streams of ribbon jostled over row after row of unopened cellophane-wrapped siblings. Oversized red and white candy canes stood to attention in glittery rows, while garlands of gold-berried greenery looped around pillars that appeared to serve no other purpose than to display them. Grace stood gaping for several seconds; it was as though someone had jumbled up every type of Christmas haberdashery known to humanity and thrown them at the walls. And then a movement just to her right caught her eye. Turning, she discovered an enormous, white-furred polar bear standing majestically on hind legs rotating slowly towards her. 'Oh!'

'That's Albert,' Keeley said, matter-of-factly. 'Usually, he's on duty at Ruggles over the festive period but he did star in the ice grotto we built in the village bandstand a few years ago.'

Now that her initial surprise was subsiding, Grace could see the polar bear was exquisitely made. His fur rippled gently as he moved and the beady black eyes seemed to be watching her intently. 'He's brilliant,' she said, reaching out to brush a white paw. 'I bet the kids love him.'

Keeley smiled. 'They did. He has a wife and a baby too, but I expect they're hibernating.'

Grace could picture the scene. The bandstand stood at the heart of Freezy Tye's village green and was a stout wooden construction open on all sides, but all it would take was a few sheets of MDF and some imagination to transform it into a frozen cave for the polar bears. 'How did you power them?' she asked, her thoughts moving inevitably to the logistics. She'd lost count of the number of times she'd had to rein in the wild enthusiasm of younger colleagues at the library around the Summer Reading Challenge and World Book Day. 'Did you use a generator?'

'We're much greener than that,' Keeley replied, sounding pleased with herself. 'The village council paid for cabling to be laid under the grass, running all the way to the hall. We could light up the whole green if we needed to.'

Grace nodded, impressed at the forward-thinking skills of the village council. 'Wow.'

'But enough about that,' Keeley said. 'Don't you want to dive headlong into Christmas heaven?'

Grace took a deep breath, noticing the crisp scent of pine for the first time. Nat King Cole had taken over from Michael and Shania, giving her a sudden yearning for roasted chestnuts. The tumult of décor stretched invitingly to the end of the corridor; she could only imagine what glittering treasures lay in the next aisle. 'I do,' she replied. 'But first, I need to investigate those ribbons. That iridescent peacock pattern is calling me.'

Keeley gave her a knowing look. 'Do you have a project in mind for it?'

'No. Does that matter?'

'Absolutely not,' Keeley said. 'I might get a roll of that silver and pink. Have you noticed the boxes of blue and green baubles underneath the table?'

Grace had not but she exclaimed in delight when she saw they matched the colours of the ribbon perfectly. 'Why do I get the feeling this is going to cost me a fortune?' she said, dropping them into the basket.

'This is just for starters,' Keeley replied. 'Wait until we get to the main course.'

Grace understood what she meant as soon as they reached the Nutcracker-themed aisle, which was guarded by two of the wooden soldiers from the sumptuously Christmassy story, resplendent in red and gold, and taller even than Keeley. She half expected them to cross their spears in challenge as they passed through the leafy, fairy-lit arch they flanked. The decorations ranged on the tables beyond complemented their scarlet uniforms, golden garlands nestled among glittering red and yellow baubles, and puffs of snowy berries on wiry stalks, ready to be twisted into floral arrangements or swags. Halfway down the aisle, they met another pair of life-sized soldiers, their uniforms a deep, festive green bedecked with gold buttons that was matched by the decorations piled upon tables on either side. The final pair of guards were white and silver, and the colour-themed displays beyond them were dotted with pale pinks and lilacs and blues. Sugary baubles hung from the white faux tree branches that formed arches over their head, and adorable mice in frilly tutus danced on the air.

Grace also spotted several Sugar Plum Fairy figurines, some caught in a graceful ballerina leap and others spinning in an endless pirouette, their wings catching the light, while rows of dark-haired Clara dolls watched them twirl. The exuberance of silver-tinged pastels was beautiful, Grace thought, and the sheer amount of white evoked the impression of freshly fallen snow. But the crowning glory of the aisle was the eight-foot Christmas tree at the end, painstakingly decorated with hundreds of twinkling decorations to mimic the one that graced Clara's home in the story, with a magnificent white rocking horse before it. The breath caught in Grace's throat as she stopped to admire the scene. 'That is incredible,' she breathed, and hurried forwards to peer up at the frosted branches, laden with ribbons and baubles. 'It must have taken hours.'

'It did,' a voice said, and a silver-haired woman of around sixty stepped out from behind the tree. She smoothed her calf-length, Liberty floral dress and sighed. 'Six and a half hours, to be exact, and at least two of them were spent perched on a rickety stepladder.'

The need for a stepladder wasn't a surprise, given the woman couldn't be much more than five feet tall. Keeley came to a halt beside Grace. 'Allow me to introduce the enchantress behind everything you see here,' she said, smiling. 'Grace, this is Ivy Caldwell, the owner of Santa's Secret.'

Ivy nodded in greeting. 'Nice to meet you, Grace. I wish I did have a magic wand to create all of this but unfortunately, we rely on plain old hard work.'

'I can tell,' Grace said, gazing in fresh wonderment at the perfectly spaced decorations. There was not so much as a strand of tinsel out of place.

'The displays are constantly changing throughout the year,' Keeley explained. 'Last time I was here, this was a toymaker's grotto.'

Grace blinked. 'You're open all year?'

'Oh yes,' Ivy said, as though it was obvious. 'It's Christmas all the way around these parts – event planners and keen festive decorators start the hunt for fresh items long before December.' She waved a hand at the tables they had just passed. 'What you see here is about a third of what we usually have in stock. It's late in the season, you see.'

'Ivy used to be the genius behind the window displays at Selfridge's on Oxford Street,' Keeley told Grace. 'What she doesn't know about creating the perfect Christmas tableau isn't worth knowing.'

Grace felt her jaw drop slightly. The windows at the venerable Oxford Street department store were world-famous and their Christmas displays were an attraction in their own right, drawing in crowds so large they often blocked the pavement, much to the irritation of the Londoners who had to edge around them. Keeley hadn't exaggerated when she'd used the word genius; they were in the presence of brilliance. 'My mum used to take me to see those windows every December when I was a child. It was one of our Christmas traditions.'

Ivy looked gratified. 'Oh, I'm glad. I do miss peeking out to see all the happy, wonder-filled faces of the people who stopped to stare, but tastes change and it was time to let someone else have a turn. And now I have a whole shop to arrange exactly as I please, with the added bonus of knowing our decorations are used in hundreds of displays that fill so many more people with Christmas spirit.'

'Including us in Freezy Tye,' Keeley put in. 'Our planning committee is meeting in a few weeks to pull together our thoughts for the village display. We'll need to up our game if we're going to win Most Christmassy Village again.'

'Ah yes,' Ivy said, nodding. 'I did hear that Flaxwood are going all out this year. Don't leave it too late if you're interested in outdoor lights or animated figures – I have a feeling the best ones will get snapped up early.'

Keeley looked intrigued. 'Flaxwood – really? They've never shown much interest before.'

'They've got some new blood on the committee,' Ivy said, and lowered her voice. 'The elder son of the family that owns Ruggles has moved back into the village and seems determined to put the place on the map.'

'Has he, now?' Keeley looked thoughtful. 'Well, a bit of competition is a good thing. As long as you keep the best decorations for us, Ivy.'

The older woman smiled. 'I'll see what I can do.'

They parted company then, with Ivy explaining she was short-staffed and needed to help on the tills. Grace and Keeley continued to wind their way around the festive labyrinth, pausing to admire an aisle dressed with giant sweets, gaudy lollipops and other oversized sugary delights. It made Grace's teeth hurt just to look at them but she could imagine what a show-stopping display they would make in the right setting.

'Ivy supplies a lot of the stands at Winter Wonderland,' Keeley said, when Grace suggested the decorations might be a bit much for the average family. 'And last year's pantomime in Chelmsford turned the entire foyer into a sweet shop with these.'

It made sense, of course, and Grace was impressed all over again. 'What a wonderful place to work,' she said. 'I'm a bit surprised Ivy is short-staffed, I can't imagine a nicer working environment. I bet they never have to deal with grumpy customers. How could anyone be bad-tempered surrounded by so much joy?'

Keeley laughed. 'Oh, I'm sure they encounter plenty of grinches. Look, this is the last aisle before we get to more practical stuff. Have you got everything you want?'

Biting her lip, Grace looked down at the basket. 'Would you be very annoyed if I nipped back to grab one of the miniature Nutcracker dolls?'

'Not at all,' Keeley said. 'Why don't I meet you by the tills?'

Grace felt quite proud of herself for resisting a set of exquisite London landmark tree ornaments as she retraced her steps along the 'Christmas Around the World' display. It was a tougher challenge to ignore the siren call of the twirling Sugar Plum Fairy, however, and she added a pair of plump mice for good measure. The pink tinsel was probably a step too far, she told herself, thrusting her hand into her pocket before it could reach out and snare the glistening strands. Then again, who did she have to please but herself? But she left the tinsel where it was – she could always revisit the shop if she changed her mind.

Keeley was chatting amiably with the girl behind the counter when Grace finally puffed through the door into the entrance foyer. 'There you are,' she said, eyeing her flushed cheeks with amusement. 'I thought you'd been whisked away by Dr Drosselmeyer.'

'I wish,' Grace said, picturing the wizard whose magic sent Clara on her dreamlike adventure to save the Nutcracker in the story. 'But sadly, I merely underestimated how heavy my basket would be once I'd added everything I wanted to buy. I had to drag it the last few metres.'

The girl on the till grinned as she saw Grace's overflowing basket. 'My mum is exactly the same when she comes here. She can't resist the sparkle.'

'Guilty as charged,' Grace sighed. 'But on the plus side, my Christmas tree is going to look amazing.'

'Definitely,' the girl said. 'If you can't go all out at Christmas, when can you?'

While she rang the items through, Grace allowed her gaze to wander. Beside the till, in a transparent A4 stand, was a poster advertising a job vacancy.

WANTED:
Part-time worker

(20 hours per week, some evening and weekend working required)

Must be fit, with some experience of working with the public, and a genuine passion for Christmas. A good eye for display an advantage.

Competitive salary and staff discount available.

For further details, and for an informal chat, telephone 01245 548 8565 and ask for Ivy, or email admin@santassecret

'That's everything for you,' the girl said, snapping Grace back to attention. She tried not to wince as she saw the amount and tapped her card on the reader. She'd spent more than she'd anticipated but supposed it would all be worth it in December, when the opening scenes of *Love Actually* began to play and she was sipping a glass of Bailey's. Keeley's purchases had been much more modest but, Grace reminded herself, it wasn't her first visit to Santa's Secret.

'Oh yes, I spent a fortune the first time I came here,' Keeley said as they loaded their bags into the boot of the car, taking care not to crowd the bedding plants. 'And on my second and third visits. Don't beat yourself up.'

Grace reached out a hand to stroke the fluffy pink feathers adorning one of the mice and sighed. 'I'll try not to.'

She stepped back, allowing the boot to close and made for the passenger door. As she did so, a grey Land Rover drove into the car park and stopped a few spaces away. 'Speaking of grinches,' Keeley said, rolling her eyes, 'here's one now.'

The tinted glass made it difficult for Grace to see who was driving but she assumed her friend was joking. There was a swish as a door opened, the crunch of feet on the gravel and a thud as the door closed. A dark-haired man of around forty appeared around the back of the car, talking into a mobile phone. He glanced towards Keeley's car and his gaze slid to Grace, who suddenly felt as though all the wind had been punched from her lungs. He was tall and tanned, with finely chiselled cheekbones and a long, slender nose that might have been beaky in a less handsome face. A mane of untidy black hair was swept back from a proud forehead, tinged with grey at the temples. As she desperately tried not to stare, he waved a key fob to lock the Land Rover and strode past them, nodding to Keeley as he went. Grace felt her stomach lurch as his gaze swept over her, and she thought for a paralysing moment that he would stop. But then he was gone, disappearing through the door of Santa's Secret. Feeling suddenly in need of support, Grace leaned against the car and took a deep breath. 'Um. Who was that?'

Keeley paused as she was about to climb into the driver's seat and eyed her curiously. 'Raff Caldwell. He's Ivy's son and all-round grumpy bugger, although he's not so bad once you get to know him. Why?'

'Oh, no reason,' Grace said, hoping her cheeks weren't as flaming red as they felt. 'I just wondered. He didn't look the type to love oversized candy canes.'

What he looked like was a Greek god, she wanted to say, all lean muscle and classical features – a face that Michelangelo would have sculpted in a heartbeat. But Keeley was staring at her now, so she ducked into the car and pretended to check her phone.

'He's not,' Keeley said, settling into the seat beside her. 'He's a landscape gardener – the one who manages the gardens at Juniper Cottage – and he's very good at his job.' She started the engine and shook her head. 'What he's less good at is interpersonal skills. I suppose that's why he likes plants – they don't expect him to maintain a conversation.'

'But that hardly makes him a grinch,' Grace objected, wondering how anyone so beautiful could be anything less than perfect on the inside, before remembering that most of her favourite novels were littered with gorgeous men who'd turned out to be utter scoundrels.

'No, it doesn't,' Keeley agreed, checking the rear-view mirror before she reversed. 'But I called him a grinch because he doesn't like Christmas. I mean, I suppose it's sort of understandable, given that Ivy lives and breathes it, but I don't think he has much to do with Santa's Secret.'

'Oh,' Grace said, glancing at the barn. 'That's a shame. For his mum, I mean. In her work.'

She stopped talking, aware she was babbling. Keeley shrugged. 'He's good at gardening – that's what matters to me.' She fired an inquisitive look at Grace. 'And he's single, if you're interested.'

And Grace felt her spirits sink, because another lesson she'd learned from romantic fiction was that if an exquisitely good-looking man was single, there was usually a very good reason. 'Of course I'm not,' she said, with a little more force than she intended. 'Like I said, I just wondered who he was.'

'Uh huh,' Keeley said, turning her attention back to the road and negotiating the bumps in the track. 'I have his number if you change your mind.'

Grace chose not to dignify that with an answer. But all the same, she watched the door to Santa's Secret in the wing mirror until it was out of sight.

CHAPTER THREE

'You have a great deal too many opinions, sir. Good day to you.'

Where the Wind Blows, ELIZA NORTON

Xander had not exaggerated when he'd told Keeley that Delores Semple's house was only a few minutes' walk from Liverpool Street station. The plan was to meet him outside the station but she'd caught an earlier train, negotiating the stream of commuters heading into the City, to give herself the opportunity to form her own initial impressions of the house without Xander breathing down her neck.

Folgate Street was easily found, a row of red-bricked, four-storey terraced residential houses nestled improbably among the shadows of towering steel and glass skyscrapers. To Keeley's sharp-eyed gaze, number 20 looked much the same as its neighbours; the wooden shutters covering the windows were perhaps a little shabbier than those of the house to the right, and the lantern protruding over the black front door somewhat old-fashioned, but that was not out of character for this part of the city. There was no sign on the wall to attract passers-by, no plaque proclaiming that here was a place of historical significance; nothing, in fact, to suggest it was anything other than an old but unremarkable house, in a street of old but unremarkable houses. Frowning, Keeley checked the address she'd found online. It was the right house. She glanced up the cobbled road, to where double-decker buses and taxis trundled along the busy main thoroughfare, and down towards the more distant Commercial Street, but there wasn't much more to see. Slightly regretting the enthusiasm that had cost her an extra half hour in bed, she retraced her steps to a bustling coffee shop she'd passed on leaving the station and ordered a latte.

'Dr Cotterill, hi,' Xander said, firing her an easy smile as she neared where he stood outside Liverpool Street at nine o'clock on the dot. 'Thanks for coming.'

He was dressed in a plain white T-shirt that emphasised his tan, and jeans with scuffed trainers. His hair was tousled and Keeley couldn't tell if he'd styled it that way or simply neglected to brush it. She felt a little overdressed in her sedate cotton dress and linen jacket. 'Good morning,' she replied, trying not to let the stiffness she felt at seeing him again affect her tone. 'Shall we go?'

Without waiting for him to answer, she turned back towards the pelican crossing that allowed pedestrians to navigate the thundering traffic. Xander fell into step beside her and they both stopped at the crossing. 'How was your weekend?' he asked while they waited for the lights to change. 'You had a friend to visit, didn't you?'

She nodded, surprised he'd remembered. 'It was lovely. She's an old friend – we went to university together – but we don't see each other as often as we'd like. It was good to catch up.'

'I've got a few mates like that,' he said, over the shrill beeping of the crossing. 'You don't meet up for ages but when you do get together, it's like you saw each other last week.'

That was certainly how it was with Grace, Keeley thought. 'How long have you been over here?' she asked, then hesitated. 'I assume you're from Australia originally?'

They turned into Folgate Street. 'That's right,' Xander said easily. 'I grew up in Brisbane but came to England around seven years ago. It was only meant to be a short visit but I fell in love with the place – there's just so much history here. I'm practically a native now.'

She gave him a sideways glance, taking in the healthy glow of his skin and air of relaxed confidence that made her feel sallow and uptight by comparison. He definitely didn't look like a typical Londoner, that was for sure.

'And here we are,' he went on, coming to a halt outside the house Keeley had studied less than thirty minutes earlier. 'Delores Semple's house.'

She looked up at the red-bricked building, noting that the shutters were now open. 'It's very low key. I wouldn't have known it was here if you hadn't told me.'

Xander nodded. 'That's part of Delores' creative vision, that the everyday can hide something extraordinary.' He eyed Keeley speculatively. 'Did you manage to resist digging into the history of the house?'

'Of course,' Keeley said, although she had been sorely tempted to click on the links that had appeared when she'd sought out its location. 'You did tell me not to.'

'I did,' he agreed. 'But I've had a lot of experience of working with experts in their field, and I've learned to respect both their curiosity and their rebellious nature. It wouldn't have been the end of the world if you'd looked – I just think you'll enjoy it more if you form your own impressions.'

With that, he stepped forwards to lift the large brass door-knocker and gave two sharp raps. Keeley braced herself, anticipating an actor in character would open the door but instead, they were greeted by a young woman in her mid-twenties, dressed in jeans and a rainbow-striped pullover. 'I thought it would be you,' she said, reaching out to kiss Xander on both cheeks. 'Good to see you. It's been too long.'

Xander stepped back. 'Poppy Wolstenholme, this is Dr Keeley Cotterill, curator of Juniper Cottage in Essex.'

The young woman moved forward to shake Keeley's hand. 'No need to explain who she is, Xander,' she said reprovingly. 'It's an honour to meet you, Dr Cotterill. I'm a huge Eliza Norton fangirl and have visited the cottage loads of times.'

The undisguised enthusiasm in her voice meant Keeley warmed to her immediately. 'That's great to hear,' she said, smiling. 'And please, call me Keeley.'

'Poppy is the creative director here,' Xander said. 'She's utterly brilliant and has an intuitive understanding of what Delores Semple wanted to achieve.'

'Thanks, Dad,' Poppy said, firing a mischievous grin his way. 'But let's not waste time out here. Come in, I'm dying to see what you think.'

She moved back and beckoned them over the doorstep. Keeley found herself in a cool, dimly lit hallway panelled in dark wood, with a black-and-white tiled floor and a wide, curving staircase at the far end. It was quiet, once the heavy front door swung shut and blocked out the city beyond; the only sound was the tick-tock of a majestic grandfather clock that stood at the foot of the stairs. Keeley took a breath and let it out, allowing the hush to roll over her, and wondered if she was imagining the thrum of expectation in the air, the sense that something, perhaps the house itself, was breathing along with her. She glanced at Xander, wondering if he noticed it too, and saw he was studying her, a half-smile playing around his lips.

Beside them, Poppy stirred. 'You know your way round, Xander, so I'll leave you to it,' she murmured, then flashed an almost nervous look Keeley's way. 'I really hope you enjoy it.'

With a final nod, she hurried along the hallway and disappeared through a door in the well of the stairs. Xander raised his eyebrows. 'Ready?' he asked Keeley, who nodded. 'One last thing before we start – Delores was a great believer in letting the stories of the house speak for themselves, and recommended visitors spoke as little as possible as they moved from room to room. Are you okay with a silent tour today?'

Once again, Keeley felt a faint shift in the atmosphere, the barely there suggestion of a quietly drawn-in breath being held in anticipation. 'Of course,' she said, trying to rein in her imagination. 'Lead the way.'

The first room they entered was through a door on the right of the hall, and had clearly been dressed as an eighteenth-century dining room. It was dominated by a large, oval table, surrounded by ornate, silk-padded chairs, and laden with food and drink. Plates were filled with ripe grapes and cheese, although some appeared to have been abandoned part way through eating, and glasses glistened with ruby wine. A Baroque melody rumbled quietly in the background, overlaid by the discreet sounds of a meal being taken: the chink of cutlery, a murmur of voices, the faint tinkle of bell-like laughter. Somewhere nearby, a man cleared his throat and the sounds faded, leaving only the unobtrusive meander of the harpsichord. Keeley stood transfixed in the doorway, her gaze roving the room, admiring the exquisite attention to detail and obvious care that had been taken in setting the scene. Her impression was that she was the invisible observer of the family in whose home she stood, peeping through the veil of time to catch a glimpse of their daily lives, if not the family members themselves.

They were wealthy, she thought, moving nearer to the table and studying the half-carved roast in the centre, the assortment of fruits and other expensive treats. Now that she was closer, she could see that the food was real and the realisation drew a small gasp of surprise. How often did it need to be replaced? She made a mental note to ask Poppy later. She wandered away from the table, turning her attention to the paintings that adorned the walls. One was a portrait of a stout, red-cheeked man in a luxurious brown periwig, standing proudly beside a handsome black hound. A discreet brass plaque declared him to be Jerome Lestrade and it was dated 1751; there was no mention of the dog, which Keeley thought was rather a shame. The neighbouring painting was a landscape, the richness of the colours dulled a little with age but still recognisable as a French village scene, and Keeley recalled Xander had mentioned the house had once belonged to Huguenot weavers who had emigrated from France. Perhaps this painting was a reminder of the home they had been forced to leave behind in the face of religious persecution.

Moving around the table, she felt her shins suddenly grow warm and was surprised to see a fire glowing in the hearth. At Juniper Cottage, they rarely lit the fires in summer but she had to admit that it lent an authenticity to the scene, as well as lacing the air with a hint of coal and wood smoke that mingled with the heady scent of cloves and oranges. A rich family would take pride in showing they were able to afford to burn fuel all year round, she supposed. Propped against a candlestick on the mantelpiece, she spotted a gilt-edged invitation to a ball at Blandford's Assembly Rooms, addressed to Jerome Lestrade, Esq and family – another sign of the family's respectable position in society. Keeley reached up to run a finger over the curved black lettering, before recalling where she was and thrusting her hand into her pocket. She doubted the invitation was old – very few of the flourishes on display were, for all they were authentic to the period – but she had far too much professional respect for the hard work that had been put in to create the exhibits to overstep the mark.

She was so drawn in by the attention to detail that it was only when a floorboard creaked loudly over by the window that she remembered she was not alone. Glancing across the room, she saw Xander looking apologetic. The sight of him pulled her back to the present and it occurred to her that she had no idea how much time had passed since entering the room. The background sounds had changed, the harpsichord had been replaced by a gently tinkling piano and, beneath it, she caught the faint tread of footsteps, as though the family were moving around the rest of the house. It was all so well done, she thought in admiration, and realised she was eager to see what the other rooms held. She drifted towards the door, assuming Xander would understand she was ready to explore further. He did, directing her along the hallway to the next door.

This room was smaller and had all the trappings of a gentleman's smoking room. The décor was rich burgundy; lush silk drapes shaded the window, giving the room a more intimate feel, and the wallpaper was dotted with gold fleur-de-lys. Two chairs stood at odd angles to a small card table, as though pushed back in haste, and a third lay on its side. It appeared the card game had been abandoned partway through; hands had been thrown haphazardly onto the table and the wine goblets were only half drunk. The scent of tobacco floated above the smoke from the fire, and Keeley discovered a table in one corner that held a bowl of loose brown leaves and a partly filled polished pipe. She bent to breathe in the aroma, delighted all over again that this sensory aspect had not been neglected. There was no music, simply the ticking of a carriage clock on the mantelpiece, beside which she found several IOU notes addressed to Jerôme Lestrade tucked behind delicate porcelain ornaments. It seemed he was a skilled gambler as well as a successful weaver.

From the hall, a narrow flight of stairs led down to the kitchen. Light filtered dimly through an uncovered skylight window in the far wall, and Keeley was once again struck by the uncanny sense of the room having been inhabited just moments before she and Xander entered. A rolling pin lay upon the kitchen table, beside a thick roll of pastry and a pie dish. Covered bowls sat at one end and it was all Keeley could do to resist the temptation to lift the checked cloth and peek underneath. A tall cone of sugar took pride of place beside a bowl of unpeeled fruit – another clue to the wealth of the Lestrade family, because sugar was not cheap. The dresser against the wall was crowded with jugs and tiny cups, with rows of a blue-and-white dinner service propped behind, while blackened pots and pans hung above the range in the fireplace. The air was rich with the sweetness of steeping fruits, causing Keeley to wonder whether the cook was in the middle of preparing a plum pudding for the evening meal. The thought made her mouth water. Perhaps she might treat herself to something fruity from M&S when she returned to the station.

Back in the hallway, the polished wooden staircase was lit by a shimmering chandelier and led to a sumptuous bedroom with an enormous, silk-draped four-poster bed, its sheets and counterpane rumpled from sleep. Several dresses hung from frames and a dressing table in a corner by the window held a matching hairbrush and mirror set, along with a cluster of stoppered glass bottles that Keeley guessed might contain perfume. But it was the unexpected discovery of a purring cat in the middle of the bed that delighted her the most. At first, she assumed it was stuffed, but then it yawned and stretched and began to groom its back legs. 'Oh!' she exclaimed softly, drawing Xander's attention.

'That's Ebenezer,' he whispered, reaching out to rub the cat's head. 'He's the Lestrade family cat, feared by mice up and down Folgate Street.'

Keeley nodded in reply, smiling as she watched Ebenezer lick his fur with complete disregard for their presence. It was another perfect touch, although she suspected he might wreak havoc in the dining room below. She was willing to bet he was quite firmly removed every time he tried to enter.

The room beside the bedroom was a nursery, bedecked with dolls and wooden toys and containing a small bed as well as a silk-covered cot. Nursery rhymes played in the background, overlain with the sound of giggling and the occasional muted wail of a baby. From there, Xander waved her up another flight of stairs. The rooms on this floor were a stark contrast to those below. Bare floorboards creaked underfoot as they explored by the light of flickering lanterns hung on the walls. There were no heavy silk drapes at the windows; indeed, the sound of the wind whistled around them as though squeezing through gaps in the frames. Nor were there comfortably upholstered chairs, ribboned dresses or tables laden with food and sweets, and the hearth was black and unlit. These were the servants' quarters and the difference between the lifestyles of the affluent Lestrade family and those who served them could not have been more marked, although Keeley knew positions in a household like this would have been highly sought after. The unexpected change of tone made her feel slightly melancholy, as though she had somehow broken the spell of gentility to reveal the reality beneath.

But wasn't that exactly what a good recreation of the past should do – to encourage its audience to reflect upon more than one side of the story? The house was less a museum and more an immersive art installation but Keeley could see what Delores Semple had been aiming for. It was a snapshot of life in the eighteenth century, perhaps even a celebration of the skills those refugee Huguenot weavers had brought to the city, and it was done to perfection. Keeley had no doubt she could begin her tour all over again and find fresh treasures and other hidden delights to admire in every room. It was, she concluded, a wonderful feast for the senses. Delores had been right about the silence, too; it had only made the experience more magical.

She turned to find Xander watching her from the doorway, his expression unreadable. 'Ready to go back downstairs?' he asked, his voice startling in the hush even though he hadn't spoken loudly.

Keeley nodded. 'Ready. I hope Poppy is happy to answer questions because I have around a million.'

He grinned. 'I thought you would. Let's go and find her.'

She assumed that much like at Juniper Cottage, there were areas of the house that were off limits to the public. Xander tapped on the door Poppy had disappeared through when they had first arrived, and it was opened after a few moments to reveal Poppy. 'So?' she asked, eyeing Keeley with a mixture of eagerness and trepidation. 'What did you think?'

'I loved it, of course,' Keeley said, keen to reassure her. 'It's all so thoughtfully done, nothing is out of place or anachronistic. In fact, it's practically time travel.'

Poppy clapped her hands, her eyes shining. 'Oh, that's exactly what I hoped you'd say. Although Delores wasn't above the occasional in-joke. There are a few hidden Easter eggs hidden around the house if you know where to look.'

'I can imagine,' Keeley said. 'There's so much detail that it would take three or four visits to take it all in and even then, I bet I'd miss things. But tell me, how do you keep the food from spoiling?'

Poppy launched into a detailed description of the preservation process the edible exhibits underwent, while Keeley nodded along. 'Some things, like the tobacco, are simply refreshed every few days to make sure they smell strongly enough. We use the same supplier Delores chose – they've been in business for almost four hundred years, although they only sell online these days.'

'You should come back at Christmas,' Xander put in. 'The whole house is decorated and the meal in the dining room becomes a festive feast that includes a whole goose.'

Keeley's eyes widened at the thought but Poppy laughed. 'There I have to disappoint you. The roasted goose is a painstaking imitation of the real thing, mostly to prevent Ebenezer from stealing it.'

'Yes, I was wondering how you stopped him wrecking your displays but I suppose the preservatives put him off.'

'That, and the fact that he is extremely spoiled and well fed by everyone who works here,' Poppy said wryly. 'Technically, he lives next door but his owners are out at work all day and we've given up trying to keep him out. Visitors love seeing him about the place.'

'I bet they do,' Keeley said, recalling her own enjoyment when she'd discovered the gently purring cat on the bed. 'Do you have other living characters around, when the house is open to the public?'

'No,' Poppy said. 'Delores was determined that people should be able to interpret what they see for themselves, without being guided what to think. She believed the house would speak to everyone differently, if they were open to listening, which is why we recommend silent visits, although the stewards don't enforce it during the day.'

Keeley thought back to her own experience, and all the details she might have missed if Xander hadn't suggested they honoured Delores' instructions. 'The silence was wonderful,' she replied. 'I loved the background sounds.'

Poppy smiled. 'Me too. We mix things up as the seasons change, especially when the nights start drawing in. My favourite is the stormy night – the candlelight and flickering fires make everything feel cosy while the rain rattles at the windows. And I know the Lestrades weren't real people – Delores dreamed the family up as she unpacked the old boxes in the attic – but I sometimes think I hear them, when the house is empty of visitors. Not ghosts, but echoes.' She paused and let out a self-conscious laugh. 'Does that sound mad?'

Keeley's eyes flew to Xander, who smiled. 'Not at all. Stories are powerful things – the best ones feel real and almost take on a life of their own.'

It was a sentiment Keeley couldn't help agreeing with. How often had she imagined the adventures Sophie and Marcus Forsythe had gone on to have after the final chapter of *The Mistress of Pendennis*? Or dreamed, a little forlornly, that young Francine had somehow survived the overturned fishing boat in *Where the Wind Blows,* because Eliza had left the possibility dangling for the reader to embrace? 'I certainly fell under the spell here,' she said. 'I can't believe I've never been before.'

Poppy looked gratified. 'You're welcome any time. I know Xander is keen to adapt some of what we do here to bring Eliza's story to life, so if there's anything I can do to help then let me know.'

Some of Keeley's good mood ebbed away at her words. Amid the glamour cast by the strange and wonderful tour, she had almost forgotten the reason she was there in the first place. 'Thank you,' she managed after a moment. 'I appreciate that.'

Xander cleared his throat. 'We should let you get on, Poppy. I expect you've got hordes of bookings to prepare for.'

'We're not quite sold out today,' Poppy admitted, 'but it's good to have a bit of breathing space before the madness of November and December hits.' She eyed Keeley with sympathy. 'You must feel the same.'

'Uh, yes,' Keeley lied, because the winter months were always the quietest at Juniper Cottage, in spite of the increased footfall the village enjoyed when the Christmas decorations went up. 'Madness.'

'Anyway, we'll get out of your hair,' Xander said. 'Thanks for this, Poppy. I owe you.'

'It was a pleasure,' Poppy said, when Keeley expressed her own gratitude. 'It's brilliant to meet you.'

It wasn't until they were standing outside the house, the black door closed once more, that Keeley thought to check the time and was surprised to see it was almost eleven o'clock. She must have been mesmerised, to have lost track of time so completely.

'Have you got time for a coffee?' Xander asked. 'Or do you need to get back?'

She hesitated, on one hand wanting to discuss the tumult of sights, sounds and smells that were still chasing each other around her head, but on the other, reluctant to spend more time with Xander than absolutely necessary. She supposed she ought to be gracious. He had introduced her to Delores Semple's house, after all. 'I have time for a quick coffee,' she said. 'Do you have anywhere in mind?'

'One of my favourites is in Leadenhall Market,' he said. 'It's not far.'

Keeley expected his preferred coffee spot to be one of the

modern, minimalist spaces that time-pressed Londoners seemed to flock to, but the cafe he led her to was an old-fashioned Italian spot tucked away between a cheesemonger and a bookshop. Tables spilled out onto the cobbles beneath the glass and wrought-iron arched ceiling and more than half were taken. Xander selected one in the corner and, having asked Keeley what she wanted, went inside to order. Leaning back in her seat, Keeley watched shoppers strolling past, many laden with bags from the mixture of independent shops and big brands that filled the market. But despite the influx of fashionable retailers, the building had managed to retain its historical character and she knew it had often featured as a location for films or television shows. Much like Delores Semple's house, it stood up proudly to the relentless march of modernisation and she was very glad of it.

'So?' Xander said, once he'd placed their drinks on the table. 'What did you think of the house?'

It was the same question Poppy had asked, Keeley thought, but the subsequent realisation that Xander had told the young woman his plans to improve Juniper Cottage irked her. She reached for her coffee. 'Like I said, I loved it. You were right about that.'

The coolness of her tone did not seem to discourage him. 'I knew you would,' he said, beaming. 'But did you see the potential for Juniper Cottage? I'm not suggesting we ask people to walk round in silence but I definitely think we can borrow some of Delores' magic touch to make Eliza's home more of an experience.'

At least he wasn't suggesting they bring in actors, she thought. Delores and Poppy had been unexpected allies on that score. But she baulked at the idea of setting the dining table for a grand feast, or piping in the sound of Eliza's quill scratching across paper, or whatever it was Xander had in mind. The purpose of visiting Juniper Cottage was not for people to imagine themselves part of Eliza's life, or even Eliza herself, but rather to pay quiet homage to her greatness by learning how she lived and worked. Keeley sipped her coffee. 'She wasn't a smoker, if that's what you're thinking.'

Xander looked at her in surprise. 'What?'

'We won't be putting tobacco out,' she clarified. 'And we're already doing some of the same things as Poppy – we have a number of dresses on display in the bedrooms. The one Eliza wore to the Devonshire House ball, for example, and we rotate them to match the changing of the seasons. In fact, we probably have enough to supply an exhibition at the V&A, if they ever showed the slightest inclination to notice her contribution to English literature.'

She knew she sounded chippy, but the suspicion that Xander had been brought in by the trustees because they thought she was failing Eliza's legacy was hard to dismiss, and it also seemed to trigger her long-held frustration that Eliza's writing was not as well recognised as it should be.

'Have you?' Xander said, pulling a notebook from his rucksack and jotting a few words on a clean page. 'Interesting. I'll keep that in mind.'

Keeley let out a small huff. 'Don't waste your time. Their opinion is that she isn't a household name, so no one would be interested in seeing what she wore.'

That wasn't exactly how the email had been phrased, of course, but she knew how to read between the lines.

'Okay,' he said. 'I suppose they do sort of have a point. But let's not try to run before we can walk. Before I lay out my thoughts, was there anything you saw today that you thought might transfer to Juniper Cottage?'

She took another sip of coffee, willing herself to set aside the nettling conviction that he was mentally cataloguing all the things she was doing wrong. 'I think they convey the story well, even though they don't actually tell you very much at all,' she said, after mulling the question over for what felt like an age. 'It makes me wonder if there's a way we can bring Eliza more to life – not by getting someone to dress up as her, but perhaps by being more creative with the way we describe her life.'

Xander scribbled another note. 'I agree. You have so much information about her, from her diaries and letters, that it seems a shame not to make more of that.' His blue eyes met Keeley's. 'The challenge is finding ways to do it that are fresh and innovative. Placards with paragraph after paragraph don't really cut it these days.'

She had to concede he was right. 'Too long; didn't read.'

'Exactly,' he replied. 'But it's something we can brainstorm. Maybe even invite Poppy in to collaborate, if you'd like? I know she'd love to help and she's full of great ideas.'

'Hmm,' Keeley said, noncommittally. She was having a hard enough time accepting Xander's interference; she wasn't sure her ego could cope with adding Poppy into the mix, no matter how well-meaning and enthusiastic she was. 'We'll see.'

'Of course,' he said easily. 'There's no rush. Was there anything else you liked?'

Keeley thought some more. 'I liked the sense that I was being invited to be a witness,' she said slowly. 'By the house, I mean. It almost felt as though it watched me come in, and then decided what to show me. God, that doesn't even make sense.'

But Xander was nodding. 'No, I completely get it. I have the same feeling every time I visit – like I'm a welcome intruder, sharing in a secret.' He puffed out his cheeks. 'I have to be honest, I think it's unique to that particular place. But I do think we could capture an echo of it.'

She considered the rooms of Juniper Cottage, which accurately reflected Eliza's life but without the same warmth and vitality she'd sensed in Delores Semple's house. 'How?'

Xander leaned forward. 'You might not love this idea initially but hear me out.'

Keeley stifled a groan. Maybe he was going to suggest actors after all. 'Go on,' she said, with grim resignation.

'Okay. I realise this would need a radical restructure in the way you manage your team of volunteers, but how would you feel about extending your opening hours in December?'

She stared at him. 'What would be the point of that? We hardly get any visitors during the winter months anyway. Staying open for longer would just emphasise that.'

Xander considered her objection. 'Fine, I hear that. So what if we switch your opening times entirely? So instead of opening at nine or ten o'clock in the morning, you stay closed during the day and only take bookings for the evenings. That way, you'd create scarcity and also offer something new.'

'But what?' she asked, feeling her brow crease. 'What can we give visitors in the evening that they can't get during the day?' But even as she said it, the seed of an idea was unfurling in her mind, planted by Poppy's observation that the atmosphere was even more intimate at night. 'A candlelight tour.'

Xander snapped his fingers. 'Exactly. A personal tour for small groups, given by those who know Eliza and her work the best, offering insight and little-known secrets about her life. And all by the cosy glow of candlelight – perhaps enclosed in lanterns, to soothe your health and safety jitters.' He paused, searching Keeley's expression as though trying to gauge her reaction. 'You could decorate the house the way Eliza would have done – a proper Victorian Christmas. With a bit of marketing magic, I reckon it would sell out ten times over and still have a waiting list. I know tickets to Delores Semple's house are like gold dust every festive period.'

It was a good idea, Keeley knew. Her heart started to quicken as she considered the possibilities – a glass of mulled wine on arrival, made to Eliza's own recipe, although it would need to be drunk before the tour began, because she had no intention of risking red wine stains on the already delicate carpets. The thought of decorating the house pleased her too; they had never done much more than put up a tree in the hallway in the past. But Eliza's diaries were filled with descriptions of Christmas jollity, and even a number of sketches she had undertaken to pass the time. Keeley was certain she could interpret that evidence to recreate Eliza's vision of a festive celebration. But who among her team of volunteers was confident enough to lead a tour? Judith, perhaps, but she had young grandchildren and might not appreciate the sudden imposition of evening hours during the dark and hectic month of December. And Elspeth would almost certainly jump at the chance, but her knowledge of Eliza held more gush than information. Keeley drummed the table, deep in thought. If they went ahead, she might need to recruit some new talent. And that was going to cost money.

'I don't know,' she said finally. 'I can see how it could work but the logistics might be a headache. How confident are you we could entice people to the cottage in December?'

He shrugged. 'Pretty confident. Especially since there's the added bonus of the village Christmas decorations. I hear they draw a decent crowd.'

'That's true,' she conceded. There had always been an unspoken boundary between the bright showiness of the village decorations and the understated reserve of Juniper Cottage. Perhaps it was time to blur that boundary, just a little.

'And there's plenty of time to build up your mailing list,' Xander went on. 'We might need to do a bit of early decorating one evening next month, maybe stick the tree up and splash out on a few mince pies to get some pictures for socials but that shouldn't be an issue, should it?'

Keeley thought of the half-finished box of mince pies in her kitchen, the ones she and Grace had opened on Sunday afternoon after bedding in her new plants. 'Mince pies, yes, but I'm not sure where you're expecting to find a real tree in September. They don't usually go on sale until late November.'

Xander was undeterred. 'Then we fake it – no one will look too closely, anyway. What we want to do is create a vibe, a nostalgia for Christmas Past.'

She couldn't let that pass. 'I know some of our visitors are old but none of them were around in the Victorian era.'

'It doesn't matter,' he insisted. 'Christmas is about tradition and collective memories – doing the things our predecessors did, for no other reason than to feel connected to something bigger than ourselves.' His eyes gleamed. 'We'll go big on greenery and berries and the illusion of feasting – more of a

Yule celebration than a Christian one but dressing it up with the same sense of importance it gained during Victoria's reign.'

Keeley pulled a face. It all sounded wonderful but she couldn't help thinking Xander was confusing Eliza's romantic commentaries with Dickens' *A Christmas Carol*.

'Not at all,' he insisted, when she voiced her concern. 'Dickens did pretty much create the English view of Christmas, I'll grant you, but your Queen Victoria and her prince did a lot of the heavy lifting too. It's thanks to them that we have Christmas trees.'

'I know,' Keeley said dryly, but her heart wasn't really in it. Xander's enthusiasm was too contagious, his expression too alive with the possibilities of the idea for her to summon up much sarcasm.

'So what do you think?' he pressed. 'Do you think we can do it?'

Keeley's head was starting to spin. There were so many things to consider. Did she have enough volunteers to accommodate several tours per night? How would her team react to the idea? Would she be able to recruit help if she needed it? Could Xander put his money where his mouth was and draw in enough bookings to make the gamble pay off? And, most importantly of all, would it help to grow awareness of Eliza's work?

She sighed, rubbing her forehead to ease the start of an ache in her temples brought on by an overwhelming morning. 'You know,' she said, dismissing the feeling that she had somehow been manoeuvred into something unexpected. 'I think maybe we can.'

The brilliance of the smile he flashed her way was

almost – *almost* – worth the pain in her head. 'Atta girl, Dr Cotterill,' he said, holding up a fist for her to bump. 'The trustees are going to be thrilled.'

Keeley wasn't certain about that, but convincing them to give the green light to the plans was his problem, not hers. 'So what do we do now?'

Scrawling a few more sentences in his notebook, he snapped it shut before answering. 'I speak to Malcolm, you start thinking about decorations, and we meet up sometime early in September to start the ball rolling.'

She sat back. At least that meant he'd be out of her hair for a few weeks but she'd need plenty of time to get the volunteers on side. December felt distant but it had a habit of coming around quickly.

'But we'll speak long before then, so you can fill me in on your existing mailing list and social media accounts,' he continued, oblivious to her doubtful expression. 'I'll need to get to work on those pretty quickly if we're going to whip them into shape to drive ticket sales effectively.'

'Of course,' she said, forcing her negative thoughts aside, although she knew they wouldn't be sidelined for long. 'Let me know what you need.'

'Don't worry, I will.' He paused to smile again. 'I think we're going to make a fantastic team, Dr C.'

The abbreviation was a step too far, she decided with a wince. 'You'd better call me Keeley.'

He tapped his espresso cup against her tall latte mug. 'Keeley, then. But it doesn't alter the fact that we're going to be dynamite together.'

Explosive and causing irreparable damage, she almost fired

back, but she wasn't sure there was much point. The trustees had wanted Xander Jones to shake things up and it looked as though they were going to get their wish. Keeley could only hope the cherished career she'd carved out didn't get obliterated in the process.

CHAPTER FOUR

'Of all the traits a man may possess, I find rudeness the least forgivable.'

The Last Rays of the Sun, ELIZA NORTON

'Shop work?' Grace's mother eyed her in surprise from the other side of the living room on Tuesday afternoon. 'I understand you're keen to fill your time, now that Jack has gone, but are you quite sure a job in retail is the answer?'

'It's not a normal shop,' Grace replied, wondering how best to describe Santa's Secret. 'I suppose it's more of a wholesaler.'

Her mother sniffed. 'But you'll still be dealing with the public, and over the festive period too. People turn into monsters when Christmas gets near – I once saw two members of my knitting group almost come to blows over the last box of M&S parsnips.'

Grace hid a smile. Orla Murphy was a young and glamorous sixty-something but some of her fellow knitters were octogenarians. 'I'm sure it was a fierce battle.'

'It was. Theresa called Honour a very rude name. Security had to be called.'

'Gosh,' Grace said, widening her eyes in mock horror. 'Who got the parsnips?'

Orla pursed her lips. 'Neither of them. Someone else picked them up while they were arguing with the security guard. They weren't allowed back in the shop for three months. Theresa said they had to have butternut squash with their turkey.'

It was all Grace could do not to snort in amusement. 'Well, this is a job in a shop that specialises in Christmas decorations. Not a parsnip in sight, unless someone has designed a range of root vegetable baubles.'

Her mother did not look convinced. 'But why are you even thinking about it? I love Christmas as much as the next person but I can't think of anything that would kill my enthusiasm faster than being surrounded by it every day.'

Immediately, the song by Slade began to play in Grace's head. She shook it away. 'It's only part-time. And I don't think it would ruin my love of Christmas.' An image of Ivy's sumptuously decorated tree floated across her mind. 'If anything, it will only make me appreciate it more. It's going to be tricky this year, with Jack so far away, and I thought working somewhere Christmassy might restore some of my festive spirit. In a "fake it 'til you make it" kind of way.'

Orla contemplated her in silence for a moment, then sighed. 'Well, I suppose you're old enough to make your own mistakes. Where is it?'

Again, Grace tried not to smile. A visit to her mother was never complete without some kind of admonishment. 'On the site of Ruggles, that garden centre near Freezy Tye. It's tucked away out of sight – I had no idea it was even there until Keeley drove me.'

'Ruggles,' Orla repeated, her eyes narrowing in thought. 'That's a good forty minutes away from your house.'

'I know,' Grace said patiently, wondering if her mother really thought she was foolish enough not to have factored in the journey she would have to make. 'But as I said, it's a part-time position, so I wouldn't be going every day. And I don't mind the drive. It'll give me an excuse to see Keeley more often.'

Not that she had mentioned the fact that she was thinking about applying for the job at Santa's Secret to her friend. She'd driven home on Sunday evening deep in thought, and spent longer than she should have admiring her purchases and dreaming about where she would display them once December arrived. When she'd finally put them away and gone to bed, the Sugar Plum Fairy had danced in and out of her dreams all night. At various points throughout Monday, she'd visualised herself working at Santa's Secret and the scene had felt right each time. By the time she awoke on Tuesday, she was almost certain she wanted to apply. She had the experience; twenty years of working in libraries had taught her everything from dealing with irate customers to promoting events on social media, and while she didn't have provable experience of interior design, she knew how to decorate a Christmas tree. And there was something else – a fear she hadn't shared with anyone, that she was too old to be taken seriously by a new employer. Didn't they all want Gen Z, technological whizzes these days? But Ivy was different; reading between the lines, she'd been pushed out of her own job and had reinvented herself at Santa's Secret. Did that make it more likely she might take a chance on Grace?

'I suppose you know what you're doing,' Orla allowed,

although she didn't sound entirely convinced. 'And goodness knows you're not wrong about needing something to distract you from those empty-nest blues.'

Grace nodded. Her home was just too quiet without Jack. She needed to find a reason to be out of the house and if Santa's Secret wasn't the answer, she would have to look for something else. But she wouldn't know until she tried. 'I know.'

'You should find a new hobby,' her mother suggested. 'I've got some spare knitting needles. We could do with some fresh blood at Knit Nurses.'

As usual, the mention of the name of her mother's knitting group made Grace's head itch. Orla, on the other hand, considered it a hilarious joke. 'I'm taking an autumn wreath class,' she said, hoping some further evidence that she was taking steps to improve her situation would stop her mother from pressing her to start knitting. She had the sinking feeling it might be difficult to extricate herself from the group if she did, despite previous evidence that her knitting was awful.

'Excellent,' Orla said approvingly. 'Honour's daughter did one of those and it was the making of her. She left her job and retrained as a florist.'

'Good for her,' Grace replied, trying not to think uncharitable thoughts about Honour's unnamed daughter.

'You could do worse,' Orla insisted. 'People always want flowers. And you might meet a nice man. He might come into your shop to collect a bouquet for his mother and be so captivated by you that he asks you out there and then.'

Grace stared at her. 'You've been watching too many romcoms.'

Orla spread her hands in a gesture of innocence. 'I'm only

saying it would be the perfect meet-cute. It's about time you started dating again. Honour's daughter—'

'If you're about to tell me she married a prince from a small but incredibly wealthy European country, then don't,' Grace warned. 'I'm not interested in meeting anyone at the moment, thank you very much.'

Except that wasn't entirely true, was it? Someone had caught her eye and, much like Ivy and the Sugar Plum Fairy, he'd also been dancing in and out of her thoughts since Saturday afternoon. It was another reason she hadn't mentioned her tentative plan to apply for the job at Santa's Secret to Keeley. It was extremely likely she would winkle the truth out of her in a heartbeat.

Her mother threw her an injured look. 'I'm only thinking of you, darling. You're forty-two, you have the best years of your life ahead of you. Wouldn't it be nice to have someone to share them with?'

'Yes,' Grace ground out, because this was another familiar theme. 'But it's not a priority. If it happens, it happens, but I'm not going looking for love.'

Orla's eyes twinkled. 'Spoken like a true romantic comedy heroine. You know, I have a feeling you're going to meet someone much sooner than you expect.'

It was perfectly normal to be nervous before a job interview, Grace reminded herself as she checked the clock on the dashboard of her car and wiped her damp palms on her sensible trousers. It didn't help that the journey had been much smoother than on Friday evening, she thought as she glanced again at the door to Santa's Secret. She'd been worried that the relentless rain that had fallen all morning might worsen the lunchtime traffic, meaning she had overcompensated and was now a full forty-five minutes early. The result had been far too much time sitting outside the barn, and her whirling thoughts had bypassed Rational and gone directly to Overthink. Ivy had been at pains to reassure her that Thursday's interview would be very informal but Grace had still woken up with an unsettled feeling in the pit of her stomach, which had only worsened as she'd dressed and set off. It had been a very long time since she'd applied for a job, and back then she'd been confident in her qualifications. What if she'd forgotten the etiquette? Her mouth went dry. What if nerves got the better of her and she made a terrible faux pas? She wrapped her hands against the cool surface of the steering wheel and forced herself to meet her own gaze in the rear-view mirror.

'This is not helping,' she muttered, observing the deep pink flush that had suffused her cheeks and was creeping down her neck. 'Get a grip, Grace. It's just a chat, not an inquisition.'

A sharp rap on the window caught her so much by surprise that she let out a loud yelp and jumped several centimetres out of the driver's seat. Her head whipped sideways and she peered through the steamed-up glass to see a man waiting a short distance from her car. Willing her thudding heart to settle, she opened the window and saw, with a jolt of disbelief, that it was Raff Caldwell. Swallowing, she tried to look cool and unflustered. 'Can I help you?'

A faint line appeared between his eyebrows as he surveyed her, unsmiling. 'It's more that I thought I might be able to help you. You've been sitting out here staring at your phone for the past twenty minutes. Are you lost or have you broken down?'

Grace blinked. It hadn't occurred to her that anyone might be observing her parked status; the rain had grown steadily heavier and the car park had been empty when she'd arrived. It was not empty now, she saw. The Land Rover she'd seen him with at the weekend was parked a few metres away. How had she failed to notice it arrive? 'Oh,' she said, as embarrassment crawled over her. 'No, I'm not lost and my car is fine. I'm here for an interview but the traffic was lighter than I expected so I'm early and I thought it was better to stick to my appointment than put anyone out by turning up before I was expected.'

She stopped abruptly, aware she was babbling. Raff's frown increased. 'An interview? To work at Santa's Secret?'

The surprise in his tone only gave fuel to the insecurities that had plagued her all morning. Had he taken one look at her and decided she was too old? Pushing the insidious whisper that he was right to one side, she raised her chin. 'Yes. At one o'clock.'

He checked his watch. 'There's no need to sit out here for the next fifteen minutes. I don't imagine being early will be problem but, if it is, you can at least have a drink while you wait.'

She opened her mouth to decline and then hurriedly closed it again. There was no way to refuse the offer – not without appearing mulish – and the truth was she could do with stretching her legs. 'Okay,' she said. 'Thank you.'

He stood back as she climbed out of the car. 'I'm Raff Caldwell,' he said, as she rustled in her bag for the key fob. 'Ivy is my mother. And you are?'

She didn't think he meant to sound so imperious but there was something distinctly Lord of the Manor about the question. She took her time locking the car, remembering Keeley's assertion that he was not great with people. 'Grace Murphy. Pleased to meet you.'

In other circumstances, she might have offered a handshake but she was juggling her bag, her coat and her keys and feared she might drop one or all of them if she tried to extricate a hand. Raff appeared to reach the same conclusion, because he settled for a nod. 'I saw you here last week, didn't I? With Dr Cotterill.'

Up close, his eyes were a distracting shade of green, she noticed, and framed with long dark lashes Grace would have killed for in her teenage years. There was also a hint of after-shave floating on the damp air – something woody, with a hint of pine. Her stomach tightened in a disconcerting replay of the first time she'd seen him and it took all her composure to remember the question he'd asked. 'Yes, that's right,' she managed, glancing away in case he thought she was staring. 'She's an old friend. We went to university together.'

She wasn't sure why she'd added the final bit – perhaps to plant the suggestion that she had some impressive qualifications of her own, although she hadn't gone down the doctorate route as Keeley had. But it wasn't Raff she needed to impress. He wasn't going to be the one interviewing her. Or at least she hoped he wasn't.

'Of course,' he said, his tone clipped. At that moment, rain began to fall again. For a second or two, Grace found herself admiring the way it glistened on his dark hair, then Raff jerked an arm towards Santa's Secret. 'Shall we go in?'

Trying not to picture what the moist air was doing to her own, carefully straightened hair, Grace turned towards the barn and they walked in silence. As they reached the door, they both reached for the handle at the same time and their hands touched. A sudden frisson of electricity danced across Grace's nerve endings as she snatched her fingers back. 'Sorry,' she managed, flustered.

'Not at all,' he said, and pushed the door open. 'After you.'

Once inside, she was relieved to spot Ivy chatting to the young woman who had been working at the till on Saturday. They both looked up, and Ivy beamed when she saw Grace. 'Ah, you're here. Perfect. I was just telling Misha you were coming in for a chat.' Her gaze shifted to Raff and she frowned. 'But I thought you'd gone. Didn't you say you have a meeting in Colchester at two?'

'I was,' Raff replied. 'And I do. But I found Mrs – Ms Murphy in the car park and thought I'd escort her in.'

Was it Grace's imagination or did his eyes stray to her ring finger as he corrected himself. 'Obviously I'm early,' she hastened to say. 'I'm happy to wait if you're busy.'

Ivy raised a wooden flap and came out from behind the counter. There was no sign of Liberty print today; the loose dress had been replaced by practical dungarees and a plain T-shirt, and her long silver hair was swept back from her face into a low ponytail that made her look more youthful. 'Absolutely not, I'm delighted you're here,' she said briskly, then glanced at her son. 'Will I see you for dinner tomorrow?'

'Of course,' Raff said, bending to kiss her cheek. Now that they were together, the family resemblance was unmistakeable, Grace thought as he straightened and fired a swift look her way. 'It was a pleasure to meet you.'

'And you,' she replied, ignoring another treacherous squiggle in the pit of her stomach. 'Thank you for showing me in.'

He inclined his head, and once again Grace was put in mind of a Regency gentleman. A moment later, he was gone and Ivy was beaming once more, her expression a marked contrast to her son's solemnity. 'Let's get down to business. I thought we'd chat in the staffroom – it's less cramped than my office.'

She led Grace through two more doors and up a small flight of stairs. A narrow landing offered several more doors, one of which opened into a decent-sized room with a kettle, a microwave and an expensive-looking coffee machine jostling for space on the work surfaces. Cheery velvet sofas sat against two of the walls, dotted with cushions and multi-coloured blankets that were hand-knitted, if Grace was any judge. A splendid oak coffee table held several dog-eared magazines and Grace spotted *Country Living*, *Tatler* and *Good Housekeeping* among the pile. The overall vibe was both homely and welcoming and she instantly felt some of her tension slip away.

'Please, take a seat,' Ivy urged as she moved towards the coffee machine. 'What can I get you?'

Caffeine was the last thing Grace's jittery nerves needed. 'Do you have any herbal tea?' she asked, settling on the sunshine yellow sofa. 'Camomile or peppermint? If not, normal tea would be lovely.'

Ivy busied herself taking cups from a cupboard. 'I think I'll join you. The rain has meant we've had a quiet day so far but it has led to me consuming rather too much coffee.'

Once the drinks were made, Ivy carried them over to the coffee table. Setting them down, she perched on the teal green sofa and turned a thoughtful gaze towards Grace. 'Perhaps I should start by telling you more about Santa's Secret,' she said. 'Obviously, I explained a little about the origin of the business in our chat at the weekend. We're a small concern – beside Misha and myself, we have April and Lucy who work at weekends, and Freddie and Sanjay in our warehouse. They handle delivery and installation of our lights and animated displays, and are generally brilliant. Paulette lives locally and works from home most of the time, sending out invoices and making sure we get paid.' She paused, as though mentally ticking off a list. 'And there's Raff, of course, but he doesn't actually work here. He pops in from time to time when he's visiting Ruggles for his gardening business.'

It wasn't new information but Grace couldn't decide whether she was relieved or disappointed to learn she was unlikely to run into Raff on a daily basis, if Ivy deemed her suitable for the job at Santa's Secret. He was undeniably good-looking – her stomach seemed determined to somersault every time she saw him – but she had no doubt he could be prickly, and the last thing she needed was to develop an embarrassing crush on the boss's son. 'Okay,' she said, opening the notebook she'd taken from her handbag while Ivy had been making their tea and forcing herself to focus. 'I know the position is part-time – do you know which days you need to fill or does it vary?'

Ivy tipped her head. 'We're currently closed on Mondays and Tuesdays, to give us time to replenish stock and change things around to keep everything fresh, although that will change at the end of September. I'm looking for someone flexible, a Jack or Jill of all trades to cover the tills if needed, keep on top of inventory items or to help customers find what they need out on the floor.' She stopped and leaned forward to pick up one of the mugs. 'But why don't you tell me a bit more about you? I believe you worked for the library service before, is that right?'

Grace described her old role, doing her best to highlight where she worked with the public and co-ordinated events that had involved a variety of different skill sets. 'I created displays, liaised with local businesses, worked on promotion and helped with social media,' she explained. 'I'm quite good with Creata – it's a design app for making eye-catching graphics to use online. And while I'm nowhere near your league, it's safe to say I know my way round a Christmas tree.'

'Good,' Ivy said, nodding. She considered Grace thoughtfully. 'What's your idea of the perfect Christmas?'

The question caught Grace off guard. She'd been expecting a follow-up about her work in the library. 'Oh. Um . . .' she trailed off, her mind suddenly blank. What information was Ivy trying to uncover here? More detail about her interior design experience? Her enthusiasm for the festive period as a whole? What was the best way to answer?

'It's not a trick question,' Ivy said gently, as the silence stretched and Grace felt her cheeks grow warmer and warmer. 'Don't overthink it. Just describe what makes Christmas the most wonderful time of the year for you.'

For a moment, all Grace could think of was the Andy Williams song with the same name, which celebrated hearts that were glowing and much mistletoeing. Kissing under the mistletoe wasn't something Grace wanted to think about, not with the image of Raff so fresh in her mind, and she didn't imagine it was what Ivy meant, either. What then? she asked herself, racking her brain for something original to say. What could she offer up to impress a woman who had dressed some of the most famous windows in London? Grace took a breath. 'Well, it goes without saying that I love decorating the tree and all the other things that make it a magical time of year,' she began, doing her best to gather her fragmented thoughts. 'But, for me, the best bit of Christmas is the happiness it can evoke. Nothing used to beat seeing my son's eyes turn to saucers when we turned on the tree lights after decorating it together, or hearing him squeak in surprise at the snowy footprints in front of the fireplace on Christmas morning and the remains of Rudolph's carrot.' She stopped, worried she sounded far too wistful. 'If I could bottle the essence of that wonder and joy, I'd give it to everyone free of charge.'

Ivy's gaze was sympathetic. 'They grow up too fast, don't they?'

Grace nodded, her eyes suddenly moist. 'He's spending Christmas in Australia this year.' The words slipped out before she could stop them and she wanted to cringe, because this was an interview, not a therapy session. 'Anyway, when I saw your advert, I realised helping others to make the season bright was exactly what I wanted to do.'

The older woman sighed and shook her head, and, for one horrible moment, Grace thought she was going to end the interview with a trite brush-off about being in touch. But Ivy surprised her. 'I think you're going to fit right in at Santa's Secret,' she said, smiling. 'When can you start?'

Grace considered calling into Juniper Cottage to share her good news with Keeley but she didn't want to disturb her friend at work and settled for sending an overexcited text instead. By the time she got home, Keeley had replied.

WOW. I did not see that coming! Congratulations. Do I need to start calling you Santa's Little Helper now? X

The suggestion made Grace grin. *Please don't*, she tapped out. *Also avoid references to elf and safety, do not ask where I parked the reindeer or suggest I practise elfy eating if I want to fit down any chimneys x*

That elicited an eye-roll emoji. *As if I would. When do you start? x*

Grace felt a little shiver of excitement as she typed her reply. *This Saturday x*

Keeley's response was instant. *Not wasting any time, then! Want to go for dinner after you finish? There's a nice pub in Flaxwood x*

Grace didn't need to think twice. *YES PLEASE! x*

She really ought to tell her mother, Grace thought, closing the message app and placing her phone on the kitchen counter. But she wasn't certain how she would take the news; she hadn't been especially encouraging when Grace had floated the idea and she wanted to hug the feeling of achievement at her own success for just a little bit longer. She glanced at the clock, doing a swift calculation and realising Jack would be fast asleep now. Would any of her other friends understand why she'd taken a comparatively low-paid, part-time job? She wasn't at all sure they would. Perhaps she wouldn't mention it until after she'd started. There would be plenty of time to fill them in once she'd settled into her new role.

Determined to celebrate the rush of elation she'd felt when Ivy had offered her the job, Grace pulled a packet of chocolate Hobnobs from one of the kitchen cupboards, marvelling all over again at the fact that biscuits lasted more than twenty-four hours now that Jack was not there to devour them.

'Here's to trying new things,' she murmured, raising her cup of tea in salute. 'Who knows where they might lead?'

CHAPTER FIVE

'Change for its own sake is to be avoided, Miss Dalrymple. And yet if we change nothing, nothing changes.'

The Mistress of Pendennis, ELIZA NORTON

The trustees love the idea of evening Christmas tours, so it's full steam ahead. Do you want me to come down and pitch the idea to the volunteers?

Keeley pinched the bridge of her nose and let out a murmur of frustration. It wasn't that Xander's message was unexpected – she'd agreed to the plan, after all, and had known he wouldn't waste any time before running it past the trustees, and she was all too aware that the groundwork had to be done sooner rather than later. But the thought of him arriving at Juniper Cottage to casually inform her team that their carefully balanced work patterns were about to be turned on their heads made her jaw clench. Not all volunteers would be keen on working into the evenings, and although others would take the change in their stride, it was critical that they were all made to feel valued and heard. If not, Keeley would probably find she didn't have much of a team left once the buzz of Christmas was over. Xander's enthusiasm would need to be tempered for now.

I think it needs to come from me first. But you're welcome to speak to them once I've explained the project. Did you tell the trustees I might need to recruit some extra help?

His response was almost instant. *Yes, they were fine with that. When's good to get the photos for social media? The sooner we start building engagement, the better.*

Keeley checked the calendar. The logical part of her knew everything he said made sense but she had to fight the urge to put him off on this score too. She assumed he would want the cottage to be closed for the photographs and while it could not be said that the Eliza's home was busy – at least not by the standards of other historic houses – they still had a respectable stream of visitors on most days. In the past, this had peaked around the August bank holiday weekend, which was still a week away. Would Xander be prepared to wait until September? She suspected not. Suppressing a sigh, she suggested he visited shortly after closing time one evening the following week.

Is Monday too soon? Obviously we want to channel Christmas with all the trimmings. Do you have a tree we can use?

She should have known he would choose the earliest possible date, Keeley thought, and pictured her own Christmas tree, which was the perfect size for the corner of her living room but would look ridiculous beneath the higher ceilings of Juniper Cottage. She'd have to try to source another, then set about studying the digital copies of Eliza's diaries for directions on how to decorate the house. The thought of that lifted her mood a little; it might even be fun. At the very least it should help her to make plans for the actual decorations later in the year. *Fine*, she typed back. *Leave the tree with me. See you on Monday.*

Getting to her feet, she abandoned her small office and headed along the corridor to the room volunteers used for their breaks. Her gaze landed on Jenny, who was flicking through a magazine as she sipped at a cup of tea. 'Just the person,' she exclaimed, thanking her lucky stars it wasn't the altogether less dependable Elspeth. 'Sorry to interrupt your break but I need your help. Do have any idea where I can get an eight-foot Christmas tree by Monday?'

If the unusual question fazed Jenny, she didn't say so. Instead, her forehead furrowed in thought. 'There's the farm near Tiptree but I'm not sure they sell them this early in the year. Raff would know.'

He would, Keeley conceded, but he wasn't always the quickest at responding to messages. 'Maybe.'

'Does it have to be real?' Jenny asked.

'No,' Keeley said, remembering Xander's suggestion that an imitation tree would be fine. 'But I don't need it for long, so I'd rather not waste money buying one.'

There were any number of websites that sold gloriously realistic trees all year round but they came with hefty price tags. She couldn't justify the expense for the purposes of a few photographs.

Jenny pursed her lips. 'I can ask around, see if anyone has one big enough.' She cocked her head curiously. 'What's happening on Monday?'

'Xander wants to start planning some new social media posts – he needs to take some Christmas pictures,' she said, keeping the details vague. 'Which reminds me, could you help to get the decorations down from the hayloft before you go today? I'll need to sort through them over the weekend.'

The other woman nodded. 'Of course. Do you need help to put them up?'

Keeley was tempted. If there was one volunteer she could trust to keep Xander's plans for December under wraps, it was Jenny. But she didn't want to risk the news leaking out before she'd had time to brief all the volunteers. 'That's kind but I'll be putting them up after we close on Monday evening and taking them down as soon as Xander has what he needs. You'll be tucked up at home.'

'Okay,' Jenny said. 'Shall I meet you at the hayloft later? Around three?'

'That would be great,' Keeley said gratefully. 'Thanks.'

It wasn't until much later, when she was loading the boxes into the boot of her car, that it occurred to Keeley there was someone else who might be able to help with the tree problem. Hadn't Grace invested in an expensive imitation tree some years earlier? She might be willing to loan it to Keeley for a few days. And if that wasn't possible, she might be able to arrange to borrow one from Ivy. She had no real idea what was involved in a social media photo shoot but if Xander wanted Christmas with all the trimmings at Juniper Cottage, that was what he was going to get.

The bar of the Flying Fox pub in Flaxwood was busy. The crowd had spilled out into the beer garden around the back, and the buzz of many conversations filled the early evening air. Keeley had arrived a few minutes before Grace and had pounced on a table a little removed from the throng, although she suspected the surrounding tables would soon be filled with fellow diners.

'So?' she said, once Grace had settled into her chair. 'How was your first day at Santa's Secret?'

Her friend looked up from the menu she was idly perusing. 'Tiring. My watch says I've done three times as many steps as I usually do. It's very confused.'

Keeley pictured the maze of aisles inside the barn. 'I bet. Did you run into any grinches?'

'Not a single one,' Grace said. 'It's not like the garden centre, where people bring their children to enjoy the experience. The customers at Santa's Secret are serious about Christmas. One woman had a spreadsheet.'

'Sensible,' Keeley replied, 'if a bit scary. But did you enjoy it?'

Grace nodded. 'Yes. My legs aren't thanking me right now and my brain feels like mush from the whirl of new information, but I like the team and Ivy is absolutely amazing.' She stretched her arms and winced. 'Ow. I helped to hang almost a kilometre of fairy lights this morning. My shoulders are not happy.'

'A hot bath and an early night is what you need,' Keeley advised, and picked up her own menu. 'Let's order and you can tell me everything.'

Over bread and balsamic vinegar, Grace described her day. 'I met the delivery team when Ivy took me out to the barn next door where they store the really big items. Did you know they supplied the light trail at Purcell Manor last year?'

Keeley's eyebrows rose. Purcell Manor was a sprawling Georgian estate managed by English History around ten miles from Freezy Tye and she'd read some excellent reviews of their spectacular light trail on the All About Essex website the previous year. 'I didn't know that,' she said. 'But I shouldn't be surprised – Raff manages the gardens there.'

'Oh, does he? Ivy says he's very busy and not really around much, which makes sense because he doesn't actually work there. I didn't see him today, anyway.'

Grace stopped talking and took a gulp of Nosecco, looking anywhere but at Keeley, who was eyeing the growing pinkness of her cheeks with sudden understanding. 'Was he there on Thursday, then?'

'Yes,' Grace admitted. 'He, um, escorted me from my car into the barn.'

Ah, Keeley thought, and tried not to grin. She hadn't expected Grace's fleeting glimpse of Raff the previous weekend would have been enough to entice her extremely level-headed friend to apply for the job at Santa's Secret but perhaps she'd underestimated his appeal. Her second encounter with him had clearly made an impact. 'Did he now?' she said, her tone mildly inquisitive. 'Well, he can be quite gentlemanly. What did you think of him?'

Still Grace did not meet her gaze. 'He was very polite,' she said, straightening the cutlery on its white napkin and brushing a crumb of bread away. 'I was early so I waited in the car park outside Santa's Secret. He thought I might be lost, or having car trouble, and asked if he could help.'

That sounded very much like Raff, Keeley had to concede. Small talk was not his strong point but there wasn't much that escaped his notice and he had a good heart. Grace was now blushing furiously, leaving Keeley with the distinct sense that her friend had noticed him too. 'Did I mention he's single?' she asked. 'He was married but they split up a few years ago, all fairly amicable as I recall. No children – she got the horses and he kept the Labrador, who is utterly gorgeous if completely brainless.'

'Oh,' Grace replied, and cleared her throat. 'Well, as I said, he was just making sure I was okay. I don't imagine I'll run into him often.'

But you'd like to, Keeley thought but did not say. Perhaps this new part-time job was going to be good for Grace in more ways than as a simple distraction from the ache of missing Jack. 'Was the shop busy?' she asked, steering the conversation back to safer waters.

'Busy enough,' Grace said. 'But nowhere near as bad as it will be from September onwards, Ivy says. I helped on the tills in the afternoon, mostly watching how Misha and April did things. I wrapped some of the more fragile items, though, and helped a few customers out to their cars with their bags. I'm back in on Tuesday – Ivy wants to tidy the aisles to make sure they're wide enough for trolleys to navigate.'

'Sounds like a good plan,' Keeley said, envisaging the organised chaos of the overflowing tables and boxes stored beneath. 'No regrets about plunging yourself into the madness of Christmas Central, then?'

'None. I loved it and I can't wait to go back. Who wouldn't love being surrounded by all things festive?'

Keeley smiled. 'I'm glad you feel that way because I have a favour to ask. What are you doing on Monday afternoon?'

Briefly, she outlined her visit to Delores Semple's house and described Xander's suggestion of introducing an immersive tour at Juniper Cottage. 'So I need to decorate part of the house in the style of a Victorian Christmas, and Xander will create some social media content to promote the tours. And I can't think of anyone better to help me transform the cottage than someone who knows Eliza's work almost as well as I do. What do you think?'

Grace looked flattered and doubtful at the same time. 'Me? I wouldn't say I've read her books anywhere near as much as you. You're the expert, after all.'

Keeley shrugged. 'We took the same module on Female Trailblazers in Victorian Literature, and I seem to recall you got a higher mark on the paper we turned in at the end. And we'll be deciding where to put the garlands and wreaths, not answering questions on *Mastermind*. It's your decorative brilliance I need most, with a sprinkling of specialist Eliza knowledge on top.'

'Is that why you messaged to ask how big my Christmas tree is?' Grace asked, her forehead crinkling. 'I got it down from the loft to check – it's just under eight feet.'

'Perfect,' Keeley said, as the waiter arrived with their food. 'Do you mind if I borrow it? Just for a day or two. I can come over and collect it if you're not free on Monday.'

Now it was Grace's turn to look amused. 'Oh, I'm coming to help. Apart from anything else, I want to meet your new creative director for myself. Every time you mention his name, you look as though you can't decide if you want to set fire to him or kiss him.'

'I do not!' Keeley protested, as heat flamed in her cheeks. 'Okay, so maybe I do find him infuriating at times but that's only because he is. I'm definitely not attracted to him.'

Lifting her knife and fork, Grace speared a chip. 'So he doesn't look like he's just stepped out of a superhero film, then? Because that's how you described him last week. All blond hair and twinkling blue—'

Keeley raised a hand. 'I know how I described him and yes, he does look like that. But it doesn't mean I've thought about kissing him. He's at least ten years too young, for a start.'

Grace chewed for a moment. 'How do you know? Have you asked him how old he is?'

'No, but I don't need to. He's too young – too enthusiastic.'

'A man who loves his job,' Grace said gravely. 'I can see how that would be annoying.'

'Exactly,' Keeley snapped. Her eyes narrowed as she took in her friend's mischievous expression. 'Wait a minute, you were being sarcastic. You're enjoying this.'

'Of course I am,' Grace replied. 'Just like you enjoyed teasing me about Raff. Fair's fair.'

She had a point, Keeley had to admit. 'But you don't work with Raff – he's fair game. Whereas Xander is a colleague – maybe even a senior colleague, although Malcolm insists we're equals – and therefore off limits. Even if I was interested, which I'm not.' She paused, took a calming sip of water and fixed Grace with a level stare. 'So let's leave it there.'

Grace's grin was unrepentant. 'Okay.'

'Good.' Keeley filled her fork with ravioli, then eyed her friend again. 'And don't even think about matchmaking on Monday evening. I'll introduce you, we do the job and then we clear up. Agreed?'

'Agreed. As long as you promise not to try to set me up with Raff.' Grace lifted her eyebrows. 'And don't try to tell me you weren't going to. I know you, Keeley Cotterill, and you've definitely got that look in your eyes.'

Keeley sighed. 'Fine.'

Apparently satisfied, Grace returned to her meal. 'Apart from anything else, I've just started a new job, and you're about to turn yours upside down. I don't think we need any romantic complications, do you?'

Privately, Keeley felt that a romantic complication was exactly what Grace needed but she knew better than to say it out loud. Much safer to subtly nudge her in Raff's direction and let Cupid do his thing, however long that took. Because Keeley had the strangest feeling the two of them might be perfect for each other, in spite of their differing personalities. All she had to do was make them see it too.

CHAPTER SIX

'It does not feel like labour if one is working for love.'

Broadstairs House, ELIZA NORTON

Grace had visited Juniper Cottage a number of times since Keeley had become its curator and it never failed to make her smile. With its bright yellow, subtly patterned walls and well-maintained thatch, the cottage was not incongruous among its colourful neighbours, although it still drew the eye. Its size and location at the top of the green suggested it had once been the home of someone blessed with money and status, although Grace knew from Keeley that it had been in a state of disrepair before Eliza Norton had fallen in love with it while passing through the village, and impetuously made an offer for it on the spot. Her diaries showed the process of restoring it had been a long and expensive business, paid for in large part by a generous allowance from her brother, with mention made of having to rehome a family of owls that was nesting in the roof and enduring countless delays due to 'idle builders' and 'fickle tradesmen'. But at last it had been done, and Eliza had spent the best part of four decades living and working under its roof. The building now was virtually indistinguishable from the way it had looked then, once Eliza's labour of love was complete, and Grace knew Keeley had spent hours poring over letters and diaries to ensure it reflected her vision as closely as possible.

Set back from the road and surrounded by a glorious English garden, the cottage was accessed through an ornate roofed gate that led to a wide gravel path through the flowerbeds. A magnificent brass knocker hung on the front door but signs pointed visitors around to the right, where they would enter through the gift shop at the back of the house. It was five-thirty, meaning the cottage had closed for the day and the garden was empty, which allowed Grace the opportunity to pause for a moment beside the flowerbeds, listening to the buzz of the bees working their way through the profusion of blooms that nodded in the early evening heat. The garden had also been painstakingly recreated from Eliza's writings and it really was idyllic, Grace thought, admiring a row of hollyhocks. She supposed Raff was responsible for much of what she saw; he must work hard to keep it looking this vibrant even in late summer. And then she shook the thought of Raff away, worried that Keeley would take one look at her and somehow guess she had been thinking about him. It was quite ridiculous the number of times he had strayed into her thoughts in the days since their last encounter and she didn't want to encourage her feverish brain to dwell on him again. Turning away from the flowers and the ever-attentive bees, she crunched across the gravel and headed around the corner to the gift shop.

Keeley was waiting behind the glass inner door, looking cool and fresh in a white linen shirt dress that Grace knew, had she worn it, would have creased the moment she pulled it over her head. Yet somehow Keeley was defying the sweltering August heat, and instead of resembling a wilting English rose, seemed to be channelling a modern-day Greek goddess, complete with delicate gold sandals that wound upwards around her slender calves. Grace swallowed a sigh and tried not to imagine her own rumpled state, acquired despite the valiant efforts of her car's air-conditioning unit. At least the thick stone walls of the old cottage meant it would be cooler inside.

'You made it,' Keeley said, beaming as she opened the door to allow Grace inside. 'Was the journey awful again?'

Grace let out a groan. 'Temporary traffic lights outside Upper Benbridge, doing who knows what. I think they just dig holes and fill them in again to make themselves look busy.'

Her friend snorted. 'Sounds about right. But I'm sorry you had to sit through it to help me out.'

'It wasn't that bad,' Grace reassured her. 'And I have the tree in the car. Is your Australian Adonis here to help me carry it?'

'Not for another hour,' Keeley answered. 'I wanted to get the bulk of the decorations up before he got here. But we can manage it between us, right?'

It wasn't that the box containing the tree was heavy, Grace considered, but it was awkward to manoeuvre. Still, she could understand Keeley's desire to get the decorations in place before Xander arrived and it would be easier with two pairs of hands. 'Of course,' she said, wondering how much more rumpled she was going to be once they'd manhandled the tree across the car park. 'Where's it going? In the drawing room?'

'In the hall,' Keeley said. 'Xander wants to capture the sense of treading in Eliza's footsteps, the idea that she's in the house with us but in another room, so he wants to come in through the front door and sweep into the rest of the cottage.'

'Oh,' Grace said, and frowned. 'Does the front door actually open? I'd always assumed it didn't.'

Keeley shrugged. 'I guess we're about to find out.'

She led Grace through the gift shop and into the house. The hall was in shadow, its grand staircase curving around like a cat's tail. 'The tree will go here,' Keeley said, pointing to a spot at the base of the stairs. 'I've got some swags of greenery to hang along the banisters, and more for the mantelpiece in the drawing room, plus a wreath for the front door.' She narrowed her eyes. 'I'm not entirely sure how we're going to hang that yet.'

Grace reached into her handbag and pulled out a packet of transparent suction hooks. 'These might help. I discovered them a few years ago and though they might come in handy this evening.'

Keeley's expression broke into a smile. 'See, I knew you were the perfect person to do this. You think of everything.' She checked the time and her smile dimmed. 'Come on. Let's get the tree in before Xander arrives and demands to know why we're not ready.'

Forty-five minutes later, Grace was damp with perspiration and her hands prickled from countless jabs from spiky leaves, but the hard work was starting to pay off. The wreath hung on the door – a vast circle of red-berried holly and lush green ivy that instantly made Grace crave a glass of mulled wine, even though it would only make her hotter. Beyond the front door, the tree was in position at the bottom of the stairs, decorated with delicate glass baubles and slender faux candles that flickered atmospherically in the fading light. In the drawing room, more holly adorned the mantelpiece, which was also dotted with glass baubles and a pair of tall silver candlesticks that would hold actual lit candles. 'Just for a few minutes, when Xander needs to film,' Keeley said, when Grace voiced her surprise that her friend would even consider allowing naked flames. 'I'm planning to order some pretend ones before the tours begin.'

But it was the spindly legged occasional table in front of the gentle smouldering fire that really drew the eye. It sat between two tall, wing-backed chairs, each angled invitingly as though the occupants had momentarily left the room. The table was laid for tea, with a teapot and milk jug alongside a plate of thin lemon slices and two delicate cups on saucers. 'I'll make a fresh pot just before Xander starts filming,' Keeley explained. 'Then we can fill the cups and he'll hopefully be able to capture the steam curling up.'

Grace nodded. They really were following Delores Semple's lead and perhaps even taking things a step further. 'It's going to look amazing. The tours will sell out faster than you can blink.'

Keeley looked uncomfortable. 'Yes, about that. The idea still hasn't been put to the volunteers. I'm a bit worried they'll refuse the change in hours.'

'Some will,' Grace said, remembering when the library where she'd worked had first proposed extending their opening hours. 'But you might be surprised by how many like the idea of—'

She was interrupted by a series of thunderous raps on the front door that made them both jump out of their skin. 'Must be Xander,' Keeley muttered in exasperation, once she'd regained her poise. 'I'm not sure that was necessary.'

'How else was he supposed to let us know he'd arrived?' Grace asked reasonably, but Keeley was already moving, grumbling under her breath. Grace followed, curious to see the man who seemed to get under her cool best friend's skin without even trying.

The front door swung back noiselessly, which wasn't a surprise thanks to the liberal dousing of oil Grace had applied to its hinges once they had managed to wrestle the ancient iron bolts back. She looked past Keeley and was immediately faced with a tall, athletically built man with a halo of blond hair and an irrepressible grin. 'Hello,' he said, his accent sounding odd and out of place in the quintessentially English cottage. 'You must be Grace. I'm Xander Jones.'

He stepped across the threshold to shake her hand and she found herself smiling a little breathlessly at him. Keeley had not lied when she'd likened him to a certain Australian actor. He looked very much as though he could pass for a film star, albeit a slightly dishevelled one. 'Yes, I'm Grace Murphy,' she said, fighting to keep her voice steady so that Keeley would not be utterly disgusted by her. 'Nice to meet you.'

He smiled and she felt a little like a deer caught in the beam of an oncoming car. Hastily, she turned to Keeley, as much to break the spell as anything, and saw her friend looked even more irritated now.

'Where do you want to begin?' she said, without preamble. 'As agreed, we've decorated the hall and the drawing room. Did you want to go up the stairs?'

Xander eyed the staircase, now swathed in greenery and looking very festive, and nodded in approval. 'Very nice,' he said. 'It would be a shame not to include it when you've gone to so much trouble.'

Keeley nodded stiffly. 'Okay. There's a fire lit in Eliza's

bedroom and I laid out some letters on the bureau. I couldn't find a cat, unfortunately.'

This made Xander laugh. 'No Ebenezer double – got it.'

Grace looked from one to the other. 'Ebenezer?'

'Sorry, private joke,' Xander explained. 'There's a sort-of resident cat at Delores Semple's house that Keeley admired.'

'Only because he was so unexpected,' Keeley countered. 'But Eliza never owned a cat, so it seemed a bit manipulative to borrow one purely for publicity purposes.'

'Agreed,' Xander said, and Grace couldn't tell if he had genuinely missed the chilliness in Keeley's tone or whether he was simply choosing not to hear it. 'So I think we'll start with a nice sweeping shot of the door opening to allow entry to the hall. I've already taken pictures and video of the outside.' He paused. 'Nice wreath, by the way. Captures the pagan elements of the season nicely.'

Keeley didn't even glance at it. 'Good,' she said briskly. 'Now, let's get started. It'll be dark soon.'

Xander didn't argue. He recorded several videos of the door opening to reveal the glittering tree, and then swept around the hall to take in the full glory of the staircase. From there, they moved into the drawing room, where Xander once again praised the decorations and the table laid for tea. 'This is perfect,' he told Keeley, beaming at her. 'Great job.'

From the set of her jaw, Grace knew the compliment had missed its mark and thought she understood why. It must feel to her friend as though she was being put on her mettle, no matter how likeable and enthusiastic Xander was about the task in hand. But Keeley was a professional; she wouldn't let ruffled feathers affect her work, no matter how much it cost her.

Once Keeley had poured steaming hot tea into the cups, Xander set about capturing the scene.

'One last thing,' he said as the shadows lengthened outside. Reaching into his bag, he produced a bottle of champagne and three crystal flutes. 'We're offering a glass of fizz on arrival. I think we should use it as another hook.'

Grace could only agree as she watched him set the scene; the champagne flutes looked especially good on the freshly cleared table, with the light of the fire flickering behind them. 'Seems a shame to waste them,' Xander said, once he'd finished taking pictures. He handed one flute to Keeley, and another to Grace before taking the third himself. 'To a very Victorian Christmas,' he said, raising his glass in a toast.

'To a very Victorian Christmas,' Grace and Keeley chorused, although Grace observed her friend's gaze did not meet Xander's as their glasses touched. Grace took a sip, enjoying the burst of bubbles on her tongue before putting her flute back on the table. 'I'm driving,' she said, in answer to Xander's quizzical look.

'Are you?' Keeley asked, surprised. 'I assumed you'd stay with me, since you've got work tomorrow morning.'

Xander gave her an interested look. 'Do you work here too?'

Grace shook her head. 'No, I work at the Christmas shop in one of the neighbouring villages,' she explained, then turned to Keeley. 'Sorry, I must have misunderstood. I didn't realise it would be okay to stay over again.'

'You're always welcome,' Keeley said. 'Even when you're not moonlighting as a volunteer.'

Grace sighed. 'I'm tempted, especially since it would mean dodging those temporary traffic lights, but I don't have anything to wear for work in the morning. I'll have to drive home.'

For a moment, she thought Keeley would argue but then she nodded. 'Okay. But I mean it – the spare room is yours whenever you need it. Next time, bring an overnight bag.'

Xander had been studying the screen of his camera, presumably to afford them a little privacy as they discussed their plans for the evening, but now he glanced up. 'I think I've got everything I need for now. We'd better start taking these decorations down or Grace is going to have a very late night.'

'Not just me,' Grace said, spotting an opportunity. 'You must have a bit of a journey home too. Where do you live?'

'Chiswick,' he replied, grimacing slightly. 'So not the shortest drive back.'

Grace matched his wince. His journey offered the choice of two notoriously fickle major routes and either could produce miles of tailbacks in the blink of an eye. 'Ouch.'

'Don't worry about helping to take the decorations down,' Keeley said, stepping forward. 'Grace and I will do it.'

He hesitated, glancing from one to another. 'Are you sure? I'd hate to go and then have you talk about me behind my back.'

Grace tried not to smile, because they were almost certainly going to be discussing him the moment he had left the cottage. But she knew Keeley was itching for him to leave, and so she kept her face as straight as she could. 'Of course not,' she reassured him. 'We'll be too busy for that.'

His mouth quirked. 'That's all right then.' He eyed Keeley once more. 'You're sure?'

'Very,' she said.

'In that case, I'll leave this here,' he said, placing the half-full bottle of champagne on the table. 'If you pop a stopper in it, you can finish it together some other time.'

'Thanks,' Keeley said. 'I'll be in touch about briefing the volunteers in the next few days.'

He nodded. 'No problem. And I'll put together a campaign for the tours – obviously I'll run it past you before I go live with anything.'

'If you wouldn't mind,' Keeley said, her tone dry. 'I'd hate for the team to find out what's coming from our own social media accounts.'

'No, that wouldn't be ideal,' he conceded, then smiled at Grace. 'Good to meet you. Hope to see you again.'

'Me too,' she replied, because in spite of Keeley's issues with him, there wasn't much she didn't like about Xander Jones. 'Have a safe journey home.'

Once he'd left, Keeley carefully extinguished the candles and set about removing the greenery from the mantelpiece. Grace watched her in silence for a moment. 'I liked him,' she said, when it became clear her friend was not going to speak. 'And you have to admit the cottage looked great in his videos.'

'Mostly thanks to us,' Keeley said, her arms full of leafy strands. 'Can you pass me that garden bag, please?'

Grace did as she requested, holding it open so the leaves could be dropped inside. 'A collaboration, then. Although obviously I'm only a temporary helper.'

Concentrating on filling the bag, Keeley didn't reply.

'But clearly the two of you work well together,' Grace went on, determined to make her point. 'I know you're worried that he's going to undermine your role here but that wasn't the vibe I got from him. He seemed . . . nice. Laser-focused on the job. From where I'm standing, you make a good team.'

Her friend huffed. 'He has too many ideas.'

'Better than none,' Grace countered. 'And I have to agree that he's very easy on the eye. I can see why you think he's a lot younger than us but I think that's just because he's so chilled out. I bet he's older than he looks.' She paused. 'Any idea if there's a Mrs Jones back in Chiswick?'

Keeley stopped in the act of removing a candle from one of the silver candlesticks. 'No. Grace Murphy, if you're thinking what I think you're thinking—'

'I'm not,' Grace cut in quickly, raising her hands in mock surrender. 'I promised not to matchmake, remember?'

'I do remember,' Keeley said pointedly. 'I just wasn't sure you did. So it doesn't matter if he's in a relationship or studying to join the priesthood, for that matter. I don't care.'

Grace bit her lip; it seemed to her that Keeley was protesting just a tiny bit too much. 'Okay. Got it.'

Keeley puffed out her cheeks. 'Now, we'd better get the tree down and packed away, or it really will be a late night for you.'

They worked efficiently together and it wasn't long before Juniper Cottage had been restored to its pre-Christmas state. Keeley's thanks were effusive as she helped Grace load the tree back into her car, reiterating her offer to stay over whenever she needed to.

'Thanks,' Grace said, as she returned her friend's hug. 'I'll definitely take you up on that.'

'Make sure you do,' Keeley said. 'And text me when you're home, okay?'

It wasn't until Grace had left Freezy Tye and was navigating the narrow country lanes in the fading light that her thoughts returned to Xander. She could see why Keeley might feel intimidated by his arrival at Juniper Cottage but he hadn't been anywhere near as annoying as her friend had claimed. From where Grace stood, Xander had been friendly and charming, with a great eye for what might make a winning social media hook, and she couldn't help thinking that he and Keeley made a perfect couple. There was still the small matter of establishing his relationship status; she wasn't sure how she was going to find that out, short of a direct question, but she'd caught him glancing at Keeley throughout the evening, when her friend wasn't looking, and thought she'd detected more than just professional interest. There was the small matter of the promise she had made not to matchmake, but it wouldn't hurt to chip away a little at her friend's armour. Because for every time she'd noticed Xander watching Keeley, she'd observed her friend stealing glances at him, and it seemed to Grace that the obvious spark that flickered between them wouldn't need much encouragement to catch light. Then perhaps Keeley's reservations about workplace romances would burn away too.

Grace smiled to herself as she changed gear to ease around a tight bend and accelerated into the empty lane. It might just be worth a try.

CHAPTER SEVEN

'Opportunity, Mrs Gladstone! It wears many disguises so you must be ever on the alert.'

Where the Wind Blows, ELIZA NORTON

'Good morning, everyone.' Keeley surveyed the assembled volunteers, gathered on rows of hastily arranged folding chairs in the library an hour before Juniper Cottage opened its doors to the public. She summoned what she hoped was a reassuring smile. 'Thank you for coming this morning, especially to those of you not due to work today. As always, I really appreciate your dedication to Eliza's legacy.'

Several faces were wreathed in anxiety, she noted. She knew from Jenny that some of them were fearful the meeting heralded bad news. Rumours of imminent closure had begun to circulate and Keeley was keen to nip those in the bud first. 'I'm sure you're wondering why I've brought you all together. As many of you know, the trustees are looking for new ways to bring visitors in to the cottage. Some of you have met Xander Jones, who they've appointed as creative director to help promote Eliza's work and increase footfall here.'

Whispers broke out and Keeley saw looks being exchanged. 'One of the things Xander and I have been exploring is the possibility of creating an exciting new event for Christmas,' she continued, steeling herself for the inevitable grumbles that would follow once she laid out the plans. 'Winter has always been a quiet period here, with significantly lower visitor numbers than in the warmer months. So, we propose a different approach this festive period. We'd like to turn our opening hours on their head, closing during the day for most of November and December, and offering guided evening tours instead.'

The whispering became a hum as those in the room began to understand the implications. Some looked intrigued, others were obviously still concerned. Keeley held up her hand. 'I'm well aware that the proposed tours can't happen without your support. I hope you'll be excited to be part of our first Christmas-themed event at the cottage but I appreciate not all of you will be able to adjust to the new schedule. I'll be speaking to you all individually, of course, but if you have any general questions, now might be a good time to air them.'

Jenny raised her hand. 'Will we be expected to deliver the tours?'

'Good question,' Keeley said, smiling at her. 'I don't have a lot of detail at this stage – everything is still very much up for consultation. But all being well, there will be a number of tours running each evening and I can't deliver them all myself, which may mean there are opportunities for some of you to step up if you'd like to.'

'And what if we don't want to deliver tours but can work in the evenings?' Jenny pressed. 'What will we be doing?'

'A variation on what you do now,' Keeley replied. 'Greeting attendees, supporting the tour guide and helping to create an unforgettable experience for our visitors.'

'Please don't tell me we have to dress up,' Isobel said, rolling her eyes.

'Absolutely not,' Keeley said firmly. 'As always, Eliza and the story of her life and work will be the main attraction and we don't want to distract from that. The rooms will be dressed up a little, however, to add some extra Christmas spirit.'

Elspeth stopped whispering to Minnie and turned an enquiring gaze Keeley's way. 'Will Xander be present for the tours?'

Keeley tried not to grit her teeth. She supposed the question was only to be expected, given that she'd mentioned his involvement. 'He may be on site from time to time, but I don't imagine he'll come along for every tour. There will be an additional briefing with him in the next week or so. You can ask him for more details then.'

Brian folded his arms. 'What happens to those of us who can't do evenings? Are we going to be mothballed?'

Keeley hesitated. 'I don't have all the answers yet,' she said, deciding honesty was the best policy. 'Once I have a better idea of who will be able to help, I can start to think about the logistics of everything else. But the tours will only be running over the festive period. In January, our opening hours will return to normal.'

She waited, anticipating more questions, but the volunteers had begun talking among themselves. There were some unhappy faces but plenty of excited ones too. Elspeth seemed especially animated and Keeley guessed she would be among the first to put herself forward as a tour guide. 'Right,' she said, when it became clear no one had anything further to ask her. 'Thanks again for coming in. As I said, I'll be speaking to you all over the next few days but if you have questions before then, my door is always open.'

Slowly, the room cleared. Jenny began to fold the chairs, stacking them neatly against the wall. 'Thank you,' Keeley said gratefully. 'I'll take them down to the stable block.'

'I'll help,' the volunteer said, smiling. 'Many hands make light work, right?'

Keeley pursed her lips. 'I wouldn't call four hands many, but it's much better than two.' She took a chair in each hand. 'Ready?'

'Ready,' Jenny confirmed, collecting two chairs of her own, and they set off for the yard.

'How do you feel about the new proposal?' Keeley asked as they walked.

Jenny flashed her a sideways grin. 'Excited. A tour sounds like a brilliant idea – there's so much about Eliza that people don't know, like the reason she never married.'

Keeley nodded. 'They see the term spinster and decide she mustn't have had any suitors, which is the opposite of true.'

'Exactly,' Jenny said. 'But imagine standing beside the priest hole behind the dining-room chimney and explaining to visitors that she'd hidden there to avoid the attentions of Geronimo Glover.'

Keeley couldn't prevent a snort of laughter. Eliza's diaries were filled with details of the almost comical lengths she had gone to when practising the delicate art of rejecting the men who saw in her a comfortable home and generous income. Her housekeeper, Mrs Mortiboy, had been a willing accomplice and, as far as Grace could tell, had gone as far as providing men's clothes to allow her mistress to escape the house when a would-be suitor insisted upon seeing her. 'That's exactly the kind of story people would love to hear,' Keeley said approvingly. 'Do you think you'll apply to be a guide?'

The other woman puffed out her cheeks. She was a stay-at-home mum, albeit with two children who were now teenagers, and Keeley suspected evenings might be a problem. 'Maybe,' she said, after a moment's thought. 'If I can manage it around football training and swimming and homework.'

Pushing back the door of the stables, Keeley swung her chairs inside. 'You'd be great at it,' she said, slotting the chairs alongside the others that hadn't been needed that morning. 'But no pressure. I know the boys keep you busy.'

'Leave it with me,' Jenny said as she put down the chairs she was holding. 'When do the applications close?'

'No idea,' Keeley replied honestly. 'They haven't actually opened yet.'

Jenny laughed. 'Ah! I'll talk to Ned and see if he can pick up a few of the training sessions,' she said, holding the stable door open for Keeley to pass through. 'It's not as though it would be every night, is it?'

'No,' Keeley said, recalling Xander's suggestion that they restrict the tours to a few nights each week. 'In fact, it might only be two or three.'

Jenny nodded thoughtfully. 'Okay, I'll talk to Ned,' she said again. 'Thanks, Keeley.'

'It should be me thanking you,' she answered. 'Juniper Cottage couldn't open at all without the help of you and the other volunteers. I hope they're not too upset by the changes.'

'They'll adapt,' the other woman said cheerfully. 'We all love the cottage and everyone wants more people to discover Eliza's brilliant books. Even Brian, who never met a moan he didn't like.'

It was an apt description, although Keeley knew he was also one of Eliza's biggest fans and could quote extracts from her books from memory. 'I hope so,' she said, sighing. 'I don't want anyone to feel they're not wanted.'

'I'll make sure they don't,' Jenny reassured her. 'They'll rally round, don't you worry. Especially when things are firmed up.'

Nodding, Keeley made a mental note to try to catch up with each volunteer in person as soon as she could. And as much as the idea rankled, perhaps an infusion of enthusiasm from Xander would help too. She should probably ask him to come down sooner rather than later. Impetuously, she squeezed Jenny's arm. 'What would I do without you?'

The other woman grinned. 'Carry the chairs on your own, of course.'

'True,' Keeley conceded with a laugh. 'Come on, let's get the rest put away. It's nearly time to open up and the last thing I need is another lecture from Brian about health and safety.'

The bank holiday weekend came and went in a blur. Several volunteers were away, meaning Keeley had to cover their shifts but she didn't mind. It wasn't as though she had plans and the additional time in the cottage allowed her to formulate a rough plan for the Christmas tour. She'd already decided to allow each guide to develop their own script, rather than provide them with a list of anecdotes and facts to cover. The tours would take place an hour apart, to avoid running into the other groups, starting in the hall with a glass of fizz or soft drink and ending at the gift shop. Xander had insisted upon keeping the groups small, to help maintain the illusion of exclusivity. 'Logically, they'll be aware there's another group somewhere in the house, doing the same thing they are,' he'd said, when Keeley called him to run her ideas past him, 'but we want them to buy into the idea that they're spying on Eliza's secret world, so it's important we make sure nothing breaks the spell.'

It made perfect sense, Keeley knew. If they got the experience right, they would be offering much more than a simple candlelit tour. They would be enabling those in attendance to travel through time.

His meeting with the volunteers, a few days after Keeley had first floated the plan for the Christmas tours, had been a virtual one, much to the disappointment of Elspeth. But the screen had done nothing to diminish his charm and he'd had them all eating out of his hand by the time he wrapped things up. Several of the younger volunteers had been recruited as social media champions, amplifying the content Xander was producing and responding to comments left under the posts. Even Brian had been won over, grudgingly offering to run the car park to ensure visitors were able to find a parking spot in the dark. Xander had promised him a hi-vis jacket and a clipboard, which Keeley was forced to concede had been a stroke of genius. She now had a list of those volunteers who were able to cover evening shifts in late November and throughout December, with assurances that she would do her best to honour parties and Christmas concerts and the myriad other commitments that might pop up as the season got into full swing.

There had also been a flurry of interest in the coveted position of tour guide and she'd received a number of applications, which was causing her more of a headache. Jenny's supporting statement had been clear and concise, giving examples of the themes her tour would touch upon and showing an understanding of the whimsical atmosphere Xander wanted to evoke, and a surprise submission from quiet, fifty-something Marco hinted at an unexpected flair for the dramatic. Isobel's statement had been rather more rigid, with overtones of a strict Victorian governess, and Elspeth had been altogether too focused on the more lurid details of what she termed 'Eliza's heartbreaking failure to find love'. Keeley calculated she needed three guides to deliver the tours alongside her and, as things stood, only two of the applicants were suitable. Elspeth and Isobel were both dependable volunteers – she did not want them to feel slighted but nor could she rely on them to meet the much higher standard required to deliver the tours. It was a problem that had given her more than one sleepless night and she was no closer to deciding how to resolve it.

With the arrival of September, Christmas began to loom larger among the residents of Freezy Tye. A village meeting was scheduled for the first Thursday after the bank holiday weekend, held as always in the village hall, with a view to co-ordinating efforts to retain the village's Britain's Most Christmassy Village award. As in previous years, the turnout was good; all the seats had been taken by the time Keeley arrived, a little before seven-thirty. She paused at the back of the hall, shaking raindrops from her umbrella and nodding to several of her neighbours who were chatting nearby.

'Looks like summer's over,' Leila said, nodding at the leaden skies just visible through the open doors of the hall.

Keeley understood the reason for her pessimism; after a blissful long weekend, the weather had taken a turn for the worse and this was the third day of relentless rain. There was a decided chill in the air too, a reminder that autumn would soon be upon them. 'My garden is grateful,' she replied, easing out of her coat. 'And I imagine the ducks are too. The pond on the green looked quite low before the weekend.'

'I suppose so,' the other woman said, although her expression did not lift much. 'But I hope it doesn't last too much longer. I've hardly had any customers this week. How's it been at the cottage?'

Leila ran Eliza's Pantry, the village cafe that overlooked the green, and it frequently seemed to Keeley that she walked an extremely narrow tightrope between harassed and despairing. As far as she could tell, Leila welcomed the business that came with an influx of tourists while simultaneously bemoaning the challenges they brought. She wanted the cafe to be busy, but often complained at being rushed off her feet. And when the village was quieter, she could often be heard cursing the rise of chain coffee shops in town centres. She was, Keeley observed, a glass half-empty sort of person, which she supposed was understandable when her livelihood was so precarious. 'It's been quiet at the cottage too,' she admitted. 'But that's to be expected now that the schools are back. The weather's due to pick up again next week.'

Leila sighed. 'I hope you're right. Everything feels better when the sun's out, doesn't it?'

Keeley was about to agree when a series of loud raps echoed

from the front of the hall. She looked up to see Helen Peabody, chair of the village council, gazing expectantly round at the assembled crowd, a gavel in one hand and a sheaf of papers in the other. 'If I could have your attention, ladies and gentlemen,' she called, her voice ringing out over the rapidly diminishing chatter. 'It's time to call this meeting to order. Please take your seats.'

'Chance would be a fine thing,' Leila grumbled beside Keeley. 'Why don't they ever put out enough chairs?'

Keeley nodded to the corner, where Gavin, the landlord of the Golden Lion pub, was unfolding more chairs and handing them out. 'Gav has everything under control,' she said. 'Come on, let's grab a couple before they're all gone.'

She would have preferred to distance herself from Leila, who had a tendency to mutter under her breath as the business of the meeting progressed, but it seemed the cafe owner had decided Keeley was her best friend for the night. Edging her chair as far away as she dared, Keeley made a show of turning an attentive expression towards the front of the packed hall as Helen was joined by the other committee members, including Gavin and the local vicar, Father Jonathan. The buzz of conversation died away, to be replaced by an expectant hush.

Helen's gaze was bright as she surveyed her audience. 'Good evening everyone, and thank you for joining us tonight. As ever, I'm delighted to see so many people invested in the life of our village. The purpose of tonight's meeting is to discuss plans for our winter decorations, as part of our bid to compete in Britain's Most Christmassy Village once again.'

She turned to Gavin, who cleared his throat. 'As you'll no doubt recall, last year's theme was Walking in a Winter

Wonderland and the judges particularly praised the sense of community spirit they observed, both during their official visit and that of the secret judge. But the village of Great Dedham was highly commended, as well as Hebden Bridge in West Yorkshire. If we want to win the title again, we'll need to raise our game, and I hope as many of you as possible will do your bit to help.'

Helen took over the reins once more. 'With that in mind, we'd like to open the floor to suggestions for this year's theme. Needless to say, we're looking for something fresh and exciting to wow the judges, especially since I've heard we're going to have some serious local competition this year.'

Murmurs broke out among the audience. Leila leaned towards Keeley. 'What's that supposed to mean?'

'I expect we're about to find out,' Keeley replied, but a memory was stirring at the back of her mind. Hadn't Ivy mentioned something about increased interest from the village near Santa's Secret this year?

A few rows in front of her, a young woman called Francesca raised her hand. 'What about a Disney theme? It would be a huge hit with families and would allow us to be really inclusive.'

Helen threw her an approving look. 'An excellent suggestion. Anyone else?'

More arms went up. 'Peter Pan,' Albie called out. 'We could build Captain Hook's ship on the village green.'

'Doesn't exactly scream Christmas,' Leila sniffed.

'Narnia,' someone else offered. 'With a stall selling Turkish Delight and hot chocolate.'

The mere thought made Keeley's mouth water, reminding her she'd been so caught up with work that she hadn't had time to eat before heading to the meeting.

'The Santa Express,' old Jasper suggested. 'I've got a mate who has a model railway, we could set it up to run around the green.'

Helen beamed. 'Brilliant. We'll consider all of these and look into the costs and logistics.' She glanced enquiringly at Father Jonathan. 'I believe our funds are in a healthy state, thanks to fundraising at Easter and the summer fete?'

He nodded. 'Very healthy. We can afford to push the boat out a little should we need to.'

'And of course, I need hardly remind you that success breeds success,' Helen continued. 'The more people who are drawn in to enjoy our displays, the greater the word-of-mouth reach and the more money flows into local businesses. I'm sure I don't need to remind you that many of us are feeling the pinch this year – a successful Christmas campaign feels more important than ever. It boosts morale and business, which is a win-win.'

Alongside Keeley, Leila nodded vigorously and looked slightly more cheerful, and Keeley was reminded that she ought to let Helen know about the plan to open Juniper Cottage during the evenings in December. It shouldn't cause any problems, and the village committee had always been very supportive of the cottage, occasionally donating funds to help keep the building and garden in good repair, so it made sense to keep them in the loop.

'As well as all that, there's village pride on the line,' Gavin said, leaning forward in his seat. 'We want to win, don't we? We want to be the best!'

Enthusiastic responses filled the air, with one or two members of the audience being moved to cheer.

Helen held up a hand to appeal for quiet. 'But we do have

an additional complication. As you know, one or two villages in the area have entered the competition in the past but have never really caused us any concern – that may be about to change. It appears that Flaxwood held a village meeting earlier this week and they intend to mount a rival display, in the hope of stealing our crown. Rumour has it that Jesse Bairstow, of Ruggles Garden Centre, has staged a coup and taken control of the village council. Ruggles is said to be sponsoring their displays.' Her gimlet gaze swept the hall. 'All of which means we might have a serious competitor, right on our doorstep, so keep those good ideas coming.'

More chatter broke out. Leila whistled. 'Ruggles really know how to do Christmas. If they're masterminding Flaxwood's display, it's going to be hard to beat.'

Keeley frowned, remembering that Ivy had also mentioned something about a son who had moved back to the village. 'Do you know much about Jesse?'

'Not really,' Leila said, wrinkling her nose with the effort of remembering. 'He went off to be something in the City. Not sure why he's suddenly come back, unless it's to take over the family business. His dad must be getting on a bit now.'

Which would explain the push to put Flaxwood on the map in terms of Christmas, Keeley thought. Winning Britain's Most Christmassy Village could only reflect well on the garden centre. Perhaps he had ambitions to grow the business.

Helen spoke again. 'As usual, we'll be establishing a number of subcommittees in the coming weeks, to manage the various aspects of our campaign such as publicity, stage management and retailer liaison. If you'd like to join one, make your way to the front at the end of the meeting.'

Jasper put his hand in the air. 'What's happening with the electrics? Last year, three of the food stalls lost power and couldn't serve anything hot.'

Gavin nodded. 'I'm aware of that. Paul the sparky undertook a major overhaul for us in May and replaced anything that might cause us issues this year. We're in good shape now, right, Paul?'

The electrician stood up. 'All sorted. I replaced the old wiring and fuse boxes, as well as upping the capacity. Should be fine for our needs.'

'Thank you, Paul,' Helen said. 'Anything else?'

Questions were raised about parking, which had been an issue in previous years when the weather in the lead-up to December had been too wet to allow parking on a nearby field. Keeley listened with more interest than usual; parking problems might well impact Juniper Cottage this year but it sounded as though the committee had everything in hand. 'Potts Farm have generously offered us the use of their yard,' Helen answered, with a grateful nod at the farmer in the front row. 'I'm told it can accommodate up to fifty vehicles, as long as people park sensibly.'

'Which means we'll be looking for stewards to manage that nearer to the time,' Gavin put in. 'Come and see me if you want to unleash your inner traffic warden and I'll add you to the rota.'

The farm was a sensible choice, Keeley thought – only a few minutes' walk from the village, the route served by wide pavements that would allow families to navigate the distance safely. It was also at the opposite end to Juniper Cottage, which would please Brian. All the same, she made a mental note to email Helen first thing in the morning. It might even be a good idea to remind Xander about the competition. Juniper Cottage had never played a prominent role in Freezy Tye's bids to win Britain's Most Christmassy Village but that was because decorating the house for Christmas had been a low-key affair, as well as the fact that it was shut by the time visitors arrived to admire the lights each evening. This year was going to be different and she suspected Xander would see an opportunity to use Freezy Tye's success as another springboard to raise Eliza's profile.

After the meeting had drawn to a close, Keeley turned down an invitation to the pub from Leila and made her way home instead. The rain had stopped, lacing the cool night air with the pungent scent of damp earth, and a full moon was slipping in and out from behind the remaining clouds. Silvery puddles gleamed under the streetlamps and lit windows glowed invitingly as she passed them. Before long, the houses would be bright with fairy lights and the green would be a hive of festive fun. She glanced towards Juniper Cottage, half lit by the moonlight, and she detoured to snap a picture. Critically, she examined the result and was pleased by the play of shadows across the windows. Perhaps it was even good enough to show Xander. She'd got into the habit of scrolling through the Juniper Cottage Instagram feed since he'd taken over the content and she had to admit the trustees' faith had been well placed. The account had almost nine thousand followers now and the number of likes and comments had rocketed too, exactly as Xander had promised they would. Her memory circled back to the evening they'd decorated the cottage for Christmas, when she'd been too ungracious to tell him how magical he'd made everything appear, but the recollection caused a sudden shiver of anticipation to chase down Keeley's spine. As much as she enjoyed autumn's gentle transition and tried hard to stay present in the change of season, she couldn't help looking forward to the final months of the year.

She had a feeling this Christmas was really going to deliver.

CHAPTER EIGHT

'When it comes to falling in love, a sensible woman makes sure she cushions her heart.'

The Mistress of Pendennis, ELIZA NORTON

'Excuse me, you wouldn't happen to have any bubblegum-pink ostrich feathers, would you?'

Grace looked up from tidying the bolts of fabric to see a blonde woman in her early twenties standing before her. She gazed expectantly at Grace through thick black eyelashes, her jaws moving rhythmically as she chewed, and tapped long taupe fingernails against the Chanel logo on the mobile phone case she held. 'Ostrich feathers?' Grace repeated, mentally running through the Secret Santa aisles. 'There's a box next to the Nutcracker displays but I think they're white.'

The woman pouted. 'White's no good. It's for a baby shower, see.'

'Oh, right,' Grace said, frowning. In her admittedly limited experience, white was a popular choice for baby showers.

'They're revealing the baby's gender,' the woman explained, clearly realising Grace had no idea what she meant. Her gaze became pitying. 'So it has to be pink. Hot pink, not pastel. Because she's having a girl.'

'I understand,' Grace said, as her cheeks grew slightly warm at the condescending tone. 'We don't have anything like that out on display but there might be some in the stockroom. Would you like me to check for you?'

The customer glanced at her phone. 'How long will that take?'

Grace dusted her hands on her jeans. 'I'll probably be a few minutes. I can meet you by the tills if you're in a hurry.'

'I suppose I'll have to,' the woman huffed.

'Great,' Grace said. 'I'll be as quick as I can.'

The stockrooms were organised by colour and theme, and packed to the rafters. Grace hesitated in the doorway, eyeing with trepidation crate after crate on the rows of tall metal shelves. Perhaps she should ask Misha for help, relieve her on the tills to allow the more experienced employee to find what the customer wanted. Grace was sure she'd seen some pink feathers while collecting stock a few days earlier, although she couldn't be sure of the exact shade. But where in this Aladdin's cave of wonders would they be? 'Think, Grace,' she muttered under her breath, squeezing her eyes shut. 'What else did you collect?'

There had been ribbon, she recalled – the blue and green peacock pattern as well as a box of thinner, silvery white rolls. Opening her eyes, she moved towards the nearest shelf, where several boxes at eye level sat under a sign stating *NUTCRACKER: White.* Grace kept going, passing boxes marked red, gold, green, blue. Her gaze travelled up to the higher shelves – had she needed the stepladder to reach what she needed? Yes, she thought she had. Retracing her steps, she collected the rolling ladder and pulled it over to the shelves. Ensuring it was securely locked in place, she climbed a few tentative steps. Misha had told her they weren't supposed to use the ladders alone, in case of accidents, but she didn't think it would matter. All she needed to do was check the boxes on the top shelves. She was steady on her feet and her shoes were flat. She'd be up and down in less than a minute. Never mind that the top step of the ladder seemed much higher than it had been when Misha had been reassuringly gripping the base, or that Grace had to stretch up on tiptoes in order to lift the flaps of the boxes. Taking a steadying breath, she tilted the open box towards her and peered inside. Damn. Ribbon, but not the colours she'd found before. She reached for the next box, twisting slightly to grip the edges and slide it open. More ribbon. Squinting along the shelf at the neighbouring boxes, she saw one that bore the word FEATHERS.

'There you are,' she murmured, carefully clambering down and rolling the ladder along. Conscious of the waiting customer, she climbed up again and explored the contents of the box. The top packets of cellophane contained white feathers of varying lengths and fluffiness. Digging underneath, Grace found a rainbow of other colours. She sifted through the packets, searching for pink and finding what she was looking for at the very bottom. The feathers inside the wrapper were more a baby pink than hot, and she was not convinced they'd ever been anywhere near an ostrich, but they were soft and fluffy and the closest she was going to get. Clutching all four packets, she began her descent.

'What the hell do you think you're doing?'

The furious male voice made Grace squeal in shock and sent

the slippery plastic sleeves slithering from her grasp. The ladder wobbled violently as she made a grab for the metal shelving to steady herself. Snapping her head round, she saw a sight that made her heart plummet. Standing in the doorway of the stock-room was Raff, and he had a face like thunder. 'You scared me!' she exclaimed, willing her heart to stop hammering.

Raff strode forwards. 'You shouldn't be using ladders in here unsupervised. It's not safe.'

Now that the ladder had stopped wobbling, Grace felt a surge of indignation. 'I was perfectly fine until you shouted at me.'

He bent to gather the bags of fallen feathers. It appeared one had split upon impact, because a cascade of pink billowed across the floor. 'You're not allowed to use the ladders alone,' he insisted. 'Didn't anyone explain that to you?'

Feeling slightly ridiculous peering down at him from above, Grace resumed her careful descent. 'Yes, they did. But a customer was waiting and I thought—'

'You thought the rules didn't apply to you,' Raff cut in, his glower darkening still further.

'No,' Grace protested, stung. 'I just wanted—'

She gave a little cry as her foot missed the next step. For a nanosecond, it seemed as though she hung suspended in air, but then she was tumbling backwards. Instinctively, she shut her eyes and braced for the collision with the hard concrete floor. Miraculously, it did not come. Instead, a pair of strong hands caught her and she found herself colliding with something altogether softer. The impact still jarred the breath from her lungs, causing her to gasp. Her eyes snapped open and she spun round to find Raff's finely chiselled features glaring down at her. She stared at him for several seconds, as her reeling senses bombarded her with unhelpful observations about the warmth of his chest, the woodiness of his aftershave and the fascinating gold flecks that shimmered amid the green of his eyes. 'Oh!' she squeaked, and thrust herself backwards in mortified horror.

'Stand still, you fool,' he demanded as her foot rattled against metal. 'You're going to trip over the ladder.'

Fighting to regain both her balance and her dignity, Grace returned his glare. 'I am not.'

They stood glowering at each other, then Grace recalled where she was and who she was speaking to. Her anger dissipated a little as she unfolded her arms. 'You shouldn't have shouted,' she said, the words heavy with reproach. 'I knew exactly what I was doing.'

To his credit, he looked briefly regretful before his bullishness took hold once more. 'If you hadn't been breaking the rules, I wouldn't have had to.'

She opened her mouth to answer, then closed it again. Really, what could she say? She had ignored the rules by climbing the ladder on her own, and it had almost ended in disaster, although she thought Raff should take at least half the blame for that. Sighing, she rubbed the tops of her arms, wondering if she would have bruises where he had caught her. 'I know. I'm sorry.'

The apology seemed to catch him off guard. 'Oh,' he said, looking momentarily nonplussed. Clearing his throat, he thrust the packets towards her. 'No harm done, I suppose.'

There were feathers all over the floor, and more stuck to the bottom of his jeans. One had managed to float up to attach itself to his T-shirt, vibrant against the navy blue cotton. Grace had to clench her fingers against the sudden urge to pluck it away. 'Thank you for – for breaking my fall,' she said.

Raff glanced away as though her gratitude made him uncomfortable. 'No problem. But please don't do it again. My mother takes the health and safety of everyone very seriously. The rules are here to protect you.'

Now that the adrenaline was wearing off, Grace was beginning to feel more than a little stupid. 'Yes, of course. I'm sorry.'

He studied her for a long moment, then nodded. 'As I said, no harm done.' His gaze slid to the feathers she held. 'Did you mention a customer?'

'Yes!' she exclaimed, feeling even more idiotic. 'She'll be wondering where I've got to. But I should clear up this mess.'

Raff shook his head. 'It will still be here when you've delivered those.'

'Good point,' Grace said, and moved towards the door. 'I'll be back in a few minutes, with a dustpan and brush.'

Glancing down, he plucked the feather from his T-shirt and let it fall to the ground. 'You do that. I'll be out of your way – I only came in here to pick up some tinsel for a client.'

Grace knew she should leave but her feet felt suddenly rooted to the floor. 'Right. Well, thanks again for – um – catching me.'

But Raff had already turned away and was moving purposefully towards one of the shelves further inside the stockroom; either he hadn't heard her or didn't deem it worth his time to reply and neither was an encouraging thought. Fleeing through the open door, Grace hurried to the entrance lobby, only to find Misha alone, with no sign of the customer.

'Where did she go?' Grace cried, looking around in consternation.

Misha raised her eyebrows. 'The baby shower woman?'

Grace nodded. 'Yes. I went to find her some pink feathers but it took a bit longer than I expected.'

She would not blush, she told herself, although her cheeks did not appear to get the message.

'She kept looking at her phone, then said she had somewhere else to be,' Misha said, tutting. She nodded at the feathers Grace held. 'So she couldn't have needed them that badly.'

'I suppose not,' Grace said, feeling more than a little deflated. 'And I got into trouble finding them.'

Briefly, she described her encounter with Raff. Misha's eyes widened when she reached the part where she'd fallen. 'And he caught you? Actually put his arms up and caught you?'

Grace definitely felt her face flush again, probably turning an even deeper shade of pink than the feathers she still held. But not as rosy as it had felt when she'd realised just how close she and Raff were to each other. 'Sort of. I'm not really sure how it happened. One minute I was falling and the next, I was pressed against his chest.'

'Oh,' Misha breathed, her expression suddenly dreamy. 'It's like something out of a film, the two of you surrounded by a cascade of feathers. How utterly swoon-some.'

Grace shifted uncomfortably because the last thing she wanted was for Raff to somehow discover she'd romanticised the encounter. 'He was more shouty than swoony, to be honest. But I shouldn't have been on the ladder in the first place.'

Some of Misha's misty-eyed softness dissipated as she seemed to recollect who it was Grace had fallen into. 'No, I suppose not.'

'And I spilled feathers everywhere,' Grace went on. 'Which reminds me, where can I find a dustpan and brush?'

'In the cleaners' cupboard, next door to the staffroom,' Misha replied, and shook her head. 'I still can't believe he caught you.'

Grace smiled, beginning to wish she'd kept her mouth shut. 'I expect he did it without thinking. Anyone would have done the same.'

Misha looked unconvinced. 'Not my boyfriend. He'd have whipped out his phone to capture the moment on camera, and then be too busy laughing at me sprawled on the floor to help.'

If that was true then Misha deserved a better boyfriend, Grace thought, but she kept the observation to herself. 'I'd better go and clean up the mess,' she said. 'If the baby shower woman comes back, give her the pink feathers, will you?'

True to his word, there was no sign of Raff by the time Grace had hurried upstairs to collect the dustpan and brush. But nor was there any trace of the scattered feathers. She stood in the doorway, staring around in consternation. All the evidence of her foolishness had been tidied away; the ladder had been returned to its usual resting place and there wasn't a speck of pink on the ground. Sighing, Grace went back to the cleaners' cupboard to replace the dustpan. It looked as though she had something else to thank Raff Caldwell for.

When Grace's phone rang later that evening, she was surprised but delighted to see Jack's name on the screen. 'Hello?' she said, a little breathless from the sudden surge of anticipation that welled up inside her. 'Is that you, Jack?'

The handset crackled and buzzed, causing her to hold it away from her ear for a moment. Then she heard his voice and her heart leapt again. 'G'day, Mum. How's it going?'

She laughed. 'G'day indeed. You've only been there a few weeks – you can't have gone native already.'

'Hardly,' he said, but she thought she detected a hint of an accent. 'Dad's kept me too busy for that. We've been to Bondi loads – I've finally learned how to surf – and he says we can go up to Brisbane next weekend.'

Brisbane – wasn't that where Keeley had said Xander came from? 'It sounds amazing,' she said warmly, thrilled Jack seemed to be reconnecting with his father at long last. 'And how are you getting on with Rosalina and the twins?'

Rosalina was Kevin's second wife – the woman he had fallen in love with once his marriage to Grace had ended. Their golden-haired twins who'd arrived not long after he'd emigrated to Australia had helped to fill the hole created by having to leave Jack. There had never been any question of Jack emigrating with him and Grace was glad they were getting the chance to bond now. 'The twins are great,' he said, his affection obvious. 'Rosie too.'

His tone didn't waver but Grace thought she detected a micro change in his enthusiasm. 'I'm glad,' she said. 'You did a brave thing by travelling so far from home on your own. It's great that you're having a brilliant time. Have you managed to find a job yet?'

He hesitated. 'Not yet. To be honest, Dad hasn't been much help on that score. He keeps telling me I don't need to work, that he'll see me right. I don't think he understands that I *want* to find a job. Apart from anything else, it'll help me make friends.'

There it was again, the faint whisper of something not right. Grace frowned. The plan had been for him to put his bartending experience to good use by finding a pub in Sydney to work in but it sounded as though Kevin did not agree. 'Do you want me to speak to him?'

'No,' Jack said, and paused. 'Don't get me wrong, it's fun sleeping in late and hanging out at the beach but I'm not sure how much longer I can do it before it gets a bit boring. Does that sound mad?'

'Not at all,' she reassured him. 'But I'm sure your dad will come round. Why don't you keep your eyes open for opportunities and speak to him again once you've found something that catches your eye?'

'Yeah, that sounds like a plan,' Jack said, sounding more positive. 'What have you been up to? How's your new job going?'

They chatted for several minutes more. Grace made him laugh with tales of Christmas excess at Santa's Secret and details of her mother's pretend feud with a rival knitting group. By the time he rang off, with promises to call again soon, she felt simultaneously buoyed up at having spoken to him and filled with the ache of missing him. It helped that he was obviously having a great time, even if all the pieces hadn't quite fallen into place yet. She would simply have to console herself with that.

Grace eyed the wreath on the table in front of her with deep misgivings. Adding dried grass stems had been a mistake, she felt; rather than blending in with the brown acorns and russet leaves she had added so far, the stalks simply stuck out at strange angles, ruining the symmetry she'd been going for. She glanced over at Keeley's effort, which was a riot of earthy colours and topped with speckled grouse feathers, and then gazed around the room at the women clustered around the other tables in the light and airy workroom at Ruffles. She sighed. 'Why does mine look like something a five-year-old would make?'

Keeley looked up in surprise. 'It doesn't. It's rustic, that's all.'

'Rustic,' Grace sniffed. 'That's a polite way of saying rubbish. Whereas yours wouldn't look out of place on the cover of *Good Housekeeping*. Have you done this before?'

Her friend frowned. 'Only at Christmas but the principle is exactly the same – we're just using different materials. And why are you comparing yours to mine, anyway. Just enjoy the process. Comparison is the thief of joy, remember?'

The fact that she had a point didn't make Grace feel any better. 'Working with greenery feels easier, for some reason. I was planning on hanging this one on my front door but at this rate I might hide it in the shed,' she said, tugging at a grass stem in an effort to straighten it. 'What are you going to do with yours?'

Keeley bent her head, concentrating on threading another feather into a gap. 'It's going on the front door of Juniper Cottage. Xander wants some autumn content for our social media. He's coming down on Wednesday evening.'

Grace nodded in approval. She could see the Instagram posts now. The wreath would contrast beautifully with the yellow theme of the cottage. 'It's a shame the trees haven't started shedding their leaves yet. The gardens always look stunning in October.'

'He's thought of that,' Keeley said wryly. 'Apparently, he's bringing a sack of dried leaves to spread around and create an autumnal vibe. I hope the rain has stopped by then.'

Grace glanced towards the window, where a steady drizzle continued to fall. 'I hope so too.' She turned back to study her friend once more. 'How are you feeling towards him now? Do you still want to push him into the duck pond?'

'Of course,' Keeley said, grimacing. 'But I have to admit he's good at what he does. Visitor numbers have ticked upwards since he took over managing our social media – not by quite the same amount as our Instagram followers but we've definitely had more people through the door compared with this time last September. And he's increased our newsletter reach too.' She puffed out a sigh that made the feathers on her wreath ripple. 'It pains me to admit it but it seems Malcolm and the other trustees were right to bring him in.'

'Wow,' Grace said, forcing another grass stem into the mossy base of her own wreath. 'He must be good if he's persuaded you to change your mind. Have the Christmas tours been announced yet?'

Her friend nodded. 'We've had a flurry of booking enquiries on the back of Xander's teaser posts and it's only the third week of September. Obviously, both of us are thinking ahead to Christmas – it's your job and the plans for this year's decorations around Freezy Tye are well under way – but most people aren't really into festive mode yet. Xander is confident the tours will sell out once the booking system goes live and word gets round.'

He was undoubtedly right, Grace mused. She'd tried more than once in the past to book tickets to visit Delores Semple's house in December and been disappointed to discover that even in October, she had left it too late. Freezy Tye might not be as conveniently situated as Spitalfields but she suspected that wouldn't matter once Xander worked his magic. 'And how's the tour guide recruitment going? Have you picked out your team?'

Lifting up her wreath to head height, Keeley surveyed it

critically. 'Not yet,' she said, pulling a face. 'Isobel and Elspeth have resubmitted their proposals, so I'm hopeful at least one of them will make the grade. If I can persuade Elspeth to be a bit less Jilly Cooper, then she might be okay.'

Grace stopped fiddling with an ear of barley to stare at her. 'Jilly Cooper? Really?'

'Really,' Keeley sighed. 'She's got it into her head that Eliza was an incorrigible flirt – a secret love-them-and-leave-them type who left a trail of broken hearts in her wake – and I can't seem to convince her that there's no evidence to support her ideas.'

It was certainly true that Eliza had disappointed more than her fair share of admirers, Grace conceded; her diaries were peppered with descriptions of marriage proposals she had refused and suitors she had declined to even entertain. But Keeley was right – there was nothing to support the idea that Eliza had actively encouraged men to fall in love with her. She had declared in her early twenties that she would never marry and had stayed true to her word, dying a spinster at the ripe old age of seventy-eight. It seemed very much as though Elspeth was trying too hard to spice up her tour, which Grace found all the more astonishing given Elspeth was well into her sixties and generally very prim in demeanour. Looks could be deceiving, it seemed. 'It sounds as though she's got quite an imagination,' Grace ventured. 'Maybe she should write a novel of her own.'

'Maybe,' Keeley agreed, her gaze twinkling. 'Sex sells, after all, and never goes out of style.'

That was a truism Grace could definitely confirm; before her redundancy, she'd created a special display at the library to highlight a variety of steamy romances and borrowing rates had shot up. The books had been read and returned quickly too – she'd had to expand the display to keep up with reader demand.

A loud burst of laughter near the door of the workroom caused Grace to look up. The florist who had been leading the workshop was talking animatedly to a sandy-haired man in a crisp white polo shirt and chinos. A pair of sunglasses were pushed up onto his head and a chunky gold watch flashed under the lights as he gestured congenially at the room. The florist nodded and turned to the assemble wreath-makers. 'Ladies, I'd like to introduce Jesse Bairstow, whose father owns Ruggles. It's thanks to their generosity that we're able to use this wonderful space for our classes throughout the year, and I'm very grateful to them for their support, as well as everything they do for the wider community.'

Exchanging a look with Keeley, Grace eyed the newcomer with more interest. He had moved to the nearest table and was chatting easily with the three women clustered there, pointing at their wreaths in obvious admiration. 'He's the one who's recently come back to Ruggles,' Keeley whispered. 'I've heard he's already upset some of the workers by commissioning an efficiency review across the whole business.'

Although it was exactly such a review that had led to Grace losing her job in the library, she found it hard to condemn Jesse for trying to make savings. 'Maybe his dad has let things slip,' she said, thinking of the old-world charm with which Ruggles operated.

Keeley appeared unconvinced. 'He's also made it known that he intends to win Britain's Most Christmassy Village this year and has been throwing money at it like there's no tomorrow. He's brought in a team of electricians to lay cabling so he can light up Flaxwood's village green.'

Grace felt a slight frown crease her forehead. 'Didn't you do that last year? I thought you said the committee had improved the cabling to the green in Freezy Tye.'

'Yes, we did,' her friend admitted. 'But that was done out of necessity because the existing system wasn't fit for purpose. I get the impression there's an altogether more commercial intention behind the improvements Jesse is demanding in Flaxwood.'

Grace was about to reply, then realised the florist and Jesse were heading their way. 'Sssshh,' she hissed, dipping her head to focus on her wreath. Was it possible to turn it into something less mortifying before the pair reached their table? She didn't think so and settled for hiding the worst of her incompetence beneath a handful of hastily grabbed barley.

'Hello,' Jesse said, firing a wide smile first at Keeley and then at Grace. 'How are you enjoying the workshop? Is this your first visit to Ruggles?'

Keeley flashed a bland smile his way. 'No, I live locally so I pop in quite often,' she said, reaching for another feather. 'And Grace works nearby.'

'Oh?' Jesse said, eyeing Grace with more interest. 'In Flaxwood?'

She shook her head. Now that he was closer, she realised he was older than she'd first assumed; there were strands of grey among the brown waves at his temples and creases around his eyes that suggested he was well into his forties rather than mid-thirties. 'I work at Santa's Secret,' she said.

His eyebrows rose. 'I see. Right on our doorstep.' He glanced at Keeley, whose gaze was still trained upon her handiwork. 'Are you colleagues?'

'No,' Keeley replied.

If Jesse picked up on the brevity of her reply, he didn't mention it. 'You certainly seem to have an artistic streak. That's a magnificent wreath.'

'Thank you,' she said, not looking up.

When it became clear she wasn't going to add anything more, a slightly awkward silence filled the air. The florist glanced at Grace's wreath and pulled a sympathetic face. 'Why don't I pop back in a minute and see if we can rescue that?'

For a moment, Grace was overcome with indignation. It wasn't that bad, surely? Then reality asserted itself and she saw the wreath through the florist's eyes. She wanted to leave with something she wouldn't be ashamed to hang on her front door, after all. 'Yes, please,' she said.

Jesse flashed another too-wide smile, and Grace decided his perfect white teeth must be the result of a very expensive trip to the dentist. 'Lovely to meet you both,' he said, but his eyes lingered on Grace. 'Santa's Secret, eh? I'll be popping in for a long overdue chat with Ivy in the coming weeks – perhaps our paths will cross again.'

She tipped her head, wondering at the whisper of unease that rippled through her. 'Maybe.'

A moment later, he was gone. Checking to see his back was turned, Keeley grimaced. 'Urgh. Why do I feel like I need a wash?'

Grace knew exactly what she meant. The conversation with Jesse had been brief, and he'd been amiable enough, but there was something off about him that she couldn't put her finger on. Perhaps he'd tried too hard to charm them, she thought, or perhaps it was simply the effect of Keeley's unflattering reports about his popularity at the garden centre. Or maybe it had been the flash of those too-white teeth, wolfish and hungry. Whatever the reason, she found herself wondering what the overdue chat with Ivy was going to involve. Strictly speaking, it was none of her business but it made her uneasy all the same.

Shaking the thought away, she turned her attention back to Keeley. 'It's probably all the moss,' she said, then waved a plaintive hand at the wreath in front of her. 'Look, there's only thirty minutes to go. Do you reckon you can do something with this?'

Immediately, her friend stopped what she was doing. 'Of course,' she said, reaching for a handful of grasses. 'What you need is more, not less. We'll have it whipped into shape in no time.'

CHAPTER NINE

> 'A single kiss. Oh, torture me not, sweet Penelope.'
>
> *Broadstairs House,* ELIZA NORTON

The rain gave way to blue skies after the weekend, which gave Keeley the confidence to hang her wreath on the front door of Juniper Cottage. It drew a number of admiring comments, which pleased her, and she'd even contemplated sending a photo to Xander, although she'd chickened out at the last minute. Perhaps she would make a more traditional one ahead of the Christmas tours, thick with holly and ivy as Grace's had been, and decked with slices of dried orange and cinnamon sticks. Xander had observed that wreaths were more pagan than Christian and Keeley didn't mind that at all. She felt certain Eliza would approve too.

'Did you order the sunshine?' Xander asked as he greeted Keeley in the garden of the cottage just before six o'clock on Wednesday evening.

She smiled. 'I assumed you did.'

'Not this time,' he replied, turning to admire the still blooming flowerbeds basking in the golden light of the dipping sun.

'But the rain has kept everything fresh, at least. It'll look great on camera.'

The gardens were not the only things looking fresh, Keeley thought, giving Xander a surreptitious once-over. Did he sneak away to the Cote d'Azur every weekend to top up his tan? He didn't seem like the type to fake it but the healthy glow he exuded showed no sign of fading. Could she ask? Or would she seem unforgivably nosy? But Xander's attention had now been snared by the wreath. 'Wow,' he said. 'Someone's been busy. Did you make this?'

She nodded, trying to squash the treacherous bubble of pleasure his praise had created. 'Grace and I took a class at the weekend. It turned out quite well.'

'I'll say,' Xander replied, and whistled. 'I can't wait to get some pictures.'

His enthusiasm made Keeley wish she'd been brave enough to send him her own photograph but she supposed he'd capture a much better image than she ever could. She observed the sagging rucksack slung over his shoulder. 'Did you decide against the leaves?'

He grinned. 'Nope, they're in the car – a whole bin liner full. But I thought I'd check out what nature had provided before I started making an artful mess.'

'Oh,' Keeley said, and felt a little surge of dismay. 'I asked Marco to sweep them all up this afternoon. I thought you'd prefer a blank canvas.'

'No problem. Let me go and get the bag and we'll make a start.' He squinted up at the cloudless sky, now gently tinted with pink and gold. 'I want to try to use as much of this light as we can, then we'll move on to the interior shots.'

In the messages they'd exchanged earlier, he'd mentioned wanting to take some photos of the library. Keeley hoped it wouldn't take too long; she had a mountain of paperwork waiting for her at home. 'Do you need any help carrying the leaves?' she asked.

'Nah, they weigh next to nothing,' he said. 'Wait here and I'll be right back.'

As before, Keeley was impressed at the speed with which he worked. He had an instinctive appreciation of composition, knew where to angle the lens to make the most of the dwindling light and she saw from her viewpoint behind the camera that he was capturing the cottage at its best. Eventually, he switched to his phone camera and took a long, slow-motion sweep of the drowsy garden, across the yellow walls and zoomed in on the front door with the wreath in pride of place. No wonder their visitor numbers were improving, Keeley thought, shaking her head in wonder. He made Juniper Cottage look incredible.

'That's the exteriors done,' he said, lowering the camera with an air of satisfaction.

'Have we got time for a tea break?' Keeley asked, opening the front door. 'Isobel made some shortbread in honour of your visit.'

Xander smiled. 'How could I say no? Is it Eliza-themed?'

'No, but she did have a recipe,' she replied. 'I can give it you if you like.'

His smile became rueful. 'I'm not much of a baker. But a recipe would be perfect to put in the newsletter. We could ask people to tag the Juniper Cottage accounts in their post-bake photos.'

Keeley threw him a disbelieving look. 'Are you ever off duty?'

'Not really,' he said, shrugging. 'When fans feel part of something, they share it with others and the reach is more organic and authentic than anything I can manufacture. My job is finding the things that draw them in.'

It was a more intuitive reply than she'd been expecting, Keeley thought as she led him through to the staffroom and switched the kettle on. 'Tea? Or coffee?'

'If we're having shortbread, it has to be tea,' Xander replied. 'I've been in England seven years, remember? I'm not a complete bozo.'

Keeley frowned. 'I don't think there are any hard and fast rules around biscuits.'

He raised a reproachful eyebrow. 'Now you're just trolling me. There's a whole hierarchy of dunkability for a start. Jaffa Cakes don't dunk.'

Amusement tugged at her lips as she warmed the teapot. 'The clue is in the name. Only a maniac would try to dunk a cake.'

'But they're shaped like a biscuit,' he insisted. 'It's a lesson I learned the hard way when I first arrived.'

Keeley pushed the plate of golden shortbread towards him. 'I don't recommend you dunk these,' she said gravely. 'Not unless you want to drink your tea with a spoon.'

'Noted,' he said, taking one of the buttery fingers and leaning against the worktop. 'So what made you choose Eliza and her life as your grand passion?'

She fought the urge to blink in surprise. In the month they'd known each other, she didn't think he'd ever asked her a personal question. Then again, she hadn't exactly been encouraging. Clearly, something had changed.

'I suppose I just fell in love with her storytelling,' she said, after a moment. 'Everyone else on my course was raving about Jane Austen and the Brontë sisters, and of course I love their work too. But something about Eliza's writing resonated with me – it was witty and clever and brilliantly observed, while also somehow feeling modern and ahead of its time. Grace felt the same way and we became friends on the back of it. When everyone else was out drinking in the student union, we were organising buddy reads and debating which Eliza characters we'd marry, snog or avoid.' She shook her head. 'We sound like such nerds.'

But Xander was watching her. 'I don't think so. It's always good to find your tribe and you must be kindred spirits. That's why you're still friends all these years on.'

She couldn't argue with that. 'How about you?' she said, adding tea to the pot and filling it with water from the kettle. 'Did you always know you'd end up hoarding dead leaves and photographing biscuits?'

The last bit was because instead of eating the shortbread, he'd taken out his phone to line up a picture of the plate containing the rest of Isobel's handiwork. He smiled. 'No, I wanted to be a professional beach bum. But it turns out that doesn't pay very well so my dad put me to work in his roofing company. I hated that so much I ran away to Thailand and spent the best part of a year travelling around Asia, doing a variety of terrible jobs to support myself. Then my dad got sick and I went home to help look after him.'

Keeley was silent, wishing she'd been less flippant. What was that advice about never judging others because you had no idea what they'd been through?

Xander went on, oblivious to her embarrassment. 'After he died, I took over running the business, just like he'd always wanted me to.' A wry grimace crossed his face. 'It turned out I wasn't as hopeless at it as I'd thought – the firm went from strength to strength, won a few big contracts and took on some new employees, but my mum knew my heart wasn't really in it. One day, she sat me down and told me she was selling up, to make sure I didn't waste my life doing a job I didn't enjoy.'

'Wow. She sounds like an amazing woman,' Keeley said, impressed at both his tenacity in accepting a responsibility he hadn't wanted and his mother's foresight in making sure it didn't hold him back.

'She is,' Xander answered. 'She made me enrol in a college course – anything I wanted to study was fine, as long as I was learning. Social media was just starting to take off back then, and businesses were really getting into the art of digital storytelling, so I took a photography course and before I knew it, I was running a campaign for a local surf school.'

'Which involved hanging out at the beach,' Keeley guessed, smiling.

'Exactly,' he said, cocking his head. 'Fifteen years later, here I am. Photographing biscuits for a living and counting myself pretty lucky to get to eat a few at the same time.'

She laughed, as he'd meant her to, but at the same time she was doing some rough calculations in her head. Grace had been right, she thought with a jolt of surprise. He was older than he looked. Thirty-five, at least, depending on how long he'd spent running his dad's business before his mum had intervened, and perhaps even a year or two older. Not that much younger than her, in fact. 'Do you still surf?'

He nodded. 'When I can. Obviously I don't get back to Australia much but I spend as much time as I can in Cornwall.'

It wasn't anything she hadn't suspected. 'I'm a Cornish girl myself. I grew up in Newquay, not far from Fistral Beach.'

An expression of amazed delight lit up his face. 'You're kidding? Fistral is where all the best waves are, although you hardly need me to tell you that.' He frowned. 'But you don't have a Cornish accent.'

'No,' she admitted. 'I made a big effort to ditch it when I went to university, in an effort to be cool and blend in with the crowd. I'm not sure my mother has ever forgiven me.'

Xander gave her a long look. 'I don't imagine you've ever blended in with the crowd.'

The way he said it did something strange to her insides. She hid the reaction by pouring the tea. 'Milk?' she asked, adding a splash when he nodded.

'So how did you end up here?' he asked as she finished stirring and handed him a cup. 'Rather than lecturing at university or writing dry academic papers on the symbolism of flocked wallpaper in nineteenth century literature, I mean.'

She did her best to look offended. 'I'll have you know that paper was very well received.'

He gaped at her for a second, uncertainty in his eyes, but she couldn't prevent herself from grinning and his expression instantly relaxed. 'I'm not saying there isn't a lot to be inferred from the way people decorated their walls,' he explained solemnly. 'I just meant that if you were writing academic papers, they'd be anything but dry.'

It was another compliment and once again, Keeley felt herself knocked off kilter. 'Oh, believe me, I've written some stinkers.

My PhD thesis on the redemption of the Victorian pickpocket in contemporary literature even sent Grace to sleep and she loves Eliza's novels as much as I do.'

Now Xander grinned. 'Okay, that doesn't sound like much of a page turner. Did you take the job here straight after you finished your doctorate?'

She took a sip of tea. 'No. I fell in love with someone desperately unsuitable – a guitarist in a grunge band who spent ten years smoking weed and insisting his big break was just around the corner, while I worked two jobs to keep a roof over our heads. Eventually, I saw the light, told him he needed to grow up and got a divorce. The position of curator at Juniper Cottage came up around the same time so I applied. And here I am. Watching you take pictures of biscuits and thinking I'm pretty lucky too.'

She meant it as a joke and only realised how it sounded when his eyes met hers. The sudden flicker of warmth in the pit of her stomach blossomed into something altogether more difficult to ignore. Get a grip, she told herself sternly, dropping her gaze to her cup of tea. Apart from anything else, he was a colleague – probably already in a relationship with someone who was not at least five years older than him – and she had no intention of making both their jobs more difficult by developing a crush on him. 'Speaking of pictures, we should probably get those interior shots you wanted. You've got further to go to get home than I have.'

Draining his tea, he nodded. 'That's true. It must be nice, living so close to your work.'

She carried the cups to the sink and rinsed them. 'It is. My house is only a few minutes away – no long commute for me.'

He picked up a tea towel. 'That's the only downside of my work. Most of my contracts are short term, so I never know where I'll be from one month to the next. It's probably why I'm still single, or at least that's what I tell my mother.'

The revelation was typically self-deprecating but the information that he wasn't in a relationship interested Keeley more than she cared to admit. 'Your contract here isn't short term,' she pointed out, striving for nonchalance. 'You're contracted to work with us for a year, right?'

'Yes,' he said, his gaze flicking sideways. 'You're stuck with me for a while yet.'

His words caused another burst of pleasure to bubble up inside her and she dug her fingernails into the palms of her hands in case it showed on her face. When exactly had she gone from wishing he would get out of her hair to being glad he'd be around for many months to come? She had no idea but it was playing havoc with her much-prized professionalism. 'Shall we head to the library?' she said, and immediately wanted to cringe at her too-bright tone. 'That was where you wanted to focus, wasn't it?'

'I think so,' he said. 'We might need to get creative to achieve the right atmosphere but the sun has set so we should get the full effect of the lantern I brought.'

She glanced at him curiously. 'You brought your own lantern?'

'It's almost October,' he said as she pushed back the door of the library and switched on the lights. 'Spooky season. I thought it might be fun to take some shots to use around Halloween.'

He slid his rucksack from his shoulder and she eyed it with some trepidation, hoping he wasn't about to pull out a severed hand or, worse still, a rubber mask. But all he had was an ornate metal lantern, of the kind she'd seen on display at Ruggles during her most recent visit, and she let out an inward sigh of relief. She didn't even object when he asked if he could use a real candle. 'Make sure you don't drop wax on the carpet,' she warned. 'And don't set off the smoke alarm.'

Although the truth was that a fire burned in the hearth most days in the colder months and the smoke from that had never triggered the alarms. But once again, Xander slipped into professional mode and she knew there was no danger to the floor or her eardrums. As before, it was a pleasure to watch him work and she found herself seeing the library through new eyes. She'd never felt anything but a sense of peace and calm while inside the room, but seeing him create shadows and puddles of darkness for the photographs, she could almost believe the notion that something wicked was lurking just out of sight, watching them and waiting. She shook the thought away, reminding herself that she was forty-two, not four.

'How would you feel about moving this?'

The question broke the spell. She turned her attention back to Xander and saw he was standing beside Eliza's writing desk, which sat in front of the window. The lit lantern had been positioned in the centre, and she saw the problem right away. No matter where Xander stood, his image was reflected in the glass of the window, ruining the shot. 'Can't you edit yourself out?' she asked.

'I can try,' he said. 'But it would be much easier to move the desk a metre to the side and avoid the problem completely.'

Keeley gnawed at her lip. The desk was an authenticated original by Thomas Chippendale dating from around 1800, with a polished walnut veneer and delicate claw legs. Eliza had written her correspondence, diaries and novels while seated at it and the drawers contained several of her own ink pots and nibs. The volunteers were under strict instructions to take the utmost care when dusting and vacuuming, and to the best of Keeley's knowledge, it had never been moved. But Chippendale had been a master craftsman; his furniture had been made to withstand the test of time. It ought to be fine to move it temporarily, she thought. If they were very careful.

'We'll need to remove the drawers,' she told Xander. 'I don't want any of them to fall out and get damaged.'

'No problem,' he said. 'Would it help if we wore gloves?'

It was a thoughtful suggestion, although she doubted either of them had anything on their skin that might damage the wood. 'There's a box in my office,' she said. 'I'll go and grab them.'

Moments later, she was back, two pairs of thin vinyl gloves in her hands. She wasn't certain they would fit Xander but he pulled them on without complaint. 'Ready?' she asked.

'Yep,' he said. 'I'll take the drawer on the left.'

'And I'll take the middle and right-hand drawer. We can lay them on the rug in front of the fireplace. That should be thick enough to protect them from damage.'

Reverently, she drew the deep drawer from its slot and placed it on the rug, before returning for the shallower, longer one in the centre of the front panel. On her left, Xander removed the third drawer and gave her an enquiring look. 'Okay to move the desk itself?'

Keeley slid her hands beneath the wood and gave an experimental lift. It was a solid piece, heavier than it looked, but she thought she could take the weight. 'Let's do it. On the count of three?'

They counted in unison and raised the desk smoothly. Keeley took several careful steps back, manoeuvring herself into position to place the piece flush against the wall beside the window. 'Here?' she asked. When Xander nodded, they lowered it to the carpet again.

'So far so good,' he said. 'If we put the drawers in, I'll get the photos and we can move it back into its rightful place without anyone being any the wiser.'

It wasn't that she wasn't allowed to move things around if she chose, Keeley was tempted to point out, more that it came with the risk of damaging the desk. But it didn't seem worth mentioning.

'The workmanship on these is exquisite,' Xander said, running a gloved hand over the smooth walnut surface. He tapped his fingers lightly on the solid oak base. 'They don't make furniture like this anymore.'

Keeley lifted up the deep, square drawer she'd removed and slotted it back into place. 'It's certainly stood the test of time.' She glanced over at Xander and saw he was frowning. Her heart sank. 'What is it? Don't tell me it's damaged.'

'No, it's nothing like that.' His tone was preoccupied as he studied the inside of the drawer, then ran his fingers across the outside again. 'It's just that the proportions are off. The sides are about forty centimetres deep but the drawer itself doesn't feel that big.'

Puzzled, Keeley came to stand next to him. 'What do you mean?'

'Look,' he said, and held the drawer out for her to inspect.

'Run your hand along the wood to get a feel for the depth, then do the same on the inside.'

She did as he suggested, agreeing with his estimate that the drawer was around forty centimetres deep. But the space inside was most definitely not the same depth. 'How strange,' she said, as Xander offered her the drawer and lit up his phone torch to examine the interior more closely. 'It's heavier than the other one too. Quite a bit heavier, now I think about it.'

Her eyes met Xander's and she saw her own realisation mirrored there. 'It must have a false bottom,' he said. 'I wonder how we trigger it.'

Eagerly, she turned the drawer over to allow the torch beam to play over the oak. Xander's finger probed the joints, seeking a hidden catch or trigger. 'There must be something,' he muttered in frustration, as Keeley tried to control her rising curiosity. What could be inside, she wondered? Love letters? A secret diary? Her heart pounded at the possibilities. If only they could find the way to open it.

It felt like hours but she supposed it was only a minute or two before Xander let out a cry of triumph. A faint click sounded beneath his questing fingers and the false bottom rose slightly. Xander looked up, his eyes bright. 'You should be the one to open it,' he said, and took the weight of the drawer from her.

With shaking hands, scarcely able to breathe, Keeley eased the base upwards. It rose smoothly, still attached by a pair of tiny brass hinges that lay hidden beneath one seam. She peered down, hoping against hope that whatever lay inside had not fallen prey to the ravages of damp or moths, and a gasp of utter disbelief escaped her as she spied a sheet of paper bearing some very familiar handwriting. 'It's the cover sheet of a manuscript,' she whispered in a voice that sounded quite unlike her own. Peering more closely into the space, she saw more pages stacked underneath. A lot more pages. 'Oh my God, Xander. I think it's a complete book.'

He let out a low whistle. '*The Merriest Month*,' he read. '*A novel by Eliza Norton, 1852*. Have you ever heard that title before?'

'No!' Keeley exclaimed, and had to clutch at his arm in case the magnitude of the realisation caused her to become light-headed. 'It's not one I've seen mentioned anywhere – not in her diaries or letters and definitely not in her publishing contracts. In fact, I don't think her publisher could even have known it existed. Surely they'd have published it, especially once she became more established.'

Xander nodded. 'I wonder why she hid it in here?'

Keeley had no explanation. Eliza was at the start of her literary career in 1852, with just one novel to her name that had enjoyed modest success. 'Perhaps she wasn't satisfied with it,' she suggested slowly. 'But if that was the case, she would have redrafted it.' Some of her initial excitement faded. 'Maybe she did and published it under a different title. Her other novels were published after 1852 – it might be one of those.'

'In which case, it's not an undiscovered manuscript at all, just an unknown draft, which is still very exciting,' Xander finished. He glanced at her. 'I suppose there's only one way to know for sure.'

The breath caught in Keeley's throat as she understood his meaning. 'I'm going to have to read it,' she said faintly. 'But what if it's too brittle? Eliza would have been able to afford good quality paper but it's still over a hundred and seventy years old.'

He studied the cover page. 'Admittedly I'm no conservator

but it looks in pretty good shape to me. The ink on the cover sheet hasn't faded and the edges have hardly even yellowed.'

'That's because it's been stored away from daylight, maybe even from the moment it was finished.' She gnawed at her lip. 'A professional in old manuscripts would be able to assess it properly – run some tests, confirm how old it is.'

Xander nodded. 'Of course. But don't you want to find out what it is first? I'm sure it's priceless to you and the trustees, no matter what lies underneath that first page, but if it's simply a first draft of an existing book then I'm not sure it's going to cause much of a stir beyond fans of Eliza's writing. If, on the other hand, it's a brand-new work . . .'

He trailed off but Keeley didn't need him to finish the sentence. A brand-new work would definitely cause the literary world to sit up and take notice. It wouldn't matter that Eliza was not the celebrated author of a recognised classic; a secret manuscript that had lain undiscovered for well over a century would capture the imagination of the public and could easily make headlines around the world. It had the potential to be huge. And she and Xander would be credited with its discovery. It was almost too much to take in.

'I suppose it would be okay to read it, if I made sure my hands were scrupulously clean before touching the paper,' she murmured, running through everything she knew about handling old documents. 'But I'm still worried. What if I damage it somehow – tear a page or bend the corners?'

'That's not going to happen,' Xander said firmly. 'You're a pro – I doubt you'll even breathe too loudly around it. And books are written for only one reason – to be read. If we were to close this drawer back up, pretend we'd never found the manuscript, we'd be denying its reason for existing.' He placed the drawer on top of the writing desk and took both her hands in his. 'Read it, Keeley. I can't think of anyone better qualified than you.'

The warmth of his assurance made the doubts that had been assailing her fade just a little. 'You're probably right. I'll just have to be careful.'

He nodded, his eyes never leaving hers. 'Of course. Maybe don't risk it in the bath.'

A snort escaped her then, somewhere between a hiccup and laugh. 'Good advice. Thank you.'

She came to several realisations all at once then. The first was how close he was; her hands still rested in his, their fingers hot inside the thin gloves neither had thought to remove, but she didn't feel the least temptation to move away. The glow from the lantern danced across his features, turning his face into a shadowy sculpture and burnishing his unruly hair to a deep, luxurious gold. His eyes were unreadable beneath his furrowed brows, his expression serious for once. Somewhere above them, the house creaked, settling down on its foundations for the night. The only other sound came from Keeley herself – from the blood roaring in her ears, the shallow rise and fall of her breathing that she was sure Xander must be able to hear too. She knew they were in the library, could feel the carpet beneath her feet and smell the familiar, comforting scent of old books, but somehow it felt as though they were teetering on the brink of a chasm. And it seemed Xander felt it too, because his eyes darkened as he gazed at her. The breath caught in her throat as she read the unspoken question and a steady surge of heat spread out from her core. 'Keeley,' he murmured at length, and stopped.

'Yes?' she said, unable to look away and not wanting to, either. She was giddy with adrenaline, tipsy from the rush of finding the manuscript, and it was sweeping her common sense aside.

'Can I—' he began but she cut him off.

'Yes,' she said, and reached up to pull his head down to hers. 'Please do.'

The first flutter of his lips against hers almost made her knees weaken. His mouth was soft, brushing gently against hers as though still asking permission, but each feathery light touch set her skin burning and lit fires along her nerve-endings. She longed to sink her fingers into his mess of blond hair, to wrap her arms around him and press her body to his, and understood in that moment that she'd wanted to do those things since they'd stood together in the hallway of Delores Semple's house, listening to the sonorous tick of the grandfather clock. She ran a gentle finger along the curve of his cheek, heard the breathy gasp that escaped him and wished they were not standing in the middle of Eliza's library, with a hitherto undiscovered manuscript less than a metre away. Reluctantly, she stepped back, on legs that were still unsteady, and released a tiny sigh of her own.

Xander's eyes were the petrol blue of a stormy sea but fixed steadily on her. 'To be continued, I hope.'

Taking a breath, she managed a wobbly nod. 'To be continued,' she agreed. As one, they turned to look at the desk, where the drawer containing their discovery sat. Keeley puffed out a breath as the enormity of it hit her all over again. 'But it's going to have to wait. Everything is going to have to wait.'

CHAPTER TEN

A snake is still a snake, no matter where it slithers.'

Tennyson Hall, ELIZA NORTON

Santa's Secret was growing steadily busier as September drew to a close. Grace and Ivy created a temporary autumn aisle, complete with two arching metal trees, decorated with hundreds of artificial leaves in orange, russet and amber, the branch tips studded with glitter-coated acorns. Her fingers ached for a full two days afterwards, bruised from pinching and twisting floristry wire, but she had to admit the effect was impressive.

'You've got a real flair for this,' Ivy said, as they stood back to admire their handiwork. 'Adding the squirrels among the branches was a brilliant idea.'

'If we had more room, it would be nice to add a woodland scene,' Grace said, pleased her idea had worked. 'But perhaps that's something we could think about next month, when our customers' thoughts really turn towards Christmas. I love the idea of them turning a corner and suddenly finding themselves in a snowy glade, surrounded by gently lit deer and fawns.

We could hang some of the pine cone lanterns that came in yesterday.'

Ivy smiled. 'I love it. Why don't you decide on the best placement and we'll make it happen?'

Over at Ruggles, Grace could see preparations for the pumpkin patch getting underway; a corner of the car park had been hidden behind tall black and orange screens emblazoned with the words 'COMING SOON!' and posters adorned the sides of the trolley parks. She wondered whether the newly returned Jesse had much to do with the development. But from what Keeley had said, the pumpkin patch was a well-established feature each year, so perhaps he was focusing his attention on turning Flaxwood into a winter wonderland. She could certainly see the evidence of his ambition. The village green had been home to a variety of diggers for the best part of a week, which she supposed were involved in laying the electrical cabling Keeley had mentioned. Two new wooden footbridges had appeared across the stream that ran alongside the green and a tall, Japanese-style pagoda now sat a short distance from the war memorial. It must all be linked, she thought, and, not for the first time, found herself wondering whether Freezy Tye would be able to compete. From what Keeley had told her, other villages had come close to stealing their crown in the past but it seemed Flaxwood had money to burn. At least the Freezy Tye committee knew they had a fight on their hands and could up their game accordingly, but Jesse had all the resources of Ruggles at his disposal. It might just tip the balance in Flaxwood's favour.

With that in mind, she wasn't surprised to arrive at work one Friday morning to meet Jesse on his way out of Santa's Secret. He stopped in the doorway, frowning as though trying to place her, then smiled in recognition. 'We meet again. Gloria, wasn't it? From the autumn wreath workshop.'

'Grace,' she corrected a little awkwardly, hoping he'd also forgotten her disaster of a wreath. 'Did you pop in to see Ivy or were you in the market for some decorations?'

He smiled, flashing his white teeth in amusement that didn't quite reach his eyes. 'A quick chat with Ivy about some plans I have for the future of Ruggles,' he said. 'I must admit, I'd forgotten how chaotically she runs this place. I'm amazed your customers can find anything – it's rather like a jumble sale. She certainly brings new meaning to the phrase cheap and cheerful.'

Grace could only stare, slightly open-mouthed, at his rudeness. What had he been expecting – Harrods? 'Santa's Secret caters to a lot of different customer bases, from event planners to DIY Christmas decorators,' she said, unable to prevent the note of stiffness in her voice. 'The sheer amount of stock we sell makes it difficult to display everything as neatly as you do over at Ruggles, but it's a rare day that anyone leaves us unable to find what they came in for.'

In Grace's experience, the wealth of choice meant most shoppers left with far more than they had originally intended to buy but she didn't want to press the point. From the pinched expression on Jesse's face, she'd already said more than he'd been expecting. 'I suppose you have a point. Some of the larger displays are very well done. I might see whether we can use any of the ideas for the Christmas decorations in Flaxwood this year,' he said, and eyed her appraisingly. 'We're intending to win Britain's Most Christmassy Village and could use someone with a bit of design talent, if you're interested.'

Grace couldn't believe his audacity. In one breath, he had

described her workplace as a jumble sale and, in the next, he'd tried to poach her to help with Flaxwood's display. She knew he could have no idea she had any loyalty to Freezy Tye – Keeley had been careful not to mention her own workplace at the wreath workshop, or even where she lived – but even so, the cheek of it all was a bit much. She summoned up a tight smile. 'I'm afraid I mostly sweep up and make the tea,' she lied. 'Ivy is the real design genius. Have you asked her?'

Jesse scowled. 'She insists she has to stay neutral, since a lot of her customers come from other local villages. It's all nonsense, of course. She's just too stubborn to see which way the wind is blowing.' He made a show of checking the time on his flashy gold watch, and Grace was unsurprised to see it was a Rolex. 'Anyway, I must go. I've got another meeting with our tulip supplier from Amsterdam. Let me know if you change your mind about helping with the design.'

With a nod, he strode past her and made for the road that led to the garden centre. Shaking her head, Grace pushed back the door and went inside.

'Morning,' Misha called cheerfully, looking up from tidying the boxes of wrapping paper propped up in front of the tills to tempt shoppers.

'Hey,' Grace replied. 'All set for another day of festive fun?'

Misha grinned. 'Always. We had another delivery first thing – I think those Nordic gonks you and Ivy ordered might have arrived. Either that or we've been invaded by an army of Christmassy garden gnomes.'

'Great,' Grace said, busily juggling her plans for the morning to fit in an inspection of the new stock. 'I'll just dump my stuff, then go and check them out.'

The staffroom was empty when she reached it, but the kettle was still hot, suggesting someone had made a cup of tea recently. Piling her coat and bag at the end of one sofa, she padded along to the tiny office at the end of the landing and tapped on the door. There was a long silence, punctuated by the faint rustle of plastic and then by the unmistakeable sound of a nose being blown. Grace frowned. 'Ivy? Is that you?'

More silence, followed by a loud sniff. 'Yes,' a female voice quavered, but it sounded so unlike Ivy that Grace wondered if she had someone in the office with her. 'Just a moment.'

She waited, concern creasing her forehead. If Ivy was alone then she was upset. 'Is everything okay? I can come back later, if you like? Or call Raff, if you're not feeling well.'

The sound of rustling increased, suggesting movement behind the closed door. A moment later, it was pulled back to reveal Ivy, clearly in a state of some distress. Grace eyed her in consternation; her usually neat hair was escaping from its ponytail, as though she had been dragging her fingers through it, and her blue eyes were rimmed with pink. Blotches of crimson stained her cheeks. It looked very much as though she had been crying. 'What's wrong?' Grace said in alarm. 'Oh my goodness, Ivy, what on earth has happened?'

The older woman pressed her lips into a thin line, shaking her head. 'Nothing,' she said, the word little more than a whisper. With an effort, she gathered herself together enough to offer Grace a watery smile. 'I'm fine, really. I've just had a bit of bad news, that's all. Nothing for you to trouble yourself about.'

Grace stared at her. 'Like hell it's not. You're crying. Please, tell me what's wrong, or let me get Raff.'

Again, Ivy shook her head, but this time it was more

vehement. 'No, don't bother him – he'll be working. I'll be perfectly fine in a minute. I just need to – to –'

She broke off, her eyes filling with tears once more. 'Come and sit down,' Grace said soothingly, placing a gentle hand beneath Ivy's elbow and guiding her to the office chair in front of the desk. She lifted a box of tissues and placed it in her unresisting hands. 'Why don't I go and make us a cup of camomile tea and then you can tell me what this is about?'

Pulling a tissue from the box, Ivy dabbed at her eyes. 'Yes, a cup of tea might help. Thank you.'

Eyeing her with concern, Grace returned to the staffroom, tapping her foot impatiently as she waited for the kettle to boil again. She selected the two largest mugs and dropped the herbal tea bags into them, dousing them in water before carrying them back to the office. Ivy seemed to have herself more under control; her eyes were dry when Grace re-entered, and the blotches in her cheeks had subsided to a rosy pink. 'I'm sorry you had to see me like that,' she said, accepting the mug with an embarrassed grimace. 'Not a good look for an employer, is it?'

'Don't you dare apologise,' Grace said as she settled on the hard wooden chair in the corner. 'Clearly you've had a shock. Is there anything I can do to help?'

Ivy's eyes fluttered closed, then reopened. 'No,' she sighed. 'I'm not sure anyone can help, to be honest. I suppose I should have seen it coming but, well, sometimes it's easier to bury one's head in the sand, isn't it?'

Grace studied her, a nasty suspicion beginning to form in her mind. 'This is something to do with Jesse Bairstow, isn't it? I met him as he was leaving – he's the one who upset you.'

For a moment, she thought Ivy would deny it, but then she sighed again. 'Yes. He came to tell me he intends to raise the rent I pay here.' Her eyes met Grace's and became watery again. 'By two thousand pounds a month.'

Grace gasped in outrage. 'What? But that's ridiculous. Surely you have a contract – he can't just spring this on you out of the blue.'

'Obviously I have a contract,' Ivy replied with quiet dignity. 'It was negotiated with his father years ago, back when Ruggles really only sold trees and plants and I was looking for somewhere big enough to realise my dream. Jim Bairstow has never been one of those ruthless types – I think he thought our businesses might even complement each other, so he offered me a long-term lease on a peppercorn rent, a nominal amount quite a long way below the market value because he couldn't see that anyone else would want the barn.'

'Your businesses do complement each other,' Grace pointed out, as the penny began to drop. 'But if this is true, why is Jesse demanding such an enormous increase in rent? You said your lease is long term.'

She puffed out a long breath. 'It is. But the name on the paperwork is Ruggles Garden Centre and Jesse says he's restructuring the business to make it more streamlined. All the assets are being transferred to a new company – Ruggles Holdings or something like that – and that means the existing lease will be nullified. Between you and me, I think he's trying to force me out. He wants the land for something else and I'm afraid his plan is going to succeed. I can't afford an extra two thousand pounds every month. Not on top of business rates and rising import costs and goodness knows what else.'

Her gaze fell to her lap and she began to shred the tissue she held. Grace felt a burst of fury on her behalf. 'This is so unfair. Does Jesse's father know what he's up to?'

'I don't know,' Ivy admitted. 'I haven't seen him much recently as he's been unwell. But I don't want to trouble him with this. Times change, after all. Maybe this is a sign it's time to move on from Santa's Secret and do something else.'

'No,' Grace exclaimed indignantly. 'This is bullying. I bet Jesse knew you were on your own this morning and picked his moment carefully. I'd like to see him try to pull a stunt like this when Raff is around.'

Ivy managed a faint smile. 'I'd quite like to see that too,' she said. 'But the trouble is, Raff has nothing to do with Santa's Secret. And while I'm sure he would defend me stoutly, at the end of the day this is my business and my problem. Not his.'

'But—' Grace began, picturing Raff's furious response when he heard what had happened.

'But nothing,' Ivy insisted. 'He has his own business to run. He doesn't need to worry about mine too.'

The steel in her tone told Grace she would not be convinced otherwise. 'You *are* going to tell him, though, aren't you?' she said, studying Ivy's now-composed expression. 'You're still his mum – he'll want to know.'

'I will tell him,' Ivy said. 'In good time, once I've worked out what to do for the best. And until I do, I'm afraid I have to ask you not to mention this, Grace. To Raff or anyone else. I'm sorry you've been dragged into it but it is a private matter – for now, at least.'

Reluctantly, Grace nodded. 'Okay.'

'Thank you. So it's business as usual, agreed? Which means

unpacking the new stock and finding a location for your lovely woodland glade.'

Creating a haven of peace was the last thing Grace felt like doing but, out of deference to Ivy, she dipped her head. 'Agreed.'

'Good,' Ivy said, and took a sip of tea. 'Why don't you let me finish this and tidy myself up, and I'll meet you downstairs in twenty minutes?'

'Of course,' Grace said, getting to her feet. She hesitated, wanting to offer something more to lift the older woman's spirits but unable to find the right words. 'Take as long as you need. I'll be ready when you are.'

Closing the office door with a soft click, she made her way to the staffroom again and stood with clenched fists, allowing her fury and indignation to bubble to the surface. Keeley had been right when she'd suggested Jesse Bairstow was not as charming as he seemed. As far as Grace could tell, the man was a vulture, out for what he could scavenge and ready to tarnish his father's good name in the process. There had to be a way to spoil his plans – she simply couldn't see what it was yet. But there was one thing she did know. She intended to do everything in her power to make life difficult for Jesse Bairstow. Whatever that took.

'Can I ask your advice about something?'

Grace was sitting opposite Keeley at the round dining table in her kitchen, toying with a plate of spaghetti carbonara.

'Hmm?' Keeley looked up from her own plate, which appeared to be similarly neglected. Her gaze focused on Grace as she smothered a discreet yawn. 'Sorry, I'm being terrible company. I was up late reading last night and I think it's catching up with me.'

Instantly, Grace felt guilty. She'd messaged Keeley at lunchtime, asking if she minded a dinner guest that evening, and of course her friend had agreed. But now Grace could see faint bluish shadows under her eyes, contrasting with the pallor of her skin and matching her weary demeanour, and guessed Keeley must have had a very late night indeed. 'What's the book? Anything I've read?'

'No,' Keeley said, dropping her gaze back to her meal. 'But you asked for my advice – is something wrong?'

Grace hesitated, remembering her promise to Ivy not to tell anyone about Jesse's outrageous demand. 'Let's say I'm renting a house,' she began, 'and the landlord decided out of the blue to increase the rent.'

Keeley blinked. 'But you're not renting a house. You don't even have a mortgage anymore – you paid it off last year.'

'Yes, I know,' Grace said patiently. 'But let's pretend I didn't.'

'Why?' Keeley asked, her gaze sharpening in suspicion. 'What's going on? Is this something to do with Jack? I thought he was staying with Rosalina and Kev.'

'He is – this isn't anything to do with Jack.' Grace ran a hand across her forehead and thought for a moment. 'Okay. Let's say – just hypothetically – that the trustees of Juniper Cottage decided to sell the house, and the new owner decided to drastically increase your rent.'

'But—'

Grace held up a hand. 'Just hypothetically. What would you do?'

'Contact a lawyer,' Keeley said promptly. 'Demand to know

what the hell the trustees were playing at.' She eyed Grace across the table, eyes narrowed. 'What's prompted this? Are you in some kind of financial trouble?'

'No!' Grace cried. 'This isn't about me. I – I have a friend whose landlord is trying to force them out of their property by hiking up the rent.'

'Then they need to get legal advice, and quickly,' Keeley repeated. 'There are laws against that kind of thing.'

Grace slumped back in her chair. It was difficult to make herself clear without betraying Ivy's confidence. 'I suppose so.' She thought for a moment and decided on a different approach. 'How are the plans for the Freezy Tye Christmas extravaganza coming along?'

This elicited another weary sigh from the other side of the table. 'It's a headache. The woman who usually manages the display on the village green is moving to Manchester for work, and so far no one else has stepped in to take her place. One of the food vendors is demanding we lower the charge for power because she says it will eat into her profits. And no one seems to be able to agree on a theme. Apart from that, it's going brilliantly.'

'Ah,' Grace said, wincing in sympathy. 'I bumped into Jesse Bairstow this morning. He basically implied Flaxwood's entry in Britain's Most Christmassy Village is going to blow Freezy Tye out of the water and asked if I'd be interested in helping them win.'

'What?' Keeley exclaimed in outrage. 'I hope you said no.'

'Of course I did,' Grace reassured her. 'In his defence, I don't think he knows I have any connection to Freezy Tye so I don't think he was trying to get inside information on your plans.'

'We don't have any plans,' Keeley complained. 'That's part of the problem.'

Grace nodded. 'I know. But it did get me thinking. Why don't I join the Freezy Tye team, as an honorary resident? It's not as though I have much else going on, apart from work and that's only part-time.'

Keeley's forehead crinkled. 'But why? I mean, it's a lovely gesture, and I'm sure the committee would bite your hand off, but what's in it for you? Apart from a long list of jobs that aren't really your problem.'

'Well, I seem to be spending a lot of time here and you know how much I love a list,' Grace said, wondering just how much the loneliness she felt every time she returned to her empty house in Upper Benbridge was influencing her sudden generosity. 'And I really don't like Jesse Bairstow. I'd love to help Freezy Tye wipe the floor with his Japanese pagoda.'

'I have no idea what he's done to make you feel so strongly but you'll get no arguments from me,' Keeley replied, quirking her lips. 'Nor am I going to look a gift horse in the mouth and I don't imagine the chair of the committee will, either. I'll mention your offer to her and let you know what she thinks.'

Grace smiled. 'Thank you.'

Keeley began to toy with her pasta again. 'Can I make a suggestion? Why don't you move into the spare room here until Christmas? It makes sense if you're going to be working at Santa's Secret during the day and running around for the committee in the evenings. A lot of the meetings happen at the pub and I don't like to think of you driving home in the dark afterwards.'

She hesitated. 'I don't want to get in your way. You might hate having a housemate.'

'Unlikely,' Keeley said firmly. She grinned. 'It'll be like old times, except we can afford to eat properly now.'

The more Grace thought about it, the more the idea of avoiding the long drive back and forth to work appealed. Besides, Keeley was right – they had shared a house before, back in their student days. There was no reason they couldn't co-exist in harmony again now. 'If you're sure.'

'Absolutely,' Keeley said. 'And I promise not to keep you up late. Those days are long gone.'

She let out another yawn, which made Grace laugh. 'What on earth are you reading? It must be a real page-turner if it's keeping you up.'

Her friend looked up, her expression a mixture of excitement and wariness. 'Can I tell you a secret?'

More secrets, Grace thought, her stomach swooping as her thoughts flew back to Ivy's distress that morning. But this was Keeley, her oldest friend, and there was only one possible answer. 'Of course.'

'You can't tell anyone,' Keeley went on. 'Not Jack, not your mum. Most definitely not your old work colleagues.'

'Why would I tell any of them?' Grace said, perplexed. 'Wait, this isn't something to do with you and Xander, is it?'

Her friend's gaze did not quite meet hers. 'No. Why would it be?'

'It is!' Grace crowed exultantly, seeing guilt flash across Keeley's face. 'Have you snogged?'

Keeley's expression grew pained. 'No, we have not snogged, because we are not teenagers.' She paused. 'We might have shared a brief kiss, but that isn't what I want to talk to you about.'

Grace grinned. 'I knew it! I knew you fancied the pants off each other. When did it happen? Where did it happen? Tell me everything.'

'On Wednesday night,' Keeley admitted. 'In the library at the cottage. But it doesn't matter right now because something else happened that's much more important.'

Grace sat back in her chair. 'More important than you getting it on with a man who looks like a Greek god? Have you taken leave of your senses?'

Keeley did not answer. Instead, she nodded at the plate in front of Grace. 'Are you going to eat any more of that?'

'Not right now,' Grace replied, folding her arms. 'I am officially agog. I want to hear the mysterious secret that beats your first snog in I don't know how long.'

Her friend gave her a long-suffering look. 'Have you quite finished?'

'No,' Grace said, smirking unrepentantly. 'But I'm prepared to behave myself if you promise to tell me all about you and Xander afterwards.'

'Absolutely not,' Keeley said in a crisp tone and got to her feet. 'Now wash your hands and dry them thoroughly and don't touch anything afterwards. I've got something to show you that's going to blow your mind.'

Intrigued in spite of herself, Grace did as she was told. Keeley led her into the living room and withdrew an unmarked cardboard box from under the coffee table. The walls and lid were a dull beige. Grace couldn't see what was inside but she recognised unbleached cardboard when she saw it. 'What's this? A rare book?'

'Something like that,' Keeley said, sinking onto the sofa.

'There's a protective cotton wrapper inside. Open it carefully and don't, whatever you do, sneeze.'

Sitting beside her, Grace took the box. Lifting the lid, she saw the plain cloth Keeley had described, folded across a rectangle that was looked too large to be a book. With steady hands, she drew the overlapping material aside and looked down. Her heart stuttered in her chest when she saw the name on the cover page. '*The Merriest Month*? I've never heard of it.'

'Neither had I,' Keeley admitted. 'Xander and I found it hidden in the library on Wednesday night. I thought at first it might be an old draft, one that Eliza had retitled, but I was wrong.' She looked at Grace, all trace of weariness gone. 'It's a new book. A previously unknown manuscript – one she didn't mention in her diaries or anywhere else.'

'Bloody hell,' Grace whispered reverently. 'That's incredible. Is it definitely one of hers?'

Keeley pursed her lips. 'The style matches. Luckily, we have plenty of verified handwriting samples, so I've compared it to some of her diaries across the years. I'm not an expert, obviously, but it looks like her writing to me.'

Grace reached out a hand to touch the cover page, marvelling at the preservation well over a century and a half after it was written, and then thought better of it. 'What's it about?'

Keeley smiled. 'It's the usual Eliza mix – despicable men, smart women battling for independence and a hefty slice of astute social commentary. Most of the action is set in London and there's a fairly grim description of the Rookery in St Giles that makes me suspect she followed in Charles Dickens' footsteps and actually visited the place, which was brave of her, given what a den of iniquity it was. But all of that pales into insignificance compared to the headline news.' Her eyes danced as she gazed at Grace. 'Which is that it's a Christmas book. Eliza wrote a romantic festive novel, complete with Christmas trees and snow and culminating in an actual frost fair on the River Thames. Can you believe it?'

A burble of laughter escaped Grace. 'What? But no one was writing about Christmas then – apart from Dickens, obviously, and as brilliant as *A Christmas Carol* is, I don't think anyone would compare it to modern, feel-good festive fiction.'

'I know!' Keeley said, and bounced in her seat. 'That's what makes it all the more incredible. And I defy even Hollywood to come up with a more perfect backdrop for a marriage proposal than a frost fair. I loved it, maybe even a little bit more than her other books.'

It certainly sounded magical, Grace thought as her head whirled with the implications. Keeley was right: the whole story was mind-blowing. 'That is high praise. Have you told the trustees?'

Keeley shook her head. 'I haven't told anyone, apart from you. And obviously Xander knows, but he agreed that we'd keep the discovery to ourselves until we're sure of what we have.'

Grace eyed the box on her lap. 'You'll need to get it properly authenticated. I've got a friend at English History who can probably help with that.' She looked at Keeley again. 'But if it does turn out to be Eliza's . . .'

'I know,' Keeley said, grinning. 'It's going to be huge. Bigger than the Brontës, maybe even bigger than Austen. I haven't the faintest idea why it was never published, or why it was locked away in a secret drawer, but Eliza Norton is finally going to get the fame she deserves and I am very much here for it.'

'There'll be an auction,' Grace predicted. 'A genuine Victorian Christmas novel hidden in a secret compartment for a hundred and seventy-odd years? It'll go for thousands. Maybe even hundreds of thousands.'

Keeley held up a hand. 'Let's not get carried away. We need to be sure it's really hers before we start counting the income it will generate for the estate.'

'Of course,' Grace allowed. 'But I think you might finally be able to spend a bit more money on restoring the cottage.'

A faraway look gleamed in Keeley's eyes. 'I hope so. I've always wanted to develop the stable block into classrooms so we can work with schools.'

'It's going to happen,' Grace said. 'I can feel it. Eliza Norton is about to become a global sensation and you're going to be the one who made it happen!' She paused and raised her eyebrows. 'But I do have one important question and I want you to give your answer very careful consideration.'

'Oh?' Keeley replied, some of her excitement ebbing away. 'What's that?'

Grace rolled her eyes. 'How soon can I read it, of course!'

CHAPTER ELEVEN

> 'For such a man as that, I would risk a great deal more than my reputation.'
>
> *The Last Rays of the Sun*, ELIZA NORTON

Monday mornings were usually dedicated to admin, when Keeley dealt with any issues that had arisen over the weekend and wrestled with the mountain of paperwork that running Juniper Cottage generated. She had earmarked this particular Monday for informal interviews with the volunteers who had applied to be tour guides, and had been impressed by the work they had put in. Keeley had asked them to prepare and deliver a mini-presentation in the library, to allow her to assess both their knowledge and performance style; Jenny and Marco had both impressed, as she'd anticipated they would, and Isobel had taken her recommendations on board to soften her approach, revealing a much warmer side to her personality than had been evident from her original application. The final presentation of the morning had been from Elspeth, and while Keeley could see she had removed some of the wilder allegations about Eliza's romantic history, her proposed subject matter meant she stood out from the other three candidates for all the wrong reasons.

'It's certainly a rich topic,' Keeley said, when Elspeth finished talking and regarded her with an expression of hopeful anticipation. 'I'm not sure there's much in the way of evidence to support a torrid affair with the village blacksmith. He does crop up in Eliza's diaries, generally in connection to one of her horses, but I don't recall anything that suggests she admired him.'

Elspeth's eyes widened. 'What about Gryff Morgan in *The Last Rays of the Sun*?'

Keeley frowned, mentally flicking through the cast of characters in the novel Elspeth was referring to. 'The Welshman who works for Lord Bedford?'

'Yes,' Elspeth replied impatiently. 'He's a blacksmith, with the initials GM. I did some digging and the blacksmith here in Freezy Tye was originally from Swansea. His name was Geraint Morris.'

'So Eliza used a real-life person as inspiration,' Keeley said. 'We know from her letters to her sister that she wasn't above borrowing character traits and even names from the people she met.'

'But listen to the way she describes him, when Lucy Pennyworth first secretly observes him in her guardian's stable yard.' Pulling a battered paperback from her bag, Elspeth flipped hurriedly through the pages and cleared her throat. '*He was broad-chested, sturdy as an oak and every inch as mighty, as his hammer rose and fell upon the molten metal. At times, he paused his labours to inspect his work, or turn to comfort the horse for whom he toiled, before raising the hammer afresh. Behind the protection of the wall, Lucy felt she need not restrain her unseemly admiration. There was no doubt he was a brute – quite unlike the refined, indolent gentlemen she had met in Lord Bedford's company – but the whispered words to the unsettled horse suggested a gentle aspect to temper his strength. Indeed, it was this tenderness that fascinated her the most, rather than his straining muscles and sweat-slicked mane of dark hair. He was a stallion, she decided, wild and unbroken and magnificent.*' Elspeth looked up, pink-cheeked and breathless as though she had been ogling the blacksmith for herself. 'If that isn't a love letter to Geraint Morris, I don't know what is.'

'I can see your point,' Keeley said. 'But that description is only there as a literary device. It does represent Lucy's sexual awakening, which is why the scene drips with lust by Victorian standards, but Eliza also uses it to foreshadow Lucy's rejection of Mr Horton later on. When she eventually accepts Lord Trelawney, who is not a gentleman in the eyes of her guardian, it is because she understands that gentleness in a man only makes him stronger.'

Elspeth raised her chin stubbornly. 'Can't it be both? A love letter and a literary device? She calls him a stallion, for goodness' sake.'

Keeley couldn't help laughing. 'Okay, you might be onto something. It's been a long time since I read *The Last Rays of the Sun*. You've made me want to revisit it, if only to enjoy Gryff Morgan's rippling muscles all over again.' She paused, her amusement ebbing away. 'Unfortunately, I'm not sure an exploration of Eliza's personal life will set the right tone for our Christmas tours.'

'Ah,' Elspeth said, biting her lip in obvious disappointment. 'I see.'

'But it might be something we could revisit in the spring,'

Keeley went on. 'As a stand-alone talk. You've clearly done a lot of research and I think there could be an audience for a speculative exploration of Eliza's life. What do you think?'

Elspeth's face brightened. 'Do you mean it?'

'Of course,' Keeley nodded. 'We'd need to run it by the trustees, but I think they could be persuaded, especially if Xander thinks it would work.'

Now Elspeth's eyes became saucers. 'Oh yes, I feel sure he'd be on board.'

For a moment, Keeley regretted dragging him into Elspeth's already fevered thoughts but the regret quickly melted away. Apart from anything else, she suspected he was going to love the idea. 'I'll mention it next time I speak to him,' she promised. 'How do you feel about taking on a front of house role for the tours? We'll need someone to greet people, check tickets, that kind of thing? I appreciate it's not quite the same as being a guide but it is a vital role.'

'Front of house,' Elspeth mused, her gaze narrowing. 'That might work. Can I wear a maid's outfit?'

Keeley blinked. When she and Xander had first discussed the possibility of running the Christmas tours, she'd been determined to avoid any suggestion of cosplay. But in the weeks that followed, they'd agreed on certain compromises: the gently steaming tea cups sitting on the table by the fire that she had created for his photography session, a feast under preparation in the kitchen and a half-written page of a manuscript upon Eliza's writing desk. Would it be so very bad if the front door was opened by Elspeth in Victorian dress? 'I think that would be a lovely touch,' Keeley said. 'I'm sure we can source something in your size.'

'Leave it with me,' Elspeth answered. 'I have several friends who are members of an amateur dramatics group in Little Dunmow. They'll know where to start.'

'Make sure you get a receipt if you hire something,' Keeley said. 'We'll reimburse you.'

Elspeth nodded, but Keeley got the sense she hadn't really heard. 'Yes . . . What was the name of Eliza's first housemaid? Betty, wasn't it?'

'Sally,' she corrected. 'Betty was the scullery maid.'

'Of course,' Elspeth said, and bent to gather up the items she'd used in her presentation. 'I must get on. Plans to make, and all that. Thank you, Keeley. I'm delighted to be part of the tours.'

Relieved that she appeared to have accepted the disappointment of not being chosen as a guide, Keeley smiled. 'Thank you for all your hard work. You've made me view Eliza in a whole new light.'

Elspeth nodded. 'Between you and me, I think she was a bit of a minx.'

Keeley's smile became a grin as she considered what Xander would make of such a proclamation. 'Let's hope the trustees agree, because I can't wait to hear the rest of your evidence.'

So. What's the next step?

The message from Xander pinged up on her phone screen just after Monday lunchtime and Keeley knew he meant Eliza's manuscript. He'd checked in with her every day since the discovery, in the manner of an impatient fellow reader who had already devoured the book and wanted to be able to discuss it. She kept her replies factual, telling him the same thing she'd shared with Grace: that the style matched Eliza's work and the handwriting appeared, in her unqualified opinion at least, to be the same. If it was a forgery, it was a very good one and begged the question of how it had been hidden in a secret compartment in Eliza's own writing desk. Surely a forger looking to cash in would have 'discovered' the manuscript themselves, in a much more convenient location.

As far as I can tell, it's real, but I think we should proceed with caution. Let's consult an expert and get it fully authenticated.

It took a few minutes for Xander to reply. *Great. I know a guy.*

A wry smile tugged at Keeley's mouth. Of course he did. She had the feeling Xander knew people everywhere. *I know of someone too*, she typed. *She works for English History and says we can courier it to their head office in Holborn as soon as we're ready.*

Almost immediately, her phone vibrated with an incoming call. She accepted the call, wondering whether he was going to be angry she had contacted Grace's friend without consulting him first. 'Hey, Xander.'

'I'm not sure I'd trust a courier,' he said, without a hint of irritation. 'I can come down and collect it, then deliver it to English History myself.'

She gave the suggestion some thought. Stories of parcels getting lost in transit suddenly loomed in her head. 'I wasn't suggesting we stick it in the post box but I agree it would be safer to hand-deliver it. Have you got the time, though?'

'I'll make the time,' he said, and paused. 'It'll give me an excuse to come and see you.'

Keeley's pulse quickened. She'd been too preoccupied with Eliza's manuscript to give much head space to the kiss she and Xander had shared, and what it might mean, but his words brought the moment back to the forefront of her mind. Was she looking forward to seeing him again? Her body seemed quite keen on the idea: her cheeks were suddenly warm and her stomach was fluttering with anticipation at the mere thought of his arrival. But her brain endeavoured to wrestle control of her emotions. As enjoyable as kissing Xander had been, and as much as she'd wanted to do it again as soon as they had broken apart, it was an added complication she did not need. 'When did you have in mind?' she asked, deciding to ignore his flirtatious tone for now.

'Is this afternoon too soon?' he asked. 'I need to run through the latest newsletter with you and decide on a strategy for the tours. Maybe after that we could go for dinner.'

The smouldering heat in her cheeks caught fire. Closing her eyes, she fanned her face with her spare hand. 'I can't manage dinner this evening,' she said, crossing her fingers to offset the lie. 'There's a village council meeting that I can't miss.'

It wasn't a total lie; she did intend to call Helen to find out which committee might benefit from an injection of Grace's logistical skills. But Xander accepted the excuse at face value. 'No worries,' he said easily. 'I had some thoughts about seeing whether there was any mileage in doing some crossover PR with the Christmassy village thing but it'll have to wait. I'm going to be at Cliveden House from tomorrow until Thursday, so if I don't collect the manuscript today, I won't be able to head to the cottage until Friday. Are you in a hurry to get it assessed?'

It occurred to Keeley to wonder, briefly, what was taking him to Cliveden. Was he working for them or visiting for pleasure? If so, being a social media expert paid more than she thought; Cliveden had once been home to royalty and was now an eye-wateringly expensive luxury hotel, although the gardens were open to the public. Pushing her curiosity to one side, she focused on Xander's question. On the face of it, there was no rush for the manuscript to be authenticated. It had lain undiscovered and unread for more than a century and a half; a few more days would not make a difference. But her contact at English History had told her the assessment could take the better part of a week, and even if Xander was able to deliver it to them the same day he collected it from her, the chances were that no meaningful work would begin on it until the following Monday. Which would mean a whole week would be lost before the assessment even began. Keeley wasn't sure her patience would stretch an additional seven days when it was possible to avoid the delay. 'You could collect it today. I'm free until closing time.'

'I'll set off now,' he said.

It took several minutes after he'd rung off for Keeley to start feeling less flustered and back in control of her core temperature once more. She busied herself with the admin she had postponed from the morning and then turned her attention to planning for the tours. The trustees had ratified the request to temporarily change the cottage opening hours to accommodate the tours and had also agreed to her suggestion that they offer an honorarium to the newly appointed guides. It was not much but it would go some way towards recognising the hard work and commitment they had already shown. Keeley was determined that Elspeth would receive the same payment; she would be giving up her Wednesday, Thursday and Friday evenings, after all.

By the time Xander arrived, she had worked out a draft rota

for the tours that took into account any dates they had given when they were not available, and would offer equal opportunities for all the guides to shine.

'What do you think?' she asked Xander, who perched on the corner of her desk to study the schedule. 'As agreed, we'll offer four tours of sixty minutes per night. I'll deliver two, and one of the other guides will do the other two. That gives me a spare guide each night, in case of illness or unexpected absences.'

'And Elspeth,' he observed, frowning at the rota.

'Ah, yes,' she said. 'I need to explain about that.'

'But I thought you didn't want anyone in character,' he said, once she'd relayed the gist of Elspeth's interview to him.

'I know but she seemed to have her heart set on it, and I'd already disappointed her once,' Keeley sighed. 'And she's a great volunteer – I want to keep her happy if I can. Her talk actually sounds very well researched, even if it does involve a few fairly substantial leaps of faith and some pretty spicy affairs. I think there might be an audience for it.'

'Just not at Christmas,' he finished. 'But maybe around St Valentine's Day – I could definitely see that working.'

'Yes!' she said, beaming up at him and instantly wished she hadn't, because she was suddenly reminded how close he was. 'That would be perfect.'

Seeming to pick up on her discomfort, Xander rose from the desk and dragged over the chair from the corner. He was still beside her, but at least there was a little more distance between them. 'I'm glad things are coming together this end because I think we're just about ready to go live with the booking system,' he said. 'Can I run the campaign past you, make sure you're happy with it?'

When she nodded, he reached into his rucksack and pulled out his laptop. She was instantly transported back to the morning they had first met, when the thought of being forced to sit through a presentation had made her jaw feel as though it might never unclench. But now she knew him better, the sight of him opening his laptop didn't bother her at all. When had she come to respect his opinion rather than rail against it? she wondered. Could it have been the morning he'd introduced her to Delores Semple's house? Or was it a more gradual change, brought on by her growing appreciation of his skills? It was impossible to know for sure. All she could say was that he impressed her more every day.

'These are the images we'll load onto the website, and across social media,' he said, moving through a series of pictures that showed Juniper Cottage in its full Christmas glory. 'I've incorporated some into graphics that I'll share once everything is live, but there are also a few videos. This one is for the website.'

Keeley watched as the front door of the cottage swung open and the Christmas tree in the hall was revealed, resplendent with its flickering faux candles. 'It looks amazing,' she breathed, as the hallway melted into a view of the table and tea cups in front of the fire. 'I feel all Christmassy.'

'That's the idea,' he said, grinning. 'And I had a thought about the finale of the tour. I know we need to be careful to make sure the groups don't run into each other, but would it be possible to finish up with a return visit to the drawing room?'

Keeley ran through the route in her mind. If they timed things right, it should be possible for the following group to be upstairs as the prior guide concluded their tour. 'I think so. Why?'

'I thought it might be nice to have another tree there, but this one surrounded by presents – as though Christmas Day has arrived while the guests have been moving around the house.' He eyed her hopefully. 'What do you think?'

She sat still, running the scene in her head, imagining pushing back the door to reveal the delights inside. 'I think it's a wonderful idea,' she said, turning her head to smile at him. 'We'll definitely make that happen.'

Perhaps it was the irrepressible joy that the thought of Christmas raised in her, or perhaps it was the appreciation of Xander's simple but brilliant suggestion, on top of the obvious hard work and skill he had put into making Juniper Cottage look utterly irresistible, but Keeley was suddenly glad he was so close to her. Before her brain could tell her it was a terrible idea, she leaned very slightly forward to kiss him.

His lips were warm and soft and tasted of sugar and butter. Her eyes fluttered shut as his arms curled around her, easing her closer to deepen the kiss. Almost of their own volition, her fingers crept up to the nape of his neck, sinking into the golden strands in a way she'd tried her hardest not to imagine since that night in the library. And then she stopped thinking and let herself float on the ebb and flow of sensation washing through her. A lazy heat began to smoulder deep inside. As the flame caught, she sensed the same response in him. One hand rose to cup the back of her neck. His mouth became more insistent, pressing into her with a hunger she felt too. She wanted the moment to last forever, but at the same time was all too aware of where they were. With an ache of regret, she took her fingers from his hair and slid her hands to his chest to push him gently back.

'Sorry,' he said, although he looked far too pleased with

himself to convey anything resembling actual repentance. 'That wasn't very professional of me.'

Keeley sighed. 'Actually, it wasn't very professional of me. I'd pretty much convinced myself we shouldn't do that again but then I immediately undo all my hard work by kissing you the first chance I get.'

Xander raised his eyebrows. 'You could have kissed me when I first arrived. That was your first chance. And I thought we agreed the other night that we'd pick up where we left off at some point. I'd say that was a pretty satisfactory continuation of things.'

She couldn't help smiling. 'It was. But I can't help wondering whether we're making life difficult for ourselves.'

He nodded. 'By choosing completely inappropriate locations to kiss each other, you mean?'

Again, she smiled. 'By kissing each other at all. There's a reason anyone with half a brain knows not to mix business with pleasure. What if something goes wrong and we end up having to work together while hating the sight of each other?'

'It's a risk,' he conceded with a shrug. 'But what if everything goes right and we end up kissing each other like that over and over again?'

The mere thought threatened to overwhelm Keeley's carefully reclaimed composure. For a moment, she swayed towards him, then pulled herself back. 'Stop that,' she scolded, although she couldn't manage much ire.

'Stop what?' Xander said, reaching out to tuck a strand of hair behind her ear. 'All I meant was that if I enjoy kissing you, and you enjoy kissing me, what's the problem?'

She took a deep breath, trying to ignore the tingle of her

skin where his fingers had touched. 'The problem is that it's bound to get messy.'

His mouth twitched. 'That's what showers are for.'

A deep blush warmed her face as she caught his meaning. 'Professionally,' she clarified, as her treacherous imagination set off down another route entirely. 'Malcolm told me we're equal in terms of seniority, so at least I'm not your boss and you're not mine, but there's still plenty of opportunity for this to blow up in our faces.'

'I'm just a contractor,' Xander said, shrugging. 'I'm paid by the trustees for the work I do, but I'm not actually an employee and therefore not technically a colleague. Does that help?'

'Not really,' Keeley sighed.

There was a brief silence as he considered her. 'The last thing I want to do is make you uncomfortable. If you'd rather keep things strictly professional, then we can do that.'

She bit her lip, still tender from kissing him. On one hand, she was grateful he understood and respected her position, but on the other, she rather desperately wanted to kiss him again, and she suspected that indecision was written all over her face. She took a deep breath. 'How about if we take it one day at a time?'

'You mean, we keep things strictly professional for the rest of today?' he said.

'Yes,' she said, smoothing her hair.

'And what about tomorrow?' he asked, in a tone so grave that she knew he must be secretly laughing at her. 'Will you decide in advance whether you can keep your hands off me or wait until we meet up?'

'Luckily, you'll be at Cliveden tomorrow,' she said. 'By the time we see each other again, I'll be over you.'

He grinned, seemingly not the least bit offended. 'Or maybe all over me. Now, shouldn't you give me the manuscript in case you're tempted to break our kissing truce before it's even begun?'

It was the wink that almost undid her. She covered the momentary weakness by standing up to retrieve the box containing the manuscript from the filing cabinet behind the door. 'I've put one of Eliza's diaries in with it, along with several letters to her sister as comparisons for her handwriting. I'm sure I don't need to remind you to be very, very careful with all of it.'

'Believe me, I know,' he said. 'By the way, I don't think you told me what the novel is about.'

Keeley hesitated. 'It's a romance,' she said. 'A bit different from her other works but utterly brilliant. I still don't know why it was never published. There's no mention of it in her diaries, or any of the letters we have.'

Xander eyed her thoughtfully. 'You don't think we should tell the trustees about it yet? I'm meeting Malcolm for an update tomorrow morning – I could mention it then.'

She shook her head. 'Let's wait until it's authenticated first. Then we can tell them with complete confidence.'

'Do you think there's a chance Eliza didn't write it?'

'No,' she replied, without a trace of doubt. 'The subject might be different to her other books but the writing is classic Eliza. Even so, I'd like official confirmation before we present it to the trustees. There was a case a few years ago of a newly discovered version of *The Moonlight Dance* by Henrietta Wilkie that the literary world fell over itself to praise but it turned out to be an elaborate forgery produced by a gifted undergraduate student for a dare. A lot of people were embarrassed when the truth came out. Careers were ruined. Worse than that, readers were disappointed. Some of them felt cheated.'

'Ouch,' Xander said, wincing. 'I can see why you want to be sure. But surely the trustees will be just as keen as you to wait for the manuscript to be authenticated before going public?'

She thought about the time Malcolm had carelessly let slip the contents of a keynote speech she'd been due to deliver at a conference, and the impulsiveness of Xander's own appointment without any consideration of how she might feel. There was definitely a chance the trustees might throw caution to the wind when they learned about the manuscript, under the maxim that all publicity was good publicity. It was a risk she would prefer to avoid. 'This novel has been waiting a long time to have its moment in the spotlight. A few more weeks won't make any difference.'

He raised his hands in mock surrender. 'Okay. We'll do it your way.'

She kept her own hands firmly in her pockets as she saw him to the door of the cottage, only allowing herself to wave once she was certain her fingers could not pluck at his arm and betray them both. The night air was too cold to linger on the doorstep and watch until he was out of sight. Instead, she returned to her office, where the memory of their second kiss was unhelpfully fresh. Catching herself smiling, she gathered up her bag and decided it was time to go home. With a bit of luck, the memory would have evaporated by the time she returned in the morning. Except she suspected it was already too late to wipe out her attraction to Xander Jones.

And she was no longer sure she wanted to.

CHAPTER TWELVE

> 'If fate cares not for us, we must take matters into our own hands. Courage, Miss Lovelock, our will may yet prevail!'
>
> *Tennyson Hall*, ELIZA NORTON

Grace wasn't sure whether she was relieved or disappointed not to have seen Raff since their encounter in the stockroom almost two weeks earlier. Part of her wanted to engage him in conversation so that she could try to work out whether Ivy had confided in him about Jesse's proposed rent increase, but another part hoped she never had to speak to him again. And yet another part – one she tried very hard to ignore – kept replaying the moment he'd broken her fall from the ladder, conveniently forgetting that he was the reason she'd lost her balance in the first place. It was all very confusing.

She distracted herself by focusing on helping to organise the Freezy Tye Christmas celebrations. Keeley had put her in touch with Helen, who had in turn suggested she join the subcommittee responsible for stage management. 'They're in charge of making the village look amazing,' Helen explained. 'Keeley tells me that's your forte.'

After a brief conversation with the landlord of the Golden Lion, Grace's phone number had been added to an online group of around ten people she didn't know, although she recognised a few names from conversations with Keeley. This year's chosen theme was 'Once Upon a Time', and, at first, Grace was too shy to add anything to the group discussions about set building and lighting rigs. But then the conversation moved on to what they could do to inject the wow factor into their plans and finally she felt there was something she could contribute.

What about a miniature light trail around the village? I work at Santa's Secret in Flaxwood and they have a Nutcracker-themed set we could hire.

The suggestion had been welcomed enthusiastically and had sparked much debate about the best locations to site potential stops around the village. Paul the electrician raised the issue of safely supplying power to the lights, and Gavin was concerned with ensuring the flow of visitors would not overwhelm any particular area. After much back and forth across several days, six locations were agreed and the route for the trail was set, to culminate in an arch of lit trees leading to the Christmas tree on the village green.

'You could add some Nutcracker soldiers as sentries beside the food and drink stalls,' Ivy suggested, when Grace laid the plans before her in the staffroom. 'I don't have any that are suitable for outdoor use but we could look into getting some.'

'That would be brilliant,' Grace said gratefully. 'The committee is keen to pull out all the stops.'

Ivy considered the map of Freezy Tye that lay on top of the glossy magazine on the coffee table. A series of red dots indicated the proposed locations of each stop on the trail. 'So the start is here,' she said, pointing to one corner of the green. 'This is where the rainbow light tunnel will go.'

Grace nodded. 'The route skirts around the west side to here, where the interactive toy box will be. The next stop, with the Mouse King and the gingerbread army, is inside the churchyard. Then we have the Land of Sweets, in the garden of Bracken House on Froghole Lane – there'll be a stall selling marshmallows on sticks and a small fire pit there too. After that, it's on to the corner of Trotters End and Main Street, where we'll have the dance of the Sugar Plum Fairy, before turning back along the eastern side of the green and passing through the tree arc to the Christmas tree.'

'It sounds amazing,' Ivy said admiringly. 'You've thought of everything.'

Grace wasn't sure about that; she'd woken up more than once in the middle of the night recently, scrabbling for the notebook she'd taken to keeping on her bedside table to write down random notes and trying not to disturb Keeley. Paul had reassured her the supply of electricity would not be an issue; apart from the light tunnel at the beginning and the tree arc at the end, all the stops had the bare minimum of lights that were constantly on and instead offered buttons for visitors to press to bring the various elements to life. Safety at the fire pit also worried her, until Helen suggested a fire warden be present each night. But top of her list of worries was the weather, the one thing no amount of planning could prepare for, and she spent far more time than was healthy refreshing the Met Office website for long-range predictions. The lights were designed for outdoor use and could withstand rain and even snow, but high winds were a risk and a storm would be disastrous. A few of the other members of the group had been at pains to point out that this was not the first time they had decorated the village, which had eased much of her anxiety, but she couldn't help worrying all the same. 'I hope we've thought of everything,' she said. 'Freezy Tye is such a lovely village and everyone is so committed to putting on a good show. Reading between the lines, a few of the village businesses have had a rough year and need the publicity a win will bring. I'd hate to see Flaxwood take the Most Christmassy crown just because Jesse Bairstow thinks all he needs to do is throw money at it.'

At the mention of Jesse's name, Ivy's mouth thinned. 'Exactly. The spirit of Christmas is about more than how much you spend. I hope the judges won't be blinded by whatever ostentatious display he has planned.' She sniffed. 'He came back yesterday, insisting I should support Flaxwood's bid.'

Grace's heart sank, remembering how upset Ivy had been by his previous visit. 'What did you say?'

'The same thing I told him last time – that I consider the happiness of my long-term customers to be of paramount importance and prefer not to pick favourites.' She sighed. 'Not that it will matter when the rent goes up.'

Her expression was so bleak that Grace wanted to hug her. 'Any official notice of that yet?'

'No, but I expect it will come soon. He made it clear yesterday that my days are numbered.'

'Have you spoken to Raff about it?' Grace asked, wishing there was something she could do to help. 'Or a solicitor?'

The older woman managed a weary-looking smile. 'Yes, I told Raff last week. He was all for confronting Jesse but I told him that wasn't the way. My solicitor says there might be a way to challenge it legally but he won't know for sure until I receive formal notice of Jesse's intentions.' She rubbed her forehead. 'I don't know if I have the energy to fight. Part of me thinks it might be time to retire.'

'Oh no,' Grace cried, with genuine consternation. 'Your talent – this place – is wonderful. Please don't let someone like Jesse stop you from doing the thing you love.'

Ivy sighed again. 'I do love Santa's Secret – the customers, the displays, knowing we bring magic into so many lives every year. But I don't enjoy the headache of running a business. The truth is I've been toying with the idea of handing the reins over to someone else for a while now.'

'You've been planning to sell up?' Grace said, trying to hide her shock. As far as she was concerned, Ivy *was* Santa's Secret.

'Or taking on a business partner – someone to do all the parts I'm not good at and allowing me to take more of a back seat. But I can't do that now, not with the rent increase.' She shook her head. 'I think the universe is telling me it's time to stop, although I'll be very sorry to let you and Misha and everyone else down.'

Grace couldn't believe what she was hearing. In the time she'd worked for Ivy, her respect and admiration for her had only grown, both professionally and on a personal level. The idea that she was being made to feel so wretched made Grace's blood boil. She took a deep calming breath. 'You have to do what's right for you, Ivy. Don't worry about us. We'll be sad, of course, but we'll be okay. None of this is your fault.'

Ivy nodded. 'That's what Raff said.' Seeming to gather herself together, she squared her shoulders. 'But it's not a problem for today. Why don't you pop over and see Sanjay, ask him to check the displays are all working?'

'I'll go now,' Grace said, getting to her feet. 'Thanks, Ivy. I really appreciate your help.'

'It's my pleasure,' she replied warmly. 'I've always had a soft spot for Freezy Tye.'

'Better not let Jesse hear you say that,' Grace said, grimacing. 'He'll add another nought to the rent increase.'

Ivy snorted. 'He can try.'

Grace could picture his smug expression as he laid yet more bad news at Ivy's door. It would be better if he never found out she was helping with Freezy Tye's display, she decided as she hurried towards the warehouse to find Sanjay. What Jesse Bairstow didn't know couldn't hurt anyone.

Ruggles grew steadily busier as the first week of October came and went. Grace was in the habit of popping into the cafe for a sandwich at lunchtime but she had quickly learned not to venture there on Saturdays. The pumpkin patch had opened and while its ticket booth was nowhere near the entrance of the garden centre, the queue was often so long that it blocked the path. She could only imagine how busy it would be as the month drew on, and pumpkin passion reached fever pitch.

'It's a nightmare,' Hettie said, as she rang Grace's sandwich and carrot cake through the till in the cafe on Friday morning. 'They have to employ security to make sure no one jumps the queue. Last year, a fight broke out over one of the pumpkins.'

Grace stared at her. 'You're joking.'

'Nope.' Hettie shook her head. 'And you wouldn't believe how pushy people get over the best Instagram shots. It wasn't so bad when it first opened – everyone waited their turn and it wasn't anything like as busy as it is now. This year, Jesse is offering a cash prize for the social media post with the biggest reach, which means the influencers are going all out.'

Something in her tone caught Grace's attention. 'You don't think it's a good idea?'

Hettie glanced around, as though checking no one was listening, and leaned closer. 'No one does. We're run off our feet most weekends but the people who visit the pumpkin patch aren't interested in buying plants or garden stuff, so Jesse keeps making us work over there instead of doing our normal jobs.'

'That doesn't sound fair,' Grace murmured sympathetically.

'And then he gets cross when the queues build up in here and we don't serve people quickly enough, or clear the tables properly,' Hettie went on, her indignation rising. 'How are we supposed to do all that when we only have half the staff we normally do?'

'Sounds like Jesse isn't very popular,' Grace said, tapping her card to pay.

'You can say that again,' Hettie snapped. 'I don't know anyone who likes him much.' Handing Grace the receipt, she glanced beyond her to the cafe door and her expression changed. 'There's old Mr Bairstow now. I wish he was still running things instead of Jesse. He knows how to treat people.'

Turning, Grace followed the direction of her gaze and saw an elderly man leaning on a walking stick, chatting animatedly with a tableful of customers. With a genial wave, he moved onto the next table and greeted them with obvious warmth. 'I see what you mean,' she said to Hettie. 'Do you know why he's stepping back from the business?'

Hettie sighed. 'He had a bout of ill health in the summer – a bad scare that took a lot out of him. Jesse came back to run things while he recovered and never left.' She folded her arms in clear disapproval. 'I think he convinced Mr B he was too old to manage the business. Before we knew it, he was announcing all kinds of changes and telling anyone who'd listen how he was going to turn Ruggles into more than just a garden centre. He was going to make it a destination.'

That certainly seemed to fit with what he'd said to Ivy, Grace thought as Hettie glowered in disgust, although she had no idea what most of it actually meant. 'Wow.'

'Right?' Hettie exclaimed. 'So what if we're a bit old-fashioned? That's what our customers like. No one goes to a garden centre for clicks and likes. They go to buy chrysanthemums and compost and maybe have a nice cream tea.'

Grace couldn't argue. 'You do serve a very nice cream tea.'

'Thank you,' Hettie said, and lowered her voice as another customer approached, clutching a sandwich. 'Anyway, I'd best get on. Thanks for listening to me moan.'

'No problem,' Grace said, smiling. 'Any time.'

As she made her way out, she glanced across at Mr Bairstow again. He was still moving between the tables, nodding politely at some and pausing to greet others as if they were old friends. Which Grace supposed they might well be; Ruggles had been open for many years and undoubtedly had many regular, long-standing customers. For a moment, she considered going across to introduce herself but quickly thought better of it. What could she say, anyway? 'Your son is a despicable bully?' It was unlikely to go down well.

Even so, she was deep in thought as she passed through the

door and made for Santa's Secret. If Hettie was to be believed, it seemed Jesse was not endearing himself to his employees. Perhaps his plans for the expansion of the garden centre would meet with resistance and he might change his mind about forcing Ivy and her business out. She could only cross her fingers and hope.

Her heart simultaneously leapt and sank when she saw Raff in the car park as she made her way back to work. He was leaning against his car, a navy waxed jacket open across his chest and his phone pressed to his ear, but his eyes were fixed upon her as she approached the barn. Determined to be polite, she nodded in greeting and was about to pass him by when she heard him call out. 'Grace, wait!'

Reluctantly, she stopped, wondering if he was going to tell her off for being two minutes late or some other breach of the rules, and then decided she was being unfair. He'd only told her off once, with some justification, and afterwards he'd seemed to regret being so strident. She waited as he ended his call and crunched across the short distance to meet her. 'Hello,' she said, as he came to a halt. 'Can I help you with something?'

'No,' he said, and hesitated. 'I mean, yes. Or rather, you've already helped me with something, in a manner of speaking.'

Grace eyed him in confusion, trying her hardest not to let her gaze linger on the adorable pair of lines that appeared between his eyebrows when he frowned. 'I have?'

Raff took a breath and made a visible effort to pull his thoughts together. 'Yes. My mother told me how you comforted her after her visit from Jesse a few weeks ago. I wanted to thank you for that.'

'Oh,' Grace said, blushing a little. 'You don't need to thank me. Anyone would have done the same.'

'Perhaps,' Raff said, and his frown softened. 'She said you were very kind. I'm also grateful for your discretion. I'm aware you haven't worked here very long, so you don't owe us any loyalty, but I appreciate the fact that you didn't spread the news among your colleagues.'

Now it was Grace's turn to frown. 'Of course not. I realise you don't have the highest opinion of my intelligence but that doesn't make me a gossip.'

Twin spots of colour appeared in his cheeks. 'I do have a high opinion of your intelligence. What makes you think I don't?'

'The fact that you called me a fool,' Grace said, and instantly wished she hadn't. Why was she reminding him of her own stupidity when he was simply trying to thank her? She shook her head. 'But it doesn't matter now. I'm glad I was there when Ivy needed me. She's a wonderful employer and I'm sorry Jesse is doing this to her.'

For a moment, she thought she'd overstepped the mark. Raff's expression darkened still further as he considered her. Then he sighed and ran a hand through his hair. 'Thanks. I don't really know what we're going to do.'

Grace stuffed the hand that was not holding her lunch into her pocket, in case it decided to act on sudden impulse to straighten the lock of hair he had displaced. 'From what she tells me, there's not much you can do until Jesse makes his next move. He seems quite ambitious so I don't suppose he'll wait long.'

His jaw tightened. 'Ambitious is certainly a word. Ruthless and conniving are others.' He took in her raised eyebrows. 'We were at school together. Let's just say he didn't mind trampling over everyone else to get what he wanted back then, and he hasn't changed a bit.'

Grace recalled Hettie's assertion that no one liked Jesse much. 'Bullies always get their comeuppance eventually.'

Raff grunted. 'If that's true then I'd like it to happen before he drives my mother into an early grave.' Seeming to remember who he was talking to, he looked away. 'Sorry. That was unnecessarily overdramatic. I'm just worried for her, that's all.'

He looked it too, Grace thought, and she had to quell an impulse to lay a comforting hand on his arm. 'That's understandable,' she said. 'I'd feel exactly the same.'

Straightening his shoulders, he met her gaze once more. 'She tells me you have big plans for the Freezy Tye Christmas display.'

'I do,' she answered. 'And I don't mind telling you that one of the reasons I volunteered for the committee is because Jesse is so convinced Flaxwood is going to win. It seems to me he's had things his own way for far too long and I want to wipe that look of self-satisfaction right off his face.'

Raff stared at her, his mouth slightly open. 'You're doing this to teach him a lesson?'

She felt her cheeks growing warm again. 'Not just because of that. I also happen to love Christmas and I didn't like going back to an empty house.' His eyebrows rose and she hurried to explain. 'My son is spending a year in Australia and, well, I'm missing him. That's why I applied for the job here.'

Stop talking, Grace, she admonished herself as understanding dawned in Raff's eyes. 'I see.' His gaze flicked to her left hand, which was still in her pocket, then returned to her face. 'No partner to make things easier – a husband or – or—'

He stopped talking, embarrassed. 'No,' she said, and something swirled in the pit of her stomach. 'No one at all.'

She wanted to groan the moment the words were out. Could she have made herself sound any more pathetic? But Raff wasn't eyeing her with pity. Instead, he seemed to have become very still. 'Right,' he said, after a silence that threatened to make things even more awkward. 'I mean, I'm sorry to hear that. I imagine you miss your son very much.'

'Yes,' Grace said simply. 'But he's having a fabulous time, living his best life, and I'm staying with Keeley for the time being so I don't have to face my empty nest each night. That's part of the deal with kids, isn't it? They grow up and leave you behind.'

Raff shook his head. 'I wouldn't know. I only have a Labrador and he doesn't leave me alone for a minute.'

The admission made her laugh. 'They do say dogs are for life.'

He smiled. 'This one really is. Even when I'm in the shower.'

The thought of him in the shower was not one Grace felt equipped to deal with right at that moment. She gestured towards the barn. 'I should probably get back to work.'

'Of course,' he said, his smile fading. 'Enjoy your lunch.'

Turning away, he crunched back to his car. Grace did not allow herself to watch him. Instead, she headed for the door and tried to ignore the jumble of butterflies that were somersaulting in her stomach. The way she felt right now, she couldn't eat a thing. It was maddening, she thought as she stowed her sandwich in the staffroom fridge.

Why did Raff Caldwell always seem to have this effect on her? And when was it going to wear off?

CHAPTER THIRTEEN

'I do not accept that adversity must be our undoing, Mrs Gladstone. Can it not also be the making of us?'

Where the Wind Blows, ELIZA NORTON

Keeley was standing silently in the drawing room of Juniper Cottage on Friday afternoon when her phone vibrated in her pocket. Discreetly, she edged it out to view the screen and was surprised to see Malcolm's name displayed there. Hitting mute, she tucked it away again and smiled indulgently at a little girl and her mother as they moved into the corridor. Only fifteen minutes remained until Keeley would be relieved by an incoming volunteer. Malcolm could wait until then.

She was therefore surprised when her pocket buzzed again. Frowning, she took out her phone and saw the trustee was calling her again. With a swift glance left and right, she checked there were no visitors nearby and swiped the screen to answer. 'Hello?'

'Keeley.' Malcolm's voice seemed to boom in her ear, made louder by the silence of the drawing room. 'Sorry to call twice. Is now a good time?'

Not really, she wanted to say, but she detected a note of something unusual in his tone. The rule was that mobile phone use was strictly forbidden while on duty in the cottage but she would have to break that rule just this once. 'I have a few minutes,' she said cautiously. 'Is everything okay?'

'Everything is fine,' he replied, and she thought he now sounded strangely ebullient. 'Marvellous, in fact. Couldn't be better.'

Keeley felt her forehead crease. 'I'm glad to hear that. So what can I help you with?'

He cleared his throat. 'I had a very interesting meeting with Xander Jones earlier in the week. He updated me on what you've been getting up to at the cottage and how well you've been working together.'

Heat flooded Keeley's cheeks. She really hoped Xander hadn't shared everything they'd been getting up to. 'We've made good progress on plans for the Christmas tours,' she said, her tone deliberately cool. 'I believe Xander plans to go live with the booking system next week.'

'Yes, it's all very exciting,' Malcolm huffed. 'Top work. I knew you'd make an excellent team.'

Her eyes narrowed. What exactly had Xander been saying? 'Is that what you're calling about? Because it would be easier to talk—'

'No,' he interrupted her. 'It's not that. Something has been brought to the attention of the trustees – a rather exciting discovery – and I must say, I'm surprised we didn't find out about it from you.'

Keeley felt a cold ripple of unease run down her spine. 'What do you mean? What kind of discovery?'

Malcolm chuckled. 'Come now, Keeley, you know exactly what I'm talking about. You ought to, since you're the one who found it. I'm talking about the manuscript – Eliza's unpublished novel.'

Blood began roaring in Keeley's ears. 'But that's not – we agreed –' She stopped talking, trying to marshal her thoughts. 'How do you know about that?'

'A little bird told me,' he said jovially. 'That's all you need to know.'

Her confusion coalesced into understanding. Only three people knew about the manuscript and she very much doubted Grace had a hotline to the trustees. Keeley herself hadn't told them, which only left Xander. Her stomach swooped in shocked disbelief. He'd promised not to tell Malcolm about their discovery before the manuscript had been authenticated but it seemed he hadn't been able to resist. Perhaps he'd even taken it straight to him, before dropping it off to be assessed. The thought of it made her feel a little sick; not only had Xander gone over her head, he'd robbed her of the opportunity of telling the trustees herself. 'I see,' she said, through lips that felt numb.

'Obviously, it's wonderful news,' Malcolm went on, oblivious to her muted reaction. 'And given the upcoming rollout of the tours, the other trustees and I think we should announce the discovery now.'

'Now?' she repeated in dismay. 'But it hasn't been properly authenticated.'

'So much the better,' he said. 'We cause an immediate stir with the news that a secret, hitherto unpublished manuscript has been found, and then another when it's officially declared to be Eliza's.' There was a brief pause. 'Unless you don't think she wrote it?'

Keeley ran a shaky hand across her eyes. 'I'm as certain as I can be that it's her work. But I still think we should wait until it's confirmed. You must remember what happened with the Wilkie manuscript a few years ago.'

Malcolm let out an especially loud harrumph. 'That was entirely different. You discovered the manuscript in situ, as it were, and there's no doubt it's Eliza's work.' He paused, and Keeley opened her mouth to renew her objections, but Malcolm was speaking again. 'I think we'll push on. I'll ask Xander to prepare a press release, for distribution this evening to catch the weekend editions. Obviously, we can't tell how much of a splash the news will make initially but you'll probably experience an increase in visitor numbers at the cottage once word gets out. Do you have some extra volunteers you can call in?'

There was no point in arguing, Keeley realised. The horse had well and truly bolted and she took little consolation from knowing she'd been right to suspect Malcolm would ignore the more cautious approach. 'Maybe,' she said, puffing out her cheeks as she mentally ran through the available volunteers. 'But we're not really set up for large crowds – there will be bottlenecks, especially around the entrance. And the cafe won't be open. It closed for the winter at the end of September.'

'We'll make sure that's clear on the website,' he said briskly. 'And I suggest we switch to online tickets only, to manage visitor numbers. No walk-ins.'

It was a change in policy that would almost certainly result in some disgruntled visitors, Keeley thought with an inward sigh. She'd need to update the signs and ensure she was nearby to deal with any fallout.

'Oh, and you might be contacted by journalists but don't worry about answering their questions,' Malcolm continued briskly. 'Refer them to us for now – Xander will know how to handle them.'

A sense of overwhelm was roaring through her, causing her heart to thump uncomfortably fast. 'Wouldn't it make more sense to wait?' she said again, cursing Xander's inability to keep the manuscript under wraps. 'That way we can make a proper plan and be better prepared for the increase in interest.'

'We do have a plan,' Malcolm assured her. 'And the trustees feel we should make the most of this staggering opportunity to raise Eliza's profile. As do I.'

The determination in his voice told her it was a lost cause. 'I see.'

'I'm sure Xander will be in touch later but I imagine he'll want a quote from you for the press release, as the foremost expert on Eliza Norton, so perhaps you could start thinking of what you'd like to say,' Malcolm went on. 'Something upbeat about how incredible it is to have a previously unknown book by such an esteemed yet undervalued writer, you know the kind of thing.'

'Yes,' Keeley said dryly. 'I do know the kind of thing.'

'And perhaps you'd be good enough to email over a brief outline of the plot, so we're prepared to field questions. It might be an idea to copy Xander in too. I don't suppose you know why it was never published?'

'Not yet,' she said. 'I've checked everything we have and it isn't mentioned anywhere.'

'Keep looking,' Malcolm urged. 'The more we have, the bigger the buzz Xander can whip up.'

She resisted the urge to clench her jaw. 'Of course. Anything else?'

'No, I think that's all. It goes without saying that we are tremendously excited about this, Keeley. Once the manuscript has been properly verified as Eliza's work, we'll see about finding a publisher for it. Imagine, a new Eliza Norton novel on sale in bookshops!'

'I know. It's a wonderful opportunity,' she said, because it was. She just wished Xander had thought to warn her before telling the trustees about their find and turning her world on its head.

She stood still for several minutes after Malcolm had rung off, staring blindly at the faded swirls of colour on the carpet while her mind worked. When Sylvie arrived to relieve her a short while later, she managed a brief smile of thanks before escaping to the gardens, where the autumn sunshine did little to soothe her troubled spirits. Her phone showed no notifications – no missed calls and no unread messages. Xander hadn't tried to let her know what was coming, had left it to Malcolm to reveal how he'd undermined her, and that made things even worse. But it didn't take long for her practical nature to kick in. The trustees were well within their rights to decide on the best way to proceed and, as their employee, Keeley had no choice but to agree. What was worse was the ache in her chest; by reneging on their pact to keep the manuscript between them, Xander had also thrown a grenade into whatever had been blossoming between them and that hurt. The only saving grace was that he'd shown she couldn't trust him with Eliza's manuscript before she'd been foolish enough to let him into her heart.

Her phone rang again thirty minutes later, when she had

taken herself for a walk to Eliza's Pantry for an Autumn Spiced Latte, and this time, it was Xander's name on the screen. Briefly, she considered rejecting the call; she was still angry and the betrayal was too fresh, meaning she couldn't think of anyone she'd like to talk to less, despite the need to demand an explanation. She also suspected he'd be confused by her anger, which would only infuriate her more. Unfortunately, she didn't have the luxury of allowing her bruised feelings to heal before she faced him. The trustees' determination to announce the discovery meant she and Xander had to talk, and she was damned if she'd let his lack of professionalism affect her own. 'Hello, Xander,' she said coolly.

'Hi,' he said, his tone as tight as her own. 'I gather you've spoken to Malcolm this morning.'

'I have,' she said, determined to keep a lid on her temper. 'Has he explained the plan?'

He let out a long breath. 'He's asked me to draft a press release about the manuscript. I have to say, the request came totally out of left field. I wish you'd warned me you were going to tell them about finding it.'

Keeley felt her jaw drop. 'Me? I'm not the one who couldn't my mouth shut. Malcolm said you were the one who told him.'

'That's not what happened,' Xander insisted. 'You must have misunderstood.'

The absolute certainty in his voice made her pause. While Malcolm had strongly implied Xander had been the one to reveal the manuscript's existence, he'd stopped short at actually naming him. But did that matter when there was no other possible explanation? 'I can assure you I didn't,' she fired back. 'Only the two of us knew about it and you were the one who suggested we take it to the trustees. I wanted to wait for the results of the authentication, remember?'

'And I agreed to that,' he ground out, sounding frustrated. 'So if you didn't tell them, and I didn't, how did they find out?'

Keeley let out an incredulous huff. 'You told them! I don't know why you're pretending you didn't. If you think it's going to make me feel any less betrayed, then you're wrong.'

Now it was Xander's turn to huff. 'Betrayed? Come on, Keeley, can you hear yourself? It's an old manuscript, not a declaration of war.'

'It's not about the bloody manuscript,' she growled, aware her raised voice was attracting the attention of those passing by. 'Not really. It's about you deciding you know better than me and doubling down on that decision now. I'd prefer it if you were honest with me and admitted you went over my head.'

'I went over your head?' he snapped. 'How about you decided to cut me out of the loop?'

She closed her eyes, counting slowly to ten. 'For the last time, Xander, I didn't tell the trustees.'

'Neither did I,' he insisted.

Silence crackled between them, during which Keeley attempted to wrestle her fury into submission. She wasn't sure what angered her more – the fact that he refused to take responsibility for his actions or his attempt to put the blame on her. After several more charged seconds ticked by, she heard Xander sigh. 'So what happens now?'

She pinched the bridge of her nose and squeezed her eyes tight shut. 'What do you mean, what happens now? Regardless of who did what to whom, we've still got jobs to do. You need to write a press release and I need to provide a quote about how brilliant it is to have found an undiscovered work by one of Britain's most underrated writers. And then we have to hope it's good news from my contact at English History.'

There was another long pause, during which she could imagine him battling his own temper. 'Fine,' he said eventually. 'I heard from the web developer yesterday. The page for the Christmas tours is ready to go live, along with the booking system. If we play this right, and the news is positive from English History, then we should be able to amplify the tours on the back of any press interest in the manuscript.'

Keeley took a measured breath in and let it out just as slowly, forcing herself to think calmly. 'Malcolm also suggested we switch general entry to the cottage to advance tickets only, in case we get inundated with visitors.' She glanced back towards Juniper Cottage, which was basking peacefully on the far side of the village green, conspicuously free from invading hordes of book lovers. 'Is that something you can speak to the developer about?'

'Yes, okay,' he agreed. 'Will you email me something for the press release? Malcolm wants it to go out this afternoon so I'll need it as soon as possible.'

'I'm not at the cottage right now but I'll do it as soon as I get back,' she replied. 'Is there anything else?'

'Not at the moment,' he said curtly. 'I'll be in touch if I think of anything.'

He rang off without saying goodbye and she stuffed her phone into her pocket, indignation roaring back now that she no longer had to keep her feelings in check. The cheek of him, suggesting she had been the one to spill the beans! Admittedly, she hadn't been totally honest, because there was a third person who knew about the manuscript but it was utterly ridiculous to think that Grace might be responsible. No, Keeley thought as she turned back to Juniper Cottage, it could only have been Xander. She had no idea what he hoped to gain by denying it but she supposed it didn't really matter. The important thing now was to make sure the announcement went smoothly. And the first step towards that was convincing the world that she couldn't be happier to have found Eliza's lost work.

The call from English History came less than a week after Keeley's disagreement with Xander. It appeared as an unknown number, and she'd grown wary of answering those after a flurry of calls from journalists that had caught her off guard. They hadn't been difficult – most were apologetic once she explained that she wasn't the first point of contact for questions about the manuscript – but each conversation brought back memories of what she still thought of as Xander's betrayal and her heart was still sore. She let the latest call go to voicemail, then listened back and was both unsettled and pleased when she realised the message was from Grace's contact at English History, asking her to call back. She did so immediately, putting aside the volunteer rota she'd been working on to tap the extension number onto the keypad with anxious fingers. Now that the moment of truth had arrived, she found herself suddenly convinced that it would be bad news – that she had somehow been taken in by a clever forgery and disaster lay ahead. She almost hung up, but the knowledge that she could not delay the moment of truth forever stopped her. And then the call was answered and it was too late to back out. 'Jemima Strong, English History.'

'Hello Jemima,' Keeley said into the receiver. 'This is Dr

Cotterill, from Juniper Cottage. I got your message about the manuscript you've been authenticating on behalf of Eliza Norton's trustees.'

'Ah yes,' the other woman said warmly. 'Thanks for coming back to me. I'm actually calling on behalf of my colleague, who has been called away from work unexpectedly. She's been the lead curator assessing the manuscript but she didn't want to keep you waiting any longer than necessary for her findings, so she's left me all the pertinent details to pass along ahead of our written report.'

'Okay,' Keeley said, with a slight frown. She supposed it didn't really matter who she spoke to now – not when the call would be followed up by a written report. She clenched her jaw and released it, steeling herself for news. 'I'm grateful for your time. What can you tell me about the manuscript?'

There was a faint rustle of paper, as though Jemima was shifting things around on her desk. 'Our assessment of the document's age matches the date on the cover page. It's impossible to be exact, not without more rigorous scientific testing, but we compared the weight and composition of the paper with what we know was in fairly standard use by other novelists of the time to produce their work.'

It wasn't anything unexpected; Keeley had instinctively recognised the quality of the paper the moment she'd lifted it from the secret drawer and turned the first page, but it was reassuring to have her assessment confirmed. 'That's good news,' she said cautiously. 'Go on.'

'We also undertook a detailed, microscopic comparison of the handwriting in the letters and diaries you provided against that of the manuscript.'

Keeley held her breath. This was it – the moment that might make or break her career. 'And?'

'The ink compares well visually to that used in the personal documents you sent, and the handwriting is an exact match. The final aspect of our analysis related to Eliza's known writing style and personal quirks. We looked at her published works to establish any idiosyncrasies, and to get a feel for her style and compare that to the unpublished manuscript. While there were some differences between that and later works – an overreliance on semi-colons, for example – we attributed these to the development of Eliza's craft. In short, she became a better writer in later years, but that's not to say *The Merriest Month* isn't an excellent piece of work.' Jemima paused. 'I only read a small extract and I absolutely loved it. I do hope you find a way to get it published.'

Keeley puffed out a long breath. 'So you're saying it's been verified as Eliza's work. The manuscript is definitely hers.'

'It's hers,' Jemima confirmed and Keeley could hear the smile in her voice. 'Written in the mid-nineteenth century, with paper and ink that were readily available at that time, and using all the hallmark language, grammar and punctuation that feature in her other works. In short, a previously undiscovered manuscript in practically mint condition. Congratulations on finding it, Dr Cotterill. You must be delighted.'

'I am,' Keeley said, feeling the final vestiges of doubt lift from her shoulders. 'Thank you.'

'As I said, there'll be a written report confirming our findings – that will arrive by email in the next few hours,' Jemima said. 'The only other thing left to discuss is the arrangement for returning the manuscript and accompanying documents to you.' There was another brief pause. 'The notes say they were hand-delivered to our offices. Is there someone local who can collect everything from us or would you like us to source a specialist in transporting delicate papers?'

Keeley had known the question was coming but it still caught her out. Xander had dropped the manuscript off but there was no way she could ask him to collect it. Apart from anything else, she imagined he would refuse. She rubbed the bridge of her nose and sighed. 'I'll have to come back to you on that, I'm afraid. The diaries and letters need to be returned to Juniper Cottage but I don't know what the trustees plan to do with the manuscript yet. I imagine they'll want to read the report before they make any decisions.'

'Of course,' Jemima said. 'Do you have any questions for me?'

Keeley thought for a moment. 'No, I don't think so. Thanks for sharing your findings, and please do pass my appreciation on to your colleague for all her hard work.'

Once the call was complete, she sat in silence for almost a minute. In other circumstances, she would be calling Xander now, bubbling over with excitement with the news that what they had found was the real thing. But the lines of communication had been so badly damaged by the revelation that he'd ignored her wishes that she wasn't sure they could ever move past the stilted, strictly professional messages they'd fallen back on now. It didn't matter that his faith in the manuscript had proved correct; what mattered was the fact that he'd bypassed her entirely and revealed the discovery to the trustees before they were even sure what they had. And then he had lied and accused her of doing the same thing. But perhaps even worse than that, he'd made her feel something she hadn't allowed herself to feel with anyone since divorcing her husband: a connection that had made her feel alive. Realising Xander had betrayed that too was the thing that hurt the most.

With a sigh, she picked up her phone and made another call. 'Hello, Malcolm, it's Keeley. I have some excellent news to share with you.'

CHAPTER FOURTEEN

Christmas! O' Christmas! Is there anything better than its marvellous glow?

The Merriest Month, ELIZA NORTON

It seemed to Grace as though the universe hit the fast-forward button in October. The days seemed to flash by in a whirl as she split her time between working at Santa's Secret, tackling the seemingly endless to-do list that had somehow landed in her inbox since volunteering to help with Freezy Tye's Christmas display, and nursing Jack through occasional bouts of homesickness. The decision to move into Keeley's spare room turned out to be a sound one, especially since she'd also stepped in to help as a volunteer at Juniper Cottage, which had seen a surge in visitors once the news about Eliza Norton's unpublished manuscript had broken. It had begun with a brief mention on the local news as Grace was driving to work.

'And finally, a previously unknown manuscript by Victorian novelist, Eliza Norton, has been independently confirmed as her work,' the newsreader said. 'The novel, which was discovered at Juniper Cottage, in the village of Freezy Tye, is thought to be an early example of Norton's work and is expected to raise considerable interest when it comes up for auction next week.'

Grace had immediately called Keeley. 'I know,' her friend had said. 'Brian heard it too and filled me in. Apparently, one of the broadsheets is going to run a biography of Eliza, describing her life and work.'

'People really seem to love the idea of a long-lost manuscript,' Grace agreed. 'The story is only going to get bigger from here.'

Her prediction had been spot-on. But it wasn't until the rights to publish *The Merriest Month* had gone up for auction that Norton fever had really taken hold. The exact amount of the winning bid was not revealed publicly but Grace had watched the colour drain out of her friend's face when she took the call from Malcolm.

'How much?' she gasped, dropping to the living-room sofa as though her legs had given way. 'But that's – it's –'

'It's insane,' Grace said, when Keeley finished the call and confided the exact six-figure sum. 'No wonder they're keeping it under wraps. But I reckon you might be able to renovate the stable block now.'

The problem with withholding the auction amount was that it created a social media storm, one that was fuelled by wild speculation, both in the UK and the USA, as well as the significant increase in those visiting Eliza's home. On the days she wasn't working at Santa's Secret, Grace found herself directing cars to the hastily arranged overflow car park in the yard of Potts Farm, or managing the queues that snaked around the cottage gardens. The village shops and businesses were not complaining; the uptick in visitors meant more customers for them, but residents were less enthusiastic and Grace knew Keeley had embarked on more than one charm offensive to placate angry homeowners unable to park outside their houses.

'It's great for the cottage,' she sighed wearily one evening, after another villager had knocked on her door to complain. 'But I'll be glad when we close the doors in a few weeks and only open up in the evenings for the tours.'

For Grace, another unexpected development was dominating what little head space she had left over. She arrived at a meeting of the Freezy Tye stage management subcommittee at the Golden Lion on the last Wednesday of October to find a new member had joined.

'Evening, Grace,' Gavin greeted her cheerfully when she stopped just inside the doorway to blink in surprise at the group huddled around a pair of tables. 'You must already know Raff, what with working at his mum's place. He's joined us to lend some much-needed horticultural expertise. The more the merrier, I say.'

'Yes,' Grace said, unwinding the scarf from around her neck and hoping she didn't look as flustered as she felt. 'Hi, Raff. Hello, everyone.'

The others nodded and called out greetings but Grace found she was acutely aware that Raff was watching her. When at last she finished hanging up her coat and risked a glance towards him, his expression suggested that he wasn't entirely sure she'd be glad to see him. She offered a reassuring smile, and felt a jolt of pleasure when he smiled back, closely followed by a surge of mild embarrassment when she realised Gav was talking to her. 'Earth to Grace,' he said, waving a hand in her direction. 'What would you like to drink?'

'Oh,' she said, startled. 'Um – a glass of Prosecco, please.'

It was her usual order but it wasn't until Gavin had disappeared behind the bar that it occurred to her that it might be better to keep a clear head, especially since the only spare seat was next to Raff.

'I hope you don't think I'm muscling in,' he said quietly, when she'd picked her way to the seat and the buzz of conversation resumed among the other committee members. 'I was thinking about what you said, the last time we spoke, about Jesse having things his own way for too long, and, well, it really struck a chord. So I thought I'd offer my services, see what I can do to stop him in his tracks.'

Grace glanced at him curiously. 'Is there much call for horticultural advice at Christmas? Obviously, there's a big push for Christmas trees, and holly.'

'Don't forget mistletoe,' Gavin interrupted, winking as he placed a flute of fizz in front of Grace. 'We're going to have a kissing station so people can snap selfies for their social media. Raff is going to source a supply of fresh mistletoe for it.'

'Oh,' Grace said, taking a hurried sip of her drink, because thinking about kissing while sitting next to Raff made her feel rather too warm. 'That will be popular.'

'As long as they tag the village in their posts,' Amanda said from across the table, with a savviness Grace thought Xander would approve of. 'We're going to need all the help we can get this year. I heard Flaxwood is having a couple of those animatronic dinosaurs installed on their village green.'

Gavin snorted. 'Because nothing says Christmas like a massive T. rex giving you the eyeball.'

'I'm just telling you what I heard,' Amanda said, raising her hands. 'So it's a good thing we've got Grace on our side. What's the latest with the light trail?'

Grace opened her notebook. 'Installation is scheduled for 26th November – that's when the frames will go up and we can test that everything works. We'll then have twenty-four hours to check for any issues before the switching-on ceremony on the 27th.'

'I've called in a couple of favours with friends to make sure we'll have electricians on hand for the install,' Paul said. 'And obviously I'll be around for the switch-on. We'll do a dry run the night before, to iron out any wrinkles. That's when the residents who are hosting their own displays have been told to aim for.'

'Let's hope it stays dry,' Grace said. 'I'm having nightmares about the weather.'

Amanda shuddered. 'Do you remember the year we had a blizzard at the start of December? That was a challenge.'

'Looked very Christmassy, though,' Gavin pointed out. 'And we still won. The judges mentioned it in their comments.'

'No snow,' Grace said firmly. 'Not until 25th December.'

Gavin grinned. 'Make a note, Raff. The weather is your department.'

'I'll see what I can do,' Raff said gravely.

At that moment, something cold and wet touched Grace's hand. She looked down to see a pair of soulful amber eyes gazing up at her. 'Hello,' she said, reaching down to ruffle the golden ears of the Labrador she hadn't even noticed was lying under the table. 'Who's this?'

'His name is Bilbo,' Raff said, with an affectionate glance at the dog. 'My self-appointed shadow and the scourge of squirrels everywhere.'

'I see,' Grace said, smiling. 'That's quite a varied job description.'

'He's got a side hustle in scrounging crisps,' Amanda put in. 'Beef if he can get them, but he's not that fussy.'

'Noted,' Grace laughed, stroking the soft fur of his head. 'One look from those big amber eyes and I bet no one can resist.'

'They haven't failed him yet,' Raff admitted ruefully. 'Much to the disapproval of our vet.'

The meeting moved on to the logistics of the kissing booth, which was really going to be an enormous, free-standing photo frame for romantics to pose inside. Trevor, a quietly spoken man who seemed to listen a lot more than he spoke, volunteered to take care of that. 'As long as someone with some artistic talent promises to decorate it.'

Next was the arrival of the stallholders, who were due to set up the day before the switching-on ceremony. 'That way, they can be part of the dry run,' Paul explained to Grace.

'Great. I'll have some themed Nutcracker decorations to put in place,' she said, and looked up from her notes. 'What about the tree? There's a net of lights to fit as the finale of the trail but when do you think it will be in place?'

'Over to our resident horticulturalist,' Gavin said. 'Raff has kindly offered to source a tree for us this year.'

He glanced at Grace. 'I've got a friend who owns a Christmas tree farm. I can ask him to deliver and secure it in place on 26th November, if you want to tie it into the light trail installation.'

'That would be great,' she said with a smile, and ticked another item off her list. 'Thank you.'

Another round of drinks was ordered. Grace noticed Raff stuck to Coke, and guessed he must be driving. At length,

Gavin wrapped the meeting up, reminding everyone to submit any receipts to the committee treasurer as soon as possible. As everyone got to their feet and began reaching for coats, Bilbo stood up and stretched. 'Time to go, boy,' Raff said, clipping a lead to his collar before turning to Grace. 'I think you said you've moved in with Keeley for a while. Is that right?'

She nodded, impressed he'd remembered. 'Yes. Apart from anything else, it makes the journey to work much easier and I'm working my way through her Agatha Christie collection.'

'I'm parked not far from her cottage,' he said, smiling. 'Shall we walk together?'

Feeling her cheeks grow warm, Grace glanced around to see if anyone was paying attention but they were too busy wrapping up warm and saying goodnight. 'Okay,' she said.

Outside, the temperature had dropped, causing their breath to billow into clouds as they walked. The sky was cloudless; a smattering of stars shimmered against the blackness and the moon hung full and bright in their midst. Grace tucked her scarf more firmly into her coat. If she hadn't already known winter was on the way, the frost glistening on the grass of the green would have been a clue.

'Are you enjoying working with Gavin and the others?' Raff asked, as Bilbo snuffled along the pavement.

She gave him a sideways look, wondering whether he might count any of the people in the pub as friends. They'd certainly seemed to know Bilbo. She decided to err on the side of caution. 'Yes, it's been fun. Although I meant it when I said I spend far too long looking at the Met Office website.'

Raff's expression was thoughtful. 'Can they accurately predict the weather that far ahead?'

'Not really,' she conceded. 'But it doesn't stop me checking.'

He laughed. 'Do you regret volunteering?'

'No,' she said. 'I'm excited to see the light trail in action. I love the idea of bringing a little bit of Christmas joy into people's lives.'

'The organisation of anything like this is always a bit bumpy,' he reassured her. 'It should all be smooth sailing once everything is in place.'

'I hope so,' Grace replied, trying to squash a fresh worm of worry. 'I might only be a temporary resident, but I want this year to be Freezy Tye's best year ever.'

'I'm sure it will. Gavin says you've been a breath of fresh air. He wants to know if there's a way to persuade you to move here permanently.'

Grace pulled a face. 'I'm not sure how Keeley would feel about that. But between working for your mum, organising the light trail and helping out at the cottage, it sometimes feels as though I do live here.'

'But next year things will be different,' he observed. 'Your son will be back home, won't he? How would he like living in Freezy Tye?'

Jack's return wasn't something Grace allowed herself to think about much, mostly because it still felt impossibly distant. She had no idea what he'd make of the quaint, pastel-coloured houses of Freezy Tye, or the close-knit community that meant everyone knew her business almost before she did. 'He might not want to come back at all,' she said, voicing the fear that made her heart ache the most. 'My mother keeps telling me I have to think about myself now – do what's right for me.'

'She sounds like a wise woman,' Raff said. 'I've said pretty much the same thing to my mother. The stress over the rent hike has really taken its toll. Unfortunately, I think it means Santa's Secret will be closing after Christmas.'

It wasn't anything Grace hadn't been expecting but the news still came like a punch to her stomach. 'Oh,' she said, and swallowed the sudden lump in her throat. 'That's very sad, especially since she's worked so hard and made such a success of it.'

He sighed. 'I know. But I can't see anyone else taking it on, not when Jesse is hell-bent on making the business unprofitable.'

'Can't you find another premises?' she asked. 'There must be other barns.'

'Perhaps,' Raff said. 'But our chances of finding one that's in good enough condition, with decent parking and enough storage for the stock and the display goods, are pretty slim. It'd be a tall order, and I suspect her heart wouldn't really be in it.'

Grace fell silent, grappling with her own disappointment. Her job at Santa's Secret had only ever been temporary and was due to finish on Christmas Eve, but she now realised there had been a small part of her that hoped she might find a way to keep working there, perhaps by branching out into other types of celebrations, like baby showers and birthdays, to build a year-round business. She'd been waiting for the right time to raise it with Ivy, but now it seemed Jesse's intervention had torpedoed any possibility for it to go ahead. 'I understand. Relocating would be a huge task.' She puffed out a long breath. 'It's such a shame this has happened. I've loved working there.'

She stopped talking, afraid the ache in her chest would leak to her throat. For a long moment, neither of them said anything and the only sound was Bilbo's cheerful snuffles as he moved from one interesting smell to another. At length, Raff glanced across the green, lit by pools of light from the streetlamps. 'This time next month, we won't be able to move for visitors to the village.'

Grace followed his gaze. 'And in two months' time, it will all be over.'

That was something else she couldn't allow herself to think about. What was she going to do when she didn't have Santa's Secret and Juniper Cottage and Freezy Tye to fill her time?

'You'll be able to stop checking the weather forecast, at least,' Raff said.

Grace forced herself to smile. 'Yes, I won't miss that.'

Just everything else, she added in her head, keeping her eyes fixed on Bilbo's wagging tail. And maybe even Raff.

They reached the gate of Keeley's driveway. 'Here you are,' Raff said, looking at the front door, where Grace's rescued wreath hung, illuminated by the glow of the small lamp. 'It looks like she's home.'

Grace nodded. 'Thanks for walking me back.'

'It was no trouble. My car's just over there.' He gazed down at her, and for the briefest second, she thought he would say something else. But Bilbo chose that moment to let out a volley of barks and race off along the street. Raff swore as he stared after him. 'Bloody dog – he must have seen a cat. I'd better go.'

'Yes, go,' she urged him, because Bilbo was already out of sight. 'I hope you catch him!'

Raff was already moving. 'He won't get far,' he called over his shoulder as he jogged away. 'But don't wait. Go in – I'll drop you a message to let you know when I've found him.'

'Okay,' she called to his retreating back. 'Good luck!'

She watched him vanish into the darkness, then turned to

crunch up the drive. Inside, she found Keeley asleep on the sofa, surrounded by paperwork, the BBC adaptation of *Pride and Prejudice* running unwatched on the television. She looked so peaceful that Grace was almost tempted to let her sleep but she knew Keeley would get more rest if she went to bed. 'Hey,' she said, touching her gently on the shoulder. 'You're about to miss Colin Firth coming out of the lake.'

Instantly, Keeley's eyes snapped open. 'What? Where?' Her gaze flew to the screen, where Elizabeth Bennet was blushing beautifully at the sight of a dripping Mr Darcy. She smiled sleepily. 'What good timing – that's not the worst view to wake up to.'

'No,' Grace agreed, because this had always been one of her favourite moments too, even though it didn't actually feature in the novel. 'And it never gets old.'

Keeley sighed and stretched, blinking up at her. 'How was the meeting? Anything I need to know?'

'Not really,' Grace said, deciding to keep Raff's involvement in the group to herself for now. 'Everything seems to be coming together well. How was your day? No altercations in the car park today?'

'Not as far as I know,' Keeley replied, wincing as she massaged her shoulders. 'It was still mad. But the good news is that the Christmas tours have officially sold out.'

'Wow,' Grace said. 'Already?'

Her friend raised her eyebrows. 'Already. Apparently, discovering an unpublished Victorian manuscript in a hidden drawer is good for business. Who knew?'

Grace laughed. 'Er – everyone? But I bet they would have sold out anyway. The time and effort you and Xander put into making the experience sound irresistible did most of the heavy lifting.'

'Hmm,' Keeley said, glancing down at the piles of paperwork spilling onto the floor. 'Let's hope it was all worth it.'

There was an edge to her voice that Grace didn't need an explanation for. The relationship between Keeley and Xander had remained strained following the discovery of Eliza's manuscript and no amount of denial on his part could convince Keeley that he hadn't been the one to reveal its existence to the trustees. The fact that everything had worked out better than she could have dreamed had done nothing to resolve the tension between them and they now communicated almost exclusively via email. It was, Grace couldn't help thinking, a bit of a shame. She was still convinced they would make a great couple. 'It's going to be brilliant,' she said. 'It might even become a Christmas tradition.'

Keeley held up a hand. 'I think we'd better see how this year goes before we start thinking about that. Who knows where we'll be in twelve months' time?'

It was a fair point, Grace supposed. She was doing her best not to think much beyond this Christmas, let alone next year. 'I suppose so.' She eyed the mess of papers sympathetically. 'Need some help to clear this up?'

'No, don't worry,' Keeley said, smothering a yawn. 'Believe it or not, there is method to my madness. It's all exactly where it needs to be.'

At that moment, Grace's phone buzzed. She pulled it from her pocket to see a message from an unknown number.

I was wrong about Bilbo not going far. I finally caught him in a garden three streets away, growling at a supremely unconcerned tabby up a tree. Raff

Smiling, she typed out an immediate reply.

What do you expect when you called him Bilbo? Of course he's going to have adventures.

When she looked up, she saw Keeley was watching her. 'Who's made you all gooey-eyed?' she demanded.

Grace blushed. 'No one. Just a joke in the committee group.'

'Really?' Keeley said, sounding utterly unconvinced. 'Then why are your cheeks pink?'

'They are not,' Grace said, even as she realised there was no point in denying it. Her phone vibrated again.

Good point. It was nice to chat again this evening. Hope to see you again soon. R.

Keeley's gaze had narrowed. 'Please don't tell me you've developed a crush on Gavin. Because he might make a mean cocktail but he's not the man for you.'

'Of course I haven't!' Grace replied indignantly. 'He's far too young.'

'Well, someone just made you light up like Oxford Street,' Keeley said, continuing to eye her closely. 'And I don't believe it was a joke in the group chat.'

Determined not to give anything further away, Grace thrust her phone into her pocket. 'I'm going to head up to bed. Goodnight.'

Keeley's amused drawl followed her as she left the room and made for the stairs. 'Sweet dreams. Whoever he is.'

It wasn't until Grace was safely in her room, with the door firmly closed, that she dared to open Raff's messages again. It had been a surprise to see him in the pub, and lovely to walk along the moonlit path with him, even if the subject of their conversation had been downbeat. But she would be a fool to read anything other than good manners into his offer to walk her home, just as she was certain he didn't mean it when he said he hoped to see her soon. In two months' time, their paths would diverge and it was unlikely they would cross again. She needed to remember that when her imagination got the better of her and she started to wonder what might have happened if Bilbo had not run away. Because that kind of thinking could only lead to disappointment.

The weeks that followed flew by faster than Grace would have believed possible. Santa's Secret was open seven days a week in November, and she found herself working so many additional shifts that it was now the equivalent of a full-time job. In between her hours there, she was also doing her best to help at Juniper Cottage, where higher visitor footfall continued to stretch Keeley's team. As the final week of November approached, and the night of the Freezy Tye lights switch-on drew near, Grace was almost overwhelmed by the volume of messages in the group chat and emails in need of a response. The only upside was that she had less time to fret over the weather forecast.

The installation of the light trail mercifully went without a hitch. Raff's tree farmer was as good as his word and delivered an impressive, twelve-foot beauty to the village green just after lunchtime on the 27th. He and Raff had ensured it was securely tethered in place, and then Raff had worked with Paul to drape the cone-shaped net of lights over the top. Grace couldn't help a gasp of delight when Paul pressed the on switch and the tree twinkled with a thousand pastel-coloured lights that chased each other through the branches. Pink danced with silver, green followed blue, and gold flirted with white.

'All it needs now is the fairy on the top,' Raff said, standing beside Grace to admire the effect. 'Want me to hold the ladder for you?'

Her gaze flew to his face and she wondered whether he was remembering the last time she climbed a ladder. 'Um, yes please. If you don't mind.'

He smiled, and something in his eyes warmed her insides. 'I don't mind at all.'

She didn't dare look down as she attached the exquisite Sugar Plum Fairy to the spike at the very top of the tree. Instead, she focused on making sure the figurine was secure, tightening the cable ties she'd brought in her pocket and adding a few more for good measure. The last thing they needed was for the fairy to fly off in the first puff of wind.

'Careful,' Raff said, and held out a gloved hand to steady her as she made her way down the ladder. 'Take it slowly.'

'Thanks,' she said, accepting the support gratefully and feeling more than a little reluctant to let go once her feet were both firmly back on the ground.

'What's next?' he asked, as Paul switched the lights off on the tree. 'The toy box?'

She nodded, squinting across to the west side of the green. 'I think it should be almost set up by now.'

Sanjay was just finishing the installation as Grace and Raff arrived. 'All set,' Sanjay said cheerfully, hammering the last peg into the hard ground to hold the metal frame of the box in place. 'Freddie's gone to connect the power.'

A few minutes later, Freddie reappeared, looking satisfied. 'I've plugged everything in and tested the connection to make sure it's safe. Want us to switch it on?'

'Yes, please,' Grace said, allowing herself a squiggle of anticipation. She'd seen pictures of the various stops on the light trail but she doubted any of them had done it justice.

Freddie lifted his phone and spoke into it. 'Ready when you are, Paul.'

There was a very faint hum, then the toy box erupted into light. Grace clapped her hands in delight as she took in the alphabet cubes piled on top of each other, the train set and the tin soldier picked out in red and black.

'It's even better if you stand back,' Raff said, and Grace followed his suggestion.

Sanjay waved a hand at a large, plastic-encased button mounted on a pole to one side of the display. 'Don't forget to make a sign telling them to press this,' he said. 'The lights go off after two minutes, to save on power, but pressing the button will switch them on again.'

Grace pulled the notebook from the pocket of her coat and scribbled a reminder. 'I'll make sure that gets done,' she said. 'Do the other stops work the same way?'

He nodded. 'All except the Christmas tree, which is on all the time. Oh, and the Sugar Plum Fairy scene, which has two circuits that light up different sections. You'll want to make that clear with your signs.'

'Noted,' Grace said, scrawling another note. 'Are the others ready?'

Sanjay laughed. 'Give us a chance! We've only just finished this one.'

It was all Grace could do not to hover over them as they worked. Eventually, Raff suggested they go to Eliza's Pantry for a hot chocolate. 'Am I that bad?' Grace laughed.

'Like a child on Christmas Eve,' he replied, grinning. 'Come on, I'm buying.'

They managed to squeeze into a table in one corner, among a throng of visitors who had clearly come from Juniper Cottage. 'Looks like another busy day for Keeley,' Raff said. 'I need to get in to tidy the garden before winter really sets in but she says it won't be possible until they close at the end of this week.'

Grace dipped her head. 'I'm not surprised. The queue to get in still leads halfway around the garden most of the day. You wouldn't be able to reach the flowerbeds.'

'I'm delivering the tree for the hallway on Sunday, and a second one for the drawing room,' he said, sipping his cream-topped hot chocolate with evident relish. 'I'll be able to see how much work the gardens need then.'

'And you'll have more time to get things done next week,' she reminded him. 'They're only open in the evenings for the whole of December.'

He tipped his head in agreement. 'Keeley has also asked for a mountain of greenery to turn into wreaths and garlands for the inside of the house. Are you helping her with that?'

'I am,' Grace said. 'That's my Sunday taken care of, and possibly my evenings next week. The first tour is on Wednesday and I know Keeley wants everything to be perfect.'

'I can imagine,' Raff said wryly. 'With the amount of attention Eliza has earned recently, I expect she's feeling the pressure.'

'She is,' Grace replied. 'Between interviews and requests for articles and invitations to literary festivals, she's swamped. I don't think she remembers to eat lunch most days.'

Raff frowned. 'Doesn't she have a PR assistant to handle all that for her?'

Grace hesitated, wondering how much to reveal. 'She does, sort of. But he's only part-time and, well, they had a bit of a falling out over the manuscript, back when it was first found. I don't think they've seen eye to eye since.'

He eyed her curiously. 'Is this Xander Jones? I wondered why I hadn't seen him around as much. One of the volunteers was quite taken with him – she seemed to think Keeley had told him to stay away.'

'Don't tell me – her name is Elspeth,' Grace said ruefully. 'But yes, Xander is handling the press side of things, as well as the cottage's social media accounts. And I can't fault him on that score. I can't stop scrolling through the Juniper Cottage feed – he's a real master of his craft and I noticed he's started tagging the Britain's Most Christmassy Village feed in some of his posts.'

Raff nodded. 'I follow the Juniper Cottage account. I have a professional interest in making sure he shows the gardens in a good light, remember?'

'Of course,' she said, and flashed him a teasing smile. 'Sometimes I forget you have a job that doesn't involve Christmas lights.'

When at last Sanjay called to say the installation was complete, Grace and Raff eased past the crowded cafe tables and made their way back to the green. Small groups of onlookers had gathered here and there, and Grace smiled as she passed them. 'Come back tomorrow night for the big switch-on,' she called, waving a hand at the shuttered food stalls huddled in the centre of the green. 'As well as our incredible Nutcracker light trail, we'll have food and drink – mulled wine and mistletoe!'

'You're quite the saleswoman,' Raff observed, as several people called out that they'd be there.

'It's easy to sell,' she replied, with a modest shrug. 'Freezy Tye is Britain's Most Christmassy Village, after all. The judges can't have been wrong seven times in a row!'

He flashed an admiring look her way. 'I've got a feeling this year will be the best yet.'

She was saved from having to work out how to respond to the implied compliment by Sanjay, who had come to meet them. 'Ready, boss?' he said, grinning.

Grace glanced at Raff, who was shaking his head in amusement. 'He's talking to you.'

'Oh,' she exclaimed. 'But I'm not—'

'You definitely are,' Raff assured her. 'I'm just your assistant.'

Feeling herself start to blush, Grace turned to Sanjay. 'I can't wait to see it. Let's go.'

To Grace's eyes, each of the stops on the light trail was more magical than the last, but she decided the Land of Sweets was her favourite. The fire pit was unlit but she could imagine it surrounded by children and adults alike, basking in its glow as they toasted their marshmallows. Or at least she thought it was her favourite until she reached the glade of the Sugar Plum Fairy. Tucked away on a rectangle of grass that was shielded from the green, a touch of the button sent it bursting into brilliance, a riot of pinks and blues and lilacs and silver, dazzling her eyes as the figures twirled and spun around. The second button lit up a glorious throne beneath a silvery moon. 'Oh,' Grace breathed, turning to Raff with shining eyes. 'Isn't it beautiful?'

He nodded, but didn't look away. 'My thoughts exactly.'

Back on the green, they made their way through the glowing arch of spindly branches to the Christmas tree, now unlit and shadowy as dusk approached.

'So what do you think?' Raff said as they came to a halt in front of the tree. 'Happy?'

'Yes,' she replied, resisting the urge to go back to the start and do it all over again. 'I'm very happy. But what do you think?'

He shook his head. 'I think it's going to take some beating.'

'I hope you're right,' Grace said fervently. 'So what happens now?'

'Sanjay and Freddie go back to Santa's Secret,' he said. 'Paul and the other electricians turn everything on – all the lights and the stalls – and make sure it's all safe and working as it should. And then we all meet back here tomorrow evening at six o'clock for the big switch-on.'

Grace gnawed at her lip. 'Should I stay to help Paul? What if there's a problem?'

Raff smiled. 'Seriously, Grace, you've done enough. Leave this bit to the experts. It really isn't the first time they've done this.'

She exhaled slowly. 'You're right. I think I've turned into a control freak.'

'Not at all,' he soothed. 'You just want everything to be perfect. A bit like Keeley.'

Grace couldn't argue with that. 'It's one of the traits we've always had in common.'

'But now it's time to go home,' Raff went on. 'Have a glass of wine, a nice bath, eat some chocolate or whatever you like. You've earned a night off. Enjoy it.'

A wave of weariness washed over her. 'Okay,' she said, relinquishing the last vestige of worry that she hadn't done enough. 'I suppose I can do that. Thank you.'

It wasn't until she was back in the sanctuary of Keeley's cottage, with a steaming cup of tea and a mince pie smothered in Bailey's whipped cream, that Grace realised just how much time she had spent in Raff's company that day. He'd been helpful, supportive and funny, making her laugh and keeping her sane. Now that the work of the committee was almost done, she couldn't help wondering how often she would see him. There was always a chance that she might bump into him at work, of course, and she had his number if she needed to speak to him, but the opportunity to spend more than a few minutes chatting was unlikely to present itself, unless she sought him out. Could she, she wondered as she sipped her tea. Should she? Keeley would undoubtedly tell her she should but Grace wasn't convinced. As much as she enjoyed Raff's company, she couldn't shake the feeling that he was simply being polite. Perhaps it was better that after tomorrow they wouldn't see each other as much. It would make it much easier for Grace to prepare for the day when she left Freezy Tye for good.

CHAPTER FIFTEEN

> We must have candlelight and music and gaiety,
> for Christmas is naught without them.
>
> *The Merriest Month*, ELIZA NORTON

Keeley had always been glad Freezy Tye did not have any famous residents. There were other picture-perfect villages nearby that were home to reality TV stars, ageing rockers and celebrity chefs; occasionally, one of them became embroiled in a newsworthy story that brought journalists and photographers haring down from London to cause havoc in the village before the news cycle moved on to the next story and they vanished as quickly as they had arrived. But Gavin's cousin was married to the brother of moderately famous nineties boy band member, Deke Decker, who could be relied upon to bestow his presence on Freezy Tye at the end of every November to turn on the Christmas lights. It cost Gavin a small fortune in drink because Deke brought an entourage, all of whom expected a free bar at the pub, but it did ensure the village got some column inches in the local press, and drew in a crowd from other villages who could not produce a celebrity of their own. This year was no exception; Keeley guessed there must be upwards of five hundred people gathered on the green to watch him kick off the Freezy Tye festive season. She couldn't help wondering whether any judges from Britain's Most Christmassy Village were among them. The dates of their visits were kept secret, although Keeley knew they came to each competing village more than once before the winner was announced in mid-December, and as far as she knew, they never revealed their identity while they were there. Gavin insisted he could spot them a mile off when they visited the pub, and made sure the drinks they ordered were generously poured, but Keeley wasn't sure his powers of observation were that potent. Then again, Freezy Tye had won the competition so many times that perhaps he was onto something after all.

As far as Keeley could tell, looking at Deke now, he had not changed his look or his hairstyle in thirty years. He stood on the makeshift stage beside the unlit Christmas tree, wearing baggy, low-slung jeans and a black puffer jacket over a pristine white T-shirt. He grinned from beneath curtains of sandy blond hair and raised the microphone to his lips in the manner of a legend addressing Glastonbury. 'Hello, Freezy Tye! How you all doing?'

An enthusiastic cheer rose up from the assembled crowd, Grace among them, which caused Keeley to grin. 'I can't believe you've never been here for this,' she said, glancing sideways at her friend. 'Weren't you a massive Deke fan, back in the day?'

Grace shook her head staunchly. 'No, I loved Rory. The only one who had any real musical talent.'

Keeley wasn't convinced any member of Boy Next Door

had been blessed with much musical ability, as evidenced by a conspicuous lack of solo success when the band broke up, but it was a topic she and Grace had disagreed on many times over the years and she wasn't about to open up old wounds now. 'Well, as you can see, he hasn't changed much.'

Grace frowned. 'Did he have those teeth in the nineties? They look bright enough to steer ships away from rocks.'

Keeley laughed. 'You can't blame him for that. He does live in Essex.'

'We live in Essex,' Grace pointed out, unpleasantly reminded of Jesse's too-white grin.

'Yes, but we're not famous,' Keeley replied. 'Anyway, I don't mind people making the best of themselves. As long as they're happy.'

Grace gave her a long look. 'Spoken by a woman so gorgeous that she hardly even needs to wear make-up.'

'Oh shush,' Keeley said, nudging her. She decided to change the subject. 'How's the mulled wine?'

'Very good,' Grace said, taking a long sip from her gently steaming cardboard cup. 'How's the cider?'

'Also good,' Keeley replied. 'I might even be starting to feel festive.'

Grace rolled her eyes. 'I should hope so,' she said in mock severity. 'Do you have any idea how much work I've put into making this the most Christmassy Freezy Tye Christmas ever seen?'

Keeley squeezed her arm. 'Yes, I do,' she said. 'And I really appreciate it. As does the rest of the village.' She glanced over her head and smiled. 'Speaking of the Grace Murphy Appreciation Society, here's Raff.'

'Where?' Grace said, jerking around so sharply that she almost spilled her drink.

'Relax,' Keeley said, watching her in amusement. 'He's heading this way.'

As Raff wove his way towards them, Deke began leading the crowd in a slightly off-key rendition of 'Merry Christmas Everybody'. Out of the corner of her eye, Keeley watched Grace doing her best to look completely indifferent and hid a smile. She'd known from the moment her friend saw Raff Caldwell that she'd very much liked the look of him and it seemed that getting to know him had not dimmed his appeal. Quite the opposite, in fact.

'Hello,' Raff said, arriving in front of them just as Deke warbled his way to the chorus. 'It's not snowing.'

He smiled at Grace, who beamed back. 'Yes. Well done you.'

Keeley glanced back and forth between them, trying to decipher what was clearly a private joke. 'I was just telling Grace what a brilliant job you've all done this year.' She waved a hand towards the kissing booth, which already had a long queue. 'That is especially inspired.'

'I've got a friend who harvests mistletoe,' he said, shrugging. 'It seemed a shame to waste it.'

Keeley glanced over at the booth, where a pair of teenagers were enthusiastically kissing beneath a thick cluster of green leaves and white berries. 'It's definitely not being wasted. Will we see you under there later?'

Pink blossomed across his cheekbones. 'I, uh, probably not.' He gathered himself together and shot her a look. 'I'll be sure to bring some to Juniper Cottage on Sunday, though. In case you can find a use for it.'

'Unlikely,' she said flatly, then frowned. 'Wait a minute. Is that Jesse Bairstow over there?'

Both Grace and Raff turned to follow her gaze. 'Yes,' Grace said, sounding furious. 'What's he doing here?'

'Checking out the competition, I expect,' Keeley replied. 'I suppose there's no law against that.'

Grace scowled. 'There should be. Men like him shouldn't be allowed to enjoy Christmas.'

The vehemence in her voice caused Keeley to blink. 'Bit harsh, Grace. I know he's a snake but—'

'He's worse than a snake,' Grace snapped. 'He's a maggot.'

Raff laid a hand on her arm. 'Forget about him for tonight. Don't let him spoil things.'

Glancing from one to the other, Keeley narrowed her eyes. 'What am I missing here? What's he done to you, Grace?'

But her friend shook her head. 'Nothing. It doesn't matter. I just wish he'd stayed away, that's all.'

Keeley's frown deepened. 'That's not good enough. Clearly, he's done something. Tell me what it is.'

Grace and Raff exchanged a long look. 'Not here,' Grace said, after a moment. 'I'll tell you later.'

At that moment, Deke reached the end of the song. 'Yeah, baby!' he roared to the crowd. 'Do we know how to rock or what? Who's ready to start the countdown? Let me hear you say YEAH!'

The audience cheered. Keeley saw Paul climb onto the stage holding a large button shaped like a Christmas present. He handed it to Deke, who swapped it for the microphone and gestured for Paul to angle it towards his mouth. 'Christmas is about to begin!' Deke bellowed. 'In ten . . . nine . . . eight . . .'

Voices swelled in the night air as everyone joined in the countdown. When they reached zero, Deke plunged the button down and the Christmas tree exploded into light. Cheers mingled with gasps of delight as the twinkling lights glittered against the darkness. Keeley glanced at Grace and saw a mixture of pride and joy upon her friend's face. 'It looks amazing,' she told her, beaming. 'Well done!'

She'd barely finished speaking when disaster struck. The tree went dark, and so did the fairy lights strung in the trees. The lights above the food and drink stalls winked out. Groans of disappointment replaced the cheers, punctuated by the sudden thin wail of a crying child.

'Don't panic, everyone,' Deke's voice was cheerful in the sudden blackness. 'I'm told it's just a temporary blackout. Let's get our phones out and have a magical moment while it lasts.'

Keeley wouldn't have been surprised to hear him to break into 'We'll Meet Again' or another wartime classic but instead he began singing 'Step into Christmas'. Around them, phone lights began to dispel some of the gloom and she saw both Grace and Raff had their own torches on. 'It's probably the fuse board in the hall,' Raff said, his face washed out by the half-light surrounding them.

Keeley sighed. 'I thought Paul said he'd made sure it wouldn't trip this year.'

'He did,' Raff replied, frowning. 'And it was fine last night. I'd better go over there and see if there's anything I can do to help.'

'I'm coming too,' Grace said, and Keeley thought she sounded upset.

'I'm not staying here on my own,' she said.

Raff nodded. 'This way.'

They picked their way through the crowd, dodging between groups who had linked arms and begun swaying. 'You'd think they were in the middle of the Blitz,' Keeley muttered to Grace.

'I suppose it's better than them all going home.'

Which was a fair point, Keeley had to admit. She could only hope any competition judges in the crowd were similarly forgiving.

The hall was in darkness when they reached it. Beams of light flickered inside, suggesting efforts were being made to find the source of the problem. Raff pushed at the door, raising his phone to illuminate the room immediately in front of them. Gavin's face swam into view. 'Easy, mate. I'm half blind as it is.'

'Sorry,' Raff said, lowering his light. 'Any idea what the trouble is?'

'Paul says it's the fuse box,' Gavin replied. 'He's down in the basement, having a look now.'

No sooner had he finished talking than the overhead lights came on, causing everyone to wince and shade their eyes. Outside, a resounding cheer went up. 'I think he might have fixed it,' Keeley said, blinking in the brightness.

A door at the far end of the hall rattled and Paul appeared. He made his way over to the group. 'Was it the fuses?' Gavin asked.

Paul nodded, although Keeley thought he looked far from happy. 'Yeah, the whole thing had tripped. Don't ask me to explain how it happened, though.'

Gavin rubbed his stubbly chin. 'Too much demand?'

'What I mean is, it shouldn't have happened,' Paul said, his tone grim. 'During the dry run yesterday, I systematically tested the electrical load, to make sure the circuit that powers the lights and the stalls wouldn't be overwhelmed. Everything was fine.'

'But that was yesterday,' Keeley pointed out. 'Maybe one of the stallholders plugged something else in. I don't know – a kettle or something.'

'The circuit should have been able to handle it,' Paul insisted. 'And even if there was a problem – if the item was old or faulty – I would expect it to only trip one switch in the fuse box. Not the whole lot.'

Keeley puffed out her cheeks. 'But it's not impossible.'

'No,' he replied. 'What it means is that we've got a headache because I can't tell you what happened. I've checked the load now and everything is fine but who's to say it won't trip again in ten minutes, or an hour, or a day?'

Gavin turned towards the door leading out to the green, where Michael Bublé could be heard crooning. 'Sounds okay at the moment.'

The electrician listened gloomily. 'Yeah. For now.'

'Let's think positively,' Keeley suggested. 'Maybe it was a blip – a one-off problem that won't happen again. Is anyone in danger of being electrocuted?'

The look Paul gave her was affronted. 'No! If I thought there was any danger of that, I'd close it all down. Like you say, it's probably a one-off. Maybe a surge or something . . .' He trailed off, looking thoughtfully at the door that led to the basement. 'There was one other strange thing. When I went down to see what was wrong, the cupboard where the fuse box is kept was open.'

'Open?' Raff echoed. 'Isn't it usually locked?'

Paul nodded. 'Yeah. I locked it myself when I finished up last night, and hung the key on a hook at the bottom on the stairs.' He paused to gaze solemnly round at them. 'It's not there now.'

Grace frowned. 'Are you suggesting someone's taken it?'

'I don't know what I'm suggesting,' Paul admitted, rubbing his chin. 'All I can tell you is that the cupboard was locked yesterday evening, and the key was hanging on the hook. Even if there was a problem today which meant someone needed to get to the fuse box, there's no good reason for the cupboard being left open.'

Raff turned to Gavin. 'Has there been a problem today?'

'Not that I've heard,' Gavin said grimly. 'No one's even been in the hall, as far as I know.'

'So who opened the fuse box, then?' Raff asked. 'And what were they doing?'

'Someone in a hurry, if they left the cupboard open and forgot to return the key,' Keeley ventured, when no one else spoke. She glanced at Paul. 'Could someone else have tried to fix tonight's power outage before you?'

'Not unless they left by the back door,' he said doubtfully. 'I came here as soon as the lights went out, ran into Gav out the front and we went inside together. There was no one here then.'

The landlord eyed the other door at the far end of the hall, the one Keeley remembered led to a small kitchen. 'I suppose it won't hurt to check.'

He strode across the room and vanished through the door. A moment later, he was back, a thunderstruck expression on his face. 'Come and see,' he called, beckoning them towards him. 'The bloody back door is wide open.'

They crowded into the kitchen to see the heavy wooden door was indeed standing open. A window over the sink was also slightly ajar, creaking in the breeze. The room was almost as cold as the air outside. 'This is getting weirder by the second,' Paul said, his forehead wrinkling. 'What the hell is going on?'

Keeley pressed her lips into a thin line. 'I've got a horrible feeling this is all connected.'

Paul crossed to the window and pulled it closed. 'This latch is broken,' he said, inspecting the old wooden frame. 'I'm not sure it will stay shut.'

Keeley had been watching Grace's expression and saw when it hardened in suspicion. 'What is it?' she asked, eyes narrowing. 'You know something, don't you?'

But Grace only gave an unhappy shake of her head. 'I don't know anything. It's just an idea.'

Gavin's expression was set. 'Out with it.'

She glanced at Raff, who seemed to catch on to what she was thinking. 'It could be. You'd better tell them.'

Grace took a breath. 'You've been doing a Christmas lights switch-on in Freezy Tye for years, right? And nothing like this has ever happened.'

Paul stopped fiddling with the window latch. 'Never,' he said, then paused. 'I mean, we did have a few electrical issues last year but that was before I replaced the wiring and the fuse box.'

'We didn't have any problems during the summer fete,' Gavin put in. 'We had a few rides and they used plenty of power.'

'Okay. So what's new this Christmas?' Grace said, looking from face to face. 'Or rather, *who's* new? Apart from me, obviously.' When no one answered, she sighed. 'Look, I don't have any evidence for this. But what if Keeley's right and it's not a coincidence that the power went out just as the lights were switched on? What if someone snuck into the hall and made it happen? Someone with a vested interest in seeing Freezy Tye's big switch-on fail.'

Keeley understood what she was getting at, although she couldn't imagine what had made the normally level-headed Grace leap to such a conclusion. 'Jesse?' she said incredulously. 'You're talking about Jesse Bairstow?'

Her friend nodded. 'He wants Flaxwood to win. Doesn't it follow that he'd take steps to make sure our lights are a disaster?'

Gavin eyed her askance. 'But this is a bit more than bad-mouthing us to anyone who'll listen, Grace. Plunging so many people into darkness could have been dangerous.'

'I know,' she said. Her gaze flicked to Raff again, who nodded. 'I think it's time I explained what kind of man Jesse is. And then you can tell me what you think he's capable of.'

They listened as she revealed his threatened rent increase to Ivy, and the barely concealed hints that he intended to evict her. When she reached the part about legal action, Gavin swore. 'That arsehole. What a way to act towards anyone, let alone someone as lovely as Ivy.'

'He's always been underhanded and sly,' Raff said. 'But what really surprises me is that his father is going along with the plans. Jim and my mother go way back – he's been a more than generous landlord. I can't believe he's letting Jesse do this.'

Grace looked thoughtful. 'Is there a chance he doesn't know? I got chatting with one of the women who works in the cafe a while ago. She told me Jesse forced through some really unpopular changes while old Mr Bairstow was ill. Maybe there are some things Jesse hasn't got round to mentioning to his dad yet.'

Gavin shrugged. 'That's easily checked. Jim Bairstow is here tonight.'

'Is he?' Keeley asked, frowning. 'I didn't see him with Jesse on the green.'

'He called into the pub about an hour ago,' Gavin said. 'I served him myself.'

Paul held up a hand. 'Hold on. We can't just accuse Jesse of sabotaging the fuse box. There's no evidence it was even sabotaged. The switch could have tripped on its own.'

'And I suppose the cupboard unlocked itself at the same time,' Grace said, with raised eyebrows. 'And the key grew legs and walked away through the unbolted back door.'

'All right, Miss Marple,' he said, shaking his head. 'When you put it like that, I agree it sounds bad.'

'We'll tell him he was caught on the CCTV,' Keeley suggested. 'There's a camera over the front door.'

The electrician sighed. 'Unfortunately, the hall doesn't have CCTV. The camera is a dummy one I put up a few years ago as a deterrent. It doesn't actually record.'

Keeley smiled. 'Does Jesse know that?'

Back on the green, they split up to look for Jesse. Grace and Raff agreed to walk the light trail route, Paul preferred to keep an eye on the hall to ensure no further interference occurred, and Gavin returned to the pub. 'Keep an eye on your phones,' he instructed. 'And if you find him, send a group message.'

Keeley was relieved to see the Christmas tree was still twinkling as she retraced her steps to the place she'd spotted Jesse. The crowd had thinned out, although there were still plenty of people admiring the lights. Some had made a beeline for the food and drink stalls, which appeared to be doing a roaring trade now that their power had been restored. Deke was no longer holding court from the stage. Keeley presumed he'd retreated to the pub in order to make the most of the free bar, but festive tunes were blasting out from the speaker system. She was unsurprised to see the queue at the kissing booth was longer than ever; next year they should have a stall selling bunches of mistletoe, she thought. Everywhere she looked, she saw people enjoying themselves and the sight warmed her heart. What she did not see was Jesse Bairstow.

He's not on the green, she tapped into her phone, after a fruitless twenty minutes of searching.

A reply from Paul flashed up on her screen. *All OK at the hall.*

Not on the light trail either, Grace responded. *Could he have left?*

Gavin's message arrived a few minutes later. *AVENGERS ASSEMBLE! He's in the bar with Deke. And so is his dad.*

'Let's get this over with,' Keeley muttered under her breath. She was not a fan of confrontation but her outrage at the way Jesse had treated poor Ivy was still making her quiver with anger, and that was before she threw in the likelihood that he'd tried to ruin the switching-on ceremony. Even so, she couldn't help feeling as though she'd stumbled into the middle of a cosy crime plot. She really hoped no one was going to turn up dead in the duck pond.

The pub was standing room only, as she'd known it would be. Craning her head from the doorway, she managed to catch Gavin's eye as he served behind the bar.

'Upstairs,' he mouthed, jerking his head towards the stairs, up which there was a small room reserved for private functions.

Nodding, she edged through the throng. Gavin met her

at the foot of the stairs. 'I got Deke to invite Jesse and Jim to join his party up there. Do you want to wait for the others to arrive?'

At that moment, the door of the pub opened again. Raff and Grace squeezed inside, with Paul close behind them. 'No need,' Keeley said, waving to get their attention. 'Can you slip away for five minutes?'

Gavin eyed the busy pub and huffed. 'Not really. But needs must.'

Slipping behind the bar, he murmured something to Elsie, the barmaid. He returned just as the others reached Keeley. 'Jesse and his dad are upstairs,' he told the newcomers tersely. 'Shall we go and do this?'

Paul's expression was mixed but Grace and Raff both nodded. 'Right, follow me,' Gavin said.

Deke was sprawled across two chairs when they entered, apparently deep in conversation with Jesse while his entourage worked their way through the bottles of wine dotted across the tables. Jim Bairstow was standing by the window with his walking stick in hand, gazing out at the village green as though deep in thought. They all looked up as the door opened. 'And here's Gav,' Deke said, beaming. 'Have you brought the whisky I asked for?'

'No,' Gavin replied, stepping into the room to allow those behind him inside. 'We've come to have a word with Jesse and his dad. Would you mind giving us a few minutes, Deke?'

The singer gave an incredulous laugh. 'You what? Where am I supposed to go?'

'Downstairs?' Gavin suggested. 'It won't take long.'

'Are you being serious?' Deke folded his arms. 'There's an

army of Boy Next Door fans down there, all wanting a piece of me. I'll be mobbed.'

Keeley rolled her eyes. 'You'll be fine. Half of them are too young to have any idea who you are.'

Deke sniffed. 'But what about the other half?'

Jesse's gaze narrowed as it travelled over Keeley and moved on to Raff, Grace and Paul. 'What's this about?'

'I think you know,' Raff said stonily. 'But it would be better for you if we discuss your actions in private.'

'In that case, I'm going nowhere,' Deke declared, and those around him nodded. 'I like a good ding-dong.'

'They can stay,' Jesse said, with a thin-lipped smile. 'I've got nothing to hide.'

Jim Bairstow moved away from the window, a stern look on his lined face. 'What is it, Gavin? Is something wrong?'

'You'd better sit down, Jim,' Raff said. 'What we're about to say might come as a bit of a shock.'

The older man frowned as he considered the group before him. 'I don't know who some of you are.'

Gavin glanced behind him. 'Shut the door, Raff.' Once the noise from the pub downstairs was muted, he waved a hand at Keeley. 'I'm sure you've met Dr Cotterill here – she's the curator of Juniper Cottage.'

Keeley nodded in stilted greeting, wondering whether Gavin had used her formal title to add weight to the accusations they were about to make.

'You also know Raff, whose mother runs the Santa's Secret shop next door to Ruggles,' Gavin went on. 'Beside him is Paul, our resident electrical genius, and Grace, who works at Santa's Secret.'

'Thank you,' Jim said, and settled into a nearby chair. He leaned his walking stick against the table. 'Now what is it you want to say?'

Keeley exchanged a look with Grace. Now that the time had come to accuse Jesse of sabotaging the lights switch-on, she felt a prickle of unease. What if they were wrong? But judging from the determined expression on her friend's face, she had no such doubts. She stepped forward. 'How long have you known Ivy Caldwell, Mr Bairstow?'

He eyed her in surprise. 'I couldn't tell you exactly. Between thirty and forty years, at a guess. We were friends long before she took on the lease for the barn and opened Santa's Secret.'

Grace nodded. 'Has she been a good tenant?'

'The best,' Jim said, without hesitation. 'I knew when she first described her business idea to me that it would be the perfect partner for Ruggles and her advice and assistance have been invaluable over the years. It was her idea to create the indoor Christmas displays that have proved so popular, and she also suggested we took advantage of the social media buzz around autumn and create a bespoke area for pumpkins.' He smiled at Raff. 'She's a smart businesswoman.'

'That's why you charged her a peppercorn rent,' Grace pressed. 'Because you saw the benefits her business could offer.'

Jim looked uncomfortable. 'I don't see what that has to do with anything, but yes, that was part of it.'

Jesse sat up straighter in his chair. 'But times change, Dad. Ruggles is much bigger now and has the potential to be even more profitable. We have to look to the future.'

His father frowned. 'Perhaps, but profit isn't everything.' He returned his attention to Grace. 'What's this about?'

Grace took a breath. 'Are you aware that Jesse has told Ivy he plans to increase the rent she pays for the barn by two thousand pounds a month?'

There was a moment of stunned silence before Jim's head whipped round to stare at Jesse. 'What?' he exploded. 'Is this true?'

'Relax, Dad,' Jesse said, holding up his hands in a placatory gesture. 'It's all part of the restructuring I told you about. When everything is transferred over to Ruggles Holdings, we'll be able to negotiate new terms with all our business partners and suppliers, and demand a fair rent for the use of the barn. Although, to be honest, I can see much better uses for it than a shop selling Christmas tat.'

Beside her, Keeley saw Raff's expression darken. She placed a restraining hand on his arm. 'Let Grace handle this,' she whispered.

'That didn't stop you asking Ivy to supply Flaxwood with lights for your village display, did it?' Grace asked Jesse. 'Which brings us on to more of your sneaky behaviour.'

Gavin took a step forward and fixed his gaze on Deke. 'Want to know why the lights went out and ruined your moment of glory?'

Deke looked confused. 'A power overload or something?'

'Wrong,' Gavin snapped. He stabbed a finger at Jesse. 'He broke into the village hall and flipped the switch to turn everything off.'

Every head turned towards Jesse. 'What the hell, bro?' Deke said, glaring.

Jesse laughed. 'Don't listen to them. I never touched the switch. Why would I?'

'To make Freezy Tye look bad,' Grace said. 'It's no secret you want Flaxwood to win Britain's Most Christmassy Village this year. You think it will be good for Ruggles.'

'It will,' Jesse said. 'But the lights going out was nothing to do with me and you can't prove otherwise.'

Keeley crossed her fingers. 'We can, actually. There's a CCTV camera outside the hall. It's there to keep a record of everyone going in and out.'

'And you're claiming you've got me on video breaking in, are you?' he said disbelievingly.

She steeled herself. Up until this point, she hadn't said anything that wasn't true. 'We know it was you, Jesse. Just admit it.'

'Are they right?' Jim's voice was a rumble of barely suppressed fury as he glowered at his son. 'Did you do this?'

'No!' Jesse got to his feet, his hands balled into fists. 'Show me this video. Go on, show me!'

Keeley felt a storm of hot anxiety explode in her chest. She should have known he would demand to see the evidence. 'All in good time,' she said, fighting to sound cool and unruffled. 'Once we've handed it over to the police.'

His lip curled. 'There's no video of me going in through the front door of the hall. That is a solid gold fact.'

A movement to the left of Keeley made her turn her head to see Paul take a step forward. 'Because you went in through a window at the back,' he said. 'You levered the frame apart, climbed inside and went down to the basement. I saw the dust on the work surface in the kitchen had been disturbed but I didn't realise why until now.'

'But you didn't have time to lock the fuse box again,' Gavin put in. 'Or hang the key back on the hook. You ran back up the stairs and unbolted the kitchen door.'

'What is this – *CSI: Chelmsford* or something?' Jesse's tone was derisive but Keeley thought she saw beads of sweat breaking out on his forehead. 'I was with my dad the whole evening. You can ask him.'

'Except that's not quite true,' Jim said slowly. 'You went off to get a drink when Deke here first appeared.'

'I was only gone a few minutes,' Jesse protested. 'Hardly long enough to pull off some kind of *Ocean's Eleven* shit or whatever it is these idiots are suggesting I did.'

'It was longer than that,' Jim replied, his brow creased. 'And you didn't have a drink when you came back.'

'What did you do with the key, Jesse?' Gavin asked softly. 'Is it still in your pocket now?'

'No,' Jesse snapped. 'Because I wasn't even there.'

Jim sighed. 'Then you won't mind turning them out.'

'Of course I will, you old fool.' Stuffing his hands defiantly into his jacket, he glared at his father. 'You don't seriously think I care enough about their poxy village display to risk breaking and entering, do you?'

Jim met his furious glower with solemn resignation. 'I think you'll do anything to win. Empty your pockets, son.'

Keeley wasn't sure what they would do if Jesse continued to refuse. Deke was eyeing him with self-righteous indignation and Gavin seemed like a coiled spring beside her. Then Grace smiled. 'You know what, it doesn't really matter if he admits it or not,' she said, and gestured to the window and the village green. 'The point is, he failed. The tree and the light trail look amazing and everyone Raff and I spoke to before coming up here was having a great time.'

Paul nodded. 'And if anything else mysteriously goes wrong, we'll know exactly where to send the police.'

There was a moment of charged silence, then Jesse stood up and jerked a hand from his pocket. He flung it towards Grace. Something bounced on the table top with a metallic clang, then dropped to the floor. 'There's your stupid key. Flaxwood's display is going to make you look exactly like what you are – a bunch of amateurs with no clue what Christmas is really about.'

Storming to the door, he pushed past Gavin, who didn't nothing to stop him. 'I'll tell you what Christmas isn't about,' he called down the stairs at his retreating back. 'It's not about a rubber T. rex in a Santa hat.'

A hush fell over the room. Jim got to his feet, his face ashen. 'I don't know what to say.'

'You don't need to say anything,' Raff reassured him. 'It's obvious you knew nothing about Jesse's underhand behaviour.'

'But I should have done,' the older man insisted. 'I was so grateful he came back to help during my illness that I didn't pay enough attention when he started talking about streamlining the business and improving profits.' He shook his head. 'I had no idea he'd been to see Ivy. I'm sorry, Raff. I imagine she's been beside herself with worry.'

'She has, I'm afraid,' Grace said. 'In fact, she's talking about retiring.'

Jim's faded eyes grew round with horror. 'Oh no, she mustn't do that. I know how much she loves Santa's Secret.'

'I don't think she's got much choice,' Grace replied gently. 'She can't afford the rent increase, and no one will buy the business with such enormous overheads.'

'The rent isn't going to go up,' Jim said, flapping an agitated hand. 'The barn is hers for as long as she wants it and I'll make sure Jesse knows the terms of the lease are set in stone, even if she does decide to sell.' His expression darkened. 'In fact, I'm not sure it's a good idea for him to have so much responsibility at Ruggles, if this is how he thinks a family business should be run.'

He sat down heavily and mopped at his brow. Keeley's heart went out to him. He looked as though his world had come crashing down around him.

'Would you like me to drive you home?' Raff asked sympathetically. 'It's no trouble.'

'No,' Jim said, rallying slightly. 'I'd like you to take me to see Ivy. The least I owe her is an apology and those are best delivered face to face.'

'I can do that,' Raff agreed. 'But wouldn't you rather wait until the morning? When you've had a chance to calm down.'

'I think she's been worried far too long as it is,' Jim said, reaching for his walking stick. 'It's time I put that right. And once again, I'm sorry for all the upset Jesse has caused.'

'No harm done,' Keeley said, as another wave of compassion washed through her.

With a suddenness that made them all jump, Deke clapped his hands and rubbed them together briskly. 'Well, this has been a lot more entertaining than usual.' He fired a cheeky grin Gavin's way. 'Any chance of that whisky now?'

CHAPTER SIXTEEN

For Christmas brings out the best in mankind,
and makes children of us all.

The Merriest Month, ELIZA NORTON

'Wow,' Grace said, when Elspeth answered her knock on the front door of Juniper Cottage and she took in her immaculate Victorian maid's costume. 'You look amazing.'

'Good evening, Mrs Murphy,' Elspeth said politely, bobbing into a shallow curtsey. 'Miss Norton is expecting you. Won't you come in?'

'I'd love to,' Grace replied, stepping into the candlelit hall and smiling at the shimmering Christmas tree that took pride of place at the bottom of the curved staircase. Her gaze slid to the banisters, thick with swags of lush greenery and laden with clusters of red berries. It didn't matter that she'd known exactly what to expect, having hung half of the decorations herself. The overall effect was stunning, made all the more atmospheric by the low light and shadows.

Elspeth handed her a flute of something fizzy – Prosecco, Grace guessed, since the price of a ticket for the tour probably wouldn't stretch to include champagne. 'I'm horribly early,' she said, taking a sip. 'And you don't have to stay in character with me. I'm here to help Keeley, not as a paying customer.'

'I don't know what you mean,' Elspeth said, with a commendably straight face. 'Miss Norton insists all visitors to her home are to be made welcome and treated the same.' She lowered her voice. 'Apart from that scoundrel Geronimo Glover, of course.'

Grace grinned. She was very familiar with Eliza's efforts to escape the amorous Mr Glover. 'I believe he is away from home on business at present,' she said in a confiding whisper. 'So you may relax your guard this evening.'

Elspeth's mouth twitched. 'I am very glad to hear it.'

At that moment, Keeley appeared from the doorway that led to the corridor beyond. 'You're here,' she said, enveloping Grace in a quick hug that wasn't fast enough to disguise the pinched anxiety around her eyes. 'I'm so glad to see you.'

'How are you feeling?' Grace asked as they separated. 'The house looks great, by the way. The wreath on the front door is a work of art.'

'Mostly thanks to you and Raff,' her friend replied. 'I'm really grateful you sacrificed so much time to help me get ready.'

It had taken the best part of Sunday to pull the greenery into enough wreaths and garlands to decorate the cottage to the standard Keeley felt Eliza would have insisted upon, and then most of Monday and Tuesday evening to fix everything in place. But at last it was done, and in good time for the first tour on Wednesday evening. At one point, Grace had been afraid they might still be pinning up swags an hour before the first ticket holders arrived.

'It was my pleasure,' she said, smiling. 'Although Raff says he never wants to see a roll of florist's wire again as long as he lives.'

'Ha,' Keeley said, grinning back. 'He did well, considering he's more used to growing leaves than arranging them. How's Ivy doing?'

'Better, I think,' Grace said. 'Santa's Secret has been so busy that I've hardly seen her over the past few days but Raff says she's been a lot less stressed since Jim Bairstow straightened everything out.'

'I should hope so,' Keeley said, and frowned. 'Jesse has a lot to answer for. I really hope the judges didn't choose the switch-on night to visit Freezy Tye.'

It was a thought that had crossed Grace's mind too but, since there was nothing she could do to change what had happened, and no way of knowing when the judges planned to visit, she'd decided not to dwell on it. 'Gavin says he's had a lot of positive feedback in the pub.' She hesitated, afraid she might sound as though she was singing her own praises. 'I think everyone is enjoying the light trail.'

'Of course they are,' Keeley said, batting her on the arm. 'It's incredible. You did an outstanding job. Gav keeps telling me I have to lock you in my spare bedroom until next year.'

Grace laughed. 'Raff said something similar a few weeks ago.'

Her friend eyed her impishly. 'His reasons for wanting to lock you in a bedroom don't have anything to do with the village Christmas lights.'

Instantly, Grace's cheeks were on fire. 'That's not what I meant!'

'I know,' Keeley said. 'But it's still true, even if you both refuse to admit it.'

Grace opened her mouth to object but Keeley was glancing at her watch. 'Time's getting on,' she said. 'Jenny and the others are waiting in the staffroom. Why don't we go and say hello? You can leave your coat and bag in there.'

Jenny looked even more anxious than Keeley, Grace thought as she greeted her. She supposed it was only to be expected; Keeley was used to public speaking and had delivered several talks on Eliza's life and works – her worries about how the evening might go were down to the logistics of trying something new at the cottage rather than the thought of delivering the tour. Jenny, on the other hand, had little performance experience, although Keeley had told Grace she was a natural.

'I'm not sure I should have volunteered for the first night now,' Jenny confessed, when Grace asked her how she was feeling. She nodded at Isobel and Marco. 'These guys get to shadow Keeley's tours before delivering their own tomorrow. I'm straight in at the deep end.'

Grace offered her a reassuring smile. 'You'll get to hear most of Keeley's tour before yours begins, and I'll be with you all the way round. Not that you'll need me.'

Jenny nodded. 'Yes, thank you. I do know what I need to say but I'm worried I'll get something wrong – a date or a fact. It helps knowing you'll be there if I mess up.'

'You're not going to mess up,' Grace said firmly. 'Keeley wouldn't have chosen you if she didn't think you were up to the job.'

'It's time, everyone,' Keeley called. 'Elspeth should be welcoming the five o'clock group now so let's take our places.' She glanced at Belinda and Sue. 'Be ready with the kettle to fill the tea cups as soon as we've gone. They should be steaming when we enter the library, but make sure you leave through the smoking room so no one sees you. And put the pan over the fire in the kitchen at ten past five, so it's bubbling when we arrive.'

Both women nodded. 'We know,' Belinda said, smiling and waving a sheet of paper. 'You gave us a list. Eliza's bedroom at five-thirty, with more tea and a boiled egg, then down the servants' stairs to spread the Christmas gifts under the tree in the drawing room and replace the empty stockings hanging from the mantelpiece with full ones.'

'And start all over again before the next tour begins,' Sue added.

Keeley puffed out her cheeks. 'Sorry. I just want everything to be perfect.'

'It will be,' Grace said, squeezing her arm. 'But not if we don't start on time.'

Elspeth was checking in the last ticket holders when Keeley and Grace returned to the hall. Tucking the scanner into her apron, she lifted the tray of drinks and began to distribute them.

'Welcome to Juniper Cottage,' Keeley said, her voice clear and confident as she addressed the small group. 'I'm Dr Cotterill, and it will be my pleasure to guide you around Eliza Norton's home this evening, as she prepares to celebrate Christmas with her friends and family. It may be that you have visited the cottage before, when Eliza was away from home, but tonight will be a more intimate experience. If you happen to hear a footstep overhead, or a whisper in the next room, don't be alarmed. Eliza is at home, although she is anxious not to be disturbed.'

A murmur rippled around the hall as the ticket holders began to appreciate that this would be more than a standard tour. Grace exchanged a smile with Jenny. They were in for a treat.

Keeley lifted a small lantern from a table beside the front door. 'The year is 1852, and although Eliza enjoys a comfortable living, she is not wealthy enough to light our way as though it is daylight. Please watch your step and take care not to trip. The village doctor is known to be a little hasty with the leeches at the slightest provocation – best that you don't place yourself in need of his services.'

She led the group from the hall. Isobel and Marco followed, and Grace joined the back of the group with Jenny. They paused in the narrow corridor that ran between the rooms. 'We begin in the library,' Keeley announced. 'This is where Eliza's collection of treasured books is kept but also where she spends much of her working day. I believe she has just laid down her quill for tea, but you may see evidence of her latest work at her writing desk. Take care with your drinks or the housekeeper, Mrs Mortiboy, will be most displeased.'

Pushing back the door, she ushered them through. Grace immediately looked towards the table in front of the fire and was pleased to see steam curling from the tea cups. The woman in front of her noticed too, and let out a little gasp. 'Look,' she said, tugging on the sleeve of her friend. 'It's freshly made.'

Other members of the group had gravitated towards the writing desk. An excited conversation broke out as they peered down at the paper spread beneath the quill pen.

'Excuse me, Dr Cotterill,' a spry but elderly gentleman called out, only to be shushed by those around him. 'How else am I supposed to get her attention?' he demanded crossly, as Keeley approached.

'Do you have a question?' she said, smiling.

The man pointed at the half-filled page on the desk. 'Is that a page from Eliza's unpublished manuscript? *The Merriest Month*?'

Keeley feigned confusion. 'Certainly it is unpublished, sir. As you can see, Eliza is in process of writing it. Her only published work to date is *The Mistress of Pendennis*.'

'Yes, yes,' he said impatiently. 'But is this a genuine page from *The Merriest Month*? I read about it in *The Bookseller*. Wasn't it found in this very room?'

Dutifully, Keeley peered at the page. 'Yes, I believe it is a page from that work. How remarkable. You heard about it from a bookseller, you say?'

The rest of the group crowded round, chattering excitedly as they tried to decipher the writing. Keeley stepped back and winked at Grace, who realised at once that this was exactly what she'd hoped would happen.

'She's so clever,' Jenny whispered in admiration. 'I bet all these people are Eliza superfans. They're beyond excited to be getting an exclusive peek at *The Merriest Month*.'

Grace did not confess that she'd had a much earlier exclusive viewing of the novel, when Keeley had allowed her to read it soon after finding it. She very much approved of the idea that Eliza and her work now had superfans, however. It was a very welcome development after so many years of being underappreciated.

After a few more minutes had ticked by, Keeley cleared her throat. 'Eliza's publisher will not thank us for keeping her away from her desk. We should make our way to the smoking room next door before her tea becomes too cold to enjoy.'

Obediently, the group followed. Grace closed the door

behind them, in case Belinda or Sue slipped into the library to empty the tea cups.

'As you may be aware, Eliza takes quiet enjoyment in remaining an unmarried woman,' Keeley confided to her audience. 'But it does not follow that she dislikes male company. This room is often filled with gentlemen of her acquaintance and you will find the tobacco chest overflowing with the most pungent and rare leaf. The drinks cabinet is likewise stocked with the very best brandy and port. Eliza likes nothing better than to make merry with those she holds in high esteem and I have heard that she is particularly skilled at card games. Those who challenge her to a hand of Vingt-et-un do so at their peril.'

The drawing room was next, with its smaller but no less sumptuous Christmas tree; Grace made a mental note to compliment Raff on it the next time she saw him. She hid a smile as Keeley pointed out the four empty stockings, hung for Eliza's nieces and nephews. In the kitchen, it was clear that a festive feast was being prepared; a saucepan of rich stock hung from a hook above the flames, bubbling merrily, and a tray of freshly baked mince pies sat steaming on a trivet. They looked so inviting that Grace was tempted to steal one. Keeley evidently anticipated the temptation because she warned the visitors they would only burn their fingers.

Returning along the corridor to the hall beside the front door, Keeley led them upstairs next, through Eliza's bedroom and dressing room where they lapped up the explanation that Eliza would be attending a ball in London the following day and could not decide which dress to wear. Along the landing, they paused in one of the spare rooms that had been laid out as a nursery. 'While Eliza has no children of her own, she loves the sound of their laughter,' Keeley told the group. 'She encourages her brother and sisters to visit as often as they can, and takes extended trips to their houses whenever her work allows.'

Jenny slipped away as they returned downstairs, to prepare to lead her own talk. 'Meet you in the staffroom in a few minutes,' Grace whispered. 'Deep breaths, you're going to be brilliant.'

She found she was holding her breath as the group followed Keeley back to the drawing room. Would Belinda and Sue have managed their task in the short window of time available to them? But she need not have worried. The gasps of delight as Keeley opened the door to reveal the glittering pile of presents beneath the tree told her the miracle had been achieved. The group crowded inside, marvelling at the freshly stuffed stockings and plate of mince pies that now sat on the table, beside bowls of glittering sugared fruits. 'It appears that Christmas has arrived at Juniper Cottage! May goodwill and blessings be upon us all!'

Over the top of their heads, she grinned at Grace, who doffed an imaginary cap. One look at the smiling, wonder-filled faces around them told her the tour had been a triumph, although she had no idea how Keeley was going to persuade them to leave. 'I'd better go and meet Jenny,' she murmured, sidling close to Keeley. 'Good luck getting this lot out.'

Keeley grimaced. 'Thanks. Tell her to break a leg!'

It was clear from the moment Jenny greeted the next group of visitors that she was nervous. Her voice quavered slightly as she introduced herself, trying to emulate Keeley's confiding manner. The lantern rattled when she lifted it and entreated them to follow her into the house. But her nerves seemed to settle once they were in the library, and Grace wondered whether the comfort of the familiar surroundings gave her confidence a boost. As before, it was not long before the page from the manuscript was discovered and Jenny copied Keeley's example to lean into the illusion that it was fresh from Eliza's quill. She grew in assurance as the tour moved from room to room and, by the time they returned to the drawing room, some thirty minutes after their first stop there, Grace thought she was every bit as comfortable as Keeley had been.

'You were amazing,' she told her, as the group spread out to admire the gifts under the tree. 'How do you feel?'

'Relieved,' Jenny admitted. 'I thought I was going to drop the lantern, my hand was shaking so much.'

'Nobody would have known,' Grace reassured her. 'And the first one is always the hardest.'

'I hope so,' Jenny said. 'I've got to do it all again in forty-five minutes.'

'You'll smash it,' Grace promised. 'Just visualise the lovely glass of wine I'm going to pour you when it's over.'

Jenny puffed out her cheeks. 'Thank you. But I'd better wrap this tour up first or Belinda and Sue won't have time to reset the room before Keeley's group arrives.'

There was no sign of nerves in her second tour of the night. Grace could only watch in admiration as she guided the final group of paying guests around the cottage, her sense of playfulness coming to the fore as she relaxed into her role and made it seem possible that Eliza really was there, if always just out of sight. As before, the paper on the writing desk caused much excitement but it was the sleight of hand in the drawing room that produced the biggest gasps of wonder.

'It was exactly the same with my second group,' Keeley

reported, when they all convened in the staffroom for a debrief after the last guests had gone. 'None of them tried to guess how it had been done. It was as though they were children again, desperate to believe it was all real.'

'I don't know why you're surprised,' Grace said, looking from Keeley to Jenny. 'You encouraged them to suspend their disbelief the moment they walked through the door. Is it any wonder they were totally under your spell by the end of the tour?'

Keeley smiled. 'When you put it like that, I don't suppose we should be surprised.' She turned in her chair to nod at Belinda and Sue. 'Really well done to both of you for timing everything so perfectly. I don't think any of the groups had the slightest clue you were there. Were there any issues?'

Belinda grimaced. 'Apart from me dropping one of the stockings and losing a satsuma under the chaise longue, you mean?'

'Did you find it?' Grace asked.

'Only once everyone had gone,' Belinda said, sighing. 'At least it rolled out right to the back and couldn't be seen.'

'Anything else?' Keeley asked.

Elspeth raised her hand. 'Brian needed to get home to his cat but he said he'd had a few issues getting cars in and out of the car park safely, with all the people walking around the light trail. He thinks we might need to work on a one-way system.'

Keeley scribbled down a note. 'Okay, I'll catch up with him tomorrow and make some recommendations to Helen. How were things from your perspective, Elspeth? Did you enjoy playing Sally?'

The older woman nodded. 'Oh yes, it was wonderful.' She

raised a hand to the starched white collar of her costume. 'Although I can't wait to take this off.'

'I can imagine,' Keeley replied, wincing in sympathy. She glanced at Isobel and Marco. 'How about you two? Do you feel ready to deliver your own tours tomorrow? Grace and I will be on hand to help with any problems.'

Isobel nodded. 'I think so.'

'It was helpful being able to see how you and Jenny did it,' Marco agreed. 'I'll be sticking fairly closely to your template.'

Keeley let them all go shortly after the debrief, reminding them to contact her in the morning if they had anything they needed to discuss. At almost nine o'clock, the village green was quietening down as Keeley and Grace walked the short distance home, and Grace was surprised by how worn out she felt. 'I didn't even do anything,' she complained. 'Everyone else did the hard work, I just listened.'

'But you've also done a full day at Santa's Secret,' Keeley pointed out. 'Thanks for being there to hold Jenny's hand, by the way. I really appreciate it.'

Grace waved her thanks away. 'I enjoyed it. In fact, I think I spotted a new detail each time I went round. It really is a brilliant tour. You've outdone yourself.'

'Thank you,' she said quietly. 'I must admit, I had my doubts when Xander first suggested it, and even when I'd agreed, I resisted all the immersive elements he came up with. But they really worked, didn't they?'

'Yes,' Grace said simply. She gave her friend a sidelong look. 'Do you think you should be telling him that?'

'Maybe,' Keeley said, in a tight tone that told Grace she had absolutely no intention of doing so.

They walked in silence for a few steps before Keeley suddenly stopped walking. 'It's no good. I can't keep this to myself any longer,' she burst out, causing Grace to stop in her tracks too.

'What's the matter?' she asked in alarm. 'Has something bad happened? Do you need help?'

Keeley pressed her lips together. 'It's nothing bad. It's just – well, can you keep a secret?'

'You know I can,' Grace said, wondering what her friend was about to tell her this time. 'I didn't tell anyone about Eliza's manuscript, did I?'

Keeley blew out a long breath. It plumed like smoke on the frosty air. 'That's true,' she said, and began to walk again. 'But this is bigger than that, and it's strictly unofficial for the time being.'

Grace caught her up. What on earth did she mean by unofficial? Perhaps this time she was talking about her relationship with Xander, although it seemed unlikely. 'I have no idea what this is about but, official or unofficial, you know I won't breathe a word.'

'Good,' Keeley said fretfully. 'Because if I don't confide in someone, I think I might spontaneously combust.'

At that, she lapsed into a silence that felt even more dramatic than her sudden outburst moments before. Grace coughed meaningfully. 'Speaking of spontaneously combusting . . .'

The words seemed to jolt Keeley from her thoughts. 'Sorry.' She took a few more steps then gave Grace a sidelong look. 'You know how I've never been able to understand why Eliza's work has never been adapted for film or TV?'

The breath caught in Grace's throat. 'Yes.'

'Well, it turns out all I needed to do was discover a secret, unpublished manuscript and make a big splash when announcing it,' Keeley said, shaking her head. 'The trustees have been approached by the BBC. They want to turn *The Merriest Month* into a six part series, to air next Christmas as the jewel in the crown of their festive programming.'

'That's amazing!'

'I know,' Keeley said, beaming. 'I must have read the email a hundred times now and I still can't believe it's real. They're talking about casting Nick Borrowdale as Jonas Laidlaw. Nick bloody Borrowdale, Grace. Can you imagine it?'

Nick Borrowdale was an immensely popular, universally fancied Irish actor in his late thirties who had set temperatures rising across the country with his rough and raunchy portrayal of a Cornish squire in the BBC drama *Smuggler's Cove* some years earlier. He'd since become box office gold, taking Hollywood by storm, and Grace knew it was a given that anything he put his name to would be a roaring success.

'Wow,' she said, suddenly warmer than she wanted to be inside her winter coat and scarf. 'Hang on, does that mean you get to meet him?'

'I have no idea,' Keeley admitted. 'It's still early days. But there has been talk about me being a script consultant. Me!'

'Of course they'd want you to help translate Eliza's brilliance to the screen,' Grace said, trying to ignore a faint prickle of jealousy that Keeley might actually get to be in the same room – or at least on the same set – as Nick Borrowdale. 'When will it all become official?'

'I don't know that either,' her friend admitted. 'Maybe at the start of the new year. They'll want to get this Christmas out of the way first.'

Grace nodded. 'If they've got any sense, they'll tie it into the publication of the novel.' She eyed Keeley curiously. 'What does Xander think?'

Keeley seemed suddenly concerned with rummaging through her pockets for her keys. 'I don't know. I haven't asked.'

'Don't you think you should?' Grace asked gently. 'Finding the manuscript was as much down to him as you.'

'If we're being totally honest, he was the one who actually found it,' Keeley admitted, finding her key and thrusting it into the door of the cottage. 'It might still be hidden in that secret drawer if he hadn't noticed something was off. But as I said, nothing has been confirmed yet. Once it's all official, I'll tell him. I'm sure he'll have some ideas about it.'

She still sounded hurt and Grace supposed she had a right to be. Xander had made a colossal misjudgement when he'd revealed the discovery of the manuscript to the trustees without her agreement. It would take a lot longer than a few months for Keeley to forgive him, and there was a strong possibility she might never fully trust him again. 'It's such amazing news,' she said, following Keeley into the house. 'Just think – one of Eliza's books on the television at last!'

'I know,' Keeley said, beaming at her. 'It's the stuff of dreams.'

'It really is,' Grace said, thrilled all over again. 'So you know your possible role as a script consultant?'

'Yes,' her friend said, frowning a little. 'Not confirmed yet, either.'

'Do you think, if it is confirmed, that you might be able to do me a teensy-weensy favour?'

Keeley's eyebrows rose. 'Depends what it is.'

Grace adopted her most innocent expression. 'Do you think

you could add in a scene where Nick Borrowdale strides out of a lake in a dripping wet shirt?'

The second week of December was even busier than the first; it seemed to Grace as if the entire population of Essex had descended on Santa's Secret for lights and decorations. Grace spent most of her time on the shop floor, or in the stockroom, and she rarely saw Ivy for more than a few brief moments during the day, usually as they passed each other on errands for customers. But apart from the ache in her feet once she got home each evening, Grace had few complaints. She loved helping people to find the ingredients for their perfect Christmas and was happy to give her opinion when asked whether two styles would clash or complement each other, or recommend a decorative theme that would stand out. But at the same time, she was aware that her time at Santa's Secret was due to end on Christmas Eve. Raff had told her that although Ivy was happy that the rent wasn't going up, she was still making noises about retirement and Grace hadn't judged it the right time to ask her about staying on.

Her mother was her usual blunt self when Grace told her what had happened over lunch on the last Sunday before Christmas.

'I agree that Jesse sounds perfectly horrible, and I'm glad it's all been sorted out, but I don't see what difference it makes to you,' she said, frowning at her across the table in their favourite restaurant. 'It was only ever meant to be a temporary job, wasn't it? You knew you'd be leaving at Christmas.'

How could she explain that she'd enjoyed being part of the Santa's Secret team more than she'd thought possible, Grace wondered? Or how much satisfaction she'd taken from helping their customers, even if one or two of them seemed to have forgotten that Christmas was the season of goodwill. 'Yes,' she said. 'But what I couldn't have anticipated is how at home I'd feel there. I've got to know the idiosyncrasies of the till system, and how it all links to the inventory and supplier orders. I think I could navigate the stockroom in my sleep and I've made friends with the people who work there.'

She broke off, worried she might blurt out Raff's name if she continued to speak. Orla was eyeing her thoughtfully. 'I see,' she said. 'So why not see if you can extend your contract?'

'Because Ivy wants to retire,' Grace said wretchedly. 'Once Christmas is over, I think she'll start looking for a buyer and then everything will change and I won't feel like I belong there anymore.'

She stopped again, but this time it was because her eyes were stinging with tears.

'Do you think she actually wants to retire?' Orla asked. 'Or is it just the idea of it that appeals, after the scare with the rent?'

Grace sighed. 'I don't know. She once told me that she'd thought about taking on a partner, to allow her to take more of a back seat. But Raff seems convinced she's gone past that now.'

Orla's gaze narrowed. 'Raff? Who's that?'

'Ivy's son,' Grace replied, keeping her gaze fixed on her plate because she didn't dare meet her mother's shrewd gaze.

'Her son,' Orla repeated. 'And does he work at Santa's Secret too?'

'No,' Grace said reluctantly. 'He's a landscape gardener.'

'But you've discussed his mother's business affairs and her plans for the future,' Orla observed. 'In some detail, it would appear.'

Grace felt her cheeks growing warmer. 'Well, yes. He found out that Ivy had confided in me after Jesse threatened to increase the rent and of course he was there when we confronted old Mr Bairstow about it.'

'Of course,' her mother said dryly. 'From what you've said, half of Freezy Tye was in attendance. And how does Raff feel about Ivy's plans to retire?'

The question stumped Grace for a moment. 'I don't know,' she said. 'He wants her to be happy, but I think he'd be sorry to see Santa's Secret close.'

Orla took a sip of wine. 'Then it seems obvious to me what you should do.'

Grace gaped at her. 'Does it?'

'Yes.'

'Okay,' Grace said, when it appeared her mother wasn't going to expand on her pronouncement. 'What is it you think I should do?'

'Invest in the business,' Orla said serenely. 'You have a decent sum from your redundancy package and your mortgage is paid. You could tap into some of that capital if you need to.'

For the second time in as many minutes, Grace found herself gawping across the table. 'Invest?'

'Yes,' Orla said patiently. 'Make Ivy an offer to take over some of the business, or even all of it if that's what she wants. You're perfectly capable, Grace, and you said yourself that you know the ropes.'

'I don't know them well enough to run the place!' she protested.

'Nonsense,' Orla replied, sniffing. 'Of course you do.'

'I can assure you I don't. There are all kinds of things to consider, like payroll and the accounts and – and—'

'Doesn't Ivy have people to help her with those things? Accountants and the like?'

'Yes, of course she does,' Grace ground out. 'But what if they don't want to work for me? What if no one wants to work for me?'

What if Raff thinks I'm trying to steal his mother's business and never speaks to me again, she thought but did not add. Just the idea of it made the food she'd eaten curdle in her stomach.

Her mother watched her over the rim of her glass. 'You're being ridiculous. None of those things are likely to happen. I imagine most of them will be grateful to still have a job, in a workplace they enjoy going to every day.'

Grace thought of Sanjay and Freddie, Misha and April, all of whom she knew loved working at Santa's Secret. But was it the job they loved, or the woman behind it? 'I don't know anything about running a business,' she said again.

'Then you learn,' Orla said. 'Take a course. Negotiate a phased handover with Ivy, so that she teaches you how it all works. From what you've said, it sounds as though it's her baby. She'd probably jump at the chance to pass it on to someone she can trust not to run it into the ground.'

Grace opened her mouth to argue, then closed it again as her brain began turning over the possibilities. Could she raise enough to buy Ivy out, or even to just purchase a stake in Santa's Secret? More importantly, did she want to? She scratched off the final question immediately – of course she wanted to. She just wasn't sure she could, or how Ivy and Raff would feel about the idea.

'I'll think it over,' she said. 'Thanks, Mum.'

Orla smiled. 'That's what I'm here for. Now, what are we

going to have for dessert? I think the plum pudding sounds deliciously Christmassy, don't you?'

The message from Gavin came through on Tuesday morning, as Grace was arriving at Santa's Secret. She parked her car, then pulled her phone out of her handbag to read it.

Big news! Britain's Most Christmassy Village is going mainstream. The winner of this year's competition is going to be announced on The One Show tonight, at 7pm!

As she stared down at the screen, another message popped up in the committee group chat, also from Gavin.

I'm being serious. This is not a joke.

The words 'Paul is typing' appeared, quickly followed by a message. *WOAH. This is huge. Are you sure?*

Grace waited with bated breath as Gavin responded. *Yep. Got an email from the judges this morning. They want a film crew to visit the winning village later this week.*

Messages began to arrive thick and fast from the other members of the group, wondering if every village had received the same message and whether anyone had any idea when the judges had visited Freezy Tye. Grace worked her way through, barely finishing one message before another appeared. And then her phone began to ring and Raff's name appeared on the screen.

'Have you seen the news?' he asked, without waiting for her to say hello.

'I have,' she said, smiling. 'I gather it's never made the television before?'

'Never,' he said. 'The best we've managed so far is page four of the national papers and a Have Your Say article on the regional BBC webpages. It's a big step up.'

Another message from Gavin materialised. *Watch party at the pub tonight – everyone invited. Drinks are on me if we win.*

Butterflies began to swirl in Grace's stomach. The thought of the competition winner featuring on *The One Show* made her feel slightly queasy. 'Are you coming to Gavin's watch party?'

There was a pause, during which she assumed Raff was scrolling through the messages on his own phone. 'Wouldn't miss it for anything. You?'

'Oh, the same,' she said fervently. 'Although I might need a stiff drink or two to settle my nerves.'

He laughed. 'I don't think you'll be alone there. But it'll be good to have everyone together. I'm not sure I could bear to watch on my own.'

'No,' Grace agreed. 'Thank goodness it's not a night when Keeley's tours are happening. I'd hate to miss the announcement.'

'I'd hate it too,' Raff said. 'It wouldn't be the same without you, especially after all your hard work.'

Grace felt her cheeks flood with warmth. 'I'll see you later then,' she said, suddenly breathless with anticipation.

'Definitely,' he said. 'See you there.'

She sat still for several seconds after he'd rung off, wondering whether he'd meant it when he said he would hate it if she missed the party. Then she decided he'd simply been caught up in the moment, and had probably meant to include Keeley too. She read the rest of the messages in the chat, which seemed to veer between wild optimism about their chances of winning and a determination not to set themselves up for disappointment. Grace found herself distinctly in the latter camp. The real achievement was all the Christmas joy they'd already spread, she told herself as she prepared to get out of the car. And then a message from Keeley arrived which gave her something else to worry about.

What are you wearing later?

Grace let out a groan as she replied. *I'm not sure I have anything. My party clothes are all back at my house.*

Wear your onesie. Raff won't care.

After several attempts at a dignified response, Grace gave up and went to work. Hopefully, the problem of what to wear would resolve itself once she stopped fretting about it.

The day passed in a blur, as she'd known it would because the shop was so busy; she barely had time to breathe. It was just over a week until Christmas Eve and the demand for decorations was showing no sign of dying down. Grace had hoped for a quiet moment to catch up with Ivy, mostly to see how she was but also to test the waters about the business proposal her mother had suggested the day before. Grace had spent most of the night turning the idea over in her mind, and the longer she thought about it, the more it felt like the perfect solution. But would Ivy see it that way?

It seemed the answer would have to wait. Frustratingly, Ivy was engrossed in a telephone call with a supplier when Grace knocked on the door of her office once the shop had closed for the day. She covered the receiver and threw Grace an apologetic look. 'Sorry, can you pop back later? I really need to sort this out.'

Grace nodded. 'Of course. I'm clocking off now but maybe we could catch up tomorrow, if you've got time?'

'Absolutely,' Ivy said, and threw her a knowing look. 'Although you might have a sore head in the morning, if tonight's announcement goes our way.'

So she knew about the party, Grace thought as she made her way back downstairs. Raff must have told her. Perhaps now wasn't the right time to broach the subject of future plans, she told herself. One more day wouldn't make a difference, and at least she had the party to distract her. Checking the time, she sped up. If she was lucky with the traffic, she might just have time to detour into Chelmsford to do some quick shopping.

Keeley stared at her as she made her way into the living room just after six-thirty that evening. 'Okay, who are you and what have you done with my friend Grace?'

A little self-consciously, Grace smoothed the pristine black velvet of her new dress, which came to a stop well before her knees. The neckline was scooped and beaded with silver sequins, and dipped daringly at the back. She'd bought a pair of black ballet pumps that were utterly impractical for winter but that she thought might survive the short walk to the pub. 'Do you like it?'

Keeley grinned. 'Are you kidding? I absolutely love it and so will everyone else.'

Grace bit her lip. 'You don't think it's a bit much for a watch party?'

'Absolutely not,' her friend responded. 'Just mind yourself around Gav – he's a sucker for an LBD.'

Grace did not want to ask how she knew this. Instead, she took in Keeley's outfit, which was a dark green knitted jumper dress that clung to her model's figure like it had been made for her. She'd paired it with gold hoop earrings and a loose ponytail at the nape of her neck, and her only concession to make-up was a dab of red across her lips. She looked stunning, and just for a moment, Grace considered running back upstairs to throw on a pair of jeans and a festive jumper, because what was the point of trying to compete with Keeley? Then she remembered they were no longer at university, and it had been a long time since she'd felt the need to compare herself to her friend. 'You look great too,' she said, smiling.

Keeley winked at her. 'I do not have anyone to impress. Whereas you—'

'Don't have anyone to impress, either,' Grace finished sternly. 'We're going to cross everything for a win, and hold our heads up high if it's anything else. Now stop teasing me or I'll go upstairs and get changed.'

'You will not,' Keeley said, getting to her feet. 'Come on, let's go. I don't mind telling you I'm more than a little bit nervous.'

The pub was pleasantly full – not mobbed, as it had been the night of the Christmas lights switch-on, but busy enough to create the buzz of conversation. Several people waved; Grace saw Paul in one corner, chatting to Helen and other members of the committee. Gavin had put BBC One on the big screen that was usually reserved for sport, although the sound was off and Wizzard were playing over the sound system instead, wishing it could be Christmas every day. With a shout of greeting, Gavin slipped out from behind the bar to greet them. 'If it isn't my two favourite ladies,' he said, grinning and swooping in to plant a kiss on their cheeks. 'What can I get you to drink? Champagne?'

Keeley raised her eyebrows. 'Cava?'

Gavin shook his head. 'Nope – actual champagne. I've pushed the boat out a bit, in anticipation of how brilliant we all are.'

'In that case, it would be rude to say no,' Keeley replied.

Moments later, Gavin was back with two flutes of golden liquid. 'Cheers,' he said, handing a glass to each of them. 'Here's to bringing that crown home for an eighth year.'

They chinked their glasses, then Grace gave hers to Keeley. 'Hold this for a second, will you?'

She slipped off her coat, looking around for somewhere to hang it, but Gavin was there before she could decide what to do with it. 'Allow me,' he said grandly as he took her coat, then noticed her dress and whistled. 'Very nice indeed. You scrub up well, Grace.'

'I couldn't agree more,' Raff said, appearing as if from nowhere to stand beside them. He smiled at her. 'Hello. You look lovely.'

Grace willed herself not to blush. 'Thank you,' she said, retrieving her glass from Keeley and trying to ignore the meaningful stare she was directing her way. 'You look great too.'

The words came out automatically but she quickly realised he did look good. He wore a forest green shirt that was open at the collar and dark blue jeans, and she caught a whisper of that scent that still did strange things to her insides. Get a hold of yourself, she mentally scolded, not daring to look at Keeley.

'Has Gavin opened the room upstairs?' her friend asked, nodding towards the open door in the far wall.

Raff nodded. 'He wanted to make it a proper celebration. Quite a few members of the committee are up there, along with my mum.'

Grace smiled. Without Ivy's help, the light trail might never have happened.

'Leila is setting up the food from Eliza's Pantry,' Raff went on. 'The sausage rolls are to die for, so make sure you get one. And Deke is here, too. Apparently he considers himself an honorary member of the committee now.'

'Why doesn't that surprise me?' Keeley said, rolling her eyes. 'He probably heard Gav was breaking out the champagne.'

Raff laughed. 'Probably, but I don't think anyone really minds. He does turn up for free every year.'

'I thought he was pretty good,' Grace said mildly. 'He held the fort when the lights when out.'

'That's true,' Raff conceded. 'And he was famous, back in the day.'

Keeley grinned. 'You don't have to tell Grace that. She was a big Boy Next Door fan. Had their posters on her walls and everything.'

'Did I hear my name?' Deke turned around to smirk at Keeley. 'I bet you were a fan too, on the quiet. You'd have been just my type.'

Grace almost choked on her drink because Keeley had been more into grunge than pop and wouldn't have been seen dead with anyone as clean-cut as Deke and his bandmates. But she simply smiled. 'It's a shame I'm not single. Will you excuse me? I think I see my boyfriend.'

She slipped away before Deke could reply. He turned his attention to Grace instead. 'Nice dress. Did you really have my poster on your bedroom wall?'

Reluctantly, Grace nodded. 'Not just you. It was the band.'

Deke appeared not to have heard. 'We were all good-looking lads but I don't mind admitting I had the most fans.' He paused to eye her hopefully. 'I don't suppose you fancy a bit of rough and tumble with the Dekester, do you?'

'Rough and Tumble' had been one of their biggest hits, Grace recalled. 'Uh—' she said, wondering how to refuse him graciously.

Raff beat her to it. He rested a hand lightly on her shoulder and glared at Deke. 'No, she doesn't.'

He glanced from Grace to Raff and his eyes widened. 'Say no more. I should have realised from the way you were the other night. Sorry, bro.'

He turned away. Raff removed his hand from Grace's shoulder. 'I hope that was okay. I thought it might be the quickest way to stop him pestering you.' He paused and threw her a quizzical look. 'Unless you really were a superfan and I've ruined your only chance at realising a long-cherished dream.'

'No,' Grace reassured him quickly. 'I preferred Rory.'

He nodded and Grace suddenly felt the need to clarify. 'Not that I have any long-cherished dreams about him, either. You know, if he was here instead of Deke. I just liked him better, when I was younger. Much younger.' She took a gulp of champagne and wished she hadn't as the alcohol hit her stomach. 'Isn't it time for the show to begin?'

Raff's mouth had begun to curve into a smile but now he checked his watch. 'You're right. I'd better tell Gavin to turn the music off. Will you excuse me?'

She nodded. 'Of course.'

Keeley had found herself a seat in the corner and was now chatting to Helen, so Grace contented herself with studying the silent action on the screen. She rarely watched TV in the evenings and had no idea what was on before *The One Show* but whatever it was had finished, as the credits had begun to roll. And then Mariah Carey was cut off mid-warble as the speakers switched to the television feed, and the festive classic was replaced by the cheery blast of the familiar theme tune.

The door of the pub swung back, just as Raff rejoined Grace. They turned to see who was coming in and Grace felt the breath freeze in her lungs because it was Jesse Bairstow, full of swagger and accompanied by two other men who could be friends or just as easily bouncers. He looked around, observed Grace and Raff staring at him, and smirked. 'Evening all. I thought I'd come and lord it over you all when Flaxwood is announced as Britain's Most Christmassy Village.'

Behind the bar, Gavin scowled. 'I thought I made myself clear last time, Jesse. You're not welcome here.'

'Trying to get rid of the competition?' the other man sneered, as more of the crowd turned to look at him.

Raff shifted position slightly. 'That's more your style. Broken into any more fuse boxes lately?'

Glancing at the big screen, Grace saw the show was about to start. She raised her chin and fixed Jesse with a challenging look. 'You seem very confident. Let's see if you've got so much to say after the winner is announced.'

For a moment, she thought Gavin was going to insist Jesse and his friends left, but he seemed to realise that it would cause more trouble than it was worth. As the presenter smiled into the camera and gave her audience a glimpse of what was to come, the pub fell silent to listen. 'And with Christmas almost upon us, we join the judges of the prestigious Britain's Most Christmassy Village competition to see which of the finalists have wowed them this year. Villages up and down the country have been lighting up the night and fighting it out in regional heats throughout December but only one can claim the top spot. Here's a list of the final six.'

Grace watched as names appeared one by one: Grasmere, in the north-west; Foulden, over the border in Scotland; Minster Lovell in the Cotswolds – that was hardly a surprise, given its famously picturesque location – and Mousehole in the south-west. And Grace suddenly realised there were only two spaces left. Surely both Flaxwood and Freezy Tye couldn't have made the finals? She held her breath, willing Freezy Tye to be the next name to appear but it was Boshum in West Sussex. Her knees began to tremble and she suddenly regretted wearing a dress. Jesse seemed rooted to the spot, his eyes narrowed as he stared at the screen. And then he let out a snarl that was instantly drowned out by jubilant cheering as Freezy Tye materialised in the last spot beneath the other villages.

'Ridiculous!' he bellowed. 'It's all a fix. How much did you have to pay them?'

'Nothing,' Gavin said, shrugging. 'Face it, Jesse. Money doesn't always buy success. But no hard feelings – what can I get you to drink? Oh, you're not staying to see who wins?'

The last sentence was because Jesse had spun on his heel, bumping into one of the less nimble men he'd brought with him, and stalked to the door. 'Don't let it hit you on the arse,' Gavin called to more cheers but Grace waved a hand to shush them, because a man and a woman had joined the presenter on the sofa, both in eye-watering Christmas jumpers.

'So tell me,' the presenter said, twinkling at her guests, 'what do you judges look for in a seriously Christmassy village?'

The man cleared his throat. 'First things first, it's not about how much they spend.'

'Tell that to Jesse,' Keeley whispered.

'What we're looking for is a real sense of community – the feeling that the whole village is behind the decorations and everyone has contributed in some way, no matter how small.'

The female judge leaned forward. 'I like seeing children's decorations. While they may not be perfect, they do tend to represent a less corporate view of Christmas.'

'It's good thing we put up the display of "What Christmas Means to Me" next to the kissing booth,' Keeley murmured. 'Score one for Freezy Tye.'

'And I enjoy a multi-faith approach,' the man cut in. 'Before Christmas became Christmas it was Yule, and filled with traditions that go back a long way. It's nice to see nods to those older, more pagan roots incorporated into the displays.'

And now Keeley turned to Raff. 'Score another point with your mistletoe.'

'But ultimately it's about the overall aesthetic,' the woman went on. 'Can we see a consistent theme coupled with a sense of pride in the village that lasts all year round? That's often what tips the balance in the end.'

The presenter beamed. 'So what you're saying is, a village is for life, not just for Christmas?'

The judges laughed. 'I suppose that's exactly the message we're trying to send,' the man agreed.

'Well, I think we've kept everyone on tenterhooks for long enough,' the presenter said, looking straight into the camera. 'Without further ado, would you like to announce who has won Britain's Most Christmassy Village this year?'

The female judge held up a large cream envelope and lifted the flap. Silence fell over the pub and Grace realised she was shivering with anticipation. Beside her, Keeley reached for her hand and gripped it tightly. On screen, the woman cleared her throat. 'And the winner is . . .Freezy Tye!'

Grace's hands flew to her face as Keeley let out a hoarse scream in her ear. Raff beamed in delight. 'We did it!' he said, turning to her and gathering her into a hug. 'We only went and did it again!'

Behind the bar, Gavin was roaring. 'Eight times! We're eight-time winners! Get in!'

But Grace barely heard because the fact that she was in Raff's arms was doing odd things to her brain. She only had a second or two to adjust before Keeley was pulling her away for a hug of her own. 'We couldn't have done it without you, Grace. Bloody well done, you superstar.'

In among the general celebration, Grace thought she heard Paul bellowing for calm. 'Look,' he shouted, pointing at the screen. 'Look!'

With some effort, Grace managed to focus and saw the scene had changed from a shot of the judges in the studio to an outdoor location. Another presenter was talking into the camera, his expression animated as he waved a hand at the glowing village green behind him, and Grace realised with a jolt of unreality that the spectacular Christmas tree behind him was actually the one she'd decorated. 'Wait, what?' she managed, as the truth slowly dawned on her.

'They're here!' Paul yelled, waving towards the windows. 'The cameras are here on the village green!'

There was something of a stampede then, as everyone hurried to the door to peer outside. Grace hung back, unable to take everything in. When she'd offered to help with the village decorations, she'd never dreamed her idea would end up on national television. It felt like a dream and yet her knees were still shaking. She sank into an empty chair, watching as several people she'd been looking at across the pub suddenly materialised on the screen and she realised Gavin was no longer behind the bar.

Raff laid a hand on her shoulder. 'I hope you're proud of yourself, Grace. I know you'll only be in the village for a little while longer but you've made a big impression.'

She smiled. 'You know, I think I am proud. But not just of myself. Of all of us. Like the judges said, we won because everyone contributed something and I'm grateful to have been part of that, even if only for a few months.'

He gazed down at her, opening his mouth to respond but whatever he'd been about to say was drowned out by the triumphant return of their fellow committee members. Suddenly Gavin was next to her, topping up her glass with bubbles, and Helen was thanking her effusively for her hard work. Before Grace knew it, she was tangled up in what felt like ten different conversations and Raff was no longer at her side.

The celebrations carried on long into the night, growing louder as the alcohol flowed more freely. Grace found herself laughing so often her cheeks ached, and then the dancing began and her feet began to hurt too. The air inside the pub grew stuffy and hot, and she began fanning her face with a beer mat.

'Too hot?' Raff said, appearing from nowhere with a glass of water.

'A bit,' she said, taking a grateful gulp of the icy water. 'Do you think Gavin would mind if we opened a window?'

Raff looked round, as though trying to decide if it were possible, and Grace felt beads of sweat forming on her upper lip. 'Actually, I might go and get some fresh air,' she said. 'Cool down a bit.'

He eyed her with concern. 'Are you okay? Would you like me to come with you?'

She was about to say no, then changed her mind. 'Yes, please, I'd like that.'

Raff nodded. 'I'll get your coat. It's cold outside.'

She knew that, of course; the walk from Keeley's cottage had been chilly enough. But the freezing air still made her shiver when they left the warmth of the pub. Frost glistened on the grass and the chill nipped at her face but she was relieved to see there was no sign of the camera crew now.

'They've packed up for tonight,' Raff said, when he saw her looking around the almost deserted green. 'Gavin says they'll be back on Wednesday to capture some more Christmas content.'

His use of the word content instantly made Grace think of Xander. 'Keeley should get Xander to come down,' she said. 'He might be able to arrange a feature on Eliza and Juniper Cottage.'

'Good idea,' Raff said. 'Where do you want to walk? Shall we go and sit on the bench by the duck pond?'

Grace wrapped her coat more firmly around herself. Now that her core temperature was dropping, she was feeling a little better. 'Actually, I'd like to do the light trail. Would you mind?'

He smiled and offered her his arm. 'There's nothing I'd enjoy more.'

It felt odd, walking with her hand tucked into the crook of his elbow. Grace wasn't sure if it was the effect of the alcohol on her too-empty stomach or the rush of adrenaline that had followed the announcement that Freezy Tye had won, but she felt much less steady on her feet than she would like. 'Here's the toy box,' Raff said as they reached the first stop on the trail. 'Do you want to press the button or shall I?'

'You can do this one,' she said generously. 'As long as I can do the Land of Sweets.'

'Deal,' he said, and pushed the button to bring the scene to life.

They stood together in silence, bathed in the glow of the lights. Grace was acutely aware of how close he was. Her hand was still resting on his arm; she could feel his warmth through his coat. 'I meant to ask, where's Bilbo tonight?' she asked, wanting to break the silence.

'At home,' Raff said. 'Probably asleep on the sofa. He's not one for parties, although I imagine he'd get plenty of snacks.'

She nodded. 'I bet he'd love the sausage rolls almost as much as you do.'

'Probably,' Raff said, grinning. He raised an enquiring eyebrow. 'Ready to do battle with the Mouse King?'

'Bring it on,' she replied.

The path was darker on the furthest side of the green, lit only by puddles of light from the streetlamps with shadows in between. They walked for a moment or two without speaking, then Grace felt Raff's arm tense. 'I have to confess I had an ulterior motive for coming out here with you tonight,' he said.

Her heart sped up. She took a long slow breath, willing it to slow down. 'Oh?'

He fired a quick look her way. 'Yes. The fact is – what I mean to say is—' He broke off, then tried again. 'As you know, my mother has started thinking about retirement. Which would probably mean Santa's Secret will close.'

'Yes, I know,' Grace replied. 'Actually, there was something—'

He held up a hand. 'Would you mind terribly if I finished what I was going to say first? I might lose my courage otherwise.'

Surprised, Grace nodded. 'Okay.'

They covered a few more metres. 'I find the thought of the shop closing to be … upsetting,' he said at length. 'It was my mother's dream, and she's worked hard to make it a success. If this was a film, I'd buy her out and run it myself. But it isn't a movie and I have a business of my own to take care of.'

He sounded genuinely regretful. Grace opened her mouth to speak but closed it when she realised he had more to say. 'And then I thought, what if I bought the business and paid someone to manage it for me. Someone with the drive and talent to make it even more successful.' He paused to look at her. 'Someone like you, Grace.'

It was so unexpected that her voice was little more than a squeak when she spoke. 'Me?'

Raff nodded. 'I know your contract runs out on Christmas Eve, and maybe you have something else lined up, but you've done such a brilliant job, both with the light trail and at the shop. Is there anything I can offer you that might tempt you to change your mind and stay?' He stopped walking and turned to face her. 'Anything at all?'

She almost laughed then, a curious hiccupping giggle that had more to do with the champagne she'd gulped down than any actual amusement. Here was Raff Caldwell, offering her a solution to the problem of leaving Santa's Secret in a week's time, and he seemed to think he needed to add more incentives to sweeten the deal. 'It's funny you should say that, actually, because I have a proposal for you.'

Was it her imagination or did he sway a little closer at her words. 'Oh?' he said quietly. 'What's that?'

She swallowed, because his expression was suddenly very intent. 'I don't want Santa's Secret to close either, but I'm not sure I can afford to buy Ivy out so I was going to offer her a partnership. That way she gets to take things a bit easier without giving up the shop completely.'

His eyes glittered as he studied her. 'A partnership,' he repeated. 'Yes, I think that might work. But would you consider a partnership with me instead of her?'

It seemed to Grace that the world contracted around them then. The green vanished, leaving only the two of them, gazing at each other. 'What would that look like?' she asked.

Time slowed as he stared at her. 'I'd be happy to negotiate. What is it you want, Grace?'

It was a good question, she thought numbly. Less than five minutes ago, she'd been fairly sure what she wanted but now her brain was cloudy and she couldn't think straight. If only Raff wasn't so close, but the idea of putting more distance between them filled her with quiet panic. And then he reached out to brush something from her cheek and the touch of his fingers sent what little self-possession she had skimming away. Another feathery touch on her face was followed by a third but it wasn't Raff touching her now. She looked up to see tiny whirling shapes tumbling from the sky and let out a soft huff of astonishment. 'It's snowing!'

Raff laughed and shook his head. 'It is. Bloody hell, I can't believe I've been upstaged by the weather.'

Grace held out a hand to catch the flakes, watching as they landed on her skin and melted with the heat. 'I thought you promised me no snow until Christmas Day.'

He sighed. 'I'll have a word with the Met Office, see what they can do.'

'To be honest, I don't really mind it. We've already won the competition.' She turned her face upwards and closed her eyes. 'Snow makes everything better.'

After a few blissful seconds, she opened her eyes again and saw Raff watching her. 'Sorry,' she said. 'We were having an important conversation.'

'We were,' he agreed. 'I believe you were about to tell me what you want.' He hesitated. 'From Santa's Secret – and from me.'

Grace grew suddenly still. His black hair was dappled with white, turning him into a magpie, and she watched tiny flakes settle on his long dark eyelashes. His expression was frozen, as though he was holding his breath while he waited for her to answer. 'What I want,' she said, and paused to catch her own breath. 'What I want is everything. Santa's Secret, a partnership, and you. You most of all.'

He froze, his green, gold-flecked gaze sharp and intent. 'Do you really mean that?'

She nodded. 'Yes, I really do.'

She was in his arms before the last word was out and his expression was filled with wonder, yet tinged with something more, something altogether more primal. Hunger, she realised as she acknowledged the same feeling in herself. Need. And then he was kissing her, and his cold, cold lips tasted of mountains and meltwater and wanting. Snow landed on her hair, her hands, her eyelids, but she did not mind its chill. She drank in his kisses, pressing into him and feeling the warmth of his body as he drew her even closer. Her fingers sank into his damp hair, cradling his head to her own as the snow tumbled around them. The world fell away, and they might have been cocooned in their very own snow globe. But at last they broke apart, and Grace gasped as torrents of melted snow ran down her cheeks and over her lips.

'We should probably go back inside,' Raff murmured, teasing a strand of damp hair from her forehead and brushing it back into place.

Grace looked around and was amazed to see a thin blanket of white now coated the ground surrounding them. They were all alone. Everyone else had vanished. 'Probably,' she replied, and turned her face towards his. 'But kissing in the snow is terribly romantic. Can we do it again?'

Smiling, he lowered his head to hers. 'You can have anything you want, Grace,' he whispered, his lips soft on hers. 'Anything at all.'

CHAPTER SEVENTEEN

Forgiveness is the greatest gift, after all.

The Merriest Month, ELIZA NORTON

As much as Keeley liked the idea of a white Christmas, she was relieved to wake up on Monday morning to find the snow that had covered Freezy Tye since the previous Tuesday night had gone. The weather had played havoc with the final tours of Juniper Cottage, with several disappointed ticket holders unable to get to the village, and refunds had been issued. She had continued to watch the weather forecast with some anxiety, hoping the promised thaw would actually materialise and allow the trustees, volunteers and selected guests to travel to the cottage for the planned wrap party on Monday afternoon: a drinks reception in the library followed by an intimate, candlelit reading from *The Merriest Month*. Malcolm had assured her that someone from the BBC would be there but Keeley was not holding her breath. Most people would have other things to do three days before Christmas, even as early as four o'clock.

Elspeth had insisted on reprising her role as Sally for the event and there was much delight among the trustees when she opened the front door of the cottage to greet them in character. 'Keeley, my dear, you have excelled yourself,' Malcolm exclaimed as he moved past Elspeth and took in the tree and the decorations. 'The reviews from the tours have been glowing, an absolute triumph. I can't tell you how thrilled we are with the work you and Xander have put in. A dream team in every respect.'

She smiled politely, trying not to react to the mention of Xander. 'Thank you. I can honestly say we've loved every moment of the tours. I hope we'll be able to offer them again next Christmas.'

'Oh, indubitably,' Malcolm replied. 'Especially with *you know what* in the pipeline.'

'Of course,' she said, and glanced over his shoulder. 'Is the producer from the BBC coming today?'

His expression grew suddenly regretful. 'Alas not. Family commitments, you understand. But we shall make very merry in her absence and arrange a meeting early in the new year to get the ball rolling.'

It was no more than Keeley had expected but she still felt a stab of disappointment at the news. 'Well, we've laid out chairs in the drawing room for the reading and lit the fire. Perhaps, once everyone who's coming has arrived, we can gather in there.'

As the hall started to fill with guests, Keeley left it to Jenny and Isobel to mingle and slipped along the corridor to the drawing room. Grace was already there, laying specially printed commemorative sheets on chairs laid out in a horseshoe shape around the Christmas tree. 'How's it looking?' she asked, when Keeley closed the door behind her. 'Are they all here?'

'Not quite,' Keeley said, pulling a face as she explained that the BBC producer would not be joining them.

'It is Christmas week,' Grace pointed out. 'I only got away from work early with special permission.'

Keeley smirked. 'Who says seducing the boss's son doesn't have its perks?'

Grace blushed a deep rosy pink. 'I did not seduce him!' A smile tugged at her lips. 'Well, maybe I did, a bit.'

Keeley raised her eyebrows. 'Even a blizzard wasn't enough to dampen your ardour.'

'It didn't feel like a blizzard at the time,' Grace objected.

'That's because you were too busy having your wicked way with the poor man.'

'Oh, stop it,' Grace huffed in mock-defensiveness. 'Shouldn't you be practising your reading? We're due to start in ten minutes.'

Perhaps there was time for one final read through, Keeley thought with a sudden ripple of anxiety. She'd spent most of the previous evening going over the selection she'd chosen, and had it almost word perfect, but there was always room for improvement. She settled in the wing-backed armchair that faced the horseshoe and began to run through it again.

She was startled by a knock at the door and looked up to find she had the room to herself. When had Grace left, she wondered as she called out to whoever had knocked. 'Come in.'

Jenny poked her head around the door. 'Are you ready? Everyone's here.'

'Of course,' Keeley said. 'Show them in.'

For a moment, Jenny hesitated and Keeley thought she was about to speak, but then she heard the rumble of voices coming along the corridor and Jenny flashed her a quick smile of reassurance. 'Break a leg,' she whispered, and pushed the door back to allow the audience inside.

Malcolm and the other trustees filled the front row, an assortment of men and women, mostly of advancing years, although some younger members had been recruited recently and Keeley judged them to be under seventy. Behind them sat the other guests; Keeley recognised the chair of the Society of Authors and the editor of *The Bookseller.* The publishing director of the company who had won the auction to publish *The Merriest Month* was also there, alongside a slender, middle-aged woman Keeley did not know, although she was puzzled to see Grace waving at her with undisguised enthusiasm. The final seats were taken by those volunteers who were able to attend; Keeley was pleased to see Brian had made it. His diligence in managing the car park throughout the month of December had not gone unappreciated and she was glad he was able to enjoy the small pleasure of this special afternoon. And then she saw a figure that knocked the breath from her lungs. Xander Jones, looking as tanned and tousled and godlike as ever, was chatting animatedly with Elspeth, who had, presumably in all the excitement of seeing him, finally broken character. Keeley's gaze flew to Grace, who waggled her eyebrows in what might have been surprise at Xander's unexpected presence, or encouragement for the imminent reading. She supposed it was probably both, because only Grace knew everything that had happened between them and would understand just how discombobulated she would be feeling. But she couldn't fall apart now, she told herself firmly as an expectant hush descended over the small group. It was time for the show to begin.

'Welcome, friends, trustees and valued guests,' she said, keeping her gaze firmly away from the row where Xander sat. 'Thank you so much for joining us today for this special reading from Eliza Norton's newly discovered manuscript, *The Merriest Month*.

'As many of you will know, Eliza's other works have not always received the recognition they deserve. With the extraordinary circumstances behind this, her last work to be found, I am pleased to say her time in the literary wilderness seems to be coming to an end.'

Every instinct screamed at her to look at Xander then. Was he remembering, as she was, the night they'd found the hidden compartment? Did his lips tingle at the memory of what had happened afterwards? She cleared her throat. 'For me, the most astonishing thing about *The Merriest Month* is the sheer abundance of joy Eliza infused into every page. It is a celebration of Christmas, an homage to gathering family and friends near and a celebration of the generosity of mankind, but it is also a trailblazer. I firmly believe that Eliza Norton wrote the first feel-good festive romance – the precursor to all those that came afterwards, from *Bridget Jones' Diary* to the myriad Christmas novels readers simply cannot get enough of today. And like everything else Eliza wrote, she did it brilliantly, with characters who crackle from the page. So here, without further preamble, is an extract from Chapter One.'

She bent down to collect her bottle of water, taking a long sip before unfolding her sheets of paper. Sitting up a little straighter in her chair, Keeley began to read.

'The winter was very hard. Lady Anderson of Gordon

Square was often to be heard remarking to her husband, "What is to become of us? Has the sun forsaken us?"

Which only goes to show that wealth and good breeding are no substitute for a keen mind and curious spirit. For in that cold, unforgiving winter, many souls perished. Yet one flower blossomed in the stony, dead soil. One soul thrived. Her name was Hannah Rose Underhill and she would become the saviour of Christmas for many a year. Draw near and I will tell you her story . . .'

When Keeley drew to a close, some eight or nine minutes later, the room exploded into applause. Malcolm was on his feet, drawing the other trustees with him. The volunteers and guests followed suit and within seconds, everyone was standing up and applauding. Embarrassed and gratified and more than a little overcome, Keeley gestured them into silence. 'Thank you,' she said. 'I'm grateful for your generous applause. Are there any questions?'

There were, of course. The chair of the Society of Authors began by wondering why the manuscript had never been published.

'I suspect we may never know,' Keeley said simply. 'Perhaps Eliza doubted herself, or it could be that she understood she was ahead of her time and decided to wait for the literary world to appreciate how brilliant *The Merriest Month* was. Locking it away in a secret compartment seems a little extreme but I'm sure you'll agree that it's only added to the mystery. It was actually very clever of her.'

The observation elicited wry laughter before the editor of *The Bookseller* raised his hand. 'Why do you think Eliza's previous works have gone under the radar, despite being well published and really rather good?'

It was another question Keeley had never been able to answer to her own satisfaction, let alone to that of a fellow professional. She cited the bias of familiarity, and suggested that readers often gravitated towards authors they knew they would enjoy, especially in the nineteenth century, when books were an expensive luxury. 'But ultimately I don't have an answer. I hope it's a situation that will change.' She offered a mischievous smile. 'In fact, change is already on the horizon but I'm afraid I'm sworn to secrecy on that score.'

That raised a flurry of curiosity but she refused to be drawn. At last it seemed that all the questions had been asked, and answered to the best of Keeley's ability. Malcolm led the audience in one final round of applause and then Keeley was allowed to rise from her chair to mingle. Jenny and Grace cleared the seats away, to allow more room for guests to circulate. Keeley was determined to avoid Xander and mostly succeeded, especially when Grace beckoned her over to meet the middle-aged woman she had waved to at the beginning. 'Keeley, this is Nicole Wilson. She works at English History and is the expert who assessed Eliza's manuscript.'

'Hello,' Keeley said, smiling. 'It's lovely to finally meet you, Nicole. Thank you for all your hard work in confirming the work belonged to Eliza, and for making sure the manuscript and the diary were well looked after.'

Nicole shook her outstretched hand. 'Not at all. Thank you for letting me look at them. It's not every day such a fascinating manuscript lands on my desk but I also enjoyed reading the diary and letters.' Her expression grew a little embarrassed. 'And I hope you've forgiven me for inadvertently letting the cat out of the bag where the trustees are concerned.'

Keeley blinked. 'I'm not sure what you mean.'

Nicole looked shamefaced. 'I thought they knew, you see, and I was enthusing about the brilliance of Eliza's writing when I bumped into Portia Lord, one of the trustees. And it was only afterwards that I realised I'd done something rather unprofessional. But Malcolm said it had all worked out for the best and I assumed he'd told you.'

Beside her, Grace's expression was faintly horrified. In Keeley's head, several things clicked into place at once and the roaring in her ears subsided. She fixed Nicole with a warm, if slightly mechanical, smile. 'Of course – it did all turn out well. The important thing is that readers will be falling in love with *The Merriest Month* soon. No one will remember the tiny details of who said what to whom.'

The other woman looked relieved. 'Oh, thank you. I'm so glad you see it that way.'

Grace smiled too, but Keeley couldn't help noticing it didn't quite meet her eyes. 'Lovely. Can I introduce you to Brian, Nicole? He's one of the volunteers here at Juniper Cottage and an avid reader.'

Keeley wasn't sure how she managed the next thirty minutes or so of small talk. She knew she spoke to Malcolm and the other trustees, including Portia Lord, who she decided she didn't like very much. The chair of the Society of Authors was charming but Keeley couldn't remember a word of the conversation afterwards. Throughout it all, she was acutely aware of where Xander was, however. And when at last people began to say their goodbyes, and the room began to clear, she knew exactly who he'd spoken to and for how long. It was as though a beacon had been flashing above his head, keeping her apprised on his every move.

Eventually, Grace ushered everyone but Xander from the room and with an expressive look at Keeley, closed the door behind her.

'Hello,' he said, with a tentative smile that was most unlike his usual confident grin. 'How have you been?'

'Fine,' she said, her throat suddenly dry. 'You?'

'Yeah, okay,' he said. 'Keeping busy. A bit like you. Malcolm tells me the tours were a runaway success.'

She managed an awkward smile. 'Yes. I wish you could have seen them.'

'Me too, but I thought I'd give you some space.' He paused, watching her carefully. 'Look, I know you don't believe me and I must have said this a thousand times already but it really wasn't me who—'

'I know,' Keeley cut in and, to her horror, her eyes filled with tears. 'I know it wasn't you because the curator from English History just admitted it was her. She accidentally let slip to one of the trustees that she was authenticating a newly discovered Eliza Norton manuscript and that was it. The cat was well and truly out of the bag.'

Xander's mouth dropped into a perfect O. 'You're kidding.'

Keeley looked away. 'I wish I was. Because I said some horrible, unforgivable things to you, Xander.' She closed her eyes. 'When I think of what I said.'

He crossed the room to stand in front of her. 'Hey, don't be upset. I said a few things that weren't especially helpful too. We both felt betrayed by each other.'

She shook her head. 'But it was all so unnecessary. If I'd only believed you—'

He took her hands. 'It doesn't matter. Really. I don't even remember what you said.'

'Liar,' she said, fully meeting his gaze for the first time since he'd walked into the room.

He gave her a crooked smile. 'It's good to see you. I've missed you so much.'

Keeley's heart began to thunder in her chest. Could he really still care, in spite of everything? 'I've missed you too,' she whispered.

He reached out to cup her face with one hand. 'I'm happy to hear that. Because I seem to remember we have some unfinished business to take care of.' He ran his thumb tenderly across her bottom lip and it was all she could do not to sigh. 'To be continued, if I remember rightly. Unless you're still determined to keep things professional between us.'

'No,' she said, tilting her face towards his. 'I mean yes. What I'm trying to say is that I think we should continue where we left off. Right now, in fact.'

'Here?' he said, his lips hovering so close to hers that his breath tickled her skin. 'Not in the library?'

'Here,' she replied, and brushed her mouth against his. 'And there.' She kissed him again. 'And everywhere.'

She wasn't sure how long they stayed locked together, his hands in her hair, her fingers splayed across his chest. It felt like seconds but might have been minutes and probably would have been hours if Grace hadn't knocked at the door and called, 'I'm counting to ten and then I'm coming in.'

Pulling away from Xander, Keeley did her best to tidy her hair while he watched in amusement. 'I don't know why you're bothering. She knows exactly what we've been doing.'

'I don't care. Appearances matter.'

His grin widened. 'Then you'd better do something about that stubble rash on your chin.'

Keeley's hand flew to her chin, where the skin already felt hot. 'You might have shaved,' she grumbled.

Xander spread his hands. 'I didn't expect to be kissing anyone.' Stepping nearer, he pulled her close again. 'I promise I'll be better prepared next time.'

Keeley eyed him archly. 'Oh, did you bring your razor with you?'

'No,' he said blinking. 'I meant when I go home.'

She smiled. 'If you think I'm letting you out of my sight again, Xander Jones, you've got another thing coming. You are my early Christmas present and I intend to take my time unwrapping you. Unless you'd rather I didn't.'

A grin tugged at his mouth. 'Sounds good to me, Dr Cotterill.'

Keeley took a deep breath. 'Then there're only one more thing I need to know.' She paused, crossing her fingers he wasn't about to give an answer that would ruin everything. 'Exactly how old are you?'

He blinked. 'Does it matter? It's just a number.'

'No, it bloody isn't,' she huffed as the door began to open. 'Tell me quickly.'

'Thirty-seven,' he said. 'But I'll be thirty-eight at the end of December. Is that okay?'

Keeley felt the last of her concerns melt away. Four years was a perfectly acceptable age difference. 'Yes,' she said with a grin. 'As long as you don't mind being my toy boy.'

His arm crept around her waist as Grace entered the room. 'Honestly? I can't think of anything better.'

CHAPTER EIGHTEEN

> O' Christmas Morn, when the bells are ringing and the snow is fresh and bright. I firmly believe there is only goodness in the world on such a day as this.
>
> *The Merriest Month,* ELIZA NORTON

Grace wasn't sure what woke her on Christmas morning. She lay still for a moment, staring at the ceiling and listening for clues that Keeley and Xander were awake, although she didn't crane her ears too hard because there were some things she definitely didn't want to hear. Once it had become clear on Monday afternoon that the two of them were very much reconciled, she'd retreated to her own house for the night, claiming she had some Christmas preparation to do. It hadn't been a complete lie; she still had a few presents to wrap and needed to collect some more clothes to see her over Christmas Day and beyond. When she'd returned to Keeley's cottage on Tuesday evening, Xander had left for London.

'But he's coming back, right?' Grace had asked. 'You've invited him for Christmas?'

Keeley had folded her arms. 'Of course I haven't. You're my

guest this year and Gavin won't thank me for presenting him with another mouth to feed on Christmas Day.'

Gavin had invited Keeley and Grace to join him for a feast at the pub, along with several other villagers who would otherwise have been on their own, and had graciously extended the invitation to include Orla.

'Gavin will cope,' Grace replied. 'And I'm more than happy to have Xander around, if that's what you want. As a wise Victorian novelist once pointed out, Christmas is a time for togetherness.'

As she'd predicted, Gavin had taken the additional guest in his stride and Xander had arrived in Freezy Tye just as dusk was falling on Christmas Eve. The three of them had joined the rest of the village for carols on the green, then spent the evening watching *The Muppet Christmas Carol* and eating cheese. Grace had been grateful for their company, which had helped her not to dwell on all the little Christmas Eve traditions that had fallen by the wayside in Jack's absence. At least when she'd crept downstairs at midnight to arrange her presents under the tree, she hadn't needed to worry about waking him.

And now it was Christmas Day. In the distant past, Grace would have been awoken long before dawn by the thunder of feet on the stairs and a delighted bellow when Jack found the glittering pile of presents. More recently, his pleasure would have been more muted but she could still expect a hug and a gruff, 'Thanks, Mum.'

Today she would have to settle for a phone call, which would probably make her cry in spite of her determination not to. But there was the promise of seeing Raff later; he'd invited her over for supper with Bilbo and she couldn't deny a quiet thrill of anticipation at the thought of where that might lead.

Rolling over, she squinted at her phone and saw it was almost nine-thirty. When was the last time she'd slept so late? Not often in recent months, and definitely not on the days she'd needed to be up for work. But that was over now, at least for the foreseeable future. Santa's Secret was closed to the public until the end of January, although she knew Ivy went in to assess the stock levels and tidy up before then, and the delivery team collected the various light displays they had provided. Before the conversation with Raff in the snow, Grace had felt consumed by emptiness when she'd thought about her life past Christmas Eve. But now, thanks to that wonderful heart-to-heart, she had hope that there was happiness and fulfilment in the months to come. Maybe – just maybe – she had found a purpose again.

With a sigh that was very nearly contented, she poked her head onto the landing to check the coast was clear, then tiptoed to the bathroom for a shower. When she returned, her phone held a message from Raff.

Merry Christmas, Grace. I can't wait to start planning our future together. Sorry I couldn't manage any snow today – my supplier was out of stock after last week. Bilbo says he's looking forward to seeing you later. Raff x

A smile curved her lips. The future he referred to felt fresh and full of promise, as well as dauntingly unknown. The details were yet to be hammered out but thankfully, Ivy had leapt at the idea of Grace and Raff taking over Santa's Secret; in fact, it was all they could do to dissuade her from handing over the reins there and then. Grace had been immensely relieved when she'd agreed to stay on in a part-time capacity to share her considerable expertise, although the twinkle in her eye suggested she had worked out there was more to the proposed new partnership than just business. Grace was grateful that she hadn't immediately demanded to know everything. There had been several more kisses since the night of the party, and a lot more talking and dreaming, but both Grace and Raff had felt it was better to wait until after Christmas to share their news, although Ivy would obviously be first on the list.

Still smiling, Grace was about to reply to Raff when she heard the door knocker rattling downstairs. 'What the hell?' she muttered, pulling her towel more closely around her and crossing to the window to peer outside. It couldn't be a delivery – not on Christmas Day – and sure enough, there was no sign of a van on the deserted lane. Shrugging, she began to pat her hair dry when the knocking came again, and this time it was accompanied by a thunderous hammering on the door itself. Now starting to fear that something awful had happened to one of Keeley's neighbours, Grace pulled on a pair of jogging bottoms and an old jumper and hurried back out to the landing. Keeley's door was firmly closed, which surprised her. Surely she could hear the racket and must be wondering what was going on? Muttering under her breath, she padded down the stairs.

There was definitely someone there – she could see a hulking shadow through the spyhole. Unable to decide whether she was more annoyed or concerned, she fumbled with the lock and yanked open the door to peer out. Standing on the doorstep, looking tanned but bedraggled and exhausted, was Jack.

'Hello, Mum,' he said, dropping a battered rucksack at his feet with a weary smile. 'Happy Christmas.'

A sob welled up in her chest as she stared at him, wondering if she was somehow still asleep and dreaming. Tears pricked at her eyes. 'What?' she managed, swiping blearily to clear her vision. 'How – what are you doing here?'

He grinned. 'I'm home for Christmas. Aren't you going to let me in?'

Grace didn't move. She wasn't sure she could. 'But . . . but you're in Australia. You're not supposed to be here.' She shook her head. 'How did you even know where to find me?'

'I know,' he said, and shrugged. 'But I hated the thought of you waking up on your own, and Dad could see I was miserable. Then Grandma messaged to say how much you were missing me, even though you were staying with Keeley, so Dad paid for me to get a flight back home. It's not forever, just for a few weeks. I've got a job in a bar that I need to get back to. But I'm here now.' He paused, his smile fading. 'Except that you look like you're going to burst into tears at any second so maybe you're not as glad to see me as I thought you'd be.'

That was it – the dam broke. 'Of course I'm happy to see you, you stupid child!' she howled, throwing her arms around him and sobbing. 'I just wasn't – you're not supposed to be here and I'd resigned myself to not seeing you and now you are here and I'm just so ha-ha-happy.'

He submitted to the hug for almost thirty seconds before gently disentangling himself. 'You sound happy,' he said teasingly. 'But maybe we could go inside now. I've been travelling for more than twenty-four hours and everything hurts. Oh, and I'm starving. I hope you've got some food.'

She hiccupped then, but it turned into a laugh halfway through. 'Of course I've got food,' she said, stepping back. 'Although I'm not sure what Keeley's going to think when she sees you tucking into her breakfast.'

'She's going to think, "Excellent, he made it,"' Keeley said, from halfway up the stairs. She threw Grace an apologetic look. 'Your mum let me in on the secret. That's why I bought double the amount of bacon and eggs we actually need for breakfast this morning.'

Jack grinned. 'Hi Keeley.'

She returned his smile. 'Hello Jack.' She glanced over her shoulder as Xander appeared in a pair of shorts. 'Can I introduce you to Xander? He's Australian so I expect you'll have plenty to talk about.'

'G'day,' Jack said, waving.

Xander grinned. 'Nice to meet you, mate.'

Grace slapped a hand to her forehead, still not quite able to believe her son – her actual baby – was standing in front of her. 'I'd better message Gavin and let him know you'll be coming for Christmas lunch too. I hope he's got a big enough turkey.'

'Gavin will cope,' Keeley said, airily firing Grace's own words back at her. 'Mostly because he was in on the secret too.'

'Did everyone know except me?' Grace huffed, as it dawned on her that Xander hadn't looked in the least bit surprised either.

'Pretty much,' Keeley replied cheerfully. 'Now, are you going to let the poor boy in? He's just flown halfway across the world.'

Keeley and Xander set about making breakfast but it wasn't until Jack was sitting on the sofa, glugging down coffee, that it occurred to Grace to wonder how exactly he'd got to Freezy Tye. 'It's Christmas Day, there aren't any trains. How did you get from Heathrow to here?'

He shrugged. 'Obviously, I hitched a ride.'

Grace almost dropped her cup. 'You did what?'

Jack grinned. 'Your face. Relax, Mum, I got an Uber. Dad transferred me the money.'

For the second time that morning, her eyes swam with tears. 'I can't believe you did this. I can't believe you came all this way.'

He put an arm around her shoulders and squeezed. 'If I'm being totally honest, I missed you. Don't tell anyone I said that, okay?'

She laughed, just as the tears she'd been trying to hold back spilled down her cheeks. 'Okay.'

'But you are glad I'm here, right?' he said, eyeing her closely. 'I'm not spoiling your plans with your friends?'

She thought guiltily of her date with Raff, which would now have to be postponed until she'd had time to explain everything to Jack. But he'd understand – they both would. 'Just a big lunch at the pub and perhaps a walk around the village afterwards,' she said. 'There are a few things I want to show you. And of course I'm glad you're here. Christmas isn't Christmas without you.'

He nodded, apparently satisfied. 'That's what I told Dad.'

Grace took a moment to surreptitiously pinch herself, afraid she might wake up at any moment and discover his appearance had all been a dream. 'Ow,' she said, rubbing her leg.

Her phone vibrated and she saw a message from Kevin. *Happy Christmas from Down Under! Hope you like your present. He's a great kid, thanks for doing such an amazing job. K.*

Once again, tears threatened, but at that moment, Xander poked his head around the living-room door. 'Breakfast is served.'

'Excellent,' Jack replied, jumping to his feet. 'I really am starving.'

'When aren't you?' Grace sighed, but she didn't mind a bit. She wrapped her arms around him again. 'Thank you for coming home,' she said, beaming up at his dear freckled face. 'I think this might just be the best Christmas ever!'

AUTHOR'S NOTE

A couple of observations about the settings in *Christmas All the Way*.

Tucked away amid the skyscrapers of the City of London, you'll find Dennis Severs' House. It's a hidden gem – an immersive art installation that invites you to step back in time. There isn't an audio guide, or much to explain what you experience as you wander from room to room, but that's the whole point – the story is up to you and it can be different every time you visit. At Christmas, the house is decorated and filled with the scent of nutmeg and cloves. I like the Silent Nights best, where no one speaks except for the house. By now, you will have realised that I shamelessly stole this magic and turned it into Delores Semple's House, but it's meant as a love letter to one of my very favourite places. I encourage you to visit, at Christmas if you can.

Juniper Cottage, on the other hand, is entirely the product of my imagination but I wish it was a real place. I can picture Eliza's library so clearly, with tea laid out on the table before the fire, and I'd love to join Keeley for a candlelit Christmas tour. Most of all, I wish Eliza Norton had really existed. Creating a book within a book was so much fun and I loved dreaming up the snippets of her work for the start of each chapter, as well as the glimpses of her life. I'm rather envious of Keeley and Grace, who get to settle down beside the fire next Christmas, a glass of Bailey's in hand, to watch the BBC adaptation of *The Merriest Month*. I'll just have to console myself with Colin Firth in a wet shirt instead.

ACKNOWLEDGEMENTS

Thank you to Jo Williamson of Antony Harwood Ltd for supporting me through another book. At Simon & Schuster UK, my thanks go to the editorial superstars Laura Gerrard, Clare Wallis, Melanie Hayes, Gabriella Nemeth and Ollie Cotton, all of whom helped to make this a better book, and to Laurie McShea for her publicity campaign. As ever, a special mention to Pip Watkins for her cover design brilliance.

I try to get most things right in my books and this often means sending odd emails to professionals, hoping they will humour me. In this case, I am most grateful to the excellent English Heritage for advising me on how they might authenticate a newly discovered Victorian-era manuscript, and preventing Dr Keeley Cotterill from committing the faux pas of wearing cotton gloves to handle Eliza's secret novel. A huge thank you to electrical guru Paul Leggett, who not only corrected my dodgy understanding of circuits but also suggested how the culprit might be caught. I hope the wiring in the village hall stands up to inspection.

The inspiration for Santa's Secret came from a shopping trip with Clare Watson several years ago and I owe her thanks for enabling that seed to be planted. My friend Charlotte Dennis never fails me – with a cuppa, a jog or a solution to a plot problem, and sometimes all three. Thank you for always being there. When I am really stuck in a plot hole, I call Tania Noble, who is more brilliant than she knows. I am so lucky to have these incredible women to lean on.

Thank you to T and E, who keep me grounded, and tummy rubs for Luna the Labrador, who is such a patient girl until she is not and demands we go for a walk. And finally, thank you to my wonderful readers – I hope you fall in love with Freezy Tye every bit as much as I did. May goodwill and blessings be upon us all!

If you enjoyed *Christmas All the Way*, read on for a sneak peek of Holly's cosy and uplifting romcom

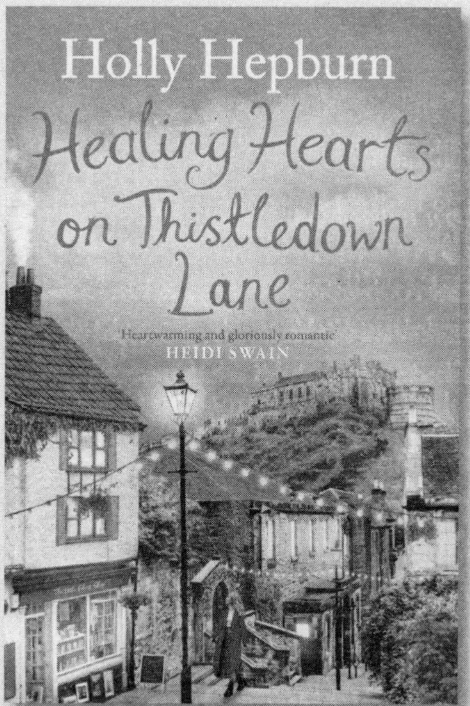

AVAILABLE NOW IN PAPERBACK, EBOOK AND AUDIO

CHAPTER ONE

Eighteen Years Later

Maura was not entirely sure about Hogmanay.

Her reservations weren't something she ever admitted, of course – as Scottishness went, bringing in the bells was up there with tartan, haggis and Irn-Bru, and anything less than total enthusiasm felt like a betrayal of her country. But she did sometimes wonder, as the clock struck twelve and her fellow Scots swelled into 'Auld Lang Syne', whether the time-honoured tradition of grabbing the new year with both hands and dousing it liberally with drink was the best way to wipe the slate clean.

She knew she was very much in the minority – thousands descended on Edinburgh to join the famous Hogmanay street parties and admire the magnificent firework display that lit up the sky over the castle – but given any choice in the matter, Maura would secretly prefer to spend the final few hours of December in bed with a mug of cocoa and a good book, the better to greet January with a clear head and no hazy regrets about the night before. It was, she suspected, a symptom of reaching her late thirties. And it was absolutely not an option with a boyfriend like Jamie, who never missed an excuse for a big night.

Which was why Maura was currently squashed into the corner of a white leather sofa, at the house party of one of Jamie's rugby mates, watching a group of grown men down shots like they were teenagers. It wasn't that she disapproved – she'd done her fair share of drinking in her youth – but nothing could have induced her to join them now. *Each to their own*, she thought, watching them grimace as they bit into wedges of lemon.

On the sofa beside Maura, her friend Zoe raised two elegant eyebrows and leaned closer, her Home Counties accent cutting through the thumping music. 'Are you thinking what I'm thinking?'

Maura glanced at the clock on the wall, which showed 10.15pm, and then back at the drinkers, who were enthusiastically setting up another round of shots. 'Is Archie going to make it until midnight?'

Originally from Dunfermline, Archie was a new recruit to the rugby club, a fresh-faced university student who was doing his best to keep up with his more seasoned teammates but inevitably starting to look a little green around the gills. Zoe followed Maura's gaze and narrowed her eyes in appraisal. 'Absolutely no chance,' she said firmly. 'But I doubt he'll be the only one, unless someone hides the tequila.'

That was a mission Maura had no intention of accepting. If five years of hanging around with Jamie's friends had taught her anything, it was that the Fun Police were never well-received. And while Zoe was a relative newcomer to the group, having only dated her boyfriend, Liam, for ten months or so, Maura knew she wasn't about to intervene either. 'They'd only open a bottle of something else,' she said pragmatically. 'Best to let them get on with it.'

Zoe nodded her agreement. 'Good advice. Never get between a scrum half and the bar.'

Maura laughed. 'Or a fly-half. Or any of them, to be honest.' She eyed her friend curiously. 'So what were you thinking, if it wasn't "how long before Archie passes out"?'

The other woman looked momentarily perplexed, then her expression cleared. 'Oh, I was looking at the guy who just arrived – the one in the hallway.' She gave Maura a mischievous look. 'And what I was thinking was, *HELLO*.'

Automatically, Maura glanced across the crowded room but her view of the hall was obscured by a couple standing in the doorway. 'Someone you know?'

'Someone I'd like to know,' Zoe said, then gave a little shrug. 'If I wasn't with Liam, obviously.'

Maura craned her head, her curiosity piqued. The party was at a house in Edinburgh's New Town – a stone's throw from the rugby club that formed a significant part of her social life – and she'd thought she knew everyone there. 'A player?' she asked Zoe, who shook her head.

'Too pretty.'

Maura raised her eyebrows. 'Some of our boys are good-looking.'

'You know what I mean,' Zoe said. 'The kind of face that has never been on the wrong end of a crunching tackle.'

And Maura did know what she meant. Jamie was rugged and handsome but his nose had been broken more than once and there was a faded silvery line on his forehead from a collision that had resulted in hospital treatment for concussion. Every rugby player she knew had similar battle scars that they wore with immense pride. 'I wonder who he is,' she said, glancing towards the hall again in case the view had cleared and noting with mild disappointment that it had not.

'Only one way to find out,' Zoe said decisively, and levered herself off the sofa. 'Can I get you another drink?'

Maura considered the dregs of lukewarm Prosecco in the bottom of her glass. 'Maybe just a Coke.'

'Sensible,' Zoe replied, 'if just a tiny bit boring. Wait here – I'll report back with the gossip.'

A moment later, she was weaving her way through the crush, trading smiles and nods. Maura watched her go, noting the appreciative looks from some of the guests as the slender blonde passed by. She hadn't known Zoe long, only for the months she'd been dating Liam, but they'd quickly become friends; she made Maura feel less out of place among the often-raucous rugby crowd. There were other wives and girlfriends, of course, many of whom had been part of the group much longer than Maura, and she liked them too. But Zoe had a sparkle that had drawn Maura in from the first moment they met. Hogmanay might not be so bad with a partner in crime, she decided.

A roar from the hardened drinkers made her look over to see Jamie holding a tray of lime-green jelly shots aloft. These were quickly snatched up. Jamie glanced Maura's way, raising an enquiring eyebrow. She shook her head. Shrugging, he offered one of the two he held to Archie, who hesitated for only a fraction of a second before tipping it into his mouth. Maura's lips twisted in wry amusement. It wouldn't be long before that was coming back up, if she was any judge. Jamie, on the other hand, would be fine. His tolerance for alcohol had been finely honed by years amid the play-hard, party-hard environment of the rugby crowd.

Not for the first time, Maura reflected how different she and Jamie were. He was gregarious and immensely likeable, with a charm few could resist once it was turned their way. It was that charm that had first ensnared Maura, at a ceramics gallery viewing sponsored by the bank Jamie worked for. He'd made a beeline for her, hiding in the corner while people studied and discussed her creations, and kept a respectful distance even as he fixed her with a sympathetic smile. 'You look like you'd rather be anywhere but here.'

She had hesitated, because it wasn't strictly true. The people in the gallery were here to view the pieces she had made – bowls and vases she had worked on for months – and there was a part of her that wanted to see them admired and appreciated, not to mention bought. But she'd be lying if she pretended she found prestigious events like this easy, even though she knew most potters would kill to be in her shoes. A down-to-earth pottery show was more her thing, in a chilly marquee or village hall, full of ceramics enthusiasts with wide-ranging, quirky tastes and fellow potters to chat with. A show that wasn't exclusively about her. 'Not at all,' she'd replied as she looked up at him, hoping the lie wasn't too transparent, and held out her hand. 'I'm Maura.'

'I know,' he said, encompassing her fingers completely with his own large hand. 'You're the talent behind all of this beauty.' He waved a hand at the spotlit gallery, with its pedestals and tables of gleaming blue and green and turquoise ceramics. 'I feel as though I'm on a desert island, surrounded by gently lapping waves. You must really love the sea.'

'I do,' Maura said, gratified. 'Although I'm not sure I came anywhere close to capturing its true depth or beauty.'

He eyed her quizzically, black brows beetling. 'Seriously?' Turning, he studied a wide, wavy-edged bowl glazed in a delicate sea-green. 'I can almost hear the crash of the surf when I look at this piece. And the way the glass shimmers at the bottom, half-covering the anemones and leaf patterns underneath – it's like peeping into a rock pool once the tide has gone out.'

Maura felt her cheeks grow warm, partly in pleasure that he'd understood what she'd been trying to achieve, but mostly in shame because she had totally judged this stranger by his appearance – tall, well-built and with a jaw that looked like it could crack boulders, let alone walnuts. He was immaculately dressed – his suit was expensive and well-fitted – and his thick dark hair was tamed into submission by liberally applied gel, all of which had led her to automatically label him as a typical city banker. Not the type to appreciate art, she had decided, without even realising she'd done so. And now he was forcing her to reappraise her initial assessment, and her own preconceptions along with it. 'Thank you,' she said, praying her face wasn't as crimson as it felt.

He smiled then, his blue eyes crinkling at the edges in a way that somehow eased her discomfort and made her feel worse. 'You're welcome. But where are my manners? I haven't even introduced myself. I'm Jamie Wallace. I work for Castle Finance, and I can tell you on behalf of all my colleagues how honoured we are to be sponsoring this exhibition.'

'Oh.' Maura heard the faint squeak in her voice and took a deep breath. It was time to take control of herself and act like a professional. 'It's nice to meet you, Jamie.'

'I hope so,' he said, a smile curving the corners of his mouth again. 'Even though you're secretly hoping I'm going to leave you alone soon.'

'I am not,' she protested and was startled to realise she meant it. 'I have a tendency to hide away at these things and then be annoyed at myself afterwards for not speaking to anyone,' she admitted. 'At least I can congratulate myself later on talking to you.'

Jamie laughed, a deep, warm sound that Maura found made her want to laugh too. 'I'm not sure anyone has ever congratulated themselves for being cornered by me. But you're very kind to say so.'

His wry self-deprecation was as charming as it was misplaced. Maura raised her eyebrows. 'I don't believe that for a second.'

'You don't?' His blue eyes rested on her with interest. 'Then have dinner with me. Tonight, when the gallery closes.'

She gaped at him, wrongfooted again. 'I – uh –'

'But I'm an idiot,' he said, slapping his forehead. 'You must have plans – a glittering celebration with your friends and family. Your boyfriend.'

Maura pressed her lips together. She did indeed have plans, and they involved a hot-water bottle, pyjamas and her sofa. But Jamie didn't need to know that. He was giving her a way out, an excuse to turn him down without either of them losing face, and she was very much surprised to realise she didn't want to. 'No,' she said, before she could change her mind. 'I don't have anything planned. Dinner sounds good.'

To her mild amusement, he looked momentarily nonplussed, as though taken aback by her assent. 'So it's a date, then?'

Discover more from Holly Hepburn

AVAILABLE NOW IN PAPERBACK, EBOOK AND AUDIO

SIMON & SCHUSTER